A SPLEN

"How long have y[...]
"Me," Jamie said. [...]
Seasons aren't the same here, it's easy to lose track, but the day is about the same length – we figure twenty-two hours. Dennis's been here maybe eight months. There are about six hundred Earth people we know of, most of them male, but for all we know there could be a million more beyond the Stinking Bucket. Oh, we call the ocean the Stinking Bucket. But I doubt if there are any other Earthers. We're mostly at a primitive technological level – you can see that. But we have decent shelter, food. I know what your next question will probably be, so I'll answer it: there aren't any intelligent natives that we know of, but there are a good many races on Fool's Hope abducted from their home worlds. So far we've counted thirty-one intelligent species. And only one's from Earth."

Books by John Shirley
* available in Mandarin Paperbacks

City Come A-Walkin'
Transmaniacon
Cellars
The Brigade
* Eclipse

A SPLENDID CHAOS

An Interplanetary Fantasy

JOHN SHIRLEY

Mandarin

A Mandarin Paperback

A SPLENDID CHAOS

First published in Great Britain 1989
by Mandarin Paperbacks
Michelin House, 81 Fulham Road, London SW3 6RB

Mandarin is an imprint of the Octopus
Publishing Group

Copyright © 1988 by John Shirley
Illustrations copyright © 1988 by Ferret

British Library Cataloguing in Publication Data

Shirley, John, *1953–*
A splendid chaos
I. Title
813'.54[F]

ISBN 0 7493 0047 7

Printed and bound in Great Britain
by Cox & Wyman Ltd, Reading, Berkshire

For Rob Hardin,
whether he likes it or not.

Special thanks to my wife,
Kathleen Woods Shirley,
for her enormous editorial help,
for her insight,
and just for her.

A SPLENDID CHAOS

THE
FIRST
PART

Disorientation
Orientation

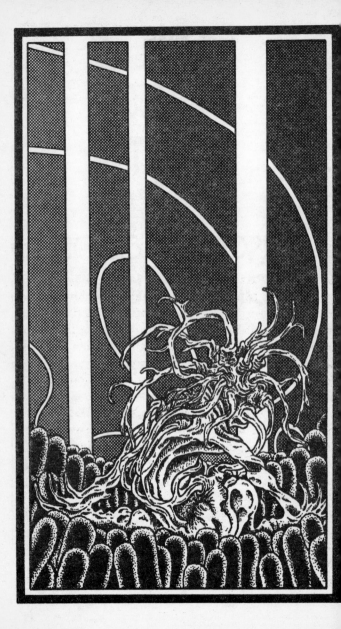

ONE

He woke into translucent green.

Zero was lying on his back, staring up into—a sky? Yeah. He saw a cloud. It was in the upper left corner of his field of vision. Creamy yellow cloud against a translucent jade sky. He saw something more, high and wide and blue-gray, out of the corners of his eyes. It was a few seconds before he got up the nerve to look directly at it. He turned his head.

"Christ!" The motion stabbed pain through his head. The throbbing subsided, and his eyes focused. He saw walls. Broken-down walls, no ceiling.

It was a ruin of some kind.

"Take a deep breath, mite," someone said in some variant of British accent. "Deep breath make you fit again, eh? Right! Deep breath—clears away the 'eadache, tidies up the 'ead."

Zero took a deep breath. The throbbing in his head went into fourth gear. But he took another breath, and another. The inhaling pressed his shoulder blades against the ground, and he felt gravel and something soft, maybe tufts of grass.

The headache passed, seeped away somewhere. He tried to sit up. His stomach clenched, and nausea roiled through him. He began to gag.

A firm hand on his shoulder rolled him over. "Go ahead, mite, 'eave it out if you want to. 'appens to all of us when we get 'ere."

But they were dry heaves. After a few moments the spasm passed. He found he was kneeling, shivering. There was a cold ache in him, deep down in his bones. An undefined yearning.

"It's adjustment, and maybe a little withdrawal, too. They put you on a drug during the trip." A woman's voice this time.

He looked around and saw them standing on his left, a man and a woman. He looked past them at the squared-off ruin. The ruin was about forty yards across, the walls mostly about twelve feet high, some of them overgrown with a climbing shrub. . . . He was in the shadow of one of the walls. The sun in the green sky was still low, occluded by the wall that had spread its shadow over him. The sunlight outlined the serrated upper edge of the broken wall with a line of white neon. It was warm, about eighty-five degrees.

"Welcome to Fool's Hope, mite," the man said. He was short, almost dwarfish, barrel-chested; his head seemed just a shade too big for his body. He grinned, showing crooked teeth. He had a jutting forehead, deep-set eyes, a stub of a nose, and a thatch of rusty-brown hair. He wore a threadbare brown plaid shirt, torn, grimy denim pants, and rotting tennis shoes. " 'ow's the boy, eh? Wot's yer nime? I'm Dennis. This 'ere's Jamie."

Jamie was about five seven, a little too heavy in the

hips and too narrow in the shoulders. She wore a short-sleeved blue workshirt, worn Levi pants, and scuffed black workboots. Her black hair was short, parted like a man's. Her features were blunt, but her eyes were lively brown and restless with intelligence. She looked affectedly masculine. Probably a dyke.

Uh-huh. Tattoo on her left biceps. A heart with the name *Trish* in it. Classic.

"May as well get you on your feet," Jamie said. "You won't like it, but . . . "

Dennis stepped nearer and helped Zero stand. "Right, up you go."

Zero's head spun, and he swayed; Dennis held him firmly.

"Come on with us," Jamie said. "Walk slowly, take deep breaths."

"Wait a minute." His voice didn't work very well. "Uh—" He cleared his throat. "What . . . I mean—" It was hard to articulate. "I wanna know, uh . . . " He looked around again, trying to find some point of orientation.

The dead, enigmatic walls, overgrown with dull blue ivylike stuff. There was no wind—it was preternaturally still, quiet, every slight noise an obtrusive echo —but the ivy seemed to rustle, all of it. As if it were adjusting its grip. There was bluish-gray moss—*was* it moss?—on the stony ground between the fallen walls. "Where am I?" he managed at last.

"Scotland, " Dennis said.

"Really?" A wash of relief. The vague memories . . . they were just a dream, then.

"No, don't bullshit him, Dennis," Jamie said. "Friend, you're not in Scotland. You're in North Dakota."

"North . . . what?"

"Come on, Jamie—let's level with 'im, eh? Mite,"
Dennis went on, deadpan, "you're in the Arctic circle
—that's why the sky's that funny color, eh?"

He looked back and forth between them, blinking.
"What?"

"Sydney," Jamie said, as if she were coming clean.
"Just outside Sydney, Australia."

"County Cork," Dennis said, shaking his head sadly
at her duplicity. "Ireland."

They're lunatics, Zero thought. "Go to hell, both of
you," he said, pulling away from Dennis.

Dennis laughed. "All right, all right. Truth is, we
don't know where we are. But the general feelin', like,
is: We're on another planet. I mean, this ain't Earth."

"No joke this time," Jamie said, nodding.

Zero stared at them for a moment. He shook his
head. "No. That's bullshit."

"I know how you feel," Jamie said. "I felt that way.
Everyone does. But you get used to it."

Zero shook his head insistently.

"Don't it *feel* all wrong to you here?" Dennis asked.
"You know—like the air's funny, the colors are wrong
—gravity's wrong. A little lighter."

It did feel that way. But it might be suggestion. Or:
"It's a drug. Somebody slipped me a drug. Hallucinogenic."

"Those are the first two stages," Jamie said, shrugging. "First you think people are putting you on. Then
you think you're dreaming or hallucinating from drugs,
schizophrenia, whatever. But after you're here for a
while, you accept it."

"This is bullshit. No one has the technology to—"

"You don't remember the disco?" Jamie asked. "That's what they used for you, right?"

Zero stared at her. He remembered.

Remembered a disco. Sure it was a disco. Only . . . it was in the middle of an intersection, right smack in the middle of the road.

They were walking along, Zero and Bowler and Angie and Cisco, looking for a way out of the sticky-hot Manhattan night and into something sufficiently distracting. Something cheap and something nearby. They'd written their term papers—"the *fucking* term papers," Zero had said—and they were trying not to think about them and how they related to grade point averages. So it was a natural, it was a prayer's answer, when they found the disco that was where it couldn't possibly be. It was shaped like a circus tent. Almost filled the wide intersection. All lit up along its tent-lines with blinking red and white lights. Or were they blue and yellow? Or what? They seemed to subtly shift their color if you stared right at them.

They knew it was a disco because it was giving out a bang-bump bang-bump bang-bump of disco beat, and because there were light-show flashes coming from inside the open front door, and because there was a doorman standing out front behind a red velvet rope. And there was a sign over the front door that said . . .

Zero squinted. He couldn't quite make it out. Highly stylized lettering. After a moment it seemed to squirm, resolved into DAYDREAMS AT NIGHT.

They stopped for a moment to stare at the place. Everyone stopped at the same instant, Zero noticed.

"Where's it getting the electricity?" Bowler wondered, looking around. The rest of the street was dark. The traffic lights over the disco were dead, dark. There weren't any detour signs around the disco, or police barriers. But there was no traffic—they'd noticed it for a few blocks. It was as if the traffic had been rerouted. So the disco had to be there with the permission of the cops, right? Didn't it?

They were walking toward it again. Zero couldn't remember deciding to walk toward it. They'd all done it at once.

The multicolored lights sizzling from the disco fanned over the time-smoothed black asphalt of the street, coiled in a manhole cover, snaked up a lamppost.

As they walked closer, the bang-bump bang-bump bang-bump graduated into *bang-bump bang-bump bang-bump.*

They approached the doorman. Medium height, black hair, regular features, mirror glasses. Like a lot of doormen at discos and rock clubs, he didn't even look at them. But he seemed to evaluate them somehow, without directly looking. He unhooked the velvet rope, stood to one side, and waved vaguely to tell them they could go in, continuing to look past them at the street. "No cover tonight," he said in a bizarrely sweet, melodious voice. His lips scarcely moved. The disco light played over his too-glossy skin.

They hesitated just outside the door.

"Open bar, too," he added.

Open bar?

They went inside.

Go into a crowded disco, impressions come in waves. A wall of sound, a wash of lights: strobes and, higher up, lasers spear and bounce from the background glitter; color splashes, light-spangled walls, mirror balls. Like all discos it was a jewelry box of chintzy light, wired softly together with smoke and dusk.

There was a knot of dancers on the small dance floor—people from this end of town, every race, all economic strata—but most of them were aged between twenty and thirty. Odd how few gays there were for a disco. Smiling people—who looked giddy drunk, starry-eyed—sat at tables too small to put both your elbows on; a cocktail waitress in tights; a bar across the room. It was a standard disco, so standard it was almost generic. The music was the latest standard dance stuff. But sometimes it would be interrupted, just for a moment, by a radio ad, which would cut off before the ad had quite got going, and another song would start. As if they had recorded it off the dance music radio station. Weird. Maybe to save money on deejays, Zero thought. He saw no deejay booth.

But the music was there, and the drinks swept them like white water into dancing. Angie was dancing around behind Cisco and kicking him, then dancing away. Not kicking him hard: Cisco was laughing. It looked pretty funny. Zero found himself laughing, too. He felt good, weirdly good. Like drugs. He found himself looking at Cisco and Bowler and Angie as if he'd never seen them before. Bowler was tall, serious, black-haired, pale—the would-be ideologue. When he danced, it was usually a way of "relating to the masses." Only now he danced like he meant it. Not normal for Bowler. Cisco was short and dark and curly haired, intuitive to Bowler's rationalist. Bowler was convinced that religion was one of the world's great evils; Cisco was convinced that we were in a New Age that would see the vindication of things spiritual. Cisco was endearingly ridiculous, seeing omens and messages from the Other

Side, making predictions based on his dreams—and he was always wrong. Willowy Angie, hair auburn, her eyes glittery, scarily intelligent, and icy blue; she was always joking but never about Certain Things. Angie, who wrote papers on feminist literature, kept her sexuality carefully contained—and now she was shaking her hips as she danced. . . . Zero feeling unlike himself. Like he'd done a hit of nitrous. Only it didn't wear off as quickly as nitrous because twenty minutes later he was still laughing, dancing with Angie now (Huh? He *never* danced with Angie—she always made fun of his moves), and drinking a pretty decent Manhattan—dry, not too much vermouth, twist of lemon peel—from a plastic glass as he danced, sloshing the stuff on other dancers, but no one seemed to care. (When had he started dancing? He didn't remember starting to . . .) It was weird that the waitresses didn't tell him not to take drinks on the dance floor, but then, everyone out there was drinking, and how come everything was free here? Must be promotional (*bang*-bump *bang*-bump *bang*-bump), yeah, must be a promotional gimmick for a mobile disco, whole thing got wheels, lifts up, skates off down the street (*bang*-bump, *bang*-bump *bang bang bang*), strange to be enjoying disco so much, usually he didn't like—

And then he stopped dancing, because of the entrance to the disco. It was closing. Sliding shut like an elevator door. Only it looked like—it was hard to tell in the shifting lights, but—it looked like it was closing *seamlessly*.

Zero yelled at Bowler, signaled him; they ran toward the place where the door had been.

The wall four feet to their right opened, and—

A man extruded from the wall.

He came out at them on a sort of metal stalk

that extended from the wall—*whirrrr*—and was suddenly standing between Zero and the place where the door had been.

The man was naked, but his body was featureless, gray, kind of rubbery looking. He had an artichoke for a face. No, it wasn't an artichoke, but it looked like one: a gray artichoke as big as a man's face—*instead* of a face. No eyes, no nose, no mouth.

The music stopped. The lights stopped whirling. Now there was just one blue light. A murmur of voices, confused dancers looking around.

Zero stared at the guy with the artichoke face. He was distantly aware of Bowler standing at his elbow. "Bowler?"

"I see it, too, man."

There was a little white metal box perched on Artichoke-Face's left shoulder. From the box came a voice that was exactly the same as the voice the doorman had. "Not yet. Sleep now."

Artichoke-Face touched something on the metal shaft he'd ridden out of the wall.

The tables and chairs suddenly pulled out from under the people sitting at them, and the sitters went sprawling, yelling in astonishment, or giggling, trying to play along. But it looked to Zero as if the chairs had moved by themselves.

"Poltergeists!" Cisco hissed as the white chairs and white tables rose to the ceiling. Seemed to meld with it. Vanished into it.

A man whimpered and then shouted hysterical incoherence.

"Sleep now," Artichoke-Face repeated.

The floor got soft.

It was softer than putty but not as soft as quicksand.

They sank into it—everyone in the club but Artichoke-Face—and everyone stopped trying to fight the sinking after thirty seconds of babbling and crying out because a sweet, seductive sleepiness came over them. They quieted, sighed, and the room was almost silent. Artichoke-Face retracted into the slot in the wall. The wall closed.

Zero and Cisco and Bowler and Angie and the others sank quickly into sticky white stuff, sank up to their chins. Stopped sinking. The sticky white stuff smelled faintly of something *almost* like peppermint.

They basked in the warm, firm stickiness around them, unable to move much and no longer trying to, as the room got darker, till there was only the faintest gray light.

They heard a distant whine and then a muted rumbling. Zero felt giddiness deep in his gut. Like being in an elevator dropping too fast.

But his sleepiness deepened till he stopped noticing the falling sensation. . . .

That was then, this is now.

"If this were another planet, we'd all die of the local microorganisms," Zero said. "We'd have no defenses built up."

"You've been immunized against them," Jamie said. "They lure you into the ship, observe you for a while, restrain you, sedate you, take off with you, undress you, inoculate you, maintain you, bring you here, dress you again, dump you here and—except for the Progress Stations—you're on your own."

When she said, "They dress you," Zero looked down at himself, frowning. His clothes were loose on him.

He'd lost weight. He wore the same black jeans outfit, but coated, in some places crusted, with dried white stuff. It was on his hands, his face. . . .

He swayed with disorientation. The world, the sky, the whole universe—all of it was spinning like a roulette wheel. Someone had spun the wheel, and he was waiting to see what number the spin would end on. The wheel spinning, the world spinning around him . . .

Oh, shit. The disco, the sticky white stuff, the rumbling . . .

"There it is, 'e's gettin' it!" Dennis crowed. "Rememberin' the trip, eh? All right, tike it easy."

Zero bent over to dry heave again.

"'ow you feel?" Dennis asked.

"Fucked. Like I've got a bad hangover," Zero said.

"You'll feel better when you get some food and water into you," Jamie said, "and get cleaned up. But I warn you: There's only one free meal here for the new arrivals. After that you earn your own."

They'd walked along a faint path that led out of the ruins, and now they were skidding down the hillside. Zero asked, "Wasn't there anyone with me? I mean—"

"They dropped your friends off first," Jamie said, "Bowler and the others, all at once. They've been here almost two weeks. They're well. A little slow to adjust. The Meta held you back a couple days. Means you were probably infected with something they had to cure."

"What the hell was *that*? That they had to—"

"Syphilis, mye-be?" Dennis suggested with a crooked leer.

"No way of telling," Jamie said. Doesn't matter; whatever it was, it's gone. But don't think there isn't disease here. They leave us some flu viruses, some other things. They'll probably test some nasty microorganism on us sometime."

Now they paused to look out over the landscape. "We call the planet Fool's Hope," Jamie said. "Well, some of the factions don't like that name. Weisman's Transcendentalist bunch calls it New Chance. Bunch of cornballs. But most of us call it Fool's Hope."

Zero shaded his eyes against the sun. It looked like Earth's sun but brassier and a fraction bigger. The plain that stretched out around the steep, anomalous hill was mostly flat and almost featureless except for big, randomly scattered craters in the neat expanse of blue vegetation. They didn't look like impact craters—almost like cookie-cutter-perfect holes, maybe forty feet across, none closer than fifty yards to another. They made Zero think of ceiling tiles. The plain was silvery-blue in the morning light, reaching into a dead-white curtain of mist that shrouded most of the horizon; through the shroud was a suggestion of something big looming up, far away. Maybe mountains. Nearer, the mist clung to the ground, and here and there, between the craters, some of it seemed almost to have clumped together, entwined to become nearly as cohesive as spun glass. As he watched, the spectral clumps—clumps? more like thin *sheaves* of mist—began to rotate, all of them counterclockwise, performing a slow waltz in the faint breeze —a breeze that smelled something like menthol and something like rotten roses.

They walked on down the hill, wending between low, lichen-crusted boulders (*was* it lichen?) to the flatlands, where a rutted blue-dirt road stretched in a straight line to what he supposed was the north. An animal yoked to a crude wooden cart, with wheels carved out of solid wood, was tethered to a ring carved into a roadside boulder. The wood of the cart looked like normal Earth wood, except it was turquoise. He was fairly sure it hadn't been painted that way. *They've gone to elaborate lengths to set up this bullshit*, Zero thought.

And then, when he was closer to the animal yoked to the cart, he saw its tail and flanks—the rear of an ordinary black horse. He nodded to himself and snorted, "So the aliens are bringing horses here, too?"

"Nope," Jamie said.

"Horses just happened to evolve here?"

"Come on," she said, and led him around to the front of the horse.

It snapped at him with a mottled red beak.

He yelped and stepped back. Jamie and Dennis laughed.

The thing with the beak snapped at him again and took a few steps toward him. The cart creaked behind it.

"Hold up!" Jamie barked at it. It looked guiltily at at her and stopped, its head drooping.

"Okay," Zero said. "It's not Earth."

It wasn't a horse either. It's neck was too long, its skull too small, and it had eight inches of horny red beak, bisected vertically. It had protuberant, sulky red-brown eyes with wrinkly white lids. A double string of drool hung from the slit in the beak. Its skin was slick and hairless, he saw now. Its legs ended in thick gray pads. It raised its head and gave out an "oh-rooooooh!" mournfully; the call echoed across the rolling plain. From somewhere far off came a faint answering call. It lifted its head and looked in that direction. He saw no ears—unless the damp, purplish membranes behind the eyes were for hearing.

"It's an oruh," Jamie said, pronouncing it *or-ooh*.

It took a step toward the horizon, in the direction the answering call had come from. The cart gave a tentative creak.

Jamie took hold of the crude gray leather harness around the oruh's neck and tugged back on it. "Forget it, pal!"

Its head drooped.

"Come on, mite," Dennis said, climbing up onto the cart. Mechanically, Zero climbed up after him.

Zero sat between Dennis and Jamie. From a long box on the back of the cart, she took a piece of metal like an oversize carpet tack—three inches long. She bent over and thumbed it into the oruh's rump. The animal didn't seem to notice. She gathered up the reins, stretched her legs out on a wooden support, and pressed the tack with her foot as if it were an accelerator in a car. The oruh lurched forward, making a sulky horn sound like *"Oruhhhh . . . oruhhhh . . . oruhhh"* deep in its throat. It had a tail that was superficially like a horse's; but looking closer, Zero saw it was all of a piece, like a paddle.

The cart shuddered, creaked, and rolled after the oruh, bumping bone-jarringly along the rutted track. Things clanked in the box behind the seat. He held on to the bench between his legs and told his stomach to hold on, too.

He stared at the pockmarks on the swaying rump of the oruh. "Doesn't that tack thing hurt it?"

"Needs a delicate touch," Jamie admitted. "But it's got a thick hide. Anyway, don't waste sympathy on an oruh. If an animal can be a shithead son-of-a-bitch, that's what the oruhs are."

"Oh, I kinda like 'em," Dennis said. "This one

'ere's me chum." He looked at Zero. "Int 'e goin' to ask about the Meta?"

Zero sighed. "I'm scared to ask. But you better tell me."

Jamie said, "The Meta brought us here—everyone, every intelligent race on the planet. We were all brought here by the Meta. All abducted. They're aliens, we assume, and I *don't* mean wetbacks. We don't know shit about them. We know they're called the Meta—the High Clan and the others tell us that. But they don't know much about them, either. They're fairly sure the Meta aren't native to this planet. We think they just sort of use it as their game board. We don't know how they brought us here—we assume a starship, but we have no idea with what method of propulsion. One look at the stars at night tells you we're not in the same damned solar system. We don't know where we are, or where the Meta are now. We never see them, never have. We don't know what they look like. We've seen their servants, 'the Ed McMahons,' we call 'em."

"Faces like artichokes?"

"Yeah. The High Clan rep tells us they're not the Meta, they simply work for them. Entirely different race, they claim. After a while it becomes clear that's what's going on. As for why you're here, why the Meta brought us all here—I mean, I assume you want to know."

Zero glared impatiently at her.

"Okay. Well, the only thing we're sure of is, they're playing a game with us. It might be a game they're playing for entertainment, a sport."

"I love to 'ear 'er go on about this," Dennis said, looking at Jamie in genuine admiration.

"It might be a game they're playing for profit. How they profit by it is anybody's guess. It might be a game they're playing—or making us play—for scientific reasons. To learn about us.

"It might be a game they're putting us through for —well, for spiritual reasons. The Meta Makers sect believes that. You know the sort of thing: the Meta are testing our spiritual development, spiritual potential, or trying to, um, augment it. Personally, I think that's bullshit. I think they're simply sadistic. Anyway, they're playing a game with us."

"It's not a bad plice," Dennis said, "not really. Quite livable in its own way. Air's good, water's fine. Not a lot of creepy-crawlies, at least durin' the day. There's a good deal of food we can eat, if we work at it. And"—he grinned at Jamie—"and it's dead innerrestin', int it, eh?"

"Oh, yes," Jamie said with heavy irony, "it's *interesting*."

Zero didn't like the sound of that. He felt a droning anxiety, a swimming nausea of disorientation. He was going to hyperventilate. *Calm down*, he told himself. *If it's a dream, it'll end. Hallucinations end, too, eventually. Nothing you can do but adjust. More questions. Keep the mind busy, keep it coping.*

"How long you been here?" he asked.

"Me," Jamie said. "Two and a half years, about. Seasons aren't the same here, it's easy to lose track, but the day is about the same length—we figure twenty-two hours. Dennis's been here maybe eight months. There are about six hundred Earth people we know of, most of them male, but for all we know there could be a million more beyond the Stinking Bucket. Oh, we call the ocean the Stinking Bucket. But I doubt if there are any other Earthers. We're mostly at a primitive technological level—you can see that. But we have decent shelter, food. I know what your next question will probably be, so I'll answer it: there aren't any intelligent natives that we know of, but there are a good many races on Fool's Hope abducted from their home worlds. So far we've counted thirty-one intelligent species. And only one's from Earth."

He stared at her. "Thirty-one? Jesus!"

"Got 'im, too," Dennis said. "The Exodus sect worships 'im, put up a bleedin' griven image of bloody Jesus and Mary. But no one's got a Bible, so they're mikin' up their own, mis-rememberin' it and mikin' it any way they want it, like."

"Thirty-one alien races?" Zero looked around nervously. The blue vegetation stretched away to either side. Nothing moved but the mist.

"You won't see them out here," Jamie said. "Most 'em are north of our settlement. But there're some nomads who spook around it. And of course, the Murderers."

"The *what*?"

"Something the Meta gave us to keep us on our toes. Randomly placed, completely hostile, homicidal aliens. Most of the aliens are more or less friendly, but the Murderers . . . " She shrugged. "Thanks to them and some of the local fauna, like the wheelers—well, there's only a little less than half as many Earthers here as there were. Some of them didn't get a mile from the ruin. Some were killed by the Murderers or on expeditions. Or went crazy and killed themselves."

Up ahead the road climbed gradually to the top of a ridge, maybe a half-mile off. "The settlement's a little ways on the other side of that rise," Jamie said.

"How'd you know I was out there?" Zero asked.

"We could see the ship coming down. The light of

it, anyway. We know what that means. That's where they drop Earthers."

Zero was studying the vegetation by the side of the road. It was one unbroken mat, about two feet high, looking like a lawn but thicker, or like the surface of a cauliflower, but flat and dull blue. It was faintly mist-beaded; its glossiness and regularity made him think of synthetic fabrics. "It looks kept up, like somebody mowed it."

"It just grows that way. We call it the Rug," Jamie said. "For more than one reason. But it—" She broke off, staring to the east. After a moment she said, "Dennis, it's humping up over there!"

"Bloody 'ell! They know we've got to pick up our people! Ought to give us a safer plice to do it so we can at least bloody compete. Bugger 'em!"

Jamie pressed hard on the accelerator tack in the oruh's rump; the animal squealed and lurched ahead, doubling its pace. The cart jounced, and its axles shrieked in protest.

"What is it?" Zero asked, looking at the thing Jamie had seen.

It was a humped place in the Rug, fifty feet ahead and to their right. As he watched, it humped more, as if a great balloon were being inflated, lifting the vegetation without breaking it; as if the vegetation were evenly planted in something that was all one piece.

The oruh had seen the hump now. It made a long, plaintive *orrrrrr-oooooooooohhhhhhh*, stretched out its long neck, hunched its shoulders, and hurried to get past. Its pads beat a sodden tattoo on the packed ground. It was hard to stay on the cart now.

The hump began to move toward them. Like a cartoon image of a mole burrowing just under the surface, the hump sweeping toward them—no, it was like a wave, a single narrow wave on an otherwise flat sea.

Dennis reached behind them and opened a box. He handed Zero something like the metal frame of a folded-up umbrella, without the umbrella fabric. For himself he kept a sort of oversized blunderbuss with a harness instead of a gun butt. He crammed a cheesecloth bag down the bell-shaped muzzle with a stick and took a small metal instrument from his pocket. All of this Zero saw through the distorting jiggling of the cart as Jamie prodded the wailing oruh into greater efforts, and as the hump began to come parallel to them.

"What are they?" Zero asked, trying not to shout high-pitched but doing so anyway.

"Wheelers!" Dennis yelled, dumping powder into a hole in the back of the blunderbuss. "Bloody friggin' wheelers! We're usually way past 'em by this time, but the—"

"Shit!" Jamie yelled. "They've got symmetry!" She pointed at a second hump on the side of the road opposite the first, coming hard at them. They were about to be caught between the two.

And then what'll happen? Zero thought.

And then the straight edges of the Rug on either side of the road arched with a nasty ripping sound. The humps formed cavemouths in the Rug, and from the caves came a sound that was like pushing a long rough needle through your eardrums, a yodeling cacophony given off by a mass of squealing ugliness. Zero's scalp contracted when he saw them: hundreds of them.

Picture an eight-spoked wheel covered with slick black fur. Take the rim away from each furred wheel, and at the end of each spoke you put a body, a body like an oversize ferret, maybe three feet high, each with two little frantically pumping legs, each without arms, each with jaws far too big for its head, each with a double row of dagger teeth that look too big for the jaw, each with a single round adorable-brown eye in the middle of its furry head, each with long floppy ears horribly like a cocker spaniel's, each with a wet pink tongue that extends from its mouth like a razzing New Year's Eve party favor, fibrillating. Each body with a rigid, furry shaft in the middle of its back that extended behind to a furry globe containing the unifying brain. The globe was divided into two parts: the lower connected the spokes, the upper moved independently, spinning like a turntable for its faceted golden eyes. The legs on the spoke-animals frantically pumped, a blur, as they poured out of the Rug caves (Zero heard himself screaming) close beside the cart, coming at it from all sides. There was something repulsively unnatural in the way they moved, the way the backward-running parts and the forward-running parts cooperated, the way the things turned this way and that, pink tongues extended, ear-needling squealings sent in all directions and suddenly the cart was surrounded by black-furred wheel-things, jaws snapping, tongues darting in and out between snaps, the oruh's wail going higher and higher in pitch, its black blood spraying where the things gnashed its flanks . . . the things would bite, spin about so the other mouths could take a bite while the ones who'd bitten would chew what they'd bitten off (Zero thinking, *Now I know it's not real, couldn't be real, this is a nightmare*), the furry spokes overlapping one another, the spoke-animals tangling in their haste, the nearer ones climbing onto the cart, their wheel-shapes crimping so that four spokes could cooperate in the climb, spiderlike . . . Zero dizzy from gulping air; black spots swarming in his eyes, reflexively whacking at the things with the naked umbrella in his hands—

Whump. Dennis's blunderbuss thundered, its stock kicking Dennis in the middle of his chest, knocking him into the back of the cart. He forced himself up, swearing. Three wheelers were down, blown to twitching, wet-furred fragments. The oruh was somehow still running, bleeding from a dozen wounds, shrieking like a human child on fire. Jamie wrenched the umbrella-thing from Zero, yelling "Like this!" and pressed a trigger so the weapon's barbed umbrella-spines opened, curving upward like an umbrella, wind-blown, inside out. There was a spike at the top of the center shaft that she drove down onto a wheeler's brain-case from above, twisting the whole mechanism so that the jags on the umbrella-spines caught the furred spokes, ripping into them, clamping them. The thing fell back crippled. She twisted the instrument loose and went after another.

The cart stopped moving. The oruh sank to its knees in a voracious morass of snarling, squealing black fur and madly arachnidian wheel-shapes. Dennis kicked another wheeler back off the cart as he crammed more shot and dumped more powder into the blunderbuss. Zero fought an impulse to run, just run in any direction. (*Wake up now*, he told himself, *wake up*), pulled another barbed umbrella skeleton from the box, fumbled with it, trying to get it open as a squealing black-fur spoke-thing, horrible puppy-dog ears flapping, came over the side of the cart at him, thrusting three snapping faces at his eyes. And then it threw its rear four animals over its front four, so that suddenly the thing fell on him from above, making a cage of itself. The spoke-animals twisted on their shafts inward toward Zero, and the thing's brain-case pressed down on him from above —he could feel it rotating . . . jaw-snapping cyclopean fur-faces everywhere he turned, their tongues lapping at his ears, rasping on his cheeks, the back of his neck, tasting him, preparing to take a bite—

He found the trigger on the (*Wake up!*) umbrella-weapon, thrust it over his head at the furred brain-case, pressed the trigger. The mechanism flew open, its springs driving barbs into the squealing wheeler, which wrenched itself loose, raining blood on him. He twisted the wheeler away, off the cart. Another began to climb toward him.

Whump-ump. Dennis's blunderbuss blew four of the wheelers into fragments. Jamie tore another away from her; one of its spoke-animals took a piece of her thigh with it. Zero gagged at the sight.

Whump, whump, whump, and long echoes, and two more detonations, and more echoes. Zero looked up, panting. Sweat ran into his eyes. He saw men climbing off a newly arrived four-wheeled cart with smoking blunderbusses, swinging hooked pikes, driving the wheelers back into the cave-mouths of the Rug. The cart had come from the settlement to the north, probably alerted by the sound of Dennis's blunderbuss. The men on it scrambled to crush, stab, and chivvy the wheelers.

And the wheelers went back into the caves, and the caves closed up. The humps withdrew and began to sink out of sight in the Rug.

Zero found himself watching a sallow, prematurely bald man who might have been in his early thirties. He wore tattered corduroys, no shirt and no shoes, his feet blue with alien soil. He paused a few yards away and bent to pick up the limp body of a dying wheeler. One of the wheeler's spoke-animals convulsively snapped its jaws at him. He drove the sharp end of a pike into the animal's eye and twisted till it sagged. He smashed the skulls of two other spoke-animals—looking at Zero all the time, grinning—and then used his pike to pry open the thing's brain-case. The upper hemisphere popped off and fell away, almost neatly. The man reached in, scooped out some of its pasty blue brain, and ladled it into his mouth as a small boy eats a cream pie with his fingers. He shivered—and giggled.

"There's a drug effect from eating their brains," Jamie muttered, looking over. She winced as she used a strip of leather to make a tourniquet around her wounded leg. "God, I hope this doesn't get infected." After a moment she muttered, "He's probably the one who did it."

Wearily, Zero said, "You going to make me say, 'Did what'?"

She looked up to see if the brain-eater was too far away to hear her. "Started the wheelers after us. We figured they wouldn't be awake yet. He woke 'em up with a drill or something, if you ask me. No way to prove it. But I bet the little prick did it."

"Did it just to be an asshole?"

"He probably works for Fiskle."

Dennis was staring at the gutted wreckage of the oruh's body, crying. Between sobs he murmured, "Bloody 'ell. Bloody 'ell. Bloody 'ell."

The settlement was here when the first group from Earth arrived a few years back," Bowler said. He spoke absently, reeling it off as if he weren't really thinking about it. He stood staring out of the second-story window at the activity in the settlement street. For some reason the Meta depilated the facial hair from their abductees; but the rest of Bowler's hair had grown shaggy. He wore the same blue jeans and workshirt he'd worn that night in New York. They already looked ragged.

Zero sat across from him in a turquoise wooden chair. He fingered the leather strips that held the chair together and struggled against sinking into the depression opening like a bottomless pit inside him.

Bowler went on. "All the buildings were here. Empty. In one of them was some stored food—local wildlife, vegetation, fruits. And a representative from the High Clans. The High Clans are just another group of forcibly transplanted aliens, but kind of humanoid. Anyway, this guy spoke through one of those shoulder translators and told the Earthers—up to a certain point —what to expect. Told them the food that the Mc-Mahons stored here was samples of the stuff that would be safe for our species to eat—but that kind of food, those particular fruits or whatever, was all he could vouch for. People have been poisoned trying some of the other stuff, though some of it turned out to be okay. And there were a few basic tools here: a smelter, a crude machine shop. The Meta give you that much edge. Just that much." He paused. "Unless you play their game, and go for the Progress Stations. Which means fighting with the other races."

"What's at a Progress Station?"

"Progress. Different things. Bits of useful technology. maybe some device we can use for making other devices or refining chemicals—like those crappy guns we've got. The plans, the ingredients for those came from a Progress Station. A little gift that gives us just that much more edge. Better chance for survival. The carrot in front of the donkey."

Zero nodded. Feeling numb, he looked around to try to get a handle on the place. The room was high-ceilinged—too high—and the thick walls were slitted with narrow windows that stretched from close to the floor nearly to the ceiling. The late afternoon light streamed in dusty shafts through the glassless windows, which also admitted a faint drone of voices and the clank and clatter of carts. The room held five beds; each bed was made of leather stretched on a wooden frame, topped with a mattress of the cheeseclothlike stuff they'd learned to make from the bark of a local tree. A symbol of the Pioneer sect was crudely painted on the wall, in a circle: an ax-blade crossed with a blunderbuss above an hourglass shape. The hourglass represented the only moon in the planet's sky, a flawless white double-triangle configuration a quarter the size of Earth's moon. The settlers thought it was artificial, a big space station of some kind, operated by the Meta.

Zero had bathed in cold water, had rinsed off his clothes. He wore shorts of the raspy cheesecloth stuff while he waited for his own clothes to dry. He'd eaten some sort of stewed vegetable that tasted like spinach but looked like cauliflower. He'd met some of the other "settlers" and thought at least half of them were cracked. Now he felt empty and disoriented, and he was still waiting for the seams to show themselves, for the dream to show him its unreality.

Bowler was almost expressionless, but somehow he emanated a deep, profoundly dignified sadness.

Zero felt like biting through one of his own fingers just to see what would happen. He made himself think about something else. "We're fighting all the time with the other races?"

"With some we maintain a cease-fire. Some we tend

to fight with—there are skirmishes here every few months. Most of the fighting is done in the north, in competition for Progress Stations. But it's obvious that the Meta put us here because they want us to fight. There was a race of something like centaurs, but their hind parts were more like lions than horses. Beautiful to look at. A week ago they were completely exterminated, ambushed, slaughtered by a temporary alliance of the Earthers, the High Clans, and the Geck. I suppose it's true that they'd attacked one of our exploration parties; they'd attacked the High Clan and the Geck. They were probably like everyone else—half crazy from disorientation. Fierce because they were lost and scared.

"But lots of the killing is calculated. There isn't room for thirty-one domineering, intelligent, ambitious races here, and they all know it. The so-called 'Allies' are waiting for their chance to kill one another when it's more convenient. It's ugly, Zero. If we hadn't been thrown onto a hostile planet in low-tech conditions, we could've had friendly relations with most of the aliens. The Meta set us up so we'd kill one another. And they watch. That's all. They *watch*. It's—" He spat at the window.

"But we're here," Zero said, trying to accept it. "What do you think we should do?"

In a choked voice, his hands balled with anger at his sides, Bowler said, "Cisco and Angie are out now trying to organize an expedition. They're so damned stupid. They figured it's that or drudge work around here. The Earther Council rewards a successful Progress Station expedition with leisure and goods. They think they'll have it easy that way. And they think they'll meet the Meta or something.

"It's bullshit. It's fucking *bullshit!* I think we should move away from the settlement, try to ignore the Meta.

— 28 —

Maybe if we abandon their game, they'll leave us alone. Start our own commune somewhere, learn to use the planet's resources."

"We'd be killed, Bowler. The place is crawling with predators. And the Murderers . . . " He stared at the floor between his feet. It was made of the same bluish, concrete-like stuff as the walls: almost adobe, almost plaster. "I mean, everything we do here is meaningless, whatever it is. This isn't where we were intended to be. This is—" He shook his head and added bitterly, "I wanted to be a filmmaker. Can you believe that? Are the Meta going to give us film equipment at one of those Progress Stations? I wonder if they can get me a good cinematograper. Not much variety for urban locations on this planet. Can't really make a film that's set in Paris, or East L.A. . . . It might seem petty, but shit, Bowler, *that was my life*. That was my dream. Here it's living death, man."

Bowler's shoulders sagged. He turned back to the window. "Tell me something, Zero. What did you have in New York, really? Where's your family, for example? Were you close to them? Close to brothers and sisters, maybe?"

Zero shook his head. "I was an only child. My parents divorced when I was ten, and I lived with my mom. She died when I was fourteen, so I moved in with my dad. He and I—he's not a bad guy, I guess, but there was always this kind of . . . this embarrassment between us. Like he felt, 'Well, you're my kid, so I got to try to relate to you.' But it was like a couple of people stuck together on a plane making polite conversation. He was relieved when I moved out. And . . . I had one girfriend I almost married. But that broke up."

"So you had nothing on Earth, Zero."

"But dammit, the *potential* for everything was there! I'd have found my place somewhere. Or had a chance to. Here—shit. Here there's only the potential for—for *combat*. It's like being *drafted*."

"It doesn't have to be. We could find a way to break away from it and survive. The Meta are the local version of the military-industrial complex. They're imperialists exploiting us for their own purposes, purposes we don't understand and probably never will. If we—"

He broke off, staring at a thing that had floated in through the window.

It was a small silver sphere about the size of a tennis ball. It floated through a shaft of sunlight, glimmering faintly, and then moved purposefully up toward the ceiling. It seemed to hang in place for a few moments, slowly rotating. There was a little red dot on one side, and somehow Zero had the impression that the red dot was like the iris of an eye, that the sphere was watching him.

Looking at it, Zero felt like a frightened child. A child's uncut anxiety held him taut inside.

The sphere seemed to watch them for a full minute and then lost interest, drifted out the open door, and down the hall.

The tension in Zero went with it. He felt drained.

"Jamie says the Meta watch us through those things," Bowler said. "When there's a fight, a flock of 'em show up. Wouldn't the CIA and the FBI love to have a few of those?"

"Anybody try communicating with them?"

"Sure. The settlers have tried everything to communicate with the Meta. They tried talking to the surveillance spheres, the McMahons. No response. The McMahons—the ones you call Artichoke-Faces—are the

Meta's shop supervisors here. They're in the Progress Stations sometimes, or they come around to hand out fresh respirators, different kinds of adaptation gear for the aliens who need it. Sometimes the McMahons say things on their own initiative, but they don't answer questions, and they don't clue you in on what's behind the game. They just tell you the basic rules. Trying to communicate with the McMahons and the Meta is like trying to talk to the Sphinx. In the end most of the abductees—settlers, if you like—end up thinking of the Meta as a kind of cryptic but ultimately benevolent employer. Some of them even worship the Meta. But some of them—"

"Some of them hate the Meta," Zero said, and Bowler nodded.

TWO

Zero and Bowler walked down a long, echoing hallway. The building had the architectural presence of a monastery. Looking out of place, a striking young woman was walking down the hall toward them. She was strawberry-blond, pale, freckled, and dimpled. Big blue eyes. Voluptuous in a torn gingham halter-top and Levi cut-offs. She was barefoot, and she carried a wooden bowl of steaming water. She glanced at them and walked expressionlessly past into a room on the left. "She's nursing Jamie," Bowler said.

"Who is she? That face should be on the label for a jar of preserves or something. Sunny Jim's sister."

"Who is she?" Bowler repeated dryly as they walked out into the courtyard. "She's the torment of every man here. That's Trish, Jamie's girlfriend. Her wife, really."

"Shit."

"Yeah."

They paused outside a wooden door. Bowler whispered, "This is the Council room. Listen, you're not going to believe this. There's someone here you know. It's a weird coincidence that they should rake in someone else from the college. Unless maybe . . . I don't know."

"Well, who the hell is it?"

"Fiskle. Harmon Fiskle, Ph.D."

"Are you putting me on?"

"Uh-uh. Dr. Fiskle. He went to that conference at Oxford, right? Went on a side trip to Wales?"

"And disappeared. Yeah, I heard. God, this is synchronicity with a vengeance. Jamie mentioned him, but I didn't connect the name . . . She said she thought he tried to kill her, set the wheelers off."

"If he can get away with it, he probably did it. Let's hope it's not 'synchronicity with a vengeance.' He's got power here, the prick."

"Oh, great. Just great. And he brought his social theorem with him. Skinner and Social Darwinism."

"You know it. And he sees this as the ideal place to—"

The door opened. A bearded man looked out at them and said, "Are you going to stand out here whispering, or are you coming in?"

There was something ritualistic in the barrenness of the Council room. Zero thought of a gathering of tribal leaders in an Indian lodge. Bare walls, a slit in one of them for a window. Shaky light from torches oozing a ghost snake of yellow smoke. And the settlers, squatting on the floor against the wall, looking at the floor, the ceiling, staring into space. A few of them talking in low voices but not looking at one another. They were like a videotape Zero had seen of a group therapy session for the chronically depressed.

There were twelve of them. With Jamie and Trish missing, only one of them was female: Anna, a sturdy pop-eyed Puerto Rican woman. Jamie was the mayor, and normally she'd be in charge of the Council meetings. In her absence the chief of food rationing presided. That was Fiskle.

Fiskle's was the only cheerful face. Zero remembered him as a preppie and a snob. And a hide-bound behaviorist. He'd been a prodigy, a professor at only twenty-six years old. Known for immaculate suits in gray, black, or quiet blue, and for his spotless patent leather shoes. For his anal exactitude in everything, from his manicure to his demands for perfection in student papers.

But after five years he'd trimmed his classroom work to the tenure minimum, and devoted most of his energies to working at the university medical facility, correcting sociopathic behavior through a particularly rigid application of rewards and punishments. Especially punishments.

Now he wore a tunic and rough trousers of leather. His head was shaved—must be painful, shaving here—and somehow he was the only man in the room with clean fingernails. He was lean and sunburned with a sharp nose and hooded gray eyes and lips so red they looked cherry-stained. His expression was supercilious complacency.

He smiled at Zero and Bowler as they sat directly across from him to the right of the door. He was also the only man in the room who didn't have yellowed teeth. Zero imagined him searching frantically through the local flora till he found some fibrous reed that could be made into a serviceable toothbrush.

"What a pleasure it is to have two former students here. And how very curious it is, too! Perhaps someone was listening when I said—more than once, to be sure—that I wished I had some of my students alone in a foreign country, where I could make my own rules for their improvement."

"This place don't run to your rules," said a strikingly handsome blond-haired young man with a surfer's tan. He wore no shirt, perhaps to show off his perfect muscle tone.

He glanced at the newcomers. Zero's gut contracted when he saw that the right side of the man's face was missing. It looked as if it had been clawed away. There was a thin crust of red over the bone, and claw-stripes of bluish scar tissue, and a crater where his right eye should have been. He grinned lopsidedly at Zero. "Something wrong, man?"

Zero shook his head. "Um. No!"

"My rules are nature's rules, Warren," Fiskle told the disfigured blond. "And in time they'll assert themselves without my help. My only hope is to guide us into step with nature. And then, paradoxically, we'll overcome nature. Tame it. As we were beginning to do on Earth. It *wants* us to tame it."

"Let Jesus guide us!" cried a wispy man with long, dirty brown hair. Zero had assumed the man was wearing a loincloth of some kind, but looking closer he realized there was no loincloth; the man was nude. "Jesus appointed us to this new wilderness. His Eden is here. If we find our way back to innocence, Eden will—"

"Kindly put a sock in it, Smilder, will you?" Fiskle interrupted sweetly. It was venomous sweetness. He beamed at the rest of them. "Now then, the chief business of the day is to vote on the acceptance of the newcomer Martin Wirth, aka 'Zero.' Bowler has sponsored him and given us a bit of background on him. So, as we have to get on to the rationing budget, let's get this out of the way. All in favor . . . "

Zero held his breath.

He needn't have worried. He was unanimously voted in. "We need everyone we can get, you see," Fiskle said. "Everyone human and sane. So far, you're sane. And so far you're human."

Zero looked at Bowler. The look said, *What does he mean by that?* Bowler shrugged. Zero asked, "Fiskle—is there something else here I should know about?"

Warren laughed bitterly. The others shifted slightly, a rustling noise about the room, and glanced up at the window.

Fiskle looked at the window, too. "We thought it was the Meta doing it, at first," Fiskle said meditatively. "But now I don't think so. I think it's this planet. Something to do with the IAMton fields. I think, though, that the Meta know about it. I think that's why they picked this planet—to make it more interesing."

"Shut up, Fiskle," Anna said, "for god's sake."

"They don't like to talk about it." Fiskle was talking absently, as if musing aloud. "It's as if there's something dirty in being a Twist. I suppose it *is* obscene. But I suspect it makes a good deal of sense in the long run."

Bowler said, "If we're going to keep our sanity here, we've got to keep the mysteries to a minimum. Because there are too damned many already." He looked sharply at Fiskle and snapped, "So what the hell are you talking about?"

"There's a sort of . . . an indescribable convection that moves through the landscape, through the atmosphere. A kind of current moving through the fabric of reality. You can see it in the way it—ah, it makes things look different. But after its passed, they're the same as before.

Except when it reaches something that *thinks*. It changes that something, alters it, gives it a new biology—a new, uh, sense of self. To greater and lesser degrees. You haven't seen the Current, Bowler, because it comes rarely to this part of the world. Only twice in Earther memory. And the settlers don't like to talk about it. Things are, as you say, mysterious enough. But you may encounter some of those who've been altered. We call them Twists. You'll know them when you see them. You'll know the Current when you see it. Steer clear of both."

Zero and Bowler stepped out into the courtyard and paused to look around. The Fortress of the Pioneers looked like something out of an old Foreign Legion movie. Baking in the golden afternoon sun, the courtyard could almost have belonged to some nineteenth-century Cairo trader—until you looked up at the mocking green sky.

The fortress was separated from the rest of the settlement by high, thick walls that were seamlessly connected by walkways with the upper floors of the block-shaped, slit-windowed buildings they protected. The whole structure looked to be of a piece, as if it had been made by pouring something into a mold. Pioneer sect guards —eight men and two women, armed with blunderbusses, crossbows, and pikes—patroled the walkway atop the wall, two stories up.

The air was rank, partly from the sewage trench in the long shed to the left, which drained into a ditch back of the fortress. The stink of the courtyard had layers, fermenting in the heat, and the sharpest layer came from the oruh pen.

Against the right-hand wall, three oruh shifted and farted in the small wooden pen. A cloud of some of the local pests, diaphanous flying things like tiny jellyfish, hung over the pen, valving in jerky movements over the oruh and their offal. They alighted now and then on an oruh's rump, clasping like barnacles, sucking, only to zig-zag away when the oruh irritably snapped at them.

A skinny, stringy-haired, tired-eyed woman carrying a six-month-old baby hitched on one hip, used her free hand to open a wooden box strapped to the pen's fence. There was a leather sack in the box. She untied it, lifted it out, and emptied it into the oruh's feeding trough, dumping segmented, squirming creatures of shiny ochre. Some variation of roaches, Zero thought. Which the oruh, grunting happily, began to crunch and grind in their sideways beaks.

Looking hastily away, Zero followed Bowler across the courtyard to the weapons rack. Sweat beaded instantly on them when they stepped out onto the courtyard's hot griddle.

The Pioneers' sergeant at arms stood behind a rough wooden counter in the shade of the wall, to one side of the wood-post gate. He was an unsmiling black man of about thirty-five, wearing a tunic of blotchy black rawhide, probably from an oruh. Bowler showed him a square of leather stamped with the Pioneers' symbol. The man nodded and asked, "Where you going?"

"Down to the Neutral," Bowler said.

"Pikes is all, then, or daggers. Watch out for the Kiss Me Darlings."

"What the hell are Kiss Me Darlings?"

"Look kinda like overgrown orchids made out of shredded coconut. Five feet high, real pretty. Smell real nice—like daffodils, kinda. Don't go near 'em. Don't listen to nothin' they say. If you see any kinda Twist, steer way clear."

He turned to a rack of weapons made in the shops and forges on the far side of the settlement. He selected two of the lighter black metal pikes and passed them over. Each pike was about four feet long with a wicked hook on one end and a spike on the other.

Bowler nodded and took one; Zero took the other. It felt like iron. It was heavy.

Holding it in both hands, he followed Bowler past the guard, out the gate.

The road outside was rutted dirt. A few Pioneers squatted outside, wearing rawhide or the rotting clothing they had been abducted in. They were talking and smoking some local herb in wooden pipes. Looking again, Zero saw that one of the men wasn't a Pioneer, wasn't even quite human. His skin was black but not Negro black; it had the waxy blackness of licorice. His eye, or perhaps eyes, was a strip of sparkling white-gold above a nose that looked as if it had been split with a blunt knife and never sewn up. He was nude except for a metal-mesh loincloth, intricate bodypaints in floral abstractions, rather like Louis XIV wallpaper, and tennis shoes—Reebok tennis shoes he'd bartered from someone. Four silvery hoops pierced his right wrist the way earrings pierce an earlobe. A black plastic box on his left shoulder translated for him as he spoke to the others. His hands seemed entirely human, except the fingers were perhaps an inch too long.

"That one of the Twists?" Zero asked, whispering. "Looks like he might've been human once."

Bowler shook his head and murmured, "An alien. High Clan. Their trading rep, Zickorian. Supposedly one of our allies, but, like, no one quite trusts him completely."

There was a broken-down cart leaning against the wall of the building across the way. A naked teenage boy with feral eyes crouched under the cart like a dog, sniffing the wind. He was gray with dust and streaked with blood. Skinny, skin so taut over his lean muscles you could see every cord and sinew. His nose was running messily. He pissed himself as Zero watched. Zero didn't need to be told about him: the boy had gone mad. About twenty-five percent of the Meta's abductees went mad, someone had said. Zero felt a deep chill, looking at the boy. He forced himself to look away.

The wall above the cart was dark with graffiti written smearily with charcoal:

TRISH WANTS COCK
after which someone, probably Jamie, had written:
BULLSHIT JUST TRY AND GIVE IT TO HER YOU CRETIN
SHE'LL USE YOUR BALLS IN A SALAD
(and someone else had scrawled:)
WE DIED AND GOD SENT US HERE. IT AIN'T HEAVEN.

And there was more, written in a cryptic alien script.

They turned left and walked down the road that led to the Neutral, where the races met to deal and where genuine neutrality was a matter of whim.

The Meta had built the human settlement atop a long, grave-shaped hill. Between the human settlement and the next one to the west, the Ki-ips settlement, was a packed dirt road that stretched across a boggy lowland. About two miles ahead, halfway across the bogs, the ground rose into a stony maze of boulders, almost a Stonehenge of crooked monoliths a few acres across, an island of dryness in the sodden valley. Here, Bowler explained, was the Neutral, where goods were bartered, defense alliances forged, conspiracies birthed, feuds resolved, curiosity sated, and contracts for joint expeditions made. Where technologies beyond the Iron Age level—possessed by those who'd made it to the upper Progress Stations—were taboo and never the subject of barter. To give another race a technology it hadn't earned was to undermine your own race's playing position in the Meta's great game.

Bowler and Zero trudged through a cloud of blue dust raised by a group of traders trundling wheelbarrows and creaking handcarts along the road to the Neutral. The road was of packed earth reinforced by logs, stretching through the swamp from hummock to hummock. It had been there when the first Earthers arrived.

There were eight traders. All of them carried skeeter switches, like scraggly brooms, cut from the scratch tree; the switches hung from leather thongs at their belts. Like most of the settlement, the traders were young, humans of every color, and mostly male. Only one of the traders was female. The Meta didn't want their game complicated by a lot of offspring.

Zero looked around, blinking in the dull jade light reflected from the chains of small bog-ponds around the blue-mossed hummocks. Clusters of translucent blue plants edged the ponds, seemed to have grown out of the water and back down into it, perfect arcs like glassy croquet hoops. The sky was hazed over, looking like tarnished bronze, a fulsome glower in green-gold. The air was humid here, hothouse warm, cloying with the odd perfumes of alien blossoms and lewd with swamp rot. Perspiration stuck Zero's shirt to his back. He unbuttoned it, but then noticed everyone else was well covered despite the heat. Some were in the rags that remained of their original outfits; some in a kind of sackcloth; some in tunics of the local cheesecloth, some in a fine, glossy, silklike cloth with curious red and yellow lightning-stroke designs woven into it: the weave of the Whorebugs. The Whorebugs traded for metal goods; few of the settlers were so well clothed.

"Better not open your shirt," one of the traders told Zero. He was a short, haggard Japanese, maybe forty, with a slight accent; he wore a strawberry-lemon Whorebug tunic that he'd rearranged to look like a Shinto robe. He was carrying a jingling crude-cloth sack of small iron tools, presumably for trading with the Whorebugs. "The more skin you expose to the air, the more likely a jumpskeeter will smell you." He pointed at a nearby hummock, where something squatted, or a mosquito as big as a crow. Take off the crow-sized mosquito wings, Zero thought, and put proportional grasshopper's legs on it: jumpskeeter. The skeeter shifted its faceted rose-colored eyes and preened its proboscis. Zero hastily buttoned up his shirt.

Bowler nodded. "Yeah, watch out for those fuckers. One of them jump on you, you'll lose a pint of blood in less than half a second. Jumps on you, sucks it up *zip*, just like that, jumps off, all in the blink of an eye. Sometimes seven or eight of 'em travel together; they get you all at once, you're a dead man." Seeing the look on Zero's face, he added, "It doesn't happen very often."

"Not very often," Zero said dully. "Just now and then. Good. Great. Lovely."

"You okay?" Bowler asked him.

"No." He looked out at the glossy patches of the bogs. He imagined the wheelers, or worse, waiting to meet him out there, something alien crouched behind a hummock of geological wrongness. "It's all too wrong." The sky was wrong. The sun was wrong. The horizon was wrong. The color of the water, the texture of the foliage, the cast of the light, the feel of the dirt—all of it was wrong. And the smells: tantalizingly . . . almost familiar. And the *almost* made them even more wrong than if they had been completely unfamiliar. Go to a foreign country on Earth—the African veldt, the jungles of Thailand —and things are strange and disquieting. But there's a foundation of some familiarity, at least, in the colors and feel of sky and earth and water and sun. The vista seals the foreign place into your understanding, opens it up to your adaptation. But here . . .

The Japanese said, "The ground is below and the sky above. Water runs downhill, plants grow upward. It is not our world, but it is world."

Ashamed of himself for whining but unable to help it, Zero said, "Bowler, I want to go back to the town. I can't handle it out here. *Anything* could be out here."

"It's not that bad. Look, there's some fishermen. They seem okay. In harmony with the environment and all that."

Six men and a woman, muddy and squinting, stood to their thighs in a coppery bog-pond not far off the road. Zero thought of Asians working in rice fields. Four of the fishermen were lined up not far apart in the oblong, thirty-foot pond, bent to make scooping motions in the water, driving crustaceans into the grass-fiber net held by the other two. A jumpskeeter went instantaneously from utter motionlessness to a thirty-foot bound, soaring down over the woman holding half the net. The man beside her saw it coming, whipped his switch around, and caught the skeeter in midair, knocking it to the side. It fell onto the mud of a hummock

— 44 —

The woman turned and used the butt of her own switch to smash the thing to pulp. Its storage pouch burst, squirting stolen blood.

"Learn skills like that one," Bowler said, "and it won't be so bad here."

Zero shook his head. He was hot, uncomfortable, and tired, and he hadn't had enough to eat.

Also, he was on the wrong planet.

"I just don't think I'm ready," Zero complained, "to go to this Neutral thing. I've seen enough aliens, Bowler. And Fiskle will be there. I want to see as little of Fiskle as possible."

Bowler began, "No one's allowed to fuck with you in the Neutral—"

The Japanese trader looked over his shoulder and laughed. "Not fuck with you there? That's a good one. They do what they want. They're not *supposed* to mess with you, and most people—or not-people—keep it that way. But sometimes . . . " He shrugged.

Bowler said, "Yeah, sometimes the Whatevers step out of line. It's hard to enforce the Neutrality. But it doesn't close down—everyone needs it. I guess it's safer than—out there." He waved vaguely at the southern horizon. Off that way the bogs ended as the ground rose to the ridge that separated the settlement from the Rug. To the north, the bog seemed to go on forever, lost in mists a half-mile on.

They'd walked more than a mile. Zero was hot and thirsty. Blue dust was gumming his nose and throat.

It was very quiet, just then, for no good reason at all. *No Earthly reason*, Zero thought.

A quarter-mile ahead now, Zero could see the stony cluster of vertical black and gray, patchy in spots with color, that was the Neutral. They might find anything there. Zero felt panic creeping up on him, coming at him from all directions. He had strobe-swift images of wheelers snapping at his face; of the mad-eyed boy crouching under the cart; of the jumpskeeter stropping its proboscis.

Bowler looked worriedly at him. "You look as if you're going to throw up or something."

Zero muttered, "I don't know how long I can hold on, Bowler."

"Everybody goes through this when they first come here. Some snap, some don't. You won't. You can't let yourself. Nothing has prepared us for this. It's another world, and its foreignness makes Cambodia look like Kansas. And it shakes you up more than anybody figured it would. Does it to everyone. Hold on to that, man, that we all went through it. The panic passes. You adapt or you flip out. You got a choice."

"I don't have a choice. If I do, I do. I can't control—"

"You can," the Japanese said. "It's a choice between strength and no strength. Between you making a choice and letting the world make the decision for you."

Zero looked at him.

He nodded slowly and said, "What's your name?"

"Yoshio."

"Yoshio. I'm Zero. Thanks, man." And they shook hands. The Earther custom was reassuring.

Bowler lowered his voice to a whisper. "Zero, you know what happens to people who flip out here? There're no counselors here. No thorazine, no antipsychotic drugs, no emergency rooms. If you lose mental control, you get expelled from the settlement. That kid back there under the cart—they've been having trouble catching him. But they'll get him. They'll take him out

— 46 —

into the country, chase him off, and leave him out there. And he'll die. Otherwise he steals food and just . . . his presence *demoralizes* people. They can't afford you if you can't adjust. So you got to go to the Neutral. Force yourself to face the alienness. You know? Anyway, you want to see Angie and Cisco, right? They'll be there somewhere. I promised them I'd meet 'em this afternoon, once you got on your feet."

"How's Angie handling it?"

"It was rough at first. But she's kind of . . . kind of into it now. I almost think she's starting to enjoy it here."

"She, uh, say anything about me?"

Bowler snorted. "You think this is the place you're going to satisfy your unrequited love?"

Zero shrugged.

The Neutral was a twisting lane between the high boulders; awnings had been strung between boulders, some of Whorebug cloth, some of grass weave, some of leather. Under each awning, or between them, or wandering about, a dozen races were proof of the galaxy's demented variety.

A grizzly of a man in the tatters of a LAPD uniform pushed aside the crude-cloth flap of his lean-to, stepped out, and looked them over. He still had his badge and a cracked plastic nameplate: LT. DOGGO. Perched crookedly on his stubby nose were dark glasses with one of the lenses missing. He had no shoes, and his horny feet were blue from the dirt. On his right shoulder was a translation box. With him was half-faced Warren, wearing buckskin.

"You're crazy," Doggo was telling Warren. "There could be anything in there. *Don't do it.*"

"Don't do what?" Bowler asked. He and Zero stood beside the lean-to, in the shade of one of the monolithic stones. Bowler seemed to have business with Doggo.

"Warren wants to go *surfing* in the Stinking Bucket."

"It shouldn't be called that," Warren said. "It smells funny, sort of mentholated and sort of like fermented soy sauce. But it's beautiful. The water's thick and warm—prob'ly hold you up real good."

"And holds you down even better, I'll bet," Doggo said.

"And the waves on it are gigantic and perfectly shaped. Symmetrical as a mandala. Tubular to perfection. And it's, like, calling to me. I'm gonna make a board."

"Have you seen my friends, Doggo?" Bowler asked.

"Yeah. I'll take you to them. Who's this?"

"Zero. Friend of mine."

"Zero," Doggo said, "I'm the lawkeeper in the Neutral, okay? I'm the law here, humanside. Okay?" Not waiting for an answer, he turned and lumbered off. Bowler and Zero followed him.

They moved down the lane, and almost immediately something four-legged and bizarre capered up to block their way. It looked like a sawhorse with a legless, armless dwarf perched on one end where the horse's head would be. The nearly human torso was naked—or possibly it had been coated with a kind of paint that was the equivalent of clothing. Where the genital would have been was a sort of pouch with something irregular and unlike human genitals outlined in it— like a silk bag containing random parts from a gearbox.

The sawhorse part was battleship gray; the torso and head were uniformly gold, even its eyes. Its plastic-glossy legs, of duller gold, looked like two-by-fours, but they moved like things of rubber, showing no joints. Zero thought of Gumby's horse, Poky.

The alien's head was like a human's whose face had been blurred, had somehow been made clay-malleable, as if the Creator's hand had pressed the features down from top to bottom, smearing eyes into cheekbones, nose into lips.

It moved with impressive flexibility, its sawhorse-legs were springy as it bounced back and forth chal-lengingly in front of them.

Doggo turned apologetically to Zero and Bowler. "This is a Pezz. They're sorta territorial."

The Pezz's mouth moved as if it were chewing some-thing too big for it, and squeaky, off-key violin sounds emerged. The translator box strapped to its shoulder said, "You may not pass, though green is green and yel-low is yellow. This is my crèche of exquisites, and you have not the three intimacies."

"Friend Pezz," Doggo said wearily—he'd said it nine times that day already—"I bear the sigil of pas-sage, and it protects me and those with me. Anyway this is the Neutral—no one's territory. Stand aside."

"Doggo," the Pezz replied, "you have piqued my curiosity. With you is one who, if I've sorted and classi-fied your hormonal secretions properly, exudes the pur-ple odor of impossible ambition. The other reeks with the sour blue of disorientation and the red smell of irritation. He is adaptation-incompetent." This last he said looking at Zero.

Zero turned in disgust to Bowler and muttered,

"Bowler, not only do I have to talk to a fucking melted dwarf on a sawhorse, the melted dwarf on a sawhorse *giving me shit*. I can't handle this place, Bowler."

"So take a subway home," Bowler said as they followed Doggo past the Pezz. "What did he mean, Doggo, uh, about the impossible ambition?"

"You'd know better'n I would," Doggo said. "The Pezz are telepathic, in a biochemical kind of way. They study a race for a while, match up that race's hormonal secretions—which they have a sense for—with their emotions and attitudes, and they know more or less what you're up to by the excess chemicals you sweat out. You got big plans?"

Bowler said nothing.

Doggo circled well around the Pezz's booth-territory —where it traded speckled pots that it had made by combining agates and a kind of cement exuded from its pouch—and they went on, following the withing lane through yet another turn.

They emerged into a lane edged by a series of booths —a bazaar where the fabric of reality became piebald and patchy; the very air seemed uncertain of itself, crackling with the interaction of bioenergy fields not designed to mesh. A sense, walking down the lane, of passing open doors into other worlds.

There were awnings between the crooked, monolithic stones, and under each one was an alien or two, or one alien that looked like two unless you looked closely (or perhaps *was* two and yet one, depending on their mood). Each alien was hawking wares in its own fashion or attempting some variation of missionary work, religious or philosophical conversions. Some of this rhetoric appeared as miniature fireworks from craterlike pores in alien skin, or the waving of intricately interspersed banners.

The place was Hell for a seeker after consonance; the only constants were discord and a certain territorial guardedness; and even those consistencies sometimes broke down.

They passed through an industrial fugue of clamors created by a group of metallic creatures who flung themselves at one another so as to crash their brassy hides, evidently in ritual celebration—living cymbals happily colliding. But they gesticulated in protest when the tendrils of a creature the Earthers called the Jungle hung down into their niche and got in the way of their crashing, frustrating them with mufflings. The Jungle fascinated Zero's eye, a viny, red-bristled thing of iridescent foliage, stretching from its own booth to overreach several others, pulsing here and there with bladders like the ballooning underchins of frogs, its interior pregnant with shadows, its vines reminding him of those Earthly sea creatures that look like plants but are in fact animals. It was an enormous tangle—a tangle that was somehow symmetrical, almost a patterned weave—of slowly reaching, groping ropiness. It signified intelligence by twisting lengths of itself into geometrical signs, but the translation boxes were nonplussed by it. Its occasional forays into the other niches were probably attempts to communicate, Doggo said, since it consumed only air and minerals.

A scaly cold-blooded snake-eyed thing ripped off one of its own several arms and offered it cheerfully to Zero as they passed. Zero, out of politeness—really trying to adjust, honestly *trying*—began to reach for the twitching, drippy-stumped limb, but Doggo pushed him away from the niche and said, "Don't accept, or you'll have to offer it at least a finger. It's a cheat—his limbs grow back."

Zero whimpered softly to himself but held together and went on.

A thing made of ice-cream-cone-shaped layers of blue-mottled flesh approached Zero on a biologically generated magnetic field; it smelled of dirty socks and the smoke from a burned-out electrical socket. It paused and exuded translucent red pears of gel that hardened and hung from it in a group of three, waggling enticingly. "You're in luck, Zero," Doggo said. "This is a Poolsh. These guys don't come around often. Supposed to be an omen of good fortune in the long run when they come up to someone. Try one of the jelly pears." Doggo plucked a pear and bit into it and smiled, nodded as if agreeing with an imaginary speaker.

Zero looked at Bowler, who nodded gravely as he bit into a pear himself. Zero made himself reach out and pluck a jelly pear. He took a bite. The consistency was like a "gummy bear," but its taste was of a delicious iodine—iodine cannot be delicious, but this was. Then he saw a picture, a vivid image of himself spitting copiously on the Poolsh.

He shook the image from his mind and said, "Whoa. I had a disgusting hallucination."

Doggo said, "It sent you an image. It knows our brain chemistry now because it ate one of our dead—with our permission. It trades the fruit for some enzyme in human saliva it prizes. It deals with us through a chemical in the fruit that carries the message in image form. You should be around when they're in the mood to make a speech. You get a pineapple-size jelly pear and if you eat it, you get a headache from all the—wait."

He broke off, looking to the side, into a niche between two monoliths, where an organism roughly resembling a man-sized koala bear was frantically gesturing, *Come here, come here!*

"Pay for me, will you, Bowler?" Doggo said, hurrying off to the koala. Bowler nodded and spat on the Poolsh until his mouth was dry.

Zero spat on the Poolsh a few times, perhaps inadequately, then left to follow Doggo, hoping he hadn't cheated anyone.

The koala was splitting open when Zero got there, bifurcating wetly between the legs; the upper head went glassy-eyed and frozen as another face, a pasty face of gills and suckers, showed itself in the new slit, lowering on a prehensile neck. The gills began to ooze phlegm. Doggo turned to Zero, muttered, "This is Hmm, he does some spying for me. But this ain't a costume. He lives inside this other animal like clothes, but the animal's alive. They climb inside lower animals and just sort of take them over and make a few changes and walk around in them. Don't really hurt them. After a while they let go and get another. Like a living fur coat. Okay, he's got his gills cleared now."

To Zero's surprise, the thing spoke raspily in English, with aspiration from its gills, in a voice that was like a sing-song mimicry of Doggo. "Fiskle is talking about extending human control throughout settlement cluster. 'Humanity *über Alles*,' I heard someone say, but I believe they were using sarcasm. He also wants to restrain the females and force them to breed."

"Jesus!" Doggo shook his head in disbelief. "What an asshole!"

Zero said weakly, trying not to think about the face between the oozing lips of the suddenly slit koala, "He didn't say anything about this stuff at the Council meeting."

"He wouldn't. This's something he's pulling on the sly. This came down at the meeting of his New Humans group," Doggo said distractedly. "Sort of a lodge he started. I thought they were up to something subversive. Looks like they are."

He took a coil of copper wire from his pocket and put it in the koala's insensate hand, closing the koala's fingers around it. "Thank you," Hmm said, and drew his head back into the koala. The awareness came back into the koala's eyes, and it lumbered off into the shadows between stones.

"How come it spoke English?" Zero said.

"Oh, I let it tap into my brain once, as a gesture of friendship. *That* was an act of trust, let me tell you. Come on. Let's find your friends so I can get back to work. I got to do something about Fiskle."

They rejoined Bowler and continued down the lane. Doggo's lower lip pushed into his upper with worry. Only ten yards on they had to slow to work their way around the edge of a small crowd. About thirty people, mostly human, stood around a seashell-like booth contrived of intricately symmetrical many-hued arrangements of fine silky cloths, gauzes, and filigrees, a kind of enormous peacock's-tail backdrop for the two creatures who stood upright before it: Whorebugs.

If you were nearsighted and not too close, the Whorebugs looked, at first, like human women. Blink and move closer, and you saw they were human-sized insects. (No, not insects, Zero decided. They had only four limbs, and they didn't have mandibles. But there was an insectlike chiton on them, and insect exoskeletal joints in their limbs.) Their long, graceful legs, their skirted hips, and what at least appeared to be breasts made Zero think of an old Fleischer Brothers cartoon he'd seen in an NYU animation class. In it a community of peoplelike insects had lived in a town made of discarded tin cans and old shoes and the like; the "insect girls" had been sexy mergings of cute bugs and stylized human females—Betty Boops with six limbs and antennae. That was almost how the Whorebugs looked, but glossier, made of hard, interlocking parts of waxy yellow and brown, faceted insect eyes in their shiny bullet-shaped heads.

They wore bright tangerine Whorebug-cloth skirts folded back to expose their crotches, where, from something like a horizontal vagina, weblike strands of silk extruded, streaming out slowly and steadily. The Whorebugs stood with legs well apart, knees bent, hips thrust forward. Their extra-long triple-jointed arms reached between their horn-covered thighs to weave the cloth with hooked fingers in a motion faster than the eye could follow, almost magically producing the cloth piling in glossy ripples between their feet. Now and then they opened their mouths and emitted a glutinous, brightly colored syrup, by turns candy-apple red and ice blue and sun yellow. It dripped on honeyed strands to the raw material extruding from between their legs and was somehow incorporated into it, organized into marvelous patterns—patterns of candy-apple red and ice blue and sun yellow.

They looked whorish indeed, standing there spraddle-legged. Zero might've laughed if the sight weren't making him so queasy.

To one side a male (*was* it male?) Whorebug squatted cross-legged, its body squarish, its head wrapped in a three-tiered turban. It reached over and examined the cloth, held it up with a flourish for the crowd to see, then folded it, cut it neatly into swatches, and chirped something that Doggo's translator interpreted as, "The divinatory weave indicates a stage of maudlin forbearance approaching; wail over your condition, seek atonement with your gods, but forgo postures of aggression. Seek out environmental harmony . . . And friends, how better to seek out environmental harmony than with a few fine yards of [untranslatable] cloth, which can be yours for a pittance in metal or high-grade foodstuffs. . . . "

As they watched, Zero whispered to Doggo, "What you going to do about Fiskle?"

Doggo glanced at him sharply. "Listen—all that was confidential. I told you because you're with Bowler and he's with the Live and Let Live faction. Like me. But just—"

"I'm not going to say anything. I don't trust Fiskle, either."

"I don't know what we're going to do. He's got a lot of backers. If we kill him in his sleep, they'll probably know who did it. I'm still thinking about it."

Doggo, Bowler, and Zero moved past the crowd, down the lane. But one of the crowd had turned to watch them, and now he detached himself to tag along beside Zero. He was a human settler, a shaggy, gaunt, dart-eyed little guy in cracking black leathers. His hands were black with grime, his teeth mossy, but he seemed too alert, and he kept an eye nervously on Doggo, who strode on obliviously up ahead. "Hey, fren'," the newcomer piped, "you a New Fool, huh? Jus' got here, huh? I seen the ship come down. You the new one?"

"Yeah. What you want, man?"

"What makes you think I—"

"You're the same kind of guy on Earth. What you want?"

He grinned. "I'm Johnny Kelso. If it can be got on Fool's I can get it for ya. And there's one thing everybody wants after a while, am I right? There's a girl shortage here, right? Huh? I can arrange something when you're ready, my man."

"Christ. You a pimp? You sell some of that sideways Whorebug pussy or what?"

Kelso tittered. "Better'n that." He lowered his voice and looked around. They were passing something that looked like a metallic gorilla from the waist down; from the waist up it became an intricacy of chromium tentacles, barbed studs, and what appeared to be a headdress of small glassy radar receivers and green-crystalline hand fans, all of which were turned toward the sun.

As they passed the alien, Zero turned to Bowler and asked, "What was that thing?"

Bowler shrugged. "Ask *him*. Kelso's got it all. He said so."

Kelso gestured expansively. "The man's right—I got it all! Them was what we call sun-monkeys. Solar-powered animules. Up here you see the High Clansmen . . . now look, you want some of that, uh, relaxation we talked about?"

"I don't wanta break any of the local laws till I know what they are," Zero said as they walked past a group of licorice-black High Clansmen. The Clansmen were squatting around a wooden board gambling, using the skull of a small animal, painted with tiny symbols, as dice.

Kelso said, "Hey, don't worry about the laws. It ain't against the law—exactly. It's—well, see . . . " He lowered his voice. "It's a Twist. Lives off by himself."

"*Him*self?"

"Whatever," Kelso said hurriedly. "See, it's not a *he* exactly, 'cause he was altered, he—it—always wanted to be . . . well, it's got a pussy *and* a dick, a real long one so's it can fuck itself, see? It's kinda mean, though. It's got these big crab-claws. Snip off your head. Uh, so—this is the less-than-legal part, see, we hadda tie it up. But its female parts work good, and—"

"Forget it."

"I got some really primo dried wheeler-brain. I'm trading for anything you brought from Earth. Cigarettes, anything useful the Meta mighta left in your pockets."

"No, man, I don't have anything."

"Hey." Kelso's fingers were like pliers on his arm. "Listen. I'm here, okay? You're gonna need something. And listen: sooner or later, you're going to want to have a serious talk with Mr. Fiskle, you know? Things are about to change, and you're going to find yourself in a bad neighborhood all of a sudden unless you—"

Bowler broke in. "What'd he say about Fiskle? Hey, Kelso, what did you—"

Doggo had glanced back and stopped, seeing Kelso. He turned, scowling, pushed past Bowler, and took Kelso by the neck; he began to squeeze his Adam's apple. "Kelso, get the hell out of here!" He shoved him backward. Kelso staggered, coughing. "I told you, Kelso, you don't work the Neutral if you wanta keep your ass on your body, 'cause I will chop it off and feed it to the Phleg if you—"

Kelso was gone, slipped off into the shifting crowd.

"Sorry about that, friends," Doggo said, turning to Zero and Bowler. "There's a lotta sleazebags like him here, tryin' to get around workin' to survive."

"That's okay, man," Zero said. "I kinda like it. He made me feel like I was back in New York. . . . Damn!"

The *Damn!* came when Zero saw two creatures blocking the path, beyond Doggo. Zero pointed. Doggo turned to see what he was pointing at. He sighed and asked the strangers, "Well? What is it now?"

Two aliens, probably of two different worlds. The one on the left looked roughly like a pink, fleshy steamer trunk with a head-size lump in one end. In the lump was a pulsing membrane on which an image fizzed, a half-coalesced television image somehow organically produced. The creature moved on an underfringe of cilia. At the "front" end, under the lump, were four pouches and slits. It respirated through one of the slits, emitting a flute-toned *ki-ips . . . ki-ips . . . ki-ips* sound with each breath. Which, Zero supposed, meant this was what the settlers called a Ki-ips.

At its side was a bull-size, effluvia-dripping Arthropod with a gem-festooned snail shell big as a VW bug— and rather resembling one—and a respirator strapped over its breathing tubes just below its gelatinous antennae. Its mouth was a quivery, oozing triangle of slivery flesh that spoke in complex flatulences. The translator box screwed to the immense Arthropod's shell interpreted, "Doggo! We are in dispute and demand you arbitrate! The Ki-ips has indicated that its booth is unsuitable, and it wishes to move."

The Ki-ips's own translator box, screwed into the back of its video hump, interpreted the Arthropod's remarks in terms of the Ki-ips's own language, which consisted entirely of organically videotaped (and video-animated) imagery: a series of images flashing across the membrane screen. After visually interpreting the Arthropod's remarks, the Ki-ips's screen flickered through its reply. Zero saw an animation-enhanced video image of a villainous Arthropod leaping about in an enormous caldron of slime, splashing the unfortunate, innocent Ki-ips who was attempting to bask in the sun nearby. The gist of the imagery was transmitted from the Ki-ips's box directly to Doggo's, and they heard, "I said nothing of the sort! The rascal snail-thing has [untranslatable] and is certainly a boor! The truth is, this repellent hedonist was splashing me with his stench-happy wallowings—"

"Wallowings?" the Arthropod interrupted, aghast. "The dance celebrating the succession of elegant slimes can scarcely be described as 'wallowings'! I insist you move this low creature—"

Zero turned away, his stomach twisting with disorientation. *I'm not going to be able to handle this,* he thought. *Uh-uh.*

He saw a ten-by-five-foot rectangular box standing to one side, twenty feet away. It looked like something of dull metal. As he watched, its facing side slid away, revealing a shimmering interior in which the form of a man took shape—a man Zero knew. Professor Arnold Samuel Garrison, who'd lectured at New York University on the theoretical intricacies of the fourth dimension. Zero knew Garrison as a verbose eccentric. And a clothes horse. Garrison was wearing one of his Victorian suits, replete with French cuffs and top hat. As his image reified, became solid, he shot his cuffs and adjusted his string tie; his long, saturnine face flickered, then sharpened to clarity. He smiled with polite condescension at Zero. "Well, well, well—young Master Wirth."

Zero winced.

Garrison winked conspiratorially and hissed, "Come over here, my boy. I want a word with you."

Zero glanced around. Doggo and Bowler were distracted, involved in talking to the—the things. Zero shrugged and moved closer to the metal box, stood a yard from Garrison. "The Meta got you too, Professor? What's with the box? Some kind of prison?"

"The Meta? Prison? Don't be foolish, my boy. You jump to unwarranted conclusions. You're living in the ivory tower of your own presumptuousness. 'Tis you who are the prisoner, sir. I—the one and only Garrison —am here by means of teleportation. I'm just looking around. I've built a machine that has mastered space, which you see before you. If you like, you may step inside, and I'll take you back with me to Earth. Back to America, back to comfort and fast living: fast food and fast cars. Back to sex and drugs and rock and roll. Coming?"

Zero stared. "Seriously? Can you do it? Lemme get my friends—"

"Ah, young Master Wirth, I'm sorry, it cannot be. I can take only one along with me this trip. And I must go *now*. You have only to step into the box. Hurry! Are you coming, sir?"

"Fuck it!" Zero stepped into the box.

A human arm crooked itself around Zero's neck and dragged him backward out of the box, just as the box's outer edges, their metallic hardness instantly becoming impossibly flexible, began to move inward, closing like a sea anemone—clamping on the spot Zero had occupied a moment before.

Zero wrenched loose from the restraining arm, turned—and saw Cisco. Angie was with him. Both of them looked dirty and haggard but intact. "You almost got ate, Zero," Cisco said "Lucky I had an intuition about you."

"He's full of shit," Angie said. "I just happened to spot you and the Boxed Liar between the rocks."

Behind them, Doggo, having played diplomat, dismissed the quarreling aliens. They moved off, one sliding away and one oozing.

Zero glared at Cisco, demanding, "What the fuck are you doing? That was Professor Garrison!"

"That," Angie said, "was an alien. It took the professor from your mind. Used your own subconscious to cook up a lure."

Doggo, taking the scene in, nodded. "That thing would have eaten you. Plain and simple. Your friends here saved your life."

Zero pulled irritably away and turned back to the box. It had collapsed inward on itself and was now humping guiltily away, moving like a metallic caterpillar.

That close, he thought. *Just that close. I could be digesting in that thing's guts right now.*

Zero felt sick and humiliated. Angie had seen his idiotic blunder. And she was smiling at his embarrassment.

He turned away. Cisco and Bowler were talking to him, but he wasn't listening. The box had almost eaten him. Kelso was warning him. Fiskle was breathing down his neck. He'd almost been killed by the wheelers.

Get away, he told himself. *Hide.*

He began to walk. He didn't care where—he just wanted the hell out of the Neutral.

But first he needed to pee.

Zero ducked into a crowd of traders and turned onto a small path between two high menhirlike rocks. He found a suitable spot, opened his trousers, and urinated on the side of a rock. He found a mild reassurance in the act. He was making a connection with all the other outdoor places he'd peed in, on Earth.

He'd just finished, when he felt the pressure of someone's gaze. He looked up and saw an eye in the rock. An eye had opened up in it, of solemn brown, like the little eye that seems lost in the side of a whale.

It was looking at him reproachfully.

He backed hastily away.

From behind came the sound of cheering and applause. Hastily tucking his privates away, he turned and saw Doggo, Yoshio, Warren, Cisco, Angie, and a number of other settlers he didn't know, standing in a group and applauding, cheering, hooting, laughing.

"Nice goin', man!" Warren yelled. "You ain't really here till you've peed on one of th' Looking Rocks! *Now* you're a citizen of Fool's Hope!"

Would you have thought it was such a bad idea if one of the men had suggested it?" Angie asked. "I know what you think of women. Their place in the 'genetic scheme.'"

"It has nothing to do with the originator of the idea," Fiskle replied. "A bad idea is a bad idea."

Zero, Bowler, Doggo, Warren, Yoshio, and Cisco were sitting in the shade in front of Doggo's lean-to. At least shade was shade here. Yoshio was absently caressing a new bolt of Whorebug cloth laid across his lap. They were watching Angie and Fiskle, as if watching a play.

Angie and Fiskle stood facing one another. Fiskle's posture emanated condescension; Angie's spoke outrage. She looked uncomfortable in the lavender jumpsuit she'd worn when she was abducted. There was a bloodstain on the inner left thigh. Tampax were not readily available on Fool's Hope. Her hair was tangled and matted, and there were streaks of dirt on her face. Zero thought she'd never looked lovelier.

Angie stood with her arms crossed over her chest as she said, "It makes sense to try it. I wonder, Fiskle, if you don't think it's in your interest to—"

"I'm responsible for the safety of the Pioneers," Fiskle interrupted, rather hastily. "If you go out on an expedition with hostile aliens, you're at risk from both them *and* the wilderness. And the Murderers. That's an unacceptable level of risk. The Pezz have consistently attacked us—"

Doggo interrupted, "The Pezz have attacked our people only when we've wandered into what they consider to be their territory. It's a big planet. Let them have their territory. They have strict territorial rituals of pass-through—we can learn them. I really think that if we'd learn their little rituals, there'd be no trouble. I think it'd be a good idea. A joint expedition with some of the so-called 'hostile tribes.' Like the Soviet-American joint space missions back home."

"Back on Earth, you mean," Bowler said rather severely.

Doggo nodded. It was taboo to refer to Earth as home. The Council had ruled that all effort should be made to encourage pyschological adaptation to Fool's Hope—to consider it home. Any other course led to madness and despair.

"You think it's a good idea, Doggo?" Fiskle said with heavy irony. "Fine. When you're elected to head of Council, you can so rule."

"You preside, you don't *rule* over us," Angie said. "And anyway the presiding is only in Jamie's absence.

Till she heals up. Let's take it to Jamie. And to a Council vote."

"Very well," Fiskle said, looking at her stonily. The sun was setting behind him, a bloodred sunset; its rays bled between the high stones, blacklighting Fiskle, blotting his face. He stood looking invisibly at them, his head spiked in red light, his face in shadow. "But we should be looking for ways to increase our combat efficiency, for methods to undermine our enemies, not to cozy up to them." He paused and added with melodramatic finality, "If you succeed, you'll be defeating us all."

He turned and strode away between the boulders.

Doggo squinted into the shattered light. His face was a wash of red, a tint that made Zero think of a car's taillight glow.

"Sunset. Best get back to the settlement before the Frost rises," Doggo said, standing. "Let's go."

But the Frost rose in the sky while they were still a quarter-mile from the settlement The Frost was a constellation, or many constellations interwoven—a sinister jewelry-chest of them. It was a sickle shape of blazing diamond-light, as brilliant white as the sky was jet black, and hard to look at directly. It was not as bright as the sun but far brighter than Earth's moon. And as if to sound a clarion announcing the rising of the Frost, the creaks and hooters began singing. Animals or insects? Zero was not quite sure, but the creaks creaked and the hooters hooted, and now and then some other creature sounded a comical bass note like a tuba.

"This idea, that danger comes with the Frost's rise —this may be superstition," Yoshio was saying as they trudged up the road out of the bogs. He carried the roll of Whorebug cloth tucked under his left arm, on the side away from Zero. It had taken Yoshio two months to get the ore with which he'd made the tools and two weeks more to make the tools. But the cloth he'd traded them for would earn him three months of settlement food.

The pike Zero carried was a bar of pain rubbing into his shoulder. He shifted it to the other side as Yoshio went on. "I think we make our own superstitions now. We're finding this world's nature spirits. Not spirits, but—" He gestured vaguely, unable to find the words in English.

"But what people think are nature spirits? The patterns in nature?"

"Yes. Patterns. And coincidences. Here people believe that when the Frost rises in the sky, the Murderers come, or other bad things. Only while the Frost is touching the horizon. After the Frost rises above the horizon, then the moon rises. When the moon rises—and the Meta are present in the moon—then all is safe."

"Superstitions already." Zero said gloomily. "*Lord of the Flies*. We're gonna regress here. First we get supersitious and then tribal primitive. Sacrifices. Despotic chiefs."

"Not if we *progress*," Bowler said. "Not if we campaign against superstition and insist on an enlightened political structure." Said with a politico's corny conviction, but it was welcome. It was a center of orientation.

Twenty yards ahead, a silhouette in the thickening blue, Fiskle walked alone. "I don't trust Fiskle," Zero said, watching him. "I didn't trust him on Earth."

Yoshio only nodded.

Zero glanced over his shoulder at Angie, walking

— 66 —

beside Cisco, looking for signs that they might be a couple. But she looked as independent as ever, walking along with her hands in her pockets, looking moodily up at the sky. Zero told himself, *Go on, do it. Drop back and talk to her.*

But he stayed where he was, thinking how strange it was. There should be less restraining him here, light-years from Earth's social conventions. Here, where survival was in doubt from minute to minute. But it was as if he were afraid of committing some xenosocial solecism. Social conventions were avenues as much as barriers. He didn't know how to approach her on Fool's Hope. There were rules none of them knew yet.

Shit, he told himself. *Don't be such a wimp, a wuss, a faint-hearted conformist.*

But he stayed where he was.

Doggo and Warren brought up the rear. Both of them looked into the bogs. Doggo looked wary and hefted his pike. It was hard to judge Warren's expression with half his face gone. But he seemed almost to be challenging the bogs with his macabre grin. Like, *Go on, send your worst out after us.*

"The Murderers—they're out in the bogs?" Zero asked.

"Yes, and other places," Bowler said. "But they're just as likely to come at you in the daytime."

"Some reassurance. What are they, exactly?"

"Aliens. Only one each, from particularly vicious races. The Meta drop them among us just to, well, to keep us on our toes, I guess. Unless the Meta are sadistic." His voice dropped to a whisper. "One of the Murderers did for Warren's face. And killed his brother."

"The Hungry Punkin' is supposed to be the worst," Cisco said, moving up beside Zero, "the hardest to kill.

I think all the Murderers are one race: a race of demons that take on different ugly shapes. Like, on whims. You know? Okay, you guys go ahead and sneer—but the thing you haven't got yet about this place is, it's not another planet. It's a spiritual *plane* inhabited by spirits trying to teach us! The Meta are highly evolved spirits, see, and higher science is always a form of what we call supernatural."

He was cut off by groans and ridicule from Angie and Bowler. Zero spoke apologetically to Yoshio. "What you have to understand about Cisco, Yoshio, is that he's from Los Angeles. The guy carried crystal pendants around to decide his itinerary."

Yoshio smiled. The smile was a mothlike flutter in the near-darkness. "But he's accidentally right about something: that it is a mistake to bring anything to Fool's Hope with us. Anything of what we thought on Earth. To understand this world, we'll have to clear our brains, empty our minds."

"My mind's empty, man. 'Cause I haven't got a clue."

Between the bogs and the settlement, the road curved through a copse of trees. At least, Zero assumed they were trees. They looked like giant coral. Their upper branches reached gray against the sky, looking stiff, brittle.

Zero and his friends were almost to the edge of the copse. It gave off a smell of ginger and sour wine. The creaks and hoots and the tuba groan grew louder as the little group of humans approached the woods. Zero supposed that the creatures making the sounds were like crickets and small birds.

As he passed near the trees—or animal growths—

edging the road, Zero realized that the tips of the twigs were hollow, like tiny horns, and the sounds, the hoots, creaks, and groans, were coming from the twig-tips themselves. He reached up and touched one overhanging the road. It was hard as stone, unyielding. He turned to Yoshio. "There're animals in the twigs? I mean, they look hollow."

"No. The land-coral itself is singing. We don't know why."

The singing of the land-coral was loud here, almost drowning Yoshio's voice.

"Oh, God," Doggo said, trotting up ahead of them. He skidded to a stop and stared at something. Standing rigidly in the road, he was frosted in starlight. The others sensed his alarm and stopped where they were. He pointed. "The Current. The altering vector."

The land-coral's singing abruptly stopped, as if someone had switched off a tape deck. The night was silent. And the gingery, sickening smell was gone, replace by the burning smell of a dentist's drill at work— the odor of metal and bone friction, of burning teeth.

At the curve up ahead, Fiskle was passing out of sight behind a screen of the coral growths. And something was there.

There was no wind, none at all. But Zero felt a shift in the air around him. Something crackled on his arms. He looked down at himself, and his gut froze. A fringe of violet fire was playing along his forearms. He felt his hair stand on end, his scalp contract. There was a palpable electrical charge in the air. Zero was afraid to move. "The Current. Has it got us?" he asked. His voice sounded muffled. His lips twitched over the words.

"No," Yoshio said. "We feel the outside of it, maybe

displaced charged particles. But Fiskle—he is in it. Look, now—you can see it." He pointed, and miniature sunset lightnings played along his arm.

Zero saw it in the stars first; it seemed to swirl them, as in Van Gogh's *Starry Night*. And then he saw it in the coral trees. He couldn't help but think of them as trees. Like heat-wave distortions—but this movement of the trees was no mirage.

The farther trees were really, truly moving in the windless night. The nearest growths were motionless but furred in violent cracklings. St. Elmo's fire footlights for the dance going on behind them. There the land-coral undulated with a flexibility that seemed impossible for anything so large and so formerly stiff-looking. Low, slow-motion silver clouds, faintly luminous, formed in a roiling snake shape over the Current, marking its passage through the land.

Zero wanted to go to Angie, to protect her—as much as she would have resented the gesture—but he could not. He couldn't move. He was nailed to the spot, rigid and shaking, first by terror and then by an undefinable awe. He had sense that a god-sized power was passing before him with majestic casualness, taking its titanic ease, sliding effortlessly on the very fabric of reality, filling Zero's head with a quasar output of scintillant white noise.

They all knew when it fell over Fiskle. They felt its impact on him in a kind of psychic backwash, felt Fiskle's ideas, his clearly defined worldview, wash over them like flotsam on an electric tide. Zero has a brief but lucid mental image of high structures of polychromatic crystal floating by like unnaturally symmetrical ice floes. Fiskle's assumptions and almost vindictively exacting theories of social planning concretized as iridescent clusters of spines and tetrahedrons; as if, had this been Earth, some great flood had dislodged the architectural monstrosities built in the 1970s, the severely geometrical churches and art museums, and swept them by. And then they moved on; the massive geometries floated off into the darkness. Zero heard, perhaps with his ears, Fiskle's hysterical screaming: "Externalization blueprinting metastasis of stinking internal organs! Stinking internal organs! Elements of—of glue-ridden hormonal para—para—paralysis synthesized with cataleptic disorganic elegance! *Disorganic elegance!*" He screamed it so loud you could hear his larynx shredding. The words reeked with his horror. "Fatal assumptions of arbitrarily imposed ontological skeletons sucked of marrow! I said *ontological skeletons!* I said *sucked of marrow, damn you!*"

And then a guillotine silence.

Creaks and hoots, again, the tuba groan, as if nothing had happened. The trees were stiff, immobile; the gingery wine smell was nauseatingly strong now.

The great Current had gone, narrowly missing the settlement and passing into the night on its arcane tracks, like an invisible train carrying a freight of inchoate possibilities.

"That was heavy," Cisco said predictably. He hugged himself. His dark eyes were dilated. His first encounter with nonimaginary psychic phenomena had left him more shaken than the others.

Twenty yards up ahead, Doggo was bending over the two men lying in the road. Yes, two. Fiskle—and the other, Doggo told them with a shout, was Kelso. "What was Kelso doing out in the coral woods?" Bowler wondered aloud.

"His little whorehouse is out there," Zero said.

"What happened to his head?" Angie asked, her voice carefully controlled. She was scared.

Zero took a few steps closer to Fiskle and Kelso. And then a few steps more. The bodies were lying head to head at forty-five-degree angles from one another, like "casualties of airport terrorism" in a blurred newspaper photo.

Zero looked closer at Kelso and saw what Angie meant. Kelso's head was separated from his body. By only a few inches, but clearly separated, and it oozed a puddle that reflected the starlight. Kelso's hands were gripping his head, clapped over the ears. He lay utterly motionless.

But Fiskle was moving. He was getting to his knees, and softly, with a hideous knowingness, he was laughing.

THREE

He came running at me out of the woods, his face as white as a sheet, his hair standing on end. Eyes like a lunatic." Fiskle paused in his dreamy recap and smiled absently to himself, as if savoring the memory. "The muscles of his face were jumping around as if he had no control over them at all. There was drool hanging from his mouth. He was giggling. I said, 'Kelso, what the hell—' And then he fell on his knees before me and said, 'Master, I give you my essence.' "

There were snorts of disbelief around the Council room. Someone said, "Come *onnnnn!*"

Zero was sitting across from Fiskle in the cool, shadowy Council room, his back against the wall, his knees drawn up to his chest. He said, "Don't sound like the way he talked."

"That is what he said. He was in the Current. Anyone might have been speaking through him."

"What the 'ell is 'e talking about?" Dennis demanded, scowling. When he scowled, his dwarfish face looked like a gnome's, Zero thought.

"What happened after that?" Doggo asked in a cop flat voice. He sat on one side of Zero, next to Warren Bowler and Angie and Cisco sat on the other side. The were there as witnesses.

Fiskle rubbed his chin and turned to gaze at th window. His smile flickered as he said, "Then Kels fell to his knees and began to slash at his own nec with a knife. Blood everywhere. I was too amazed t interfere. And I was afraid of him. Once he got the jol started, he used the strength of his arms and legs—hi feet tucked up under his chin"—he paused and looke around the room, as if cueing everyone to disbeliev him—"to tear his own head from his neck."

There were five full seconds of silence before th jeering, the snickers began. Not everyone laughed Warren and Cisco looked like small children at thei first horror movie.

Indifferent to them, Fiskle went on. "He achieve his own decapitation with a single superhuman wrench ing. Horrible but impressive. The spine snapped awa all at once under the exertions of the arms, and o course, the signal from the brain being cut off, the bod went limp." He shrugged.

"It isn't possible," Doggo said. "Halfway throug the process he'd collapse from cutting his jugular vein or at least from damage to his spinal cord. And he didn look that strong. I don't know anybody who is."

"He was insane beyond the insanity we know, Fiskle replied coolly. "He had not only a madman strength, he had the Current's strength."

"You talk as if you're an insider," Doggo said "where the Current's concerned."

Fiskle said softly, "I have made a quiet study of th phenomenon in my spare time."

Zero found himself staring at Fiskle. He looked different, in a way Zero couldn't define. Glossier, and . . . Zero wasn't sure.

"Kelso had his hands on his head all right," Warren said. "And there wasn't no blood on Fiskle."

Doggo nodded. "Even a guy as . . . even a clean-freak like Fiskle would've got some blood on him if he'd cut off Kelso's head. He didn't really have time, either, to decapitate Kelso. He wasn't out of our sight long." He pursed his lips. "This is Fool's Hope, this isn't Earth. Maybe what Fiskle said happened could've happened here. Weird as it sounds, I believe him. So I motion we accept the story and lay the matter of Kelso's death to rest with the judgment: accidental."

Zero looked at Doggo with surprise. He'd had the definite impression that Doggo and Fiskle were on opposite sides of the fence, that Doggo regarded Fiskle as a clear and present danger to the human settlement.

"The New Humans," Bowler explained, whispering, as the *ayes* went around the room. Everyone agreed with Doggo because they wanted to put this behind them, fast. "Fiskle's new lodge. Too many of them. Doggo doesn't want a confrontation with them yet— they're too strong. They got Twists with them."

"Now," Fiskle said, immediately trying to reassert control, "there's this deplorable matter of the interspecies expedition. I urge that we don't embarrass ourselves with any more discussion of it than necessary. I motion that we veto it and go on to—"

"I think it's a bloody good idea!" Dennis interrupted. "Jamie thinks so, too. She tol' me this mornin'. You can send someone from the Council to get it from 'er straight on right now, if you want. She's for it."

"The Meta are against it!" Fiskle said sharply be-

tween clenched teeth. He looked around, making eye
contact, and then stood up. He raised a hand to quiet
Doggo's predictable question. "How do I know what the
Meta want? Common sense. They set us up here to be
in competition with the aliens. *That* is obvious. If we
defy them—and we know they're always watching us—
things could get ugly. They might do anything—and I
mean anything."

There were murmurs of agreement, noises of skep
ticism. "Sit down, Fiskle, or I'll have to stand, and then
everyone will," Doggo said.

His reluctance naked on his face, Fiskle sat.

Doggo went on. "We have no damned idea what the
Meta really want. Just as many people are sure they put
us here to find a way to get along with aliens."

"Or either one," Zero put in. "To give us a choice
and see what we do."

Doggo nodded. "We just don't know. But supposing
you're right, Fiskle. We've got to ask, do we really want
to be their sniveling punks?"

The debate went on; Zero followed only the rough
outline of it. There was an element that didn't want to
take a chance on angering the Meta. But there was also
a general resentment of the Meta. If Fiskle was right,
this was a chance to defy them, to fling the theft of their
own lives into the Meta's face.

Fear of the Meta was strong. The vote came out half
for, half against. Deadlock.

"I vote aye, in favor of the expedition," someone
said. Jamie stood in the doorway, leaning on Trish. She
was bone pale; her face sagged, and she was breathing
through her open mouth. Even with someone to lean
on, she looked as if will power alone kept her upright.

"That breaks the deadlock," Doggo said. "The expedition is on."

Jamie looked at Fiskle and managed a weary smile. "You think I don't know what happened out there? It's not over, Fiskle."

Zero realized that by *out there* she meant on the road, when the wheelers had attacked them. She'd said Fiskle's crowd had somehow prompted the attack.

Jamie turned and, Trish's arm around her, hobbled away. As if her going uncorked a jug of bees, the room buzzed with talk.

After the meeting, as they went to morning meal, Zero moved up beside Doggo and said, "You believe Fiskle's story about Kelso? Bowler says everyone's just trying to avoid a confrontation with him."

Doggo glanced around to be sure Fiskle wasn't near, then told him, "It wasn't just being careful about confrontations. It was that I believed him. I don't know why, but I knew he was telling the truth. I guess what he described sounded like the sort of pattern that comes down when the Current happens to people. And it didn't sound like something Fiskle would make up. But don't you worry, man. We'll take care of Fiskle. I'm on that one."

Zero had a lot of choices. One was to make crude-cloth out of scumballs. You picked the scumball pods sort of like picking cotton except the scumballs stuck to your hands, and if they dried, it hurt to pull them off—and then your dried them, pulverized them, and wound them into a loom. You had to learn how to use the loom, of course.

You don't want to do that? You can work with oruhs. Herding, breeding, shoveling their droppings, gathering ground mites for their meals. Slaughtering them. Scraping their hides.

Not appealing? Try crustacean harvesting—all day in the sun, bending over, back aching. Fighting off the jumpskeeters.

Or there's sewage tender, which includes water pump maintenance. Every morning you got to unclog the sewage ditch.

No? Hard to please. Okay: tater fields. Or you can try to be Army, but there's a waiting list. Cleaners of all kinds—basically means janitor. Or woodgathering, though gatherers tend to get killed in the Out There.

Something. You got to show a designated Council monitor what you did during the day to earn food, and usually that means you work for someone, and the job boss reports you were okay. . . . You want to stay in the settlement, you better pick something.

Me and Cisco've been working with scumballs, making cloth," Angie said. "You can do that. You put some oil on your hands first so the stuff doesn't stick so much, and you just get used to the . . . to all this fingerwork. I wanta go into law like Doggo, eventually, but there's only supposed to be two settlement cops, and of course Fiskle's the other one. If you don't count Army. The Army assholes are so fucking lazy."

They were squatting in the shade of a cart (the one the mad boy had crouched under, Zero thought, wondering if his being there now was an omen), across from the gates to the human settlement. Angie was wearing a pair of crude-cloth shorts stitched up the sides with leather strings. He could see the edge of her Whorebug-silk underwear, where her shorts rode up on her tanned legs. One of the guardsmen in the Army had given her the Whorebug cloth the night before. She had "a heap of stuff like that in my dorm" from other suitors. She insisted she hadn't given out anything but verbal thank-yous for the gifts yet, but Zero wasn't so sure. The thought made him cringe inside and grind his teeth.

He could smell Angie's skin, her sweat, and a hint of vaginal secretions. Her smell combined with the scent of the breeze off the plain and became—for Zero anyway —an intriguing, exotic perfume. But they were just two working people resting; polite and friendly but businesslike. She'd shown him the job centers, the settlements' various social organs, its sheds for drudgery. She had been assigned to it. It was her job today, was all. If there were warmth in it, it was because they'd known each other on Earth. "What happened to that naked kid who was out here yesterday?" Zero asked.

"A bunch of Army caught him, trussed him up, carried him into the country, and let him go. They said they untied his hands but not his legs, so he'd be occupied with all the knots and couldn't follow them back. Cute. He's probably dead. The law here . . ." She shrugged.

"They don't hassle things out long. They find Fiskle with a decapitated body and they say, 'Aw, forget it.' "

"There's too much that happens here. They can't investigate much of it. And Kelso was a greaseball. A thief, a pimp. If they *know* somebody killed someone else, though, they come down on them. Well, first they appoint a defense attorney and a prosecuting attorney, and then the Council tries the case itself. People convicted of murder are expelled from the settlement, which usually means they get killed themselves. Unless we decide that the murder was a one-time-only act of temporary insanity. There's a lot of temporary insanity here. They understand that. If that happens, the killer is restricted and watched a lot, assigned extra work. They get another chance. But if they go completely loco or even act that way a little too often, they get expulsion."

"There's already some wicked Social Darwinism here without Fiskle making it worse."

"That's what Bowler says. He talks about rehab programs." She shook her head. "It's hard enough for us to take care of people who've got it reasonably together." She looked at him. "You make up your mind what job you want?"

"Uh . . . I don't like any of them. Don't they have any clerical jobs?"

She grinned. "Council members are also scribes, they keep records with squirmer juice and dandruff-willow bark. That's it. They all work drudge jobs, too."

"I'll probably, um, work in crude-cloth. Then at least I can hang out around you." He said it as matter-of-factly as he could and tried not to look for her reaction.

"Okay, well, we better get back and tell 'em what you want to do—"

"Actually, uh," he broke in, stalling, "maybe you could tell me about the Progress Stations. Bowler only told me a little. The Stations are another possibility, right?"

She shrugged. "It's like this. There are thirty-one races we know about here, besides the occasional alien Murderer. Each is from a different world. Each is given its own settlement area. The settlements run across the continent in—supposedly—an east-west belt. But anything like map-making and geography is in the infant stage around here. Generally, though, we know the Progress Stations are to the north. The McMahons move them around for the Meta, and when someone's found one and gotten into it, taken whatever was useful in it, the McMahons take it away and put it down somewhere else—somewhere real dangerous—and you got to find it, and—what's tougher—you got to get into it. A new one's been reported up near the wastes, in the Hungry Punkin' swamp."

"What's in 'em?"

"Different things. When you get to one, the Mc-Mahons are waiting, and they hand out things that help your settlement progress, you know, technologically. So far they've given the human settlements a form of gunpowder, some medicines, and a method for synthesizing a kind of rubber compound. Jamie and the others are still learning to use it.

"Only a few of the people who were brought here have any mechanical or scientific skills. The Meta stacked it that way, I guess. We can build some stuff on our own, but even something as simple as a generator —how do you make the components? Copper pure enough, machined metal parts. There's no Radio Shack on Fool's Hope. You got to make it all from scratch, from the local stock of ore. But that's taking a long time, a lot of trial and error. We haven't got a lot of time. Because if you don't progress fast enough, the other races overtake you, get the advantage—and they wipe you out. This is what we hear happens, anyway—and we found some empty settlements with some crude stuff half built and a lot of bones—well, they were shells in that case—and it looked as if they'd been ambushed by another low technology."

"But if we could get the races to stop competing—"

"We're working on it. Some are more cooperative than others. Either way, the Progress Stations are important to us."

"So I take it there's a big reward when you come back from a Progress Station with the goods."

"You get real light duty for a year. You get some Whorebug cloth, wire, trading stuff. Hey—I see that light in your eye, Zero. Better think twice. Most people who go out to look for Progress Stations don't make it back. They die. Or if they're lucky, they end up like Warren."

"Oh."

"Yeah, oh. But if you do get to a Progress Station, you got a better chance of being elected to Council. A lot of good comes from it. So I'm still thinking about the interspecies expedition idea. But look at the shadows—it's almost noon." She stood up and stretched. He stole a look at her bare legs. "Come on. Let's report to scumballing."

It was just a shed; the heavy, still air in it was held in place by the sour Elmer's Glue smell of scumballs. There were two long, irregular wooden tables, and baskets of scumball pods against the synthetic wall to the right. *Thunk thunk thunk thunk* thunk-thunk-thunk-thunk. Like that, over and over again with the wooden mallet. Zero would spread out the heap of pasty yellow-white scumball pods, each one marshmallow-size, and remove the scumball pod-cup, toss it aside, squash a few scumballs together, compress them, then pound them *thunk thunk thunk thunk*, four times or so, hit them hard with the hammer to flatten them out some, then again a whole lot of times but fast and more lightly, all over, to make them into a kind of matzo wafer. You put that wafer, after you get it flattened enough, onto the stack in the corner of the table, then you grab another pile of pods.

You stop every couple of wafers to pry scumball gunk from your mallet, which gets too spongy with the stuff.

Zero's hands and arms ached, were beginning to stiffen up. Blisters were turning from red to white on his fingers. "You get used to it," Angie had said. She was at the far side of the room from him, pounding. Four other people he didn't know were between them.

How long had it been? They didn't have any clocks except the dripper—a couple of jars the Pezz had made. The upper one dripped into the lower one through a tiny hole, very slowly. When enough had dripped through, allowing for evaporation, Boris Chubchek, their monitor boss, would tell them it was quitting time.

There were risks in everything here. He could work his ass off and still get killed. By aliens—or through settlement politics. There were rumors of some kind of coup fermenting.

The whole planet was high risk. So why not go for a Progress Station?

Because of sudden death. Because of getting lost and sick and mutilated and enslaved.

A gleam of polished silver.

Zero looked up and saw the small silver sphere of one of the Meta's watchers floating near the ceiling of the shed, its little red dot turned toward him. The others glanced at it and ignored it. Zero reached down, gathered together a clump of scumball paste, and flipped it underhand at the sphere. It dodged at the last split-second, with no jerkiness, no indication of agitation. It continued to watch.

Chubchek said, "Zero, don't waste the pod stuff."

Zero signed and picked up the mallet. *Thunk thunk thunk thunk.*

Evening, Swanee thought. Evening in the coral gulley. One part of the world was going to sleep, another was waking up, like on Earth. But there were different players on this stage.

Swanee was a wide-shouldered man with narrow hips and thick hands that, when he wasn't using them, hung like dead things on his arms. He had a quiet body reflecting an inner stillness. Not the stillness of a peaceful man—the stillness of a trapped man, conserving his energy. He was black, with nappy hair that was going to Afro now; cocoa-colored skin; brown eyes so light they were almost yellow. He wore a fading Memphis State University T-shirt and surprisingly intact jeans. He'd only been on the planet a month.

Swanee was walking along a hollow in the forest of land-coral. The coral was just beginning to wake up and sing to the evening murk, humming here and there, tentatively. He was down in a sort of gulley, his head a few feet below the edge. The evening had made the ground a soft, faintly strobing purple. On Earth wild places, unchanged by man, somehow arranged themselves into their own garden designs; the gardener of struggle and competition and evolution, he'd always supposed, had given some wilderness places their look of having been put together like a Japanese garden. The natural beauty of wilderness could be seen on Fool's Hope if you were open to it. Only, he wasn't at all sure he wanted to be open to it.

A con trail of light zagged across his path. It was the trace of a local insect, the streakfly, that outdid the Terran firefly: it left a sulfur-yellow trail in the air behind it, a luminous stroke that lingered for a few minutes. There: another streak, zigging, crossing the first like an X. He walked through them, careful not to breathe, not knowing what the luminous gas might be made of.

Knots of mossy stuff grew from the walls of the gulley in disturbingly symmetrical patterns; tufts were arranged in diamond shapes with respect to one another. Not exact enough, probably, to have been artificial, but almost.

Another streak of light broke the symmetry. And then luminous red splashed the air as a Washcloth caught one of the streakflies and enveloped it in mid-flight, crushed it, absorbing some of the energy burst. The Washcloths were a membranous, patch-shaped creature with terry-clothlike cilia on one side, drifting through the air light as autumn leaves, then angling like Manta Rays after prey. . . . Between the diamond-alignment of moss tufts, dirty-white plants—or perhaps they were animals—shaped like ten-fingered hands would suddenly open, creating a suction that pulled small flying things toward them, with a repeating *shhh-fwoop* sound that seemed to deliberately punctuate the swelling song of the coral trees.

He wasn't at all sure he *wanted* to know the patterns sewn into this world.

He walked on. Now the coral trees grew closer to the edge of the gulley, crowding over him. The coral branches cast a crooked mesh of shadows over the ground; he could feel the shadow net closing over him, tugging him along.

It was damp down here, smelled of minerals and wet living things; the usual smells of the alien world were masked by the damp, so that when he closed his eyes and inhaled, for just a moment it was possible to believe he was on Earth. He imagined it was the woods behind his Uncle Ted's place in Tennessee, walking along the path with his brother after Sunday school, smelling the pines, kicking the ferns to make the dew flash through the air. As they neared Uncle Ted's, they smelled the barbecue, the deep, smoky, spicy smell of it, heard his uncle's booming laughter, imagined his aunt's cakes. Thinking that after dinner, if Dad wanted to stay late enough, they could watch *Have Gun Will Travel* on television. Man, that was heaven. That was—

But then a flying pig asked him his name, and he knew he was on Fool's Hope.

No, the pig-thing wasn't flying, he saw. It was hanging by something long and white and sticky that came out of its ass, as if it were a spider on a web-strand. Hanging from a tree branch. But it was a long way from being a spider. It was like a human dwarf crossed with a pig. All pink and bristly, about the size of a seven-year-old kid. Rubbery squashed-looking face, stubby little fingers. Hanging upside down in front of him like that was real comfortable for it as it looked at him and asked him his name again . . . while it lowered itself another eight inches, its voice an effeminate grunt.

"My name's Swanee," he told it. "Am I in the right place?" Stupid question.

"Yuh. Yuh inna right place, thweets. C'mon thish way." Its glutinous hanging strand parted, and it fell to the ground, landing on its back feet in the soft blue soil, belching with the impact. It did something with a stub of an arm that might have been a "follow me" gesture and waddled off to a shadow under an overhang in the dirt walls of the gulley.

What if it isn't a Twist? Swanee thought. *What if it's an alien?*

But drawn by an invisible strand of his own, he followed the dwarf-pig to the hole, a sort of cave-mouth blocked up with something.

He squinted into the dimness, looking closer, trying to see what the stuff blocking the hole was. It was like soft cloth, shiny, sort of furry. Like velvet. All rumpled but in a pretty way—styled rumpling, like the velvet the pin-up girls in the old calenders were stretched out on. But it looked as if it had more substance than cloth. As if it were flesh underneath. He reached out, touched it, felt it contract a little, reacting to his touch. The dwarf-pig was looking at him, chuckling. "Velvet. Ith nith, huh?" It stroked the rumpled blue-black velvet with its truncated fingers, and the stuff contracted some more, then blossomed out, as if erupting from the hole. Gushing without wetness.

Swanee stepped back, thinking it was an alien, something he was going to be fed to.

But it was opening to provide access to a dwelling; it was dilating, flowing out to slide over some of the dirt around the entrance, exhaling a scent of gardenias and the ocean. And giving out a glimmer of light.

"C'mon in. Fithskle—he'th inthide," the dwarf-pig said, waddling into the hole.

Swanee had to bend over to enter. And he had to force himself, because the fear was on him; sweat was beading on his face and neck, running down his back.

Inside, moving hunched over, it was like walking on a soft, thick carpet, through a living tunnel. The light slithered and blotched along the folds and rumples of the velvet walls. Looking into the back was like looking into a hole in thick clouds where you see the light coming through. The light was strong at the back of the tunnel, where the walls narrowed, but somehow it wasn't a piercing light, it didn't hurt his eyes. It washed over things without lighting them up too much. That was good: Swanee didn't want to get a better look at the three sitting with Fiskle, or at the thing at Fiskle's feet.

He knew what the thing at Fiskle's feet was, though. It was Kelso's head. Supposed to have been buried.

Fiskle stood out for his cleanliness—almost everyone else was a little grimy. And he had a certain intensity, a sense of authoritative preoccupation about him. Now his expression was simply supercilious, a good-natured contempt for everything. His eyes seemed glassy. His fingers—was it Swanee's imagination?—seemed unusually long, their movement spidery.

I shouldn't have come here. But the one they called Father had made Swanee promise. Made him promise deep inside himself. You didn't argue with Father much.

Father wasn't there, Swanee saw. Instead, sitting beside Fiskle, were three Twists. The dwarf-pig had gone back outside.

The Twists were part of a composition. That was the way it looked to Swanee. Swanee had painted murals in Nashville and sold some paintings to collectors, and he knew composition. It was as if the Twists were almost part of the walls, or worked into them, like the shapes of animals worked into the patterns of wallpaper; more like a Henri Rousseau.

The big one on the left was made of glassy beetle-wing skin, his changeless face like a knight's helmet; the body was made out of hard shell-like sections of random scrapyard things, all tucks and cross-hatchings and vents and pipes, a tumble of hard stuff arranged like a collage to shape a man. But when he moved, shifting position, you could see all the parts working together, pipes over pipes like air compression tubes; everything went click-click into place. Organic, though, not robotic.

On the right was a white-faced little kid with delicate, semitransparent fingers, soft pads at the ends, and suckers under them; attenuated face, round black eyes without any white to them, lids coming from beneath. *A newt,* Swanee thought. And then a hunched, skinny, sunburned dude—too tall for the cave, sway-backed, looking human except for not having legs: his legs had grown together, gone prehensile. And Fiskle, with the snake-legs and the newt on his left, the shiny-parts guy on his right, looked as if he were holding court, sitting on a hump in the velvet, looking nearly human.

The walls shifted when you didn't look right at them; they ran with faces, which pinched kaleidoscopically into one another. The light came from some source behind Fiskle, something hidden. A dirty secret made of luminosity.

Fiskle reached down and tousled the matted hair of the staring, severed head at his feet and said, "You look scared. Nothing to be afraid of. We're just plain folks. This"—he indicated the snake-legs—"is Purdy. My little newt here is Smythe-Wickerson." He tilted his head toward the shiny-part guy. "This now calls itself Pacific Bell. We're not aliens, Swanee."

He had to swallow hard to get his voice back. "I know you're not." He did. He sensed they were human, or had started that way; that they were Earthborn. Even the one made of all those hard pieces of this and that.

"My friends here have simply adjusted a little. The Current made them more themselves than they were before. Brought out hidden qualities in them. They're human. Everything they've become is part of the human world."

"Why'd you make me come here?"

"I didn't force you."

"You did. I didn't know it till I was in here, but Father"— his voice rose an octave—"he did something to *make* me come here. It's a kind of kidnapping. It's fucked up."

Purdy coiled himself a little tighter, as if in warning. Smythe-Wickerson said, "Phhht," softly. Pacific Bell clattered inwardly.

But Fiskle ignored Swanee's outburst of resentment. He said thoughtfully, "You don't like aliens. When you see one, you scream."

Swanee shifted his position. He was not comfortable, bent over in here. He grimaced. "Not always. I don't scream when I see just any of them. But I feel like it. Some I can pretend are just . . . are something else. Like this tunnel thing—it's just some sort of big animal."

"Yes. Tamed."

"But the aliens that think and move around, they scare me because you can't imagine what they might decide to do. So I don't normally go outside the settlement much. That's how I know he did something to my mind. To make me come here."

"You seemed ready, Swanee."

Swanee felt a deep, deep chill radiate out into his soft parts from the marrow of his bones. "I don't want to be ready."

"We're going to need your support. There are people planning an interracial expedition. Rapprochement with the aliens would be a disastrous weakening for us. We must train ourselves to the maximum survivability, which means optimizing our competitive edge. Don't you agree? You really must back us up on this."

"Uh . . ." Swanee was staring at the severed head. A long, utterly dry, rubbery pink tongue was extruding from its mouth, oozing slowly out to push at the soft floor. It moved with its tongue, like a clam's single leg, turning itself with agonizing slowness so it could look at Swanee with its unblinking, pasty eyes. Its jaws worked restlessly. Much of the face had been peeled away, exposing bone. Fiskle reached down and absently plucked at the thing's skin, pulling away another strip—

Swanee gagged and turned away. He started back toward the entrance, thinking that at any moment the tunnel would contract and begin to swallow him toward the things in the back.

"You'll need a certain fundamental shift in attitude and aptitude to survive here," Fiskle called after him. "But in essence we'll always be human, Swanee!"

His back aching from hunching down, Swanee pushed out of the entrance and was surprised that he hadn't been held back.

But there was a wind out there now, and a strong smell like teeth burning under a dentist's drill, and a tension in the air. He felt his hair stand up on his head and limbs, saw violet fires flickering over his hands and purple auroras of light outlining the coral trees against the sky. The crooked branches seemed to flex and bend in the eddying Current, their stiffness becoming comically rubbery, swaying in a macabre dance of sarcastic stateliness. He felt the great brooding presence of the Current bearing down on him, nailing him rigid to the ground so that he was a lightning-rod medium between atmosphere and the planet's soil, electrocuting him with the energies of intracellular transformation.

A great and thunderous sound exactly resembling a single high-amped electric guitar chord boomed *keerang!* and vibrated through Swanee like a living whiplash, oscillating from broad to narrow wavelengths, concentrating into more intense energies, so that sparks leaped blue-white between his teeth and fulminated from his eyes.

Oh lord, no.

Zero and Angie walked down the slope from the scumball shed, through warm semidarkness, down narrow streets, and between high walls. On their left was the outer wall of the settlement. Beyond it was wilderness.

There were irregular triangles of light every so often from the oil lamps in windows to the right. The yellow light wavered just a little. Zero could smell the oil burning—it was gathered from a pool of petroleum leakage in the bogs, a place like the La Brea Tar Pits. The smell was a stroke of comfort through him, a reminder of Earth.

Zero and Angie walked stiffly, muscles aching, down streets made of the same stuff as the buildings in the settlement; their footsteps clacked and rang off the walls.

Something small corkscrewed through the air to Zero's left and then abruptly changed course and zipped itself onto his forearm, began to screw itself in.

"*Shit!*" he shouted, and slapped at it. The corkscrew dug in deeper—and it *hurt*.

Angie said, "Hold still." She grabbed his arm just below the elbow and squeezed it hard, then used the other hand to pump the pressurized blood *hard* up the arm to the thing. The sudden pressure popped it out of its burrow. It unscrewed from him and whipped away into the air, though more sluggishly now.

"Ow! Shit!" He took a deep breath as the pain ebbed, and he watched the blood ooze; it looked black in the twilight. The laceration was small. He said, "Thanks. . . . I find it hard to believe the Meta inoculated us against every virus and microorganism on this planet. A parasite might be carrying anything."

"Maybe. Some people do get infections. So far there isn't much heavy disease, like Fool's Hope malaria. But the Meta could've blown it, of course. There could be some microorganisms they haven't got covered. This is just an experiment, after all. Experiments will go wrong."

They had begun to walk again. They could hear voices from up ahead, around the curve in the narrow street, but they were too muffled to make out. Zero said, "You think it's all an experiment?"

"What else?"

He chuckled. "Everybody's got a theory."

"Okay. You think it's stupid."

He looked at her. Insecurity? Most of the time she seemed so confident. Maybe it marked a change in their relationship. He hoped so. "No. It's not stupid. Not at all. I meant—"

He broke off as they turned the corner and came to a small courtyard, where the slope bottomed out and the street widened. A group of people were standing around a big man who had set a large oil lamp on the bed of a cart. The darkness had thickened; it pooled indigo around the yellow circle of light. The big man was backlit; the others, facing him, caught the light on their faces.

"Jesus," Angie breathed, as they got closer to the group. "Look at the size of that guy."

Zero saw a man at least ten feet tall. Maybe more. "An alien?"

"I don't think so. The way he's dressed . . . "

"Yeah." The giant was wearing baggy pressed slacks, wing-tip shoes, white shirt, dark tie, dark jacket. The tie was loosened. The whole thing looked about twenty years archaic, for Earth.

"Fred MacMurray," Zero said, thinking aloud. "*My Three Sons*. It's not Fred MacMurray but the general look is the same . . . except he's so huge. The clothes are like MacMurray's or Robert Young's in . . ." His voice trailed off as they walked up to the group, and he felt a sensation in his chest. A faint vibration in his sternum . . . and spreading out from it was a sense of relaxing, of warmth. It increased as they neared the giant.

He stopped, awed, as he looked up at the giant's face. There was no giantism disfigurement, no bulging forehead or prognathous jaw. The effect, instead, was of . . . an adult. They who looked on him were child-size.

His face was middle-aged, lined with care but benevolent. His nose a touch too small, so it looked Irish; his black eyebrows were thick, bristling slightly, salted with white hairs. His short hair was combed neatly back and might have been barbered that day. Streaks of white were at the temples. His expression was confident, quintessentially paternal.

Zero felt instantly loyal to this man. He knew he could be trusted.

"I guess," the paternal giant was saying, "I was always out of place on Earth. I feel here I can fulfill myself, find my real function." His low voice, the way he rolled the syllables, resonated deliciously with the hum of well-being Zero had felt on entering the courtyard. Zero felt himself smiling, nodding. He was aware of Angie and the other settlers around him also sharing in this moment.

"But my work is not here in the settlement," the

giant was saying, "not *this* settlement. I feel a sort of call to the other one." His smile was pleasantly mysterious.

"What other one?" someone asked. A familiar voice. Zero looked and spotted Cisco.

"The New Humans' settlement," the giant rumbled sweetly. "It's just beginning. But it's more enlightened. It's dedicated to putting the safety of humanity first. To establishing more than a sort of frantic way station. To making a home. It has room for individuality." There was just a faint tinge of irony in his voice then. "Oh, yes. But we know one thing for sure: a *close* community is a safe one."

The crowd had moved nearer to him. The giant reached with his big arms to embrace two of them, pulling them gently close. It was entirely paternal. One of them was an anemic-looking young man with straggly black hair and large brown eyes, jeans, a workshirt, a beaded leather belt. He had a sort of Santa Cruz look about him: wide-eyed, like a yogic devotee. The other was a smiling Latino with round cheeks. They both smiled like shy children as he went on. "I can't tell you everything. But I think the Meta will help us. I have reason to believe they approve of what we're doing."

A sigh, a ripple of *ahh*s when through the small crowd. *The Meta approved.*

"Web-maker and false prophet!" came a dissonant shout from the shadows. Zero looked and saw an old man crouching at the edge of the light. He seemed agitated, like a frog about to jump. His large black eyes shone. He sucked a strand from his tangled, teased-out white hair into a corner of his mouth. He tilted his head to one side. "The stink of your lies hangs in the air like the flatulence of a corpse!" His voice was as abrasive as the giant's was assuring. "You are a *Twist!* And you intend these people nothing but harm!" The little man stood and came into the light. Zero saw then that he wasn't old, particularly. His hair seemed prematurely white. His sharp, birdlike features were a little sunken, but by privation. His lips and hands trembled with passion as he spoke. "Why is this man dressed as he is? Where does he get these clean clothes, his perfect hair? They *grow* on him that way, friends, or in any way he pleases, for *he is a Twist.* Open his shirt if you want to see!"

"Shut up, lunatic! Let the man talk!" Someone yelled. Someone else muttered, "The old dude is Jack the Baptist." The nickname was spoken with ripe derision. "Ignore him."

But Zero noticed one of Meta's watchers bobbing overhead, its tiny red dot turned toward them. The giant glanced at the watcher, then at Jack the Baptist with the same expression. Raw hatred for both.

For Zero, then, the spell, or whatever it was, was broken. That glimpse into the giant's emotional core had dispersed Zero's trance, though he still felt the warmth tugging at him—even more insistently than before—as the giant recovered his composure and beamed at the Baptist. "We might even be able to restore this man's sanity if he'll let us help him," the paternal giant said.

"Open his shirt!" Jack shrieked. Someone aimed a kick at him, and he danced back. "Ask him to—"

The giant went on, his voice booming like a bass-pitched clarion, drowning him out. "Our elected organizer is Professor Fiskle. If any of you would like to go with me to meet him—"

Fiskle, Zero thought. He saw Cisco nodding, as if

he were about to volunteer to go with the giant to Fiskle. *Open his shirt!*

Zero stepped in, feeling as if he were moving upstream against a strong pull that came from somewhere he couldn't place.

He grabbed the giant's shirtfront and tore it aside.

It wouldn't part far, because it was, as the Baptist had hinted, growing out of his skin. But between the two halves of the shirt, under the tie, fully exposed in the light of the lamp, was the most hideous face Zero had ever looked on. He saw it all in a half-second.

It was an insect's face, but wildly overgrown, with something manlike merged into its features, growing from the flesh of the giant's chest. It was about as big as a cat's head. Below it was a chitinous hollow, seamlessly part of the giant's flesh, in which a purplish membrane vibrated, shivering, going quiet, shivering again.

The membrane was moving in time with the waves of well-being Zero had felt.

The people standing nearest to the giant made inarticulate sounds of disgust and moved away from him. Zero backed away, too, as the giant stood, his face contorting, his mask of paternal reassurance shorn. The insect face in his chest, exposed, gnashed its mandibles; a liquid like bile dripped from its mouth, and its eye glittered iridescent facets at the Earthers.

"He's a Twist," someone said, incredulous, hurt.

"Looks like," Cisco said, nodding, with awe.

The crowd moved back from the giant. He stood there glowering at them; the thing on its chest gnashed. The giant was an enormous beast now. The features that had been arranged for the maximum in paternal reassurance were now as cold as those of an executioner. The sensation of warmth had stopped.

"The thing on its chest," Angie said. Her voice was choked with the ugliness of the realization. "It was humming or something. We couldn't hear it—"

"But it affected us," Cisco said.

"You *fucker!*" a young man screamed at the Giant—one of the men the giant had had his arms around.

The giant moved past them, a furious blur. When he stopped, he was looming over Jack the Baptist—and he had the young man with the straggly hair and the beaded belt, had him by the neck, holding him like an unruly barnyard animal.

"Put him down and come and get *me*, Father!" Jack the Baptist yelled hoarsely, laughing up in his face. "What you going to do?"

"No fucking way!" the boy was wailing, thrashing in the giant's oversize hands. "I'll never go with you!"

"In some ways it's easier," Jack said, "isn't it? Easier than the Open Heart? But in other ways, Twist, it's going to be much harder."

The giant glared at the Baptist—and then turned away from him.

Absentmindedly, the giant reached down and broke the boy's neck. *Crick-ick.* The body spasmed once and went limp. He let it fall.

He turned to them, closing the flaps of his shirt-front. He looked at Zero. "You're among the ones he wants, or I'd kill you now." He looked up at the others. "You're going to wish you'd followed me."

He bent, picked up the body of the boy, and slung it over his shoulder. Carrying the corpse like a sack of meal, he turned, stalked to the outer wall, and leaped. He grabbed the top, did a pull-up, and then vaulted ponderously onto the wall and over.

There was a small red puddle on the street where

the corpse had been. The blood seeped into cracks in the pavement. They stared at it, and then someone yelled a name and began to weep. They began to talk all at once, a babble of voices. Several of them knew the boy who'd died; they wept for him. Thinking about the cracking sound when the boy's neck broke, the casual way the Twist had slung the body over his shoulder, Zero's stomach contracted sharply.

Angie was looking at Zero, frowning. "What made you do that? Open his shirt?"

"I don't know. Felt right. I—it feels more all the time like I want to look past the outsides of things, here."

"I knew it would be you," Jack the Baptist said. He was there at Zero's elbow, that suddenly. "I could see it in your face, even when he had you. You, my friend, could smell what Father was from the start."

Smell what the *giant* was? Zero could smell the sour of Jack the Baptist when he stood so close. But there was a defiant humor in the man's eyes, a presence about him. He had the glow of a familiar, drunken friend at a party. "You said something about the Open Heart to him," Zero said. "What was that about?"

The Baptist grinned, showing rotting, crooked teeth. "The Open Heart was a cult he created in Southern California before he was brought here. He was its father figure, its charismatic leader. He squeezed his followers dry. Made them paupers."

"You seemed crazy at first," Zero said, thinking aloud. "But you're not."

"Crazy is relative. You're crazy yourself. You're going to go on an expedition soon."

"You a fortune teller?" Angie said. She was frowning at him. "If you'd kept your mouth shut, maybe that guy would have gone away, maybe he wouldn't have gotten pissed off. Maybe that kid would be alive. I can't believe we're just standing here as if nothing happened, and that kid died just a minute ago. Must have been like, eighteen. . . ."

"I'm not a fortune teller," the Baptist said, unruffled. "Not even a mind-reader." He nodded at Zero. "His personality was on store-window display a few minutes ago. That's what told me he'd go. Once they're out of their shell, there's no stopping them. He's going on an expedition."

"We don't know if there's going to be one," Angie said, snorting.

But Zero looked at the Baptist and realized he was right.

THE
SECOND
PART

Fallout from the
Exploded Heart

FOUR

A vista of small mirrors, sunk into the soft blue of the land, reflected the jade sky. They ran together in the distance like molten silicon. The bog-ponds mirrored a translucent green sky trimmed with a fine ribwork of silvery clouds. Zero thought it was a sort of cloud formation one saw from time to time on Earth, weirdly regular in its configuration, each strip of cloud lined up with the others as neatly as plow-furrowed soil. Each gave out the moisture-dulled light of refraction.

"How can the clouds be so regular?" Zero asked, looking at Yoshio. They were in the expedition's lead cart, which rocked and shuddered over the rutted dry-mud track that led sinuously between the ponds. Zero had to be careful how he set his jaws, or a sudden jarring would clack his teeth together. "Winds are turbulent, moving like liquid, just sort of flowing around. . . . I used to wonder about this on Earth, too. So how can the clouds be regular like that?"

Yoshio shrugged. "I saw the same on Earth and wondered. Unliving things fall into patterns too."

"It's the Meta," Cisco said. He was riding in the back of the cart, sitting on a leather satchel of supplies, his head nodding with the cart's motion. "We gotta be careful. It's some kind of sign or—"

"Christ, Cisco," Zero said, "if you imagine you see the Meta everywhere, you're going to flip out. They're just clouds. It meant nothing on Earth, it means nothing here," Zero said, unaccountably irritated. "Sometimes I think you—" He broke off, and they both stared off across the bogs, hearing an animal voice cry, *Ha! Ha! Ha-ha!* High-pitched and jeering. They'd heard it five or six times that morning without ever seeing the cry's originator.

Zero glanced over his shoulder at the other carts. Angie and Dennis were in the next one. Behind them in the last cart was Zickorian, of the High Clans, beside his fellow Clansman, Calum. Calum was smaller and had fewer hoops through his wrists. Zero had the impression that he was some sort of younger relative out for a rite of passage. Not a son, but perhaps a nephew.

The Pezz trotted along behind the third cart, as he preferred to do for most of the day. Now and then he climbed up into the back of a cart and rode, squeaking listlessly to himself. Or was it *it*self? Zero could never quite decide.

The eight travelers were three days into the expedition. They were on their way, they hoped, to the Progress Station that had been reported beyond the bogs; it was said to be past the mocking veldt, on the far side of a great forest, and beyond the IAMton Wastes. The Pezz had absorbed a "map" of biochemically distilled experiences from a fellow Pezz who had been on another expedition that had been turned back by the Hungry

Punkin'. Out of nine travelers, that expedition had only two survivors.

All but the first hour of the first day had been spent trundling through the bogs. The swamp had seemed infinite, stretching ahead and behind and to either side as far as they could see. "It's as if we've slid into yet another world," Yoshio had said. "Another plane—a continuum of bog-ponds, one after another, like one of those Dali perspective planes of checkered infinity." He said things like that the way other people said, "Boy, this *bog* stuff just goes on and *on!*"

"I wish Bowler had come," Zero said, shifting on the driver's seat. His butt hurt from the jouncing. He eased his foot on the pedal-tack in the oruh's rump to slow it a little, give his pelvis a rest. The beast grunted and gave out a soft, relieved *oroooooooooh.* "Said he wanted to 'organize' the settlement. I keep telling him his politics are irrelevant here."

Zero's back was hurting from hours of sitting up. The sun had burned a spot in the back of his neck that chafed him bitterly whenever he turned his head, and Yoshio was getting on his nerves.

It's the monotony, Zero thought. It made him irritable. And fighting off jumpskeeters every half-mile or so, having to keep them off the oruh. And at night, the moss-suckers. They looked harmless, like a short piece of Spanish Moss, dull violet, floating through the air, dried up and harmless. But they steered themselves without seeming to and drifted against your bare skin. The sucker's spongy mesh extruded filaments that drew blood—much more blood than the corkscrews took. They swelled up like sponges, just getting bigger and bigger, taking root if you let them.

And the sounds of the bog at night made the Earthers light, paranoid sleepers. The sounds were like a sinister orchestra tuning up. The ground was lumpy and moist; a few hours on it, and you woke with aching muscles. The nights were almost as wearying as the days.

"Parasitism is something you'll see in many forms out there," Jack the Baptist had told them. He'd stopped them along the road, just outside the settlement, that first morning, to wish them well. "Be wary of its multiplicity of form. There is every kind of abundance on this world: you'll learn to know the abundance that resonates constructively from the kind that is poisonous to you. The capacity to know it is in you. The outside and inside are interchangeable."

"Uh-huh," Zero had said, nodding just as if he knew what Jack was talking about.

They'd driven on, and Jack the Baptist had shouted something obscured by the creaking of the carts that might have been, "See you around the hill!"

Zero had driven the cart that morning in a glow of interior excitement that matched the solar energy flashing from bogs. But then the hours and days had piled up, and tedium had rolled in like an invisible fog—and remained. And Angie seemed nervous, distant.

"This road looks as if it were made by randomly trekking Pioneers," Yoshio said, interrupting Zero's train of thought. "But I suspect the Meta may have laid it down. There's a certain engineering wisdom in its—"

Zero couldn't stand any more of it. Maybe now was the time to try getting through to Angie.

"Yeah, yeah, uh-huh, you're probably right. How about you take over driving, Yoshio? I'm gonna drop back and talk to Angie for a while."

But by sunset, she'd only said a few words to him. Maybe she was just simply scared, and tired from not sleeping much, and trying not to show it. He'd felt that way himself, the first night in camp. He made the mistake of trying to tell her that. "All I could think of that first night," he said, "was that *anything* could be out there. But then I thought, it's probably no more dangerous than Africa. Or parts of the Bronx, for that matter. I mean, we just keep thinking, This is alien, this is alien. And that makes it seem worse than it is. So I decided just to resign myself to anything that—" He broke off, seeing her look.

She snapped, "You think I need this lecture? The strong male explains things to the dizzy female?"

"No, no that's not what I—"

"Just shut up, okay?"

He shut up. The luminous orange oblong floating above the horizon turned the mirror bog-ponds into plates of hot copper. The sunset light limned one side of a great hummock up ahead. It was the first break in the monotony, and it brought with it a mixture of fear and an almost feverish curiosity.

The oruh protested as Yoshio drove the lead cart faster to find out what the thing was.

It was a small hill, as anomalous as a wart on a baby, rising about forty feet high from the bogs. It rose in a sudden arc in the midst of a clearing of bare, compacted dirt. The hill was pocked with caves, they saw as they came close. The right side of the hill looked molten with sunset light. The left side was purple with shadow. As they drew nearer still, the motion of the carts made the shadows in the caves seem to shift and flutter.

Dennis, the expedition's leader, climbed down from his cart and said, "Roit. No one moves till I have a look-see. Yoshio, stay where you are." Dennis took an oil lamp, lit it with a spark-maker—something that looked like a nutcracker with flints—and carried the lamp up to the caves. In his right hand was a blunderbuss, charged.

He approached the caves and stopped. Stared. Took a few steps closer. Bent to look into the nearest without getting closer than ten feet to it. He grunted and circled the hill slowly, looking into the caves, sniffing. He climbed up onto the hill and looked in each hole—there were about twenty.

He came back to the carts grinning. "It's perfect, it is! Sompin' used ter live there, but it don't no more. Caves go back two or three meters, and then it's blank wall. We got a perfect little shelter for the noit."

"It looks sort of like a termite hill," Angie said, looking around at the bogs as if expecting to see termites coming home. "*Big* termites."

Yoshio said, "Maybe whatever lived there leaves during the day, comes back at night."

"Neee-awwww'" Which was Dennis's way of saying no contemptuously. "No tracks. Dust undisturbed. Nothin' been there for *years*."

"I don't remember this thing from the maps," Zero said.

"Those maps are a bloody mess, they are," Dennis said.

"This place is not on Pezz maps," the Pezz said through its translation box. It squeaked and capered anxiously. The sack under its melted-dwarf scrotum inflated with a *pweeeee* sound, and then it announced, "I smell nothing but old smells from this place. They who came from these holes have not been here for a much-long."

Zickorian frowned at the hill. "I am not at ease," the High Clansman said in his taciturn way. The band of gold that replaced his eyes shimmered red in the dying sunlight as he turned his head from side to side, as if looking with his ears.

"I also am uncertain," Calum said.

Zero snorted. They'd learned that Calum echoed whatever Zickorian said.

"The Pezz know when sompin's around," Dennis said. "You can see the caves for yourself. Come *onnn*, unpack the gear. Let's mike camp!"

Weariness made the decision for them. They made camp at the base of the hill. The Pezz foraged through a bog-pond for its dinner; the High Clansmen brought out their own supply sacks, and each took what looked like a lump of rock-hard meat into his mouth and chewed it incessantly for an hour before swallowing. This was their full meal.

Hungry and tired to the core, the Earthers ate their rationed provisions quickly and silently. Afterward they sat half-slumped, wrapped in crude-cloth and leather, staring into the flicker of the oil lamp as if it were a miniature campfire. The sky went violet and then purple-black, crystal green at the horizons, like thin-sliced volcanic glass. The stars glowed through, thickened in the sky, jostling each other to get a look at the expedition. By degrees some of the weary irritability seeped from the Earthers. Cisco stretched out and fell asleep on the ground. Dennis and Yoshio looked at their crude map and spoke in low tones on the other side of the circle of lamplight.

Angie sighed and turned to Zero, whispered, "I'm

sorry about what I said. Telling you to shut up. But you were sort of patronizing."

"Guess so."

"God." She looked up, craning to take in the sky. "Those stars. One good thing about Fool's Hope—stars to beat the band. Makes Zales look shut down."

"Sort of like the Texas desert. Last time I was in Texas—visiting this friend of mine I used to correspond with—we went to a country music club out on the highway in the desert. Went in a convertible, and we got drunk. And we were looking at the stars. That was the best part. The club was a disappointment. No country music. Turned out it was Disco Night. Had all these country music trappings like a barn but everyone was dancing to Madonna and wearing—what's the matter? Oh. 'Don't talk about Earth.' "

"Right. Don't talk about Earth."

"Okay. But just one thing—I'm starting to miss it less. The planet itself is great, but the people have totally fucked it up. Ruined it." Thinking about the trashed, oil-slicked beaches, the vast dumps, the toxins in everything, the dying sea, the moronic video culture, he could almost make himself believe he was better off here. Almost.

"I don't care if you're talking about Earth negative or positive. Just don't."

He was silent till she said, "I guess you think I'm bitchy. I just feel—cheated all the time. I was going to be a dancer. I studied for two years."

He looked at her in open surprise. "I knew you were taking dance, but I didn't know you wanted to *be* a— you mean a *career*?"

"Yep. I didn't talk about it because how many people want to be a dancer or an actress or a successful musician, and talk about it, and everyone says, 'Oh, that's nice,' but secretly they think, 'Sure, sure, what are the odds *that*'ll happen?' "

"I didn't have the good sense to keep my mouth shut. Went around making big talk about the movies I was going to make. You're lucky, compared to a lot of us here. I'll never be able to make those films, but you can dance here. In fact, you can dance for every human on this planet."

He fully expected her to tell him that he didn't understand. But she said, "I never thought of that. That doesn't make up for everything. But I guess it's okay . . . " She said it softly, and he felt good.

She yawned. "I'm gonna crash. Listen—how about sharing one of those big caves near the ground? I'm —I'd rather not stay in one alone. I mean, I think none of us should be alone, in case something attacks." Her voice was utterly antisuggestive. Carefully.

But he thought, *Maybe* . . .

They got up and went to a cave and laid out their bedrolls. Side by side but not too close.

The caves were bone dry and smooth; this and the thick coating of dust made them almost comfortable to sleep in, after the bog. As Zero fell asleep, his mind flickered with fantasies like an old-fashioned peep show. He imagined both of them waking before dawn, while the others were asleep. She'd reach for him and snuggle against him, and they'd find themselves kissing. And then . . .

Well. Sh*e had* asked him to sleep next to her, hadn't she?

Outside, the dissonant orchestra began its hopeless

tuning up. Inside, the shallow cave echoed with their snores.

Swanee watched and tried to remember everything he saw.

Night in the Earther settlement. Much activity, which was itself unusual here after dark, and there was a constellation of lamps, scattered on every unused horizontal surface. The crowd of human shapes and nonhuman anomalies made Swanee think of a Chinese New Year's parade, circulating within the benevolent corral of lights. Above the walls the Frost had risen and shone balefully on them through a purple sheen.

Swanee stayed in the shadows of the settlement. He didn't want anyone to see him. He wasn't sure why. It wasn't his fear of the aliens; Fiskle had forced him to spend time looking at them, getting used to them. "They are our enemies, but they are not bugbears. If we're afraid of our enemies, our enemies win. Don't trust them—but learn to observe."

No, it wasn't fear of the aliens that made him stay crouched in the oruh stalls, peering from shadows out through the door, with the oruhs champing and defecating only a few feet behind him. It was horror of being seen by the Earthers. He hadn't completed his Twist, of course. Not yet. Perhaps there was a little extra glossiness to his skin; a change in its shade, and texture. A certain humping to his back, his eyes changing color.

But this would go unnoticed by anyone who didn't know him well. It really wasn't how he looked physically.

It was how he felt. He was sure they could sense the changes taking place inside him: the birthing of his Real Self, Fiskle called it.

So he crouched in shadow and watched. The Pioneers' courtyard and the street outside was bannered and frilled for the Interspecies Festival. Crudely dyed strips of cloth were hung from the walls, the gate, the weapons rack. A banner reading simply FRIENDS! hung over the front door of the Pioneers' dorm. Swanee had heard the Ki-ips puzzling to Jamie about it: in the language of the Ki-ips the closet analogue to *friends* was *co-conspirator*. Which race, they asked, were they planning to conspire with—and against whom?

Sounding like Abraham Lincoln's speechwriter, Jamie had said, "We're conspiring with *all* races on this planet—against conflict itself."

"That *almost* makes sense," the Ki-ips had replied.

Swanee made a mental note of everything so that he could repeat it to Fiskle later. "Because after I arrive," Fiskle had said, dispatching him on this mission, "things will be different, and much will go into hiding." It was night out, and so the Poolsh had been unable to come: they were rooted and immobile nocturnally. But the Arthropods were there, and the Ki-ips, the two known sun-monkeys, a few Whorebugs, a few Gator-Men, two or three Pezz, a thing that looked like a big koala, and four upper-rank High Clansmen.

Jamie and Trish and Doggo and Warren and a Latino named Chester Sanchez had gone in a deputation to the Neutral and had invited each race to send a few envoys to the Festival. Some understood readily that this was a sort of embassy party; others were baffled but complied for their own obscure reasons.

Swanee spotted Jamie and Trish on the other side of the courtyard. He noticed that Jamie was still moving stiffly and seemed very pale. Swanee attuned himself to them, performing the focusing trick that had come to him with the changes, filtering out all other sound, amplifying, hearing them as if they were standing nearby.

"The food was a mistake," Jamie was saying. "We put crustaceans out for the Whorebugs, but the High Clans, it turns out, have some kind of animistic kinship with crustaceans—they're like some holy animal from their home world, and they got mad because we gave them to the bugs to eat right in front of them. Then the Arthropods wouldn't eat the mashed spinach-taters we set out for them because they have to be prepared in some kind of ritual and the way we did it was 'septic.' "

"Chester warned you about all that."

"Yeah, I shoulda listened to Sanchez. He's smart. After you, he'd be the guy I'd pick to succeed me if this infection kicks my butt."

"That," Swanee muttered to the oruhs, "was a good one. A lucky one to hear."

On the left, beside the entrance to the dorms, was an improvised stage of woodblocks, on which four musicians with homemade drums sat in a semicircle. The small one, in the middle, was Chester Sanchez, who had irreverent brown eyes outlined by long, thick black eyelashes. The cheekbones of his wide face hinted at some Indian blood. His expression was always relaxed, barstool cool, but his whole body nodded to the drumbeat.

Someone stepped onto the stage with a wooden washboard, and a sixth man stepped up with a jug. In a moment the salsa/jug band was feeling its way around a rhythm. A few Earthers gathered around the stage and began to dance, rather solemnly at first, but smiling. Some of the aliens seemed to respond. The Gator-Men slapped their corrugated skin and snapped their alligator jaws shut in time; the Pezz pranced, seeming to enjoy it. (But who knew with an alien? Perhaps they were in pain.) The Arthropod began to move in ponderous circles, swaying this way and that, making O's of silvery slime on the ground. The High Clans seemed puzzled. Swanee heard one of them ask Warren, "Who is having offspring?"

Warren said, "Nobody I know of. Why?"

"We make drums only for the birthing time. This really is embarrassing. Perhaps if one of you pretended to have a child . . . ? Just to make things decent."

Swanee noticed the one they called Bowler at the far side of the courtyard from the musicians, talking to a group of six human settlers. He seemed so earnest. Perhaps it would be best to listen in.

Feeling his ears shift on his head, Swanee performed his trick: focusing, amplifying, winnowing sound.

The noise of the Festival crowd and the musicians fell into the background, and Bowler's voice leaped into aural relief. "It's not so much the way it is as the way it's going to be if we don't plan against it. We'll fall into exploitive capitalism. Already some people have cornered the market on crustaceans; others are dominating oruh skinning."

"Only because no one else wants to do it," Doggo put in.

Bowler went on. "And the people who have the most to trade are the most influential in the settlement. Eventually some concept of land ownership will develop here, with people working for other people as employees . . . we bring all those concepts with us from Earth. It was so entrenched on Earth, in the United States, it was almost impossible to consider giving it up.

But in a place like this where everything is raw and unshaped—well, the capitalism is only inside us, in our assumptions and customs. We can devalue the whole idea of ownership and capitalism and start a society unencumbered by the traps of the old."

"Why should we?" Doggo burst in, more assertively this time. "Buying and selling and owning is the natural human way, and you yourself said it held civilizaiton together."

"It held it together, but in a viciously competitive way. We can hold it together in a constructive way. Communal decentralism. There were lots of communal Earth societies, even before the Bolsheviks. We were trained to believe capitalism was the natural order of things because it was convenient for the status quo. Listen, Doggo, this planet is a great opportunity, a chance for a new society."

"Sure, and whoever organizes it is the big cheese! You'd *like* that, right, Bowler?"

"I'd enjoy a leadership role, that's true. But that doesn't devalue my leadership or my ideas. And I don't fancy a dictatorship, if that's what you're implying. All I want is to get the thing started."

Doggo snorted out another retort. The argument went on.

Interesting, Swanee thought. *This could be a wedge for Fiskle.*

But he heard something else, something that made him shiver. A sound below the other sounds. A deep thrum, announcing the coming of Father—and Fiskle.

After a few moments, everyone felt it. They turned and looked toward the front gate. Conversation died from lack of attention. Even the musicians stopped playing. Puzzled, the aliens, too, turned to look.

Fiskle had come, and he had brought his New Humans Lodge with him.

They were back-lit by something—no, it was some-*one*, Swanee saw. It was Harry "Hulk" Porter, who had been a football player on Earth, a brutish linebacker. He had, on Fool's Hope, Twisted into a slender, buxom woman. She called herself Bella; her Twist was modeled on an early 1960s movie vampiress, a mesh of Vampira and Elvira, a human pop caricature of swelling cleavage in a skin-tight black gown, of spike heels and legs in black mesh stockings and swept-back black hair; the thin, black, arched eyebrows of a Disney villainess, the clinging black gown that Morticia Addams might've worn if she'd posed for the first panels of a *Playboy* spread. Comic-book lurid makeup: dead-white skin and blood-red lips. The "clothing" and "makeup," Swanee knew, grew from the skin, like fur or scales. She was all this, and she was luminous too; emitting a sickly green glow like those light-absorbing plastic children's toys shaped like stylized Spooks; toys that glow in the dark. She was quite predatory, of course. She was a sin and a punishment for sin, in one.

Swanee basked in the sight of her. She glowed like a fluorescent sea creature; she stood there, seductively relaxed and lethally confident, like a minor goddess in the back row of the pantheon. Swanee loved her, loved her deeply, loved her achingly, from afar. She was an artfully crafted apotheosis of one of Swanee's boyhood fantasies.

The others, standing just outside the light from the oil lamps, illuminated only by their proximity to Bella, were dim figures, shapes sprung from whimsy, seen mostly in silhouette.

With Father looming protectively just behind him,

Fiskle stepped into the light. The crowd aspirated together, almost a whimper, seeing his clothing, Swanee stared. He hadn't seen Fiskle for a day—but he'd changed. So had Kelso, Swanee knew; he saw the dark hump of Kelso, like a jacket hood, hanging from the back of Fiskle's neck. Most of the crowd couldn't see Kelso at that angle. They were staring at Fiskle.

Fiskle was wearing a new suit.

Which was impossible. Where would he get a new suit?

Oh. Where Bella got her skin-tight gown, and Father his raiment.

Fiskle seemed to be wearing goggles. But with a plummeting sensation, Swanee knew that he wasn't. They weren't goggles. They were small camera lenses, like the ones on the security cameras you see in banks. And they were growing from his skull.

Had the Meta altered him? Cyborged him?

No. This thing had grown out of him. Swanee knew it, looking at the lenses. A shuddery recognition: *They had always been part of Fiskle.*

Somehow, inexplicably, they went with the immaculately clean, professionally pressed gray suit and the shiny, spotless black patent leather shoes. (How many of the staring crowd realized that the shoes were not shoes but Fiskle's feet?) And yes, the camera-lens eyes went with the tapering, four-inch mirror-painted fingernails on his prehensile, boneless fingers.

And his face. Was frozen. Trapped into one expression: Humorously supercilious, with just a faint undercurrent of cold rage, like a hint of sparks from short-circuiting wires glimpsed through a crack in the walls . . .

"I have decided to confront you with the truth of

your destiny," Fiskle said, sounding like a pompous Shakespearean actor, his voice ringing in the frightened silence. Kelso shifted on Fiskle's back and humped up onto his shoulder, pulling itself up with tiny little black bird-legs; it took its place like a parrot, suddenly in full view of everyone, and flapped its wings. The incongruity brought a sizzle of suddenly sucked-in breaths and mutters from the crowd. One of the Ki-ips made a startled *bra-aak* sound, and a Pezz squeaked in bafflement.

Kelso's face had been stripped away from the skull; only shreds of his hair remained, a stringy fringe on the remaining strip of scalp around the back of the yellow cranium. The fleshy wings were stylized, outsize versions of the wings on Mercury's helmet; grotesque outgrowths of his ears, flapping uselessly like the flattened arm-stumps of a Thalidomide child. His eyes, sans lids, bulged from the fleshless sockets, sickly pink, and perpetually staring. The rest of the face was the face of a skull. Flecks of flesh stuck to it here and there. The jaws opened, and a long black tongue oozed out, licked off a bit of rotting flesh clinging to the cheekbone, and sucked it into its mouth with a smack of enjoyment.

"They've gone alien," someone said. "They're fucking aliens."

Those words sent a sick weakness into Swanee, "No," he whispered to the oruh. "No way. No."

The thrum from Father picked up, and a shiver of quiescence went through them all. "We're human," Father rumbled, his voice deeply reassuring. "We're adaptations. Each of us with some speciality, something useful to the great pattern the Meta intend. We have in fact come to rescue you from the aliens."

"This is undeniably another world," Fiskle said,

his voice carrying theatrically. "We must not deny its needs. To be human here, we have to change, to become—"

"It's a lie!" Jamie said, stepping forward. Doggo, behind her, moved off into the crowd, signaling to the guards on the wall. They stood ready with pikes; others moved to charge their blunderbusses. Jamie yelled, "You aren't adaptations for this world. You're Twists! The Current has changed you because it does that to people, and only the Meta know why—but I don't believe it's improvement. We're not going to be intimidated by —by um . . . " Her voice faltered.

It was Father's doing. The thrum had deepened, from the hidden thing on his chest, and ripples of trust and relaxation spread out from him. He said, "We came like this hoping to shock you into accepting us—and your future." Jamie looked uncertain, as if about to give in, as Father went on. "We are your future. Those of you who want to work *with* the Meta, come with us now. Accept Professor Fiskle's leadership. Discover your Real Self, the fulfillment that you've been aching for. We understand that hollowness, that perpetual doubt you feel."

One of the Pezz stepped up to Doggo, who was staring slack-mouthed at Father. He squeaked and his box translated, "You are experiencing [untranslatable] cerebral interference. You are being [approximate translation] manipulated!"

Doggo stared at the Pezz for a second, then shook himself and yelled, pointing at Father, "The Pezz is right—he's *bullshit*!" He signaled to Sanchez, who began drumming with his hands on the crude conga vised between his knees.

The drumbeat broke up the thrum. A shudder ran

through every human there as Father's influence dissipated.

Doggo yelled over the beat, "You think I don't know about you?" He pointed at Father but turned to Fiskle. "This thing murdered one of our people—fella named Dagstrom, hardly more than a kid! He broke his fucking neck! And you got the nerve to—" He broke off and turned to shout at the walls. "I want the son of a bitch arrested!"

There was a jostle of movement on the walls as the guards headed for the stairways. Fiskle looked around. His camera eyes were whirring; the lenses extruded an inch further, their chrome collars turning, glinting. Kelso looking at the other wall, as if he were a second set of eyes for Fiskle; drool ran down his bony jaw, and his bulging eyes caught the oil-lamp light.

Fiskle barked out something Swanee couldn't make out, and two enormous Twists stepped from the shadows to flank Father. Two more stood beside Fiskle. They were what Fiskle called Phylum Twos. Eight feet tall, naked, as pink as babies with heads nearly as small as babies'—but monstrously muscled. Utterly under Fiskle's influence. Their great penises, like elephant's trunks, hung down past their knees, wagging softly with their movements. Their feet, broad as the blades of shovels, dug toes into the hard pavement as if it were clay.

The crowd backed away. Fear suffused the air like the stink of blood in a slaughterhouse. Sanchez stopped his drum patter.

Jamie put her hand on Doggo's arm. "Keep the guards back."

"Even the infinitely stupid have their moments of wisdom," Fiskle said to her, bowing slightly.

"They're very *stuuuu*-pid, very stupid, very very

stupid," Kelso chattered on Fiskle's shoulder, using its mutated larynx to make a voice somewhere between a parrot and a sneering dirty-minded adolescent street kid. "Every stupid body but baby and me. Baby and me! It nuzzled affectionately against Fiskle's cheek.

"My friends here," Fiskle said, "are very strong. It would be, as this sweet little bulldyke has suggested, unwise to attack Father or myself. The Phylum Two can take walls apart with their hands. Bodies are like soap bubbles to them. And the rest of us, the Phylum One, we have our talents—much that you might find disagreeable."

"Fine," Doggo grated. "Then just get the fuck out."

As always, Fiskle's expression remained mannequin frozen. But his camera eyes turned and clicked to themselves. Kelso whined. "Try to be friends, and they stink on us. They are not sensitive. They have brain farts. Stink for stink, stink back at them." It flapped its pathetic wings and spat a fetid oyster of bloody sputum onto the street.

"Perhaps the time has come," Fiskle began, "to demonstrate—"

Doggo broke in, "We could pike you before your lunks could protect you. We'd get you, at least. Before they got us."

Fiskle took a deep breath, then nodded curtly. "Another day, then."

He raised his hand in a florid gesture of farewell and turned. His people parted for him and followed him out the gate.

Swanee's heart ached as he watched Bella go.

Thrumming, perhaps hoping to draw a few of them along in a psychic slipstream, Father was the last to go.

Swanee felt the tug. He fought it. He wanted to stay here, and perhaps if he remained with the humans, his store of humanity would remain with him. He had glimpsed what Fiskle was, and what the others were becoming.

He found himself walking out the door of the oruh stable, pushing through the crowd. He was drawn by the thrum and the will-o'-the-wisp light of Bella, a light retreating like the glow of swamp gas, always just out of reach.

He didn't go alone. For some, Fool's Hope was simply too torturously unfamiliar a canvas to contemplate, too foreign a banquet to feast on. Half Twisted already by madness and despair, some twenty settlers followed Father's Pied-Piper thrum out the gate. Pursuing a light that was darkness.

FIVE

Zero awoke suddenly from a dream of earthquakes. In the watercolor-green light of dawn he saw that Angie was still asleep. She lay with her back to him. Her crude-cloth blanket had fallen away from her; he was sorry she slept with her clothes on. He reached for the blanket to cover her.

The tremors came, a deep rumble from below. The sound translated into motion so that dirt crumbled down on them from the ceiling of the cave.

Still dreaming?

Another tremor. A crack in the wall. A muffled scream from somewhere on the other side of it.

Zero scrambled out of the cave. Braced on a ledge, he turned, grabbed Angie's arm, and pulled her into the open like a sack of flour. She cursed and got onto her feet, blinking, her face swollen with sleep, leaning against the outer wall of the mound. "For God's sake—"

One more quick tremor, short but sharp, so that they almost lost their precarious footing, and Angie's eyes widened. She reached into the cave and scooped up their bedrolls, and they scrambled down the hill.

The others were there, Cisco and Yoshio and the High Clansmen and the Pezz, standing in a confused group by the oruh carts. The oruh champed nervously and shifted on their pads like children waiting to go to the bathroom.

Dennis was missing. "Where's Dennis?" Zero asked, looking up at the mound. None of the caves seemed to have collapsed.

"I'm round here!" Dennis's voice came from just out of sight around the curve of the mound. "Come and have a look at this!"

They walked around the curve and saw Dennis about halfway up, his head and shoulders extended from a cave just big enough for his body. He pointed to a much larger cave beside him. "This is going to be hard to believe, but there's an *entrance* in there to another place, a beautiful underground world!" He stopped and grinned at them. Foamy spittle at the corners of his mouth ran through the dust on his face, marking it like a handlebar moustache. "I found it last night. I'm in an exit from it now. You must see it —it's beautiful. I think it's where the"—he paused and stared into space, his jaw drooping—"trying to remember. The . . . " Then the animation came back into his face. "The *Meta!* That's where the Meta live! They've been waiting for us to find them, and they'll explain everything! It's so beautiful! There's a tribe of women there, and they're *so friendly!*" He winked at them idiotically. "Come on in! Look! It has to be this hole over here! You must see it!"

"Wow!" Cisco said. "That's rad, man! I mean, it's like it was always with us, underneath us, and like, I could feel it spiritually, but I didn't know what it was!" Impelled by his burst of enthusiasm, he started up the slope.

Zickorian looked at Calum and spoke in their language. The translation box said, "Let's have a look. Perhaps this is a great discovery imparting [approximate translation] karmic honor!"

Yoshio said, "I think, uh, perhaps you'd better not."

Zero stared at Dennis. The spittle had become drool. Pink drool, mixed with blood. Dennis twitched.

Zero scrambled up the slope, grabbed Cisco, and pulled him back. Cisco fell on his ass and slid down the slope. "Shit! Goddammit, Zero!"

Zero slid after him and backed away from the mound. "Dennis—what happened to your accent?"

The Pezz said, "I smell something that used to live here . . . closer now. Also [untranslatable]."

Angie backed away from the mound, one hand going to her mouth. "Oh, God. Oh, Dennis . . . "

Zero said, "We'd better get the hell out of here."

Yoshio looked at Zero. In a halting voice he said, "Zero, we can't leave him."

Zero took a deep breath and nodded. He trotted back to the carts, reached in, and brought out a pike and a charged blunderbuss. He returned to Yoshio and handed him a pike; they started up the hill, moving cautiously between the caves.

When they reached the ledge just below Dennis's cave, he drew himself partway into the cave like a startled hermit crab. "Hello, fellows," Dennis said, his eyes rolling wildly. Sweat made more streaks on his face. A little blood ran from his nose. "Hello. Ready to . . . enter the beautiful paradise . . . beautiful girls?"

Yoshio grabbed Dennis's left arm; Zero grabbed his

right, and they pulled, hard. Dennis came partway out. Zero and Yoshio dug in their heels and leaned out to enlist the help of gravity. All at once Dennis pulled free of the cave with a squelching sound.

His lower half was gone. It had been chewed away, replaced by what appeared to be a maggot as big as a large dog, whipping itself like a worm on a hot sidewalk. Rubbery bands of pinkish white. Its underside was swollen with the parts of Dennis it was digesting. Its upper half was concealed completely inside Dennis's torso like a hand hidden in a Puppet. Some tap-in filament co-opting Dennis's brain. "Beautiful girls, fellows!" the Dennis-shell was yammering. "They give their big breasts to you! Beautiful girls!"

There were shouts from the group at the base of the mound and the shrill *orooooooh!* of an oruh in fear of its life. But Zero couldn't take his eyes from the thing that had Dennis. Zero's stomach writhed to match it. The slugs had been in the mound all the time, behind the backs of the caves, hibernating. The thing flopped and whipped, slapping the ground, inching back toward the cave. "Yoshio"—losing control now—"what do we . . . "

Yoshio made a high-pitched sound mingling horror and fury—and drove the spike through the middle of the great maggot, piercing it through. Yellow paste of maggot-gut squirted. Dennis screamed.

The maggot crawled backward into the cave, pulling the spasming shell of Dennis with it. Zero watched, feeling the blunderbuss as a great leaden weight in his hands, feeling as if some part of himself were going down a drain, as Dennis's face drew back into the hole. Maybe there was just a hint of *imploring* in Dennis's eyes. . . .

"There might be some part of his brain still alive," Yoshio said huskily, "experiencing."

Zero made himself step up to the hole. He shoved the blunderbuss up against Dennis's forehead. He fired. He glimpsed blood and bone exploding, and then the sky leaped into his eyes as he bent backward, losing the gun, tumbling down the hill, fragmentary images of clouds and dirt and a hole with a hideous pinkish-white face—

He retched painfully on the packed dirt at the base of the mound.

His face was warm and wet. Tears. Angie knelt beside him, touching his cheek, but he couldn't enjoy it.

Yoshio's voice: "The mound is breaking. It's opening up. Where's the oruh for that cart?"

Zero sat up. Clods of dirt came bouncing down the mound to roll against his feet. He looked up and saw pinkish-white skin glistening in broad cracks in the mound.

One of the oruh was missing from its traces. Its black blood smeared the ground in a path that led up to a big hole in the mound. A plaintive *oroooh* echoed to them.

The cracks in the mound widened.

Zero and the others crowded on the remaining carts, driving the oruh away. The oruh—barely restrained till now by Cisco and the High Clansmen—had no need to be urged.

"What was that act you performed?" the Pezz asked. "You got out of the cart and [untranslatable]—"

Zero sighed. "That was vomiting. Regurgitation. Brought on by a shock to my nervous system." Bitterly he mocked the Pezz's clinical objectivity. "From seeing my friend half eaten, taken over by the . . . whatever it was."

"I understand the shock. Myself, seeing a herd part-

— 129 —

ner in that situation, I would have run in circles for a while. This is my version of the sickness you experienced."

"Uh-huh," Zero said. He didn't want to talk about it. He didn't want to look at the Pezz, which trotted along beside him. The Pezz was too alien; something profoundly alien had eaten Dennis's consciousness alive.

Zero was sitting beside Angie, who was driving the oruh. Cisco and Yoshio were in the back; Zickorian and Calum rode in the second cart. They'd abandoned the third cart.

The Pezz's squeaking merged indistinguishably with the squeaking of the wheels. Zero had to strain to hear the translator box.

The bog was changing. The ponds were fewer and farther apart. The ground between them seemed dryer. The moss-suckers came rarely. A few twisted trees, if that's what they were, sprouted between the bogs, competing with the glassy hoop-plants. There was less smell of waterbound life—which on Fool's Hope was very much like the smell of ponds on Earth, with a few dissonant olfactory notes—and more of another smell, brought from ahead of them on a faint breeze, a sort resinous plangency and dry dustiness: a smell of austerely dry places.

"When you first *vomited*," the Pezz said, "I thought you were praying and applying holy benediction to the road-territory." The Pezz went on, guilelessly straining Zero's patience. "That is what we do, when we vomit. But now I understand and agree: The violation of the inner person is the greatest territorial crime of all. My people will see to it that the mound is exterminated. I left a scent-swatch there impregnated with a warning. . . . I vomited it."

"Good," Zero grated, "glad to hear it."

Translating Zero's remarks, the box strapped to the Pezz squeaked and trilled. The Pezz said, "The translator box uses the third degree of semirefined sarcasm in its tonality. I confirm it in [approximate translation:] sorting through the hormonal content of your sweat-vapor. I take this to mean you are annoyed: I understand. I will mention it no further. Except to request an explanation of your attitude toward territoriality. Your people pass in and out of one another's territorial scopes without [untranslatable] or protective acknowledgment. I would have thought that the territorial instinct is as universal as the survival instinct, with which it must bear some [untranslatable] relationship."

"We have a sense of personal space and territory," Zero said, glad of the chance to abstract things away from talk of Dennis. "But I guess it's simply less extensive than yours. My physical sense of territory—unless you're talking about my, you know, residence—extends only, um, maybe twenty inches from me."

"Mine doesn't extend from me at all," the Pezz said.

Zero looked at it, puzzled. Its rubbery, melted-dwarf face, if that *was* its face, was enigmatic. When it spoke, it was like someone with a charred sheet of rubber over his features; the rubber moved about, but you saw no no mouth at work. The Pezz's speech sounded like someone trying to talk to you, high-pitched, through mummy wrappings.

Zero frowned. "It sounds like . . . you *are* your territory. The part of you the dust from the road is settling on. That's *you*, to me. Is there more?"

That's my core or reflective self, my [untranslatable] self. My exteriorized self extends to [untranslatable] distance. That self-layer is of course dented

— 131 —

when other entities intersect it with their own exterior
ized self-layers."

"Uh, are you talking about some kind of bioelectric
field? I read about—"

"No. I speak of a self of environmental interrela-
tionship."

"This sounds like it's, sort of, um, entirely psycho
logical, to me."

The Pezz was stung. "That's an offensive remark."

"It was? Sorry. It wouldn't be for us. Listen, um—
you're like, absorbing people's vapor exudations and
going through them for hormonal traces that tell about
their attitudes, and . . . well, doesn't that violate our
territories?"

"No. We investigate them only after they have emanated from your outermost self."

"Oh. That's nice. I guess." He looked at the bogs.
Fewer yet. "Where do they come from?" he wondered
aloud. "The bogs. I mean, there's no stream feeding
them like in a swamp. Why don't they just evaporate?"

"They come from below," the Pezz said. "I smell a
big water table. I don't know its source."

"You smell anything else—anything new?"

"Yes. A new ecosystem. A dryer place. For some time
now."

"That much I can smell, too."

By late afternoon they'd left the bogs behind. They con-
sulted the map, and Zickorian's crude compass, and the
Pezz—and set off across the veldt, northeast, following
the faint track.

The road, if that was what it was, wasn't rutted
and the ride was much smoother. Some of the gloom
that had come with Dennis's death lifted from the com

pany. Cisco broke out a water flask and passed it around as they sat up straighter and looked around at the new landscape.

The plain was dotted with man-high, whip-thin, feathery growths, yellow but coated on the windward side with blue dust. The desert reached away to the north; behind them, to the south, were the bogs. To the west, swallowing the horizon, was what might have been a bank of blue fog or the edge of a forest. The veldt stretched away unbroken to the east.

"All that water back there, and then suddenly a desert," Yoshio said when they stopped for lunch. "That is geologically peculiar. The ground rose a little—but not very much, really."

"This ground is barren and dusty from stripping and wind exposure," Zickorian said, "not from lack of water. Water exists under the ground, and it rains here. No, something has kept all but a few growths stripped away. This land is very much like my own, and I have looked at it and known: an animal has done this. Many such."

They went on. And after a while they were lulled to a stupor by the motion of the cart and the dull pressure of the heat, a stupor broken only by anxiety. The open spaces made them feel exposed, vulnerable. So by unspoken agreement the High Clansmen drove their cart up beside the Earthers'; the two carts trundled on side by side.

Occasionally they saw small patches of hoop-grass and something that looked like a cheap magician's paper bouquet. And near a patch of the magician's bouquet was what appeared at first to be great heaps of cow manure, each as big as a car. "Looks and smells like droppings of something," Angie said. "But . . . "

"It'd have to be something fuckin' big," Cisco said for her. "Like a dinosaur or somethin'."

"It wasn't something big that left those things," Zickorian said. "They are something big themselves."

He reached into the back of the cart, picked up a scrap of leather, and winged it at the big, crusty yellow-brown lump.

The heap humped itself and began to move away, like a misshapen inchworm, irritably questing for a more private place in the sun. On the way it paused and extended an oily brown pseudopod to a clump of the hoop-grass and magician's bouquet. It uprooted the whole clump in one easy motion, leaving a naked crater, stuffed the vegetation into some aperture on its under-side, and then went humping on to the west.

The Earthers stared—and then laughed. Laughing felt good, and Cisco, as if to perpetuate a sort of festive sharing, passed the water flask around.

Zero drank and handed it to Yoshio. "That's good." Zero said. "But God I'd like a beer."

"Uh-uh," Angie said, closing her eyes and sighing. "*Diet Pepsi*. Or better yet, a *Tab*."

"Okay," Zero said. "We'll stop and get you some. Goddamn *7-11s* are everywhere."

"They don't have *7-11s* here," Yoshio said. "They have *Plaid Pantry*."

"No, it's *AM/PM* here," Cisco said.

"No, they have *In 'n' Out*," Angie put in. "I know because I always send the Ki-ips there to get me my Silvathins."

Zickorian tapped the translator box as if trying to restart it. "The translator seems to be broken."

As they rolled on, they gradually became aware of a white noise that by degrees refined itself into what

Zero could only think of as "a cloud of cheeping," the incessant cheeping of hundreds of birds.

Minutes later, as the wind died down and the skirling dust parted, they caught sight of a big tree. It was almost twenty meters high, the tallest thing they'd encountered on the plain. And as they neared it, Zero's heart swelled with a warmth he knew was foolish. It was a tree, a real tree, and in it, thronging it, were real birds. He had seen many things flapping through the skies of Fool's Hope. Things soaring, too, and spiraling and hovering and darting. But none had been birds.

They pulled up about thirty yards from the base of the tree and gazed at it, the Earthers gaping. It looked like an oak tree without leaves. There was a bird on every perching spot on every branch. They were brown birds with rust-colored breasts, varying in size, but all apparently of the same species.

"I've seen starlings do that on Earth," Zero said. "A huge flock of them just pick a tree, or two together, settle in, and start yelling, go on for hours. For no reason anyone can figure out." The sight comforted him.

"They can't have been there long," Yoshio shouted over the wall of sound. "No guano under the tree."

The Pezz was squeaking something. They couldn't make out the translation over the noise. Zero heard only, "Wrong smell!"

Then the Pezz made a dash at the tree, as if attacking or trying to startle the birds. He stopped short, but it was enough. The birds began to flap their wings—in unison. As one. Every bird in the tree flapped in time with every other bird. And the shallowly rooted tree—not a tree at all—lifted off from the ground. Though the birds remained on the branches. Because, Zero saw as the tree took off, the birds were part of the branches.

They had no legs, nor even eyes. They were fused to the thing they sat on, and if they could see, it was through the "tree's" eye, which—golden, big as a dinner plate, and baleful—kept watch on them from between its roots as the tree flew away.

"I'm sorry I scared it," the Pezz said. "I was testing a theory. I didn't think it would go so far."

"No birds," Zero said. "Okay." He felt numb. "Fine. No birds."

"Fuck it," Cisco said. "Let's roll."

They camped a little early that night, in the partial shelter of an outcropping of rock. After they made sure it really was an outcropping of rock. The sinking sun was just beginning to turn the upper branches of the feather trees into neon fans.

The outcropping—of basalt, thirty feet high—slanted gray-black from the plain like three tombstones stacked one against another, each a little smaller than the next; the great stone made a dimple in the dust where it thrust through from the bedrock. A few smaller rocks, along the same design, studded the dust in a rough circle curving out from the outcropping.

Zero and Yoshio sat together, their backs to the stone of the biggest outcropping, gazing out at the decaying sunlight. The row of rocks stretched a picket of shadows long and black on the gray-blue plain. The dust had been swirled into wave-patterns, as if garden-raked that way. Beyond, the horizon compressed pin-wheels of dust clouds between the dirty jade sky and the ashen ground.

"It's like a Japanese garden, sort of, isn't it?" Zero said tentatively, glancing at Yoshio. Expecting Yoshio's refined disdain.

But Yoshio said, "Yes. The composition has come together."

"You know Yoshio, you have an accent—but your English, your sentence structure . . . actually, it's better than mine," Zero said, prying dust from his nose and ears. Angie and Cisco were scraping dust from themselves, too, Cisco wasting water by rinsing his eyes. The Pezz had found nothing to forage and ate pressed vegetable matter from its supply bag. It put a boardlike foot into the bag and drew the wafers out; the matter of its foreleg flowed into a grasping shape so it could thrust the food into the slit above its pouch. The High Clansmen had strolled off into the plain to "exercise mollification of animistic deities," according to the translator box. They had decided that the spirits investing the local animal life were annoyed by the expedition and needed placation.

"I was born in Japan but, after my seventh year, educated in San Francisco," Yoshio said. "Still, most of my time out of school was spent with Japanese, speaking Japanese. And every summer we went back to Japan. I lived there for three years after I graduated from college. American universities are now held in low regard in Japan—I couldn't find work I could bear. So I came back to California to work in my father's business in Silicon Valley. I was not happy there, either. I like to think about the—the potential of electronics, of computers, but I grew very tired of actually working with them on little—oh, little job puzzles all day. I wanted to make something—something artistically meaningful."

"Funny how many people here are artists of some kind," Zero remarked. "Not everyone. But a high percentage. Anyway, what happened after that?"

"I felt rigid. Trapped. It was as if I'd brought all the strictures of Japan here with me. I wanted to do something different, to meet a different kind of people. So one night I went to San Francisco, thinking maybe I could find a place where artists congregate. Writers, poets—perhaps a coffeehouse of some kind. I saw a sort of—it looked like a circus tent made of something shiny and hard. It was in a lot that had been vacant the week before, near my uncle's house. They said it was for performance art. So I went in." He shrugged.

"I know the rest."

"I thought it was performance art right up until I lost consciousness. 'A very clever performance,' I thought."

Angie stood up and said, "Okay, before the light's all gone, I'm gonna use the ladies' room. Thank God for this rock. I'm going on the other side. You guys have fair warning."

She stood up and walked around the rock, out of sight.

Cisco came to sit by Zero, grunting as he settled back against the rock. "My back hurts. My butt hurts. There's dust between my teeth. My throat itches from it. My eyes hurt. My—"

"We *all* feel that way, Cisco," Zero broke in.

"Maybe," Cisco said, it's like Zen or something. The discipline." He looked at Yoshio. "Right?"

Yoshio snorted. "I don't know anything about Zen."

"You seem so, uh, philosophical," Cisco said.

"There are lots of philosophies. I like to think about things, but I don't want to be a monk. Not unless the Meta refuse to bring any more women here."

"I'm with you there, man," Cisco said. "But whatever happens here, we got to find a way to relate to it, you know? I mean, it's all, like, a message to us, like stuff in dreams."

"*Don't you dare!*" It was Angie, shrieking in outrage from the other side of the rock.

Zero was up with a pike in his hand and running before the other two were on their feet. He ran around the outcropping—and stopped dead.

Seeing Zero, Angie hastily kicked dust over a hole she'd dug in the plain. The two High Clansmen were moving in a stiff-legged dance to either side of her. They looked like children imitating kangaroos as they danced toward one another, then smacked their fists together and turned toward her, making humping motions with their hips, dancing closer as she backed toward the rock. Clamped in Zickorian's mouth was a short blue stick carved with runes.

"I'm warning you, Zickorian!" she yelled.

Zero walked up and tapped Zickorian on the shoulder. "An emergency has come up. You have to stop your dance."

After the translator box had done its work, Zickorian stopped dancing and signaled Calum. Calum stopped dancing. Zickorian turned to Zero, aggressiveness in the abrupt movement. His vision-strip flashed like a stoplight. He took the stick from his mouth. "What emergency?"

"A danger of physical conflict between members of the expedition. Angie is about to deck you." Zero turned to Angie. "What happened?"

She snapped, "They came up to me and started making those obscene motions, and then Zickorian took a stick out of his satchel and started rubbing it on my crotch!"

Zickorian replaced the stick in his pouch with one

hand; with the other he thrust a finger into a corner of his mouth, which Zero had learned expressed puzzlement and surprise. "You mean her protestations were genuine? They seemed to translate so exactly to the ritual protestations of the matable female."

"She means it."

"Then why did she signal for a mating ritual? Just as we'd completed our mollification of the animal-invested deities. That is the proper time for the female to squat and emit musk."

"But you know perfectly well," Zero said, his voice whetted to a sharp edge, "that we're a different race with different customs."

"Yes, but some settlement Earthers have studied our customs. I thought she had studied our customs and was offering herself in our customary way as an act of interracial camaraderie, such as your people speak of with such enthusiasm."

Was there a note of sarcasm there? "So she squatted and, uh, made water, which you thought was musk, and she did this at the wrong time, and you thought—I see. You really think sex is possible between your race and—?"

"Zero!" Angie broke in. "Let's not explore every angle of this too thoroughly, shall we?"

"No, I don't think it's possible," Zickorian said, "nor desirable. We were making the ritual dance of polite disavowal."

"You were"—Zero smiled—"letting her down easy."

Angie made a grating sound deep in her throat and stomped back to the camp.

It was night on Fool's Hope.

Great shafts of blue-white light arose, quivering

faintly, from the perfectly round holes in the Rug. They stood sharply delineated against the purple-black sky, looking like translucent columns of quartz holding up the ceiling of lowering rose-edged clouds. The effect was of some enormous, luminous temple just trembling into being.

The holes punched in the smooth blue Rug-growth over the rolling plain were perfectly round but randomly distributed, each between thirty and fifty feet across. A gathering of Twists was taking place in the sixty-foot gap between two of the biggest. Swanee wheeled overhead, riding the warm updrafts. He circled the columns of IAMton light, shivering as IAMton energies tingled his bioelectric field, exciting his Twist-grown psychic sensitivity. It was warmer near the colums of shine, but not dangerously hot. He held back from them because he was afraid of the interaction of the IAMton radiation and his own mind, though he had no notion what the fruit of that interaction might be.

Flying seemed normal and natural. He'd awakened with the wings—and the other changes—only that morning. Almost immediately on waking he'd run and leaped into the air, spread his wings . . .

And flown. It was as if he'd been doing it all his life. He had—he was one of those people who dreamed often of flying. The dream and waking life had overlapped.

From up here, it was possible to pretend the congregation of Twists was a gathering of humanity, Swanee thought.

In their oddity they had become interchangeable with the aliens. Sometimes Swanee wondered: had they *become* aliens, somehow? Was there a race of creatures like Swanee somewhere?

Like Swanee: glossy black parodies of a man, with

hollow bones and rattling wings borrowed from a pterodactyl (except that those wings were not built on the frame of degenerated arms—he had his arms still, in the same place, but shaped differently now); with a face shaped into a leathery muzzle, nose flattened onto upper jaw; long prehensile fingers, three to a hand; his manhood shrunk to something that emerged from the slit at his groin when he peed and, he supposed, when some unguessable mating ritual with some unguessable mate triggered a more dramatic response. A pared-back man without a gram of fat, with lean muscles and leathery black skin stretched tightly on his light frame; a kite-man.

There were no others like him, because a Twist buried deep in his own mind had shaped him. He knew that as surely as an angry man knows he wants to hurt someone. He was alone. He was a Twist.

(And of course there were no aliens who had become Twists here; aliens who'd been Twisted kept to themselves.)

But three hundred feet above the gathering of Twists, with details blurred by distance, Swanee could pretend for a comforting moment that they were ordinary people down there, wearing costumes. One was costumed as a dwarf crossed with a pig; another as a man whose legs had fused into an enormous snake's tail, so that he sat S-shaped on it; another was a bar of flesh that flowed into this shape or that with its moods; many were Phylum Two: great eraser-pink men grown to eight and nine feet, their muscles swollen unnaturally, their heads shrunk, absurd caricatures of weight-lifters, naked and brutally sexed. There was a woman who was also a venomous reptile; beside her a man with a giant snail's underside instead of legs, his arms shrunken to pathetic flaps; there were the skate couple, a man and woman shaped like human-flesh Mantas; there was Smarg, who weighed nearly a ton, a human-skinned eight-legged triceratops; there were the diaphanous vamps, like silk scarfs in the shape of women, who were lighter even than Swanee except when they were engorged with stolen blood; there was the inside-out man, whose intestines were also his legs, whose heart beat visibly before you; there were the four air-sharks, held aboveground with their pockets of helium and their constant back-and-forthing, their wide, toothy shark-mouths open, barely restraining themselves from tearing at their fellow Twists. There was Father, looming over most of the others, and there was Sissy, the man who had become an evil little girl in a white lace dress; Oliver, the former pop star, had split into two perfected, Adonis-like versions of himself, each as golden and perfect as the David of Michaelangelo, each perpetually embracing the other, obscenely posing and posingly obscene. There, too, were Pacific Bell, Smythe-Wickerson the Newt, and Solus, who was Fiskle's prisoner: Solus of the ecstatic wounds.

And Bella. Light in darkness, every curve a wicked invitation. The pop apotheosis of her Twist came into its own here.

Swanee ached to paint Bella, to do a hundred portraits of her.

And the others; all of them needed to be painted. Some heraldic quality about the Twists . . . As if each was a figure from a card in an otherworldly Tarot deck. Each a living signifier.

Swanee hung on an updraft, gazing at a watching silver sphere that bobbed ten yards away, fifty feet over the Twists on the ground, studying the convocation.

"Why?" he asked it. Encrypted in that syllable was more he couldn't articulate. It was something like, *Am I this? Am I a man not yet thirty, a Tennessee black man raised with a cold fury in him, a painter of revolution in angry murals? Or am I a hollow-boned thing with wings and a beak? An aviator, a genius of the uppers air, happiest when diving to snap up some big-eyed tree nester, just another animal preying on the small warm furry fauna of this world? I don't feel like Swanee Jackson. I feel like the flying thing, the aerial elegance. Was the young artist from Tennessee a dream? Is there a place called Tennessee?*

As always, the watching ball gave no response, unless the swivel of its red dot was a reply.

The Twists were standing in a circle now, facing inward to Fiskle. The shivering columns of IAMton light looming beside them threw their shadows, twisted and uneasy, onto Fiskle, like an ecliptic benediction. From up here Kelso, sitting on Fiskle's shoulder, looked like a second head. But he was a living skull. Now Kelso saw Swanee looking at him; he looked up and croaked in his puerile jeer, "Swanee, big black bug, come down and play for the boss, he's calling you, and if you don't come, you stink like a seagull, one o' them seagulls in tar, yuh dirty dirty thing!"

"Yes, for the sake of your Consummation, Swanee," Fiskle said in his rolling, Shakespearean tones, "do come down."

No.

Swanee saw Fiskle's face catch the light as he looked upward. The metal of his camera-lens eyes gleamed dully; the glass of those lenses glinted sharply.

There was no change of expression on Fiskle's mannequin face; there never was. But Fiskle was summoning

Swanee. Who felt the tugging. Swanee held back, back-peddling in mid-air a few meters to diminish the tugging. Remaining aloof . . .

Swanee knew that as the kite-man he could stay out of reach, safe from most of the aliens and everyone else. Safer, he had reasoned on some cellular level, than a turtle. He could stand back and paint—mentally, if not physically. Artfully distancing, as he had always done.

"Join us."

Swanee shook his head and thought, *No.*

Joining Fiskle's congregation meant conscription into war.

"Apart from Swanee, there is only one other," Fiskle said, aloud and mentally. "And they are arriving now."

They, in this case, meant only one. That would be *El Chingadero.*

Swanee soared lower, to look. He loathed seeing El Chinga, but, like a rubbernecker at a car accident, he had to look. There she was. He was. They were.

The woman, under, was almost dead. It was a shame she'd gone Twist, with so few women in the settlement. (He chided himself for this disloyal thought.) She was Guatemalan, a dark, handsomely stocky woman, once quite pretty, before the draining had begun.

El Chinga looked, just now, like a naked woman with a naked man on her back. The man, though, was not quite there. He was a thing of transparent blue filminess, an apparition, naked and lean and the perpetual picture of lust. His face like a comic parody of Pan. Clinging to her inextricably. Fucking her from behind. Endlessly. Day and night without ceasing. She could not shake him—he was as substanceless as a hologram, if you tried to touch him. But he was not really without substance. He grew more substantial every day, as she grew weaker. He drained her, as if his ghostly penis were a vampire's fang, and after a few days of his presence she was bent, hunchbacked, shriveling, aging. On her face was weary horror and weary disgust and weary despair. But she had grown this thing herself, somehow. Some brutality endured in her past had planted this thing in her, Swanee supposed. The glimmering white thing on her back kept humping, humping, gasping happily . . . Soon she would be dead. The humping thing would find someone else, and it would not care if they were male or female.

El Chingadero joined the circle of Twists. Swanee could not see how this Twist could be of any use to Fiskle. Except perhaps—judging from Kelso's caper of delight—as entertainment value.

"Swanee," Fiskle said, "you will come. . . . We'll let it go, for a few minutes."

Swanee circled just fifty feet over Fiskle's group, spiraling up and down, looking now at Solus.

Solus squirmed at Fiskle's feet. "Solus's childish self-indulgence," Fiskle announced, sounding theatrically pompous and yet ringingly convinced of himself, "has acted in a sort of personality alchemy to change him, to debase him from gold into lead. And here he squirms. Look at what has become of him . . . what the Meta have made him."

"It was you. You have . . . done this to me," Solus croaked. "Only because I spoke up." He was so pale, his skin was almost blue; he was naked and shivering, but not from cold. He was a pudgy, round-faced man, more resembling a dog now as he lay on his back, his arms and legs in the air like a submissive beast, his belly exposed, panting, whimpering accusations. "You influenced the Current. Your mind." His voice was garishly pathetic. As if he wanted them to revile him for his weakness. "You did this to me . . . because I fought you. Because I spoke with the aliens." His face contorted as the anguish of transformation lanced through him.

Fiskle droned, "What has happened to you is the judgment of the Current. The Meta brought us for the Splendid Conflict. To decimate the Lower Aliens, to demonstrate our fittingness to survive and blossom in greater and greater Twist Frees. You defied the Meta; your defiance has taken you to Phylum Three: the living communion wafer."

"Don't!"

But he didn't fight Fiskle—couldn't, somehow—as Fiskle bent over him and placed his hands in the wounds on Solus's belly.

The wounds had not been cut there. They appeared in his skin on their own. Each big as a hand, but releasing no blood or intestines, only a slow ooze of pink mucus. Before his fall from grace, when one of the other Twists, at the behest of Solus, had placed his hand in the stigmatic slit, Solus had writhed with a jolt of pleasure—some of which overflowed into the Twist touching him.

But he had changed after his rebellion against Fiskle. Now, crueler wounds had appeared on him, everywhere but his head, and they gave out slow leaks of blood: they gave a powerful pleasure to the toucher but rewarded Solus with deep, sickening hurt.

Father's soft thrumming grew louder, like a call to mass, and the crowd gathered around Solus, kneeling, looking up at Fiskle, who squatted behind Solus's head, and like Fiskle they thrust their hands into his wounds,

— 147 —

so that he howled and writhed, and they shuddered with pleasure. And more: they were communing with one another through the medium of Solus's nervous system, using his neural pathways as their psychic telephone system.

Swanee fought a down-draft of temptation. Father's call was strong; the psychic tantalization from Solus was strong. Bella was there, and Swanee could perhaps commune with her through Solus.

But he held back, almost hovering overhead, clinging to his repugnance. Watching as Fiskle removed a hand from Solus's neck and reached instead to touch his victim's scalp in the center of his cranium. The skin parted like curtains, blood the applause; the skull cracked and shivered apart. (Swanee alighted on the ground. Was drawing near. Fighting it, but drawing nearer, slow step by slow step. The soundless music resonated with the contents of the secret black box he kept locked away in his heart.) Fiskle reached into the other's brain, between the lobes; Solus began to shake and foam at the mouth. Kelso scampered down Fiskle's arm, leaped to Solus's face and perched there, thrusting his tongue into a cleft that appeared in place of an eye. Kelso giggled.

Fiskle spoke as his hand moved lovingly in the exposed brain, as he rocked on his hands and knees, murmuring what began as a dry dissertation and then devolved into a bellowed declaration of messianic destiny:

"The revelation of a global Overmind presence has made a wreckage of my old assumptions. And then allowed me to fuse them into something new. The old principles were true: that people are biological machines to be programmed by reward and punishment; that Social Darwinism is the path to sociological and bio-

— 148 —

logical betterment. That here the struggle with the lower aliens is the congruence of that path. But a third truth has been vouchsafed me, children. The third truth is the Overmind, which uses the principles of behavioral programming and Social Darwinism as the cutting tools on its lathe."

His voice, booming now, charged with feeling, came faster and faster. "And the Overmind's raw stuff is intuition, and the emotional self—things I denied myself all my life. The realm behind the hidden doors. And lo! The door opens, and I see into the overrealm, the landscape of my own intuition, and I enter and range there, and I permit the wild horse of my emotions to gallop where it will over this landscape. And wherever the wild horse roams, it carries me, and wherever I ride I have, one in each hand, the tools: the scepter of reward and the scythe of punishment. And those who do precisely and absolutely and unquestionably as I direct: those are rewarded. And those who spurn me are *punished!*"

And so saying he squeezed Solus's brain in his fingers like a soft fruit. So that everyone communing felt Solus's death, felt him pass, and glimpsed the demolishing infinity he was sucked into. And—as Fiskle intended— perceived Fiskle as Death's doorman.

"Do you feel the Overmind running through us?" Fiskle asked them in hushed tones that buzzed with his awakened charisma.

Swanee knelt now beside Bella, whimpering as he fumbled for a gash in the still-spasming body of Solus, probing for what little bioelectricity remained in it for him.

Fiskle shouted, "Can you *feel it?*"

"Yes!" came the response, as one.

"I look at the horizon," Fiskle said breathlessly, looking to the east, "and I see the Frost rising in the sky. And at the opposite horizon the hourglass moon of the Meta. And overhead? One of the Meta's watchers, hovering. Is there any mistaking these signs? These are benedictions. They are beyond argument. They identify me, fully and forever." When Fiskle looked back at them, he was more than Fiskle as he cried out in a voice that was half bellow and half whinny, *Do you know who I am? I am the Emperor!*

There was no question about it. Swept away by his lunatic charisma; stoned on Solus's nervous system; inspired by the cathedral presence of the great shimmering columns of light around them, a temple of luminosity Fiskle had invoked into being himself; struck by the miraculous witnessing of the Frost and the Meta's silver sphere—they were convinced. *"You are the Emperor!"*

"In this great ball of chaos, I am harmony. I am the unifier, the theme, the needle that sews the patchworks into the safe blanket of society. I am the Emperor of of Harmony. I AM EMPEROR HARMONY!"

"YOU ARE THE EMPEROR!"

"I am," Fiskle said softly. "And I will bring Harmony to Fool's Hope. If I have to kill everyone to do it."

"You are the Emperor!"

In that moment, Swanee knew that Fiskle, the Emperor Harmony, would lead them into killing and being killed. That their commitment to devotion would lead them into catastrophe; that the consecration of their lives to the Emperor Harmony was a disaster, the signpost of suffering.

But it was a perfect thing in itself; the watching ball above; the columns of light; the circle of Twists; the constellation they called the Frost; the bloody communion through Solus; the contrived symmetry of Fiskle's child-vivid megalomaniacal symbols; the reveling in Fiskle's operatic excess: all the elements of their improbable situation had come together into a composition. And the composition was the reason for all of it.

Swanee was sure of it: that the Meta had brought him to this world for this moment, and this moment alone.

SIX

The dust plain was beginning to change. It had diversified with shrubs and trees, and they saw no more of the ground-stripping heaps of fetid brown. But there were long, segmented chitinous things that moved sinuously away through the blue brush-tipped grasses on what appeared to be tiny tank treads; there were furry creatures hopping like lame bats and spreading what looked like batwings. But the wings were not for flying, they were sticky blue membranes for catching small flying creatures; the batwings were portable spider webs. Mice with tentacles instead of legs swung from twig to twig in what Zero called puzzle trees. The puzzle trees were grown into shapes that made Zero think of the Find Your Way Through The Maze! puzzles he'd worked in the Sunday papers as a boy.

Still, that sun-baked afternoon, the trees were spaced well apart from one another, and the meager ground-cover was no impediment. The carts trundled through grass and over beachball-size fungal pods that burst into dun clouds, breaking with a sound that was a good imitation of a human voice, the husky voice of a drunk middle-aged man going down a child's slide: "Wheee-eee-eee. Umph." That was exactly the sound they made when run over, many times a day. "Wheee-eee-eee. Umph. Wheee-eee-eee. Umph." A minute or two later, "Wheee-eee-eee. Umph."

Zero rode beside Angie in the lead cart. She slowed the oruh as they came to a patch of rocky ground. The wheels protested as they crunched and clacked over the scree. "Those wheels are going to break soon," Angie muttered.

"We could ride the oruh if we had to, taking turns maybe," Zero said.

"They're already getting weak. We ran out of bugs on the dust plain. Maybe we'll find a nice patch of bugs to feed 'em."

Zero said, "I need a break from this heat. You think you could steer us more into the shade?"

"I'll try, but there isn't much of it. I remember when me and my mom and dad were driving through the Mojave Desert and we ran out of gas out there. My mom blamed Dad, Dad blamed Mom. My dad insisted that Mom and I had to crouch in the shade of the car while Dad tried to flag people down. It was so hot and the shade kept getting smaller. Finally Mom got up and kind of took over. She always had to take over for him. Or thought she did. I think that's why they got divorced— she wouldn't let him be in charge of things—God, I'm really chattering."

"Why shouldn't you?" he said, smiling. "I like to hear you talk. You didn't say much for the first week out here."

"I guess it's all coming out now. I was—I wasn't adjusted to being on the expedition till, I guess, after

Dennis got killed. Then, like you said, even if I hate to admit it, you either have to turn back or resign yourself. If it happens, it happens. It wasn't all that much different on Earth. It wasn't usually a matter of life and death, but there was always some bullshit problem springing at you out of, I don't know, the undergrowth of life. That sounds corny, but—"

"Sounds about right to me."

"And my mom would say, 'If you lose, you lose. Just don't turn your back on it or you'll end up a scared housewife hiding behind a man.' "

"Your mom was a feminist, sort of, huh?"

"Not sort of. She wrote papers about the sociology of sexism, sexist conditioning, sexist institutionalism. And my sister had already gone over to the other camp —'a bovine housewife,' my mother said. So I had to be the perfect little feminist for my mom." She looked guiltily at Zero and hastily added, "Not that I wasn't into it. I was. I *am*. Women have to struggle. It's hard to break out of that much—that much *history*. You do have to kind of be an asshole about it, sometimes, to get free. But my mom—she was never satisfied. I had to be the shining example for Womanhood. . . . And dating, God—she let me wear some makeup and jewelry and date a little, but she made me feel like I had to watchdog everything the guy said and did. And I did—and it discouraged them. And then I had to go see my dad, and he was trying to get me away from my mom, mostly to spite her. He was always pressuring me to cooperate with his lawyer, to testify that she was too strict, that she was driving me crazy."

"Sounds like a lot of pressure all the time. From both sides."

"It was. I was scared when I woke up on Fool's

Hope—but there was some relief, too, to be away from all that pressure. Till the settlers started in on me."

He glanced at her. She was staring grimly at a tree they were slowly passing. Something that looked like a dead, eviscerated six-legged monkey lay on its back on a bough of the tree, wedged in a crotch between two branches. Its belly had been slashed open, and the edges of the torn flesh were beginning to curl with decay.

A creature like a small leathery kite was doing a figure eight in the air over the dead monkey-thing. It had a series of lamprey-mouths on its tubular torso, under the wing membrane. Zero had seen the lamprey kites feeding on other carrion; they were the local scavengers. It made up its mind and settled down over the exposed guts of the monkey-thing—which closed over it with a *snap*. The monkey's rib cage snapped shut like a bear trap over the scavenger, crushing it. The monkey-thing sat up and began grooming itself as it digested the scavenger in its fake wound.

"Oh," Angie said, "that's it. I *wondered* why there weren't any of those spiral bugs on the dead animal." She went on absently. "I was going to go and get some for the oruhs." She shook her head ruefully. "I can't believe I'm actually thinking of scraping bugs off dead animals to feed to another animal. Yuck. Weird, the stuff you get used to."

Zero glanced in the back of the cart at Yoshio. "Hey, Yoshio—you see that one?"

Yoshio, writing on bark strips with a piece of sharpened, spongy stick dipped in homemade ink, nodded distractedly. "I'm calling it a trap-monkey. Not very imaginative, but thinking of names for animals is exhausting after the first two-thousand."

They were quiet for a while. The trees, it seemed to

Zero, were thickening, and the ground was becoming more uneven, was generally rising.

Not looking at Angie, carefully casual, Zero asked, "What kind of pressure are the settlers here putting on you? You mentioned, uh—"

She snorted. "What do you think? They want sex. And babies. They *say* it's babies. They say, 'Hey, sweetheart, come *onnnn*—we have to survive here as a species!' That sort of thing. Just before I left, there was a story going around that the Meta brought us here because there's going to be a war on Earth and everyone there'll be killed so this is our chance to preserve our species. But if they did that, why all these other species? Why the High Clans and the others? They all having World War III, too?"

"Everybody's"—he began, and then she chimed in and they finished it together—"got a theory."

He laughed. More soberly, he asked, "Hey, how *much* pressure they put on you? Anyone try to force the issue?"

"With Jamie prez? No way. Punishment for rape is expulsion. But I've been argued with, snubbed, urged, fondled, drooled on, wheedled, lied to, and once, dry-humped. If I want to have a goddamned baby, I'll decide to do it myself."

"Yeah. Especially here. No hospitals. No surgeons. One doctor—and he was only a med student—and one nurse. If there are complications—"

"Even if the delivery comes off okay, there's still the question, do I want to raise a baby on this godforsaken planet?"

"Why a baby when I can't trust anyone?" The voice was flung at them from the high grass nearby. A cruel parody of Angie's voice.

Angie's head jerked toward the brush, and she took her foot off the oruh, which stopped moving and looked questioningly over its shoulder.

The cart behind them stopped. Zickorian shouted. and they dimly heard the translator say, "What is the problem?"

Yoshio was sitting up, looking around.

"I heard it, too."

Another voice from the brush, this time a parody of Yohio's. *"It sounded mocking . . ."* And the rest of the phrase was in Japanese.

"It read my mind!" Yoshio burst out. "That's what I was thinking!"

Angie said tentatively, "I think I was thinking that the real problem with having a baby is trusting people on Fool's Hope." She added under her breath as she looked around, frowning, "There isn't much social convention keeping people responsible."

Another voice from the brush, this time mocking Cisco's. *"The spirits of this planet are finally showing up in person!"*

Cisco squeaked, "Jesus!"

At the same moment the voice said, *"Jesus!"*

Another voice, imitating Zero's, said, *"Let's get out of here!"* just as Zero said it himself.

The carts moved off as fast as they could go, which was about twice as fast as walking.

*"Shit, this's just what I need when I'm hungry and my ass hurts and my head hurts I need some fucking sunglasses in this sun and then this asshole voice—"*A mix of Angie and Zero's voices.

A parody of Cisco's voice: *"God, the spirits sound hostile, oh shit, listen spirits, don't—"*

"Fuck, what if it reads my mind about Angie and then says something—oh God! It's doing it!"

Angie glanced at Zero at that one and then looked quickly away. Zero flinched.

More voices, from elsewhere in the brush, spoke in Zickorian's languge and the squeaking of the Pezz. Now and then one of the voices said, *"Orooooooooooh!"*

The Pezz trotted up beside Zero and said, "I think I know what they are—" It broke off as the carts emerged from the area of thicker brush into an extensive clearing. Something bounded from the brush nearby, pacing them. It looked like a scorpion, but with a chitin-covered ratlike head, and it was the size of a smallish kangaroo; it moved like a kangaroo, bounding on hind legs. Its segmented tail ended in a sort of spiral scoop that took a right-angle turn halfway down so it was pointed sideways, at the expedition.

More of them bounded from the brush, eight in all, pacing the carts effortlessly. Unnervingly, the voices came from the creatures' mouths. Their faces were permanent expressions of mockery; their mouths curved into sneers as they spat back bits and pieces of their thoughts at them. *"I'd like to blast one of those little fuckers, but there's no telling what its buddies might do. . . . God, I want to stop and crap, but I can't with those things hanging around. . . . What the hell are they doing this for?"* Snatches of Japanese. Like turning a dial through radio stations.

The Pezz said, "They are mind-echoers. My people have encountered them before. They haven't got much mind of their own."

"What the hell are they trying to accomplish?" Zero asked.

"What do they hope to get from this?" came the mocking summary of his thoughts.

"We don't know," the Pezz said. "Some method for warning others from their territory, no doubt."

"You *would* give it that interpretation," Zero said. *"Damn Pezz think everything's related to—"* "Shit!" *"Shit!"* "How do we—" *"get rid of"* "the little fuckers?"

"Form mental images of devouring them alive," Yoshio suggested. "Picture it strongly!"

They did just that. They pictured it *very* strongly. Zero imagined himself dismembering the things and eating them like pieces of soft-shell crab.

A squeal like feedback burst from the mind-echoers, and they bounded away, flinging, *"Good riddance, you little fuckers!"* back at them.

They saw no more of them.

The carts continued on a track that thinned to a trickle of definition and finally dried up. Navigating with compass and the Pezz's mind-map, they bore doggedly north. The ground continued to rise. The oruh were showing strain; foam flecked their beaks, and progress slowed so much that the expeditioners found it quicker to climb down from the carts and walk beside them.

Great, improbably dense clouds moved in from the north, staking out every corner of the sky with a brooding ceiling of blue-black overcast. The weighty cloud cover looked as if it were poised to topple. It admitted light sparsely, so that the shadows multiplied into blue-tinted gloom. The expedition felt the tension of an impending storm, and the strange, unnaturally dense look of the clouds seemed to suggest that a strange, unnatural release was impending.

When afternoon was fraying into dusk, they topped

a rise and found themselves descending into a misty, thickly forested valley. The main body of the forest was below them, with the details of its purple and indigo foliage lost behind silvery veils of mist. As they approached it, the expedition grew quiet. All that was known about this forest was that not much was known about it.

The clouds rumbled overhead as the expedition zig-zagged down the hillside, guiding the oruh carefully to keep them from slipping. Warm mist deepened around them; it dewed the wrinkly, livid blossoms of a vine that choked the puzzle trees; it bowed the feather trees and pooled in the cupped leaves of more stunted varieties of growth; it rose into steam on the flanks of the weary oruh.

The slope bottomed out onto the valley floor, and they emerged into a small clearing. The ground was cracked and oddly exposed here. On the far side of the clearing was the apparently impenetrable edge of the forest. In the center of the clearing was a great fallen tree, rotten now, and in the broad cracks of its trunk wriggled thumb-sized roach-things of shiny brown and pasty white. The oruh bellowed happily, and their drivers let them browse to contentment on the things in the rotting trunk. The crunching of the roach-things in their beaks was sickening; to escape it, Angie and Zero took a short walk to the edge of the forest.

"Maybe we should camp here tonight," Angie said, looking at the forest, hugging herself.

"Probably. God knows we should be fresh before plunging in there. It'll be dark soon."

"It'll be wet before it's dark," said someone just inside the forest. Zero could see him—or her—moving in there, but it was hard to make them out clearly. It was like trying to see someone wearing cammies that fit the foliage. The voice sounded familiar, though.

"Who is it?" Angie called nervously.

She was no more nervous than Zero. He whispered, "Maybe you should run and get the blunderbuss."

There—Zero saw it again. A man-shape, just an outline, shadow in shadow. Coming closer. Zero tensed.

And then the man stepped out into the clearing: Jack the Baptist. Grinning at them. Filthy. His hair matted with twigs. A worm crawled through his grimy bangs. His face was streaked with sweaty grime and the purple ooze of plant sap. He wore torn buckskin and, still smiling, reached into his shirt and plucked what looked like a gray lump of fungus from it. One end of the thing was sticky with the Baptist's blood.

He tossed the thing playfully from hand to hand, then over his shoulder—and kicked it away on his heel.

"How the hell did you get—" Zero began.

Angie interrupted, "Are you on foot, or—I mean, how did you—?"

"I've been here all day waiting for you," Jack the Baptist said. "I came cross-country, and I walk faster than your carts move. I had some things to look into before I could join you."

"You were *waiting* for us?" Zero asked. "How'd you know we'd come exactly this way? There isn't a trail anymore."

"I had word you were coming. I could feel the funneling." He seemed bored with explanations. He looked past them at Yoshio and Cisco, walking up from the carts. "You've lost Dennis, I understand. A sadness. He was one of the nicer people here."

"Yeah," Cisco said, ogling Jack. "He was. You follow us here?"

"No, I came ahead. Something else followed you."

They stared at him. The clouds rumbled.

He went on placidly, looking at the clouds. "It's about forty feet behind me."

They looked and saw nothing but an intricately patterned wall of foliage, dense with the promise of approaching night.

"Keep looking," he said, reaching behind him. His hand closed over the long yellow Pinocchio's nose of a plant jutting from the wall of undergrowth. He pushed it down as if it were a lever. Just *exactly* as if it were a lever.

In one place, the foliage parted as if it were a curtain. Just *exactly* as if it were a curtain. For one startled second, a being was revealed, a human become marsupial: black-furred, chinless, lank, stretched between two tree limbs, its long, black, pad-tipped fingers grasped the upper limb, its long black toes wrapped around the lower; its enormous perfectly round golden eyes gazed at them in unblinking apprehension. It wore an old U.S. Army belt and the shreds of an army jacket.

Then it bared its teeth, hissing, and a virulently orange ruff stood out on its head in warning. It turned and melted into the undergrowth. The curtain of plants closed.

"That was one of the first Twists," Jack observed. "It works for Fiskle now."

Zero gaped at him. "How did you—I mean, you pulled that almost like a lever. Is this some kind of sham forest? It's mechanical, or—or what?"

Angie stepped past Jack and pushed the yellow blossom downward. Nothing happened.

She stepped back, brushing yellow pollen off her hands, and looked expectantly at him. "Well?"

"I have a certain rapport with the natural world," Jack said, shrugging. The sky rumbled, louder this time. "Maybe that was my stomach," Jack murmured. "I'm kind of hungry. Got anything to eat?"

"Yes, please come and join us," Yoshio said.

"Wait a minute," Zero said. "I want to know how you—"

Suddenly Jack looked sharply at the sky. "Uh-oh," he said.

The clouds burst. The deluge came down as if it were all of a piece, one solid thing that fell on them from an enormous aerial trap door, a tidal wave AWOL from the sea.

They cried out as they were smashed to the ground, flattened facedown by the thundering downpour. Then coughed, sputtered for air, drowning; watery hands pushed them down into instant mud. Zero saw blood curl away from his face. The weight of the rain had bloodied his nose against the ground.

The environment had been transformed in a split-second. It was as if they were instantly underwater. But it wasn't water or, anyway, not only water. It was . . . glutinous. Transparent but thick. It was like mineral oil, Zero thought, forcing himself to his knees, but a little thicker. Like a liquified slug. It smelled like a living thing. And *almost* like chicken soup.

It moved like a living thing, too. It gathered itself into wormlike threads and slid over his limbs, over the ground, back onto his limbs, searching, moving up his sides, against gravity, making tiger stripes on him with its questing.

It wasn't quite like being underwater, he found once he had got to his knees. He could breathe a little now.

But the baritone white noise of its downpour filled all the world. He gasped, looking for Angie, almost blinded by the stuff. He saw her, a gray blur a yard or two away, and he crawled toward her on his hands and knees. The wet hammering on his back made every movement a bone-creaking effort. He reached for her, but with one hand lifted he was off balance and the weight of the deluge flattened him again.

As abruptly as it had begun, the pressure let up. The rain slackened. Some of the murk cleared away, and he made out Yoshio and Jack and Angie pushing up from the sucking mud, squinting at the sky. Zero looked up and, blinking away the last of the rain, saw that the cloud cover was edged with a rippling aurora of light, the Northern Lights imported from Earth, fringing the clouds like ornament on an eiderdown blanket. And then the blanket tore itself into shreds: the cloud cover fragmented and began—not to drift away, but to *disintegrate*, dissolving into nothingness, evaporating in fast-forward. Cracks of luminous emerald sky shone through and expanded.

More rain fell, as if released when the clouds disintegrated. But it fell fitfully; it was little more than a drizzle, and less glutinous. It washed away some of the translucent stickiness that coated the Earthers. They stood and staggered to the carts. No one was badly hurt. Two bloody noses, some bruises. Jack the Baptist was sniggering, shaking his head, wagging a finger at the sky. The Pezz had smelled it coming, and had hidden under a cart. The High Clansmen had followed his cue.

Everything smelled *almost* of chicken soup. The forest around the clearing was sagging in spots, looking like cooked spinach in purple food dye, badly beaten by the sudden weight of the deluge. Mist rose thickly from it now; the bushes rustled, fussily rearranging themselves. Expanding, unfolding, shaking dry.

With the clouds' breaking up, the evening's darkness retreated a little, giving the illusion of time reversed. Zero thought of a film run backward. It grew lighter for the space of half an hour as they set up their tents, running them between the carts and the tent poles. Jack squatted nearby, not lifting a finger to help them.

"It was water and amino acids, I think," Jack was explaining to Yoshio. "Building blocks of life. A specialized local variety. The local ecology needs, ah, periodic transfusions of it, like plasma for the wounded." He beamed at them. "You were baptised in it. It was none of my doing, but I rejoice anyway."

The ground steamed. The rainbow-coated puddles shifted and squirmed like amoebas, recombining in a two-dimensional dance, a waltz in Flatland.

Zickorian and Calum set up their own tents. They were silent, seeming glum and withdrawn. From time to time they stole glances at Jack, and Zero thought perhaps they mistrusted him. Perhaps they were wondering if he was someone else to split the booty with when they reached the Progress Station.

"You know what?" Cisco said, tying a knot. "I feel good."

Zero nodded. "Me, too. Kind of exhilarated."

"The amino rains are good for you," the Baptist said. "Like Flintstone Vitamins or Post Raisin Bran." He giggled.

"Oh, no, what the hell?" Angie said, pointing at the ground. "Oh, no. Really. I've had enough for today."

The ground erupted. They were small eruptions, where the glutinous, transparent puddles had reached out pseudopods of themselves, the rain puddles nosing into the ground, searching, blindly seeking . . .

In response, the ground spat mud as something pushed up from beneath, making room for itself. It was a thing like a square peg with four faces, one on each of its four sides. They were slimy ochre toadlike faces with a circular arrangement of transparent-lidded yellow eyes above each twitching muzzle. The peg emerged a few inches from the ground—and split apart, into four identical creatures, each of its four sides going a different way, like a hideous flower opening. More of the things erupted all over the clearing. Dozens of them. Hundreds. Each one made a noise like winding an alarm clock as it split apart. Where seconds before the ground was nearly barren, now life was boiling, spreading itself feverishly; the basin of the clearing was swarming with slimy things crawling away in four directions from each hole, crawling on cilia-coated undersides and making the maddening ratcheting sounds, leaving a complex criss-crossing of slime-lines on the clearing's floor. They were heading for the brush, on all sides. They moved steadily as the expedition watched, afraid to move, and in minutes the clearing was almost empty of them.

"It's the rain, you know," the Baptist yawned, lying down to sleep by the fire that the High Clansmen had built. "Always happens like this."

As darkness fell, the forest came alive with millions of minute awakenings and transformations. A festival of metamorphosis was triggered by the living rain. Sitting by the fire, Zero felt himself open up to the forest's internal rhythms. "It's biological party time," Zero said, listening to the rising uproar of rattles, ratchetings, shrieks, whistles, pops, hoots, and *WHOPs*. In the distance something said, "Hey! Hey-hey-*hey*!"

The sounds came in a sequence and a rhythm, like a song. Rattle shriek whistle *pop* whoo!-*whop* hey-hey-hey! (Begin again.) Rattle shriek whistle pop *whoo!-whop* hey-hey-hey! (One more time.) Rattle shriek whistle *pop* whoo!-*whop* hey-hey-hey!

Carried on a wave of exhilaration—maybe from the effects of the unearthly aminos, maybe from a need to release some of the accumulated tension of the journey —Zero stood and shuffled into a dance. He moved to the rhythm of the animal sound sequence, singing along. The Earthers laughed. Zero pulled Angie to her feet, and they danced around the fire, laughing, singing, "Rattle shriek (they whistled, popped their cheeks) whoo! (clapped their hands for *whop*) hey-hey-hey!" Rattle shriek whistle *pop* whoo!-*whop* hey-hey-hey!

The High Clansmen watched respectfully what they assumed was a ritual of animistic communing. The Pezz sensed the fun of it and gamboled about them like a spring lamb, rising to its hind legs so Zero and Angie could take its front legs in their hands and . . .

Large, perfectly round golden eyes watched them from the forest.

Rattle shriek whistle POP Who! hey-hey-hey! (One more time.) Rattle shriek whistle POP.

Swanee heard the beating heart of the small warm furry thing. He heard the furry thing before he saw it. Then, spiraling lower in the light of the Frost and the hourglass moon, he spotted the warm furry thing swinging from branch to branch. It was hamster-size (or ham sandwich-size, he thought, for he was hungry), and it had one eye and little whipping tentacles instead of arms and legs. It used them to swing from twig to twig like a tiny spider monkey. He could hear the quick purr of its heart, could smell its warm-blooded essence. His mouth watered, and he dove for it, letting his new instincts take over. His claws moved of their own accord and snatched the thing from its perch. It squeaked once before he drove a talon through its faltering heart, and then he popped it into his mouth. It had a salty-fruity taste, and its life-essence, as it left the body and filtered between his teeth, luxuriating over his tongue, gave the morsel extra savor.

Swanee's wings reached for air, and he climbed above the trees. Licking blood from his talons, he prepared for another pass over the little woods, looking for another living sweetmeat.

"Swanee, my child. Come along."

It was Fiskle. No—the Emperor Harmony now. Swanee heard the summons with a mixture of fear and childlike happiness. He banked and angled for the gulley in the land-coral, two miles away.

He found the Emperor Harmony sitting on a Phylum Two in front of his den, that living hole in the ground. The exaggeratedly muscled Phylum Two was on his hands and knees, a human bench, padded with beefcake, uncomplaining and unwavering. Elbow on his knee and chin on his fist, the Emperor sat in the pose of the Thinker. The Frost was screwed into the glass and metal of his camera-lens eyes, and the moonlight filtered prismatically through the enormous diamond pinky-ring he'd acquired. (From where?) His suit had changed, too. It had become glossy black silk. Or what looked like it. There was a broad red silk ribbon across his chest, such as royalty wore at embassy parties, and an emerald stickpin on his tie (white silk now), shaped like a crown.

Bella was lolling like a sated panther at the Emperor's feet. Her sickly glow softly illuminated the Emperor and his charges, tingeing everyone a watery green. And softly the land-coral sang its alien chorale to the Emperor. Oliver, the self-cloned pop star, naked and fantasy-beautiful, was embracing himself just behind his liege, like an ornate back to Harmony's throne. The diaphanous vamps, weightless human jellyfish of the air, were dancing six feet off the ground to either side of the Emperor, magic-colored in the starlight, like living curtains to frame his throne. Father stood behind and to one side of the throne, like a eunuch guard. The air-sharks cruised in wide circles around it, moving in opposite directions, passing one another with the monomaniacal grace of beings streamlined for predation. They were the first line of protection for the Emperor. In the Emperor Harmony's pose, in his theatrical regality, was the message, *All of Fool's Hope is my throne room.*

Swanee fluttered down to alight before him, going to one knee, his head bowed, as he knew was expected. "My Emperor, my essence is yours."

"What do you think?" the Emperor asked mischievously, sitting up straight and gesturing at the array of Twistflesh around him. "Wait till you see the palace I'm going to build. *Then* you'll see some self-indulgence. I intend to live every fantasy I denied myself as a boy. I lost my boyhood, you know, raised as I was. . . . Well, that is neither here nor there."

His eyes whirring, the Emperor reached down to the corpse of a wheeler lying beside his stoic, breathing throne and dipped two fingers into the wheeler's exposed brain. Then he ate the blue brainstuff straight from his fingers, like a Hawaiian with poi. Climbing up Harmony's back, Kelso came to rest on the Emperor's shoulder, gnashing his skull teeth, sniggering, eyes glowing pink-red.

"Disturbing news reaches me," Harmony said, looking affectionately at Kelso but talking to Swanee. "I am in rapport with Golden-eyes, who informs me that the cross-species expedition, that diplomatic miscegeny, has won past the brain termites. I awoke the termites myself with a ripple and felt them take one of the expedition—the little cockney fellow, Dennis—and I felt sure the others would fall to them, too. But they didn't. They're at the edge of the forest, and they have a guide now, this Jack the Baptist creature."

"That's a drag, my Emperor," Swanee conceded. He was looking at Bella, who gazed tauntingly back at him in full knowledge of his hopeless devotion. Swanee hoped he didn't have bloody fur on his mouth.

"I need to contact someone out there, Swanee dear," the Emperor was saying languidly. "A group of aliens going after the very same Progress Station. I'd like to tip them off about the Earther competition. They might just do something about that competition. Especially if I tell them that the Earthers plan to do something about *them*."

Kelso crooned, "So creative, so, oh *soooo* creative!"

Pleased, the Emperor paused and turned to Kelso and made kissing noises at him, like an old lady with a parakeet. Kelso snuggled up closer to his Emperor's nearly changeless face. The Emperor turned to gaze at Swanee now, saying, "My agent, unfortunately, is too deep in the forest to contact. It's a sentient place, that forest, and its interference is impassable. So I need a sort of communications satellite. You."

The temperature of Swanee's blood dropped twenty degrees. "No. If I understand you, Emperor, I cannot—"

"You do. You will. You'll take to the air, fly partway to the forest. Nearby the forest are the aliens. I'll send my ripple to you, and you'll transmit it to the aliens. We'll tip them off. With any luck—and who is luckier than the living God?—they will kill the infidels. These aliens are a fierce bunch and will probably torture them first. I'd like to see them torture this Zero, and the Baptist . . . but even *I* cannot have everything. Not yet." His voice was sticky with affected humility.

Twenty degrees colder still. "No, my Emperor," Swanee said haltingly. "Aliens—to be in mental contact with them—I couldn't handle it."

"You'll merely be a relay. Anyway, it's not as if you have a choice."

Suddenly the air-sharks were there, within reach, circling Swanee with sharp sweeping motions, making slicing sounds in the air, clashing their teeth. In their small shark eyes was a compressed infinity of undiluted rapacity.

Swanee shrank within himself.

Bella's laughter tinkled; Kelso snorted derisively and yammered, "Shark bait, you're shark bait if ya don't!"

Deep inside Swanee there was a reason under the reason for not wanting to be the Emperor's psychic communications satellite. He didn't want to be the cause of the expedition's murder. He had known Angie a little, and Yoshio. Angie was lonely and uncertain of herself, a child really; Yoshio had been kind to him. He didn't want to murder them. Or anyone at all.

One of the air-sharks ducked its beveled head at him and flashed the ornament of its jaws in the Frost-light.

"My essence is yours, my Emperor," Swanee said.

SEVEN

We'll probably get lost in there," Cisco said, looking at the forest. It was no less ominous in the light of morning. The trees seemed higher today.

"How will we get the carts in?" Zickorian asked.

"Yes," Calum said, "how can we get the carts in?"

"There is a place," the Baptist said. "I'll show you."

Two hours later they were toiling through a murky corridor of trees along a narrow, claustrophobic trail between dense banks of underbrush that was feverish with renewed life. The forest here was a many-layered thing of purples and shades of violet, of sudden splashes of scarlet and dead-white. The trees rose in dove-gray shafts, each big enough to dwarf a sequoia, through tiers of foliage canopy. Their branches contained not leaves on stems but a feathering of the bark itself into something like leaves, like a bird with its plumage puffed out. The canopies were made with a profusion of branches and with interlacing parasitic plants and lesser shrubs. Things scampered and slithered and fluttered in the canopy but were rarely seen.

The dull blue light was diffuse. The outlines of things were clear; the details were not. They were blurred not only by shadow but also by the amino-rich mist that hung between the growths and added choking humidity to the dull pressure of heat. Occasionally shafts of sunlight struck through breaks in the canopy, like a spotlight illuminating a circus of dust and spores and minute flying things . . . The place smelled of damp, of dissolved minerals, of menthol and ergot and fermenting mulch, and faintly of chicken soup.

The expedition trudged beside the oruhs. Zero and Angie were at the lead cart, both of them sticky with sweat and trying not to go back to the water-skins too often. They hiked on either side of their cart's cranky beast, urging it on when they came to a place where the undergrowth bullied in too close or where the ground was choked with fallen limbs. The oruh seemed reluctant to be in direct physical contact with the forest.

"How is it that the ground is exposed here?" the Pezz asked suddenly as it dropped back from expedition point. It addressed its question to Jack the Baptist, who was walking beside Angie singing softly to himself.

As if humorously unsure that the Pezz would believe it, Jack said, "From other expeditions, perhaps? Or forest animals?"

"No, it is very fresh," the Pezz said. "It gives the appearance of being recently exposed. As if the forest drew back to make it."

Zero looked at the Baptist, wondering. Remembering.

The Baptist said, "Perhaps it recognizes the inevitability of your passage and seeks to minimize your damage to it. Your expedition is, after all, an important enzyme action in the unseen organism."

"He's starting that stuff again," Angie muttered. "He says stuff like that and refuses to explain it."

"I understand it," Cisco said pompously. "See, he means we're all One with the cosmos, and—"

"We are certainly not all One," The Baptist said. "We are all Many. There *is* a One, of course, who rides passively with us and watches through our eyes."

He's a classic Paranoid, Zero thought.

But Jack went on, with a madman's confidence, "You might say we are that One, but then again you might point out that we have our own choices to make which the One does not take part in, and thus we are quite separate. The forest, similarly, is one organism on a certain level; on another it is made up of many very combative and competing parts. It happens that, here, those parts can cooperate when they have to, when it's useful to them, through the IAMton interconnection. Myself, I tell you that the level on which we are All One will not help you, Cisco."

Cisco tried to draw him out, but the Baptist would say nothing more. Zero thought how remarkably little they knew of him. He made jokes to sidestep their questions about his life on Earth, his background. He made short forays into the forest at times, melting effortlessly into what appeared impenetrable to others, and returned with armfuls of fruit. At least, Zero assumed it was fruit. It might have been colorful eggs or . . . he preferred not to guess. The Baptist had piled the multicolored fruit into the back of the cart and said, "Take note of the type. I bring you those that won't poison you. They're nourishing. Even for the Pezz and the Clansmen. Don't eat any now, though," he had added, as Cisco reached for a mauve ovoid. "Might not be wise to eat them when you're moving."

The hours dragged. The Earthers' feet ached, and then their legs ached, and then their feet and legs and backs. Zero's breath rattled in his throat. He felt chills and wondered if he were coming down with a fever. The angle of the sun-shafts tilted as the day wore on, and were seen less often; the smothering closeness of the woods closed around them. The forest spoke to itself with its ten million denizens, but more quietly now; the chattering and rattling and hooting sometimes inexplicably dropped into silence. In those oases of quiet they'd hear only the faint rustling of things moving, just out of sight.

"This fucking woods is on my *nerves*," Angie said out of the blue, her voice shrill with stress. "And the damned trail is getting thinner." She pulled on the oruh's halter, urging it on against it will so that it cut through a corner of the underbrush crowding the turn in the trail. The oruh stepped on the bush. The bush's seeds broke under the oruh's tread. From up ahead came a rustling. Angie took a pike from the back of the cart and went ahead to use it like a clumsy machete, smashing at the vines and the smaller outthrust branches in their way. Jack the Baptist gaped at her, blinking

What's so surprising? Zero wondered.

More rustling up ahead. They completed the turn in the trail. . . .

Then the trail was gone. Just petered out and ended. They faced a wall of brush.

Jack sighed. "It's rather stupidly stubborn, you know. If you try to penetrate it like a bulldozer, it closes up and refuses to cooperate. As it has done here. If you try to minimize your damage, it plays along and lets you through. You'd think it would be the other way around." He shrugged. "But perhaps, as you're abusive, it wants you to die here so more of your sort don't come."

Zero turned to him. "You mean it's going to—" He broke off, staring at the apparition hovering over the Baptist.

It was a small pyramid, a half-yard to a side, slowly rotating in midair. It was the color of the afterimage that comes from staring at a light bulb. Its artificiality glowed against the riotously organic backdrop like a computer screen in a dark room, and Zero thought it reminded him of something that had been computer animated. That look of having been drawn without lines or conventional shading.

Was it translucent? Zero stared at it, straining to see into its interior—and it split up into two smaller pyramids, as if under the impact of his gaze; as if the process of perceiving it disturbed its shape.

"Oh," Cisco began.

Angie turned to him, snarling, "Don't you fucking *dare* say 'Oh, wow!' Understand?"

The pyramids merged again into one, which moved off, into the forest. The Baptist murmured something inaudible and followed it, keeping his eyes on it. For the first time his face showed tension—even fear.

The expedition's sodden amazement broke up into a babble of overlapping exclamations.

"Hey, what the fuck—"

"I apprehend no physical exudations from this entity."

"Where you going—"

"What is this phenomenon?"

"Maybe we oughta follow it. Maybe it wants us along, too." This last from Cisco, who started to follow Jack into the brush. Acting on instinct, somehow knowing it was the right thing to do, Zero and Yoshio reached out and grabbed Cisco by the collar, hauled him back, and held him protesting till both the pyramid and Jack were gone from sight.

"We camp here, I think," Zickorian said.

Swanee was crucified on the sunset. He had reached the apogee of his climb, had spread his wings and his arms as if he were asking the sun to burn away his guilt with photon grace, and he was silhouetted spread-eagled against the shimmering bands of tangerine, gold, and jade on the horizon.

And then he plummeted so suddenly, he nearly dove through his own shadow on the clouds. He pierced the cloud with his dive and opened his wings, emerging with a horizontal swoop into the open air, clearing his mind with the breathless exhilaration of the moment, making himself receptive, an antenna, a transmitter.

A hot flash rolled through him and squeezed perspiration from him like water from a crushed sponge as he saw the Emperor Harmony sitting on a small cloud before him. There and not there. The Emperor Harmony: Caparisoned in an ermine robe and a sapphire-studded diadem, his face shining with angelic perfection, a halo spiking bluewhite around his head, a ball of healing golden energy seething in his upturned right hand; a ball of destructive scarlet energy combusting in the palm of his left; the balance, reward and punishment . . .

This was how the Emperor saw himself, Swanee realized.

And then Swanee saw another place entirely. In it were six creatures alike, aliens, striding along the edge of a forest, circumventing it. They were noble creatures, living prisms, creatures of transparent skin because the sun loved their inner selves, knights of breathing glass who rejected shadowy places like the forest. They remained in the open, so as to remain in communion with the planet's god, the Star (Swanee realized then that his rapture in the sunlight had come from the aliens' sun-worship, a precontact psychic glimpse as the Emperor sent the first mind ripple between himself, Swanee, and the aliens), the great hydrogen-fusion warrior in the sky.

Distantly, Swanee was aware—and indifferent to the awareness—that he had begun to spiral down, recklessly descending.

Images of Zero, Angie, and Yoshio. Of a Pezz and two High Clansmen. All these springing from the forest, firing blunderbusses and flinging pikes, ambushing, fouly murdering the noble beings of soft glass.

Gone. The Emperor waved and blinked into nowhere, and Swanee's contact with the aliens was severed. He found himself diving, falling dangerously near the ground. Trees rushed up at him; the speed was like a furious hammer about to smash him onto a treetop. He banked and clawed at the air, fighting to come out of the dive. But the trees shot toward him like spears.

Then he found the lift-pressure, and the treetops tickled his stomach as he pulled up and streaked above them parallel to the ground. That close.

Heart pounding, Swanee found a perch on a natural obelisk of rock thrusting up from the woods. He settled onto it, panting, fearing a heart attack. But his heartbeat slowed as the planet heaved its horizon over the sun, drawing a soothing darkness over the antic world.

Swanee looked north and thought; *They're there. A long way north. In another forest.*

The memory of the aliens clung to his mind like a

bad aftertaste. There was, in fact, a taste that accompanied it: of vinyl. He knew them then. They were the aliens whom Earthers called Vinyls, creatures of what looked like soft transparent plastic and visible internal organs. Creatures of long, frictionless feet, skating over the ground with unnatural ease, moving over grass or dirt like an ice skater over a frozen pond. They were violent things and so utterly alien that he had backed away, biting off a scream, when he'd first seen them in the Neutral.

With a lead weight sinking through his gut, Swanee knew that he had just given them a message, a message they would take to be from their sun god. A counterfeit premonition of ambush. An imperative to do something about it.

"What did he mean, 'It might not be wise to eat them when you're moving?' " Zero asked, frowning, looking at the core of the third piece of fruit he'd eaten since making camp.

"You trust this Jack too much," Zickorian said. He'd refused to eat the fruit. "What do you know about him? He has been referred to by others of your kind as insane. Perhaps he has poisoned you."

"Yes," Calum said. "What do you know about him? He might have poisoned you!"

Angie shook her head. "More likely he meant the stuff gives you diarrhea."

They were sitting around the fire, rather close to it, their backs to the two carts. No one wanted to leave their backs completely exposed to the volatile mystery of the forest.

The Pezz had consumed two pieces of the fruit. "The fruit is nourishing and not poisonous to me. But

I cannot truly say that it is harmless. It has (untranslatable) my synapses and has given me waking dreams."

"I feel . . . kind of . . . funny myself," Zero said. His teeth ached. His skin tingled. He moved back from the fire; it seemed to burn aggressively, threatening to swell to a bonfire.

"Me, too," Cisco and Angie said almost simultaneously. They broke up into giggles, leaning on one another. Zero himself was smiling idiotically.

"I suspect," the Pezz said, sitting on its hind legs with unusual rigidity, "that since this forest stands on the edge of the IAMton wastes, its roots and water systems may carry IAMton-rich minerals to its plants. There may be an unusually high concentration of IAMtons in the fruit. Which may account for certain phenomena."

"What the hell are IAMtons?" Yoshio asked.

Zero looked at him in astonishment. He had never heard Yoshio swear.

"They are not in-the-realm-of-metaphysical-punishment," the Pezz said. "They are—wait." It turned to look at the brush. "I cannot explain today. I am undergoing an (untranslatable) experience."

"Everything is untranslatable if you try too hard to understand it," Yoshio said. "Detailed analysis is conceptual shit! We must apprehend with—" The rest was spoken in angry Japanese. His eyes were wildly dilated.

He's stoned, Zero thought. We're all stoned. What a fucked up place to be stoned in.

He looked at Zickorian, and saw firelight playing on the golden strip of his ocular organ. He imagined that Zickorian was using that golden reflection to communicate with the fire, talking to some spirit innate in fire. And what was fire? Combustion, rapid oxidation accompanied by heat and light given off when the—wait. There's someone—

Who is that? In the forest?

A face in the foliage. The golden-eyed thing? No. It was Dennis.

A chill made Zero clutch himself. And then Dennis's face became Bowler's. And then it was . . . his father's. "I should never have left, son. I know that now." Practically whimpering. All Zero's respect for the man vaporized.

His father wasn't there in the bushes. It was an hallucination.

Zero turned to Angie. She was staring into the dense wall of forest, muttering, "Shut up, Mom, goddammit. All right, all right, all right already, I hear you! Now just *shut up.*" Zero looked and saw a middle-aged woman with short black hair, her mouth moving rapidly, her face contorted.

It's not possible, Zero thought, *to see someone else's hallucination.* "Angie—did you see Dennis and Bowler a minute ago?"

She broke off her muttering and turned to him, blinking, her face vibrantly golden in the firelight. Breathlessly she said, "Yeah, I did." Her eyes looked so *big.*

"Jesus. Me, too." He stared at the forest. He heard Cisco and Yoshio talking to one another; Cisco was frightened, Yoshio was trying to calm him down but sounded scared himself, while the forest . . .

It glowed with internal energies, which somehow didn't do much to illuminate the shadowy places. It was a black-light forest, pulsing in places with tongues of ember red and cones of methane combustion; it was a fire without flame, without glare.

And the forest was moving. The vines, the plumage of the bark, the other plants woven into every passage in the living maze, were sliding in erotic lethargy, vine against leaf, branch against bole, small, shiny animals squeezed in and out—unhurt—like beads of sentient sweat.

But the movements weren't random. They formed shapes, reflecting their thoughts, one image melting into another, forming a bas-relief in the wall of living plants, animals, insects, three-dimensional and yet fluid, brutish but aware.

Zero's father was there again. His features ran like the face of a wax figure in a burning museum, reshaping, becoming someone else, a face Zero had pushed from his conscious mind for two years.

Gannywick. Hank Gannywick, in a Long Island jail on suspicion of homicide. Zero had been arrested in an antinuke demonstration at the Long Island nuclear power facility. He was doing a student film on the thing as well as taking part, and when the cops came in to bust the demonstrators for deliberately blocking the access road, he'd filmed one of them beating a coal-black Rastafarian with his nightstick after the guy had already been handcuffed. Then he'd given the film to a friend, who'd driven off with it. And he'd refused to tell the cops where they could get the film. So they separated him from the cell containing most of the demonstrators and put him in with Gannywick. "There you go, Hank," the guard had said. "You wanted some company, I told you you'd have to wait till we had one we didn't give a damn what happened to him. He's one like that."

Gannywick was a big-bellied bearded guy with a shaved head. A dent in that head, a small crater. An open bubo on his neck. Shit under his fingernails.

"You're gonna be my girlfriend," Gannywick had said. "And I wancha give yourself to me zif ya like it."

Gannywick had alternately tried to seduce and terrify him for the next seven hours before the demonstrators' lawyer finally arranged Zero's release. Gannywick had failed to seduce him but had succeeded in terrifying him, and only the timeliness of the lawyer preempted a rape.

Here on Fool's Hope, Gannywick was ten feet tall; a shrub had become his beard, a knob on a branch his head, a legless scorpion had become his mouth, his eyes were two glittering onyx bugs—but he was there. "I'm gonna make new holes in you, kid, when I get tired of th' usual ones," Gannywick whispered. Rigid with fear, Zero stared—and remembered the mind-echoers. He concentrated and visualized Gannywick exploding.

The Gannywick-bush burst like fireworks. Bits of twigs and foliage rained; a piece of legless scorpion was flung by the explosion, fell snapping to and fro at Zero's feet like a spastic mouth. Zero kicked it away, and covered his eyes with his hands.

The others, wrapped in their own contemplation of the rippling, shifting forest, scarcely noticed the small explosion, except that Cisco said "Oh, wow."

Zero tried to think of some alternative, something to keep Gannywick from coming back. Angie. The way she moved with, yes, a little self-consciousness, but never vanity; and always neatly, like a song sung a cappella by a singer with perfect pitch.

Could she move like that in the awkward displays of lovemaking? When people, caught up in the toils of instinct, became as mechanically fixated as frogs mating, or beetles? Would she still be graceful then?

He imagined her shorn of all misgivings about him,

free of all inhibitions about herself, opening her arms and legs to him, opening her mouth and eyes with no fear whatsoever, trusting him utterly. . . .

Instantly the stoned electric charge in him focused in his groin, making his cock so engorged it was painful. He fell on his side, hugging his knees to himself, curling up into the fantasy, letting it carry him.

The fruit in the drug was hallucinogenic, but was not a strong stimulant. Weariness softened the neon-edged fantasy to muted fleshtones and pastels, and then to grainy impressions . . . and the curtain closed.

Zero felt as if his body were divided up into locked rooms and the various parts could only communicate dimly, through the walls. His feet and legs were locked up in the basement; his torso was jailed in the living room; his arms and shoulders were incarcerated in upstairs bedrooms.

Grimly, he admitted to himself that it was morning.

He forced himself to sit up and move around the campsite, stumbling to the carts, ignoring the others except to walk around them; he swished water from the water-skins into his gummy mouth and spat on the blue dirt. He scowled at the moss-sucker welt on his forearm. He stumbled through everything, giving the Pezz a wide berth as it staggered, squeaking mournfully to itself, as it bumped into the wheels of the cart and the legs of the yawning oruh. Zickorian, squatting with Calum by the dead fire, chewing one of his clods of protein, could not resist saying, "The Higher Instincts of the High Clan have always saved them from such pitfalls. We are fortunate, Calum."

"Yes," Calum said. "Fortunate our Higher Instincts save us from these—"

"Oh, *fuck off*," Angie snarled, holding her head as she looked for a place to pee. She walked away from the High Clansmen as they puzzled over the translator box's interpretation of *fuck off*.

By degrees, Zero's various parts pushed through their bonds, room joined with room, and his coordination and sense of connectedness began to return. But they brought a gritty muscular ache and a throbbing headache.

So he wasn't prepared for it when Yoshio touched his arm and pointed at Dennis in the bushes.

He wasn't *in* the bushes; he *was* the bushes. They'd been rearranged like an unusually detailed topiary into his body, his smiling face. He was made out of twigs, vines, leafy things, and blossoms; the stuff was stippled into an improbably lucid mosaic. They found that if they shifted to one side or the other, they lost the image. It was like a cheap hologram that way. But it was no accident, no hallucination. It was there.

It wasn't alone. Angie's mother was there, frozen in shouting. Portions of Gannywick. One of Yoshio's ancestors, who'd died in the blast at Hiroshima. Aleister Crowley and Bowler, arm-wrestling. What appeared to be geometrical abstractions arranged around Pezz figures . . . The stuff was etched into the porous wall of the forest. Mental Polaroids caught in an environmental emulsion.

Zero turned to Angie to show her. He found her staring at something on the other side of the camp. Her mouth was open in tired outrage. It was a plant sculpture. He couldn't think of it any other way. It was more abstract than the other images but embarrassingly clear. It showed a plant-formed semblance of a nude Zero embracing a semblance of a nude Angie. The figures, looking as if someone had taken bundles of various plants and flowers and pressed them into a mold, were rendered impressionistically. But there was no doubt as to who they were.

Angie's semblance was open in cracks along the thighs and belly, giving an effect of semitransparency, showing the plumelike inflorescence of a plant resembling a marsh reed, (the male genitals) thrust into a blossom very like an orchid (obviously the vagina) . . . and from the tip of the reed grew tiny white flower-filaments like a spurt of semen. The figure of Angie had its legs locked around the Zero's back, arched in ecstatic surrender . . .

Angie turned to Zero and her expression said, *I've been violated.*

He wanted to protest, *It could've been you who made it, you know.* But they both knew it hadn't been her.

Angie moved toward the plant sculptures and made as if to kick them apart. Then, with a hiss of frustration —or perhaps confusion—she turned away and stalked back to the cart.

Zero saw Cisco wander over for a closer look. To forestall any painful remark Cisco might make, Zero stepped between the plant erotica and Cisco and said, "Uh, how we going to go on? Forest's closed off. Trail's gone."

"I dunno, man." Cisco tried to peer past him.

Yoshio returned from strapping a feedbag of bugs onto the Oruh and said, "Your friend Jack the Anointer seems to have consistently known what he was talking about."

"He didn't warn us about the fruit, except to say don't walk when you're eating it," Angie said bitterly.

"True," Yoshio admitted. "But it was clear he knew about it. I think he felt it was for the best. Because in the night I thought much about what he said. About the forest. And the—the drug, or whatever was in the fruit —it made me . . . ah, I am having difficulty expressing myself in English today. It gave me a feeling of relationship with the forest. I think I know how to proceed. But I think we will be going much more slowly. And we'll have to leave the carts."

"We will have to learn to cooperate with the forest and (untranslatable)," the Pezz said. It was still wobbly but seemed much recovered.

"Exactly," Yoshio said.

They followed Yoshio's lead. They detached the oruh from the carts and tied some of their baggage onto the animals' backs. Some they carried over their own shoulders. Then, Angie and Zickorian each leading an oruh, they followed Yoshio into the underbrush.

The going was hard at first, but by degrees they found that if they avoided damaging the brush, it loosened up and seemed to move aside for them just enough. They found a sort of slow, polite rhythm in their pressings on. In an hour the trail had widened noticeably in front of them.

Once Yoshio said what they were all thinking: "The pyramid thing might've killed Jack. Or . . . it is impossible to know. I wonder if we've abandoned him."

Zero thought about it. Finally, he shook his head, convinced. "He knew what he was doing. I'm sure of it. And he knows this forest. He'll be back."

Mercury is not here by accident," the Emperor Harmony told them. "Like all of you, he has a purpose special to me. Some of your purposes I see immediately, some show themselves to me with time and by mysterious degrees."

The entire colony of Twists was gathered that morning around the Emperor and the once-human called Mercury. Everyone but Bella—who had fallen asleep—was looking raptly at Mercury, a faceless, sexless slab of human flesh in the general outline of a man.

Mercury was lying on its back. If that *was* its back, it was identical to its front. It was shaking. A shimmy of pink flesh rose into large goosebumps down its middle. The goosebumps became a miniature mountain range of skin, which spread outward, remaking itself into the configurations of a different creature entirely. To Swanee it looked like a painting taking place in fast action, with Mercury's original form as the blank canvas. First the rough shape of the thing, then the topography of its body, then the fur, the claws, the big golden eyes, the small white teeth.

"What a lovely resemblance," the Emperor said, crooning the words over the transformed Mercury. "My messenger, you see, takes the form of that which transmits to it. Its mind-ripple reception is so much clearer than my own. It is perhaps possessed by that which transmits to it. That's a wonderful thing, don't you think, children?"

They applauded and murmured approval as he went on. "It's the very essence of art. It is method acting beyond method acting. It demonstrates devotion to my needs down to the last cell of Mercury's body. Now, that is the way to appreciate one's Emperor." He looked down at the furry golden-eyed thing that had been Mercury.

It lay there twitching, staring at the sky as if swept up by a vision. After a moment it spoke in a comical voice somewhere between a cartoon dog's talking growl and a raccoon's *chirr*: "The cross-species expedition continues. It has absorbed IAMtons and seen things with them. It has materialized its mentation with IAMtons in the forest. The expedition is in danger of becoming holy. The one called the Baptist has communicated with an alien that is unknown to me." As it spoke, its breast opened, as if it were giving birth, producing a pyramid the color of the afterimage of staring at a light bulb; the pyramid rose into the air a few inches and slowly rotated. "The alien appeared in this form." The pyramid sank back down into Mercury and melted into him. From the fur of his belly rose six figures of transparent plastic, the size of toy army men. You could see tiny organs of cherry red and metallic blue inside them. They seemed to skate along but never got anyplace. "Here are the Vinyls, who have nearly circled the forest. They are near the Hillserlive. They await the expedition; they plan an ambush to counter the ambush they believe the expedition plans."

Hearing that, Swanee's heart seemed to spin in his chest like a grieving dervish. His wings closed down over him, enwrapping him protectively.

"The Vinyls will do their bit of business," the Emperor said distantly, looking up at the dwarf-pig lowering from a coral branch by a sticky white strand. "But it may perhaps not be enough. This Baptismal with IAMtons—yes, this is the origin of the Baptist's name, though no one who uses this nickname knows it—this Baptismal could create interference patterns. It could siphon Overmind away from your Emperor."

"That ith very thad," lisped the upside-down pig.

Nodding solemnly, the Emperor went on. "And so it is necessary for us to consolidate our power in the

settlement, to eliminate all other interference patterns."
He looked down at Mercury. "Good-bye, Golden-eyes.
Well done. Continue to watch them. Get me Father on
the 'line,' Mercury."

Mercury ran within itself, shivering into a new
shape. In perhaps ninety seconds, Father was lying
there in place of the anthropomorphic marsupial. But
it wasn't Father. Father was in the settlement. This was
a simulation, his message through Mercury personified.

"My essence is yours, Emperor."

"Father," the Emperor said thoughtfully, "have you
had some success?"

"With a few of them. I have only just left them. But
there was some interference from this fellow Bowler,
who, with an ironic aptness, seems to regard you as an
imperialist."

The Emperor chuckled. "Continue to hide yourself
by day. Rest, but watch them. Mark those who are to
be killed."

Swanee could bear no more. He turned and flung
himself into the air, pulling himself up it almost vertically, like a lizard climbing a wall, his muscles protesting. But the pain was nothing in comparison to the
horror of self-realization he had experienced when he'd
heard the Emperor say, *"Mark those who are to be
killed."*

He flew away but not to warn anyone. Because even
when he was gone from the Emperor, the Emperor was
not gone from him.

EIGHT

It took them almost an hour to realize that they were walking above the ground.

They were deceived by the density of the forest around them, by the increasingly murky atmosphere, and by the interwoven solidity of the surface they trod. The slope had climbed gradually, till it had become almost steep. The forest had gradually closed in around them, literally becoming a tunnel, letting only a little light through in thin green-tinted beams; the ground was covered with woven branches and roots, so that they were walking on living plant matter, in a funnel of foliage angling up a hillside, they'd assumed.

But it wasn't a hillside, Zero discovered when one of the oruhs stepped through a weak spot in the floor of woven wood. The oruh sank up to its knee and gave out a quavering *orooooh* of pain. "Shit, I hope it hasn't broken its leg," Angie said as they gathered around the oruh to help it from the hole. Zero and Calum the High Clansman bent and grabbed its leg, pulling up, while the others nudged the beast so it leaned on its other limbs. Zero could smell the High Clansman's body this close. A smell of moldy cinnamon.

They pulled the oruh free—and then Zero's breath caught in his throat. The hole was a window to another level down. It was a hole in a floor, he saw, and the floor was also a ceiling. He was looking down into a vast chamber given top and bottom by the terraces of the jungle; at least thirty yards below him was another level made of interwoven tree limbs, roots, things he couldn't be sure of. But that distant level too was broken open in one spot, and he saw void below it.

"We're way above the ground," he said, swallowing. What if the forest decided to move the way it had that first night? It might move out from under them.

There was much exclaiming. The Pezz claimed to have known it all along and had assumed the Earthers knew what they were doing.

"Perhaps we should go back down and try to remain on the ground," Zickorian said. He was clutching at a limb in the curving, irregular wall of tangled wood grown beside him, justifiably afraid that the floor would give way at any minute.

"Yeah. There's just enough room to turn the oruh around," Angie said. "Let's just—" She clapped a hand over her mouth and stared back down the way they'd come. Zero looked, although he was almost afraid to.

The forest had closed tightly behind them. The only way out was ahead.

Somewhere above them it had rained. They had heard the rumble and the shushing of water, but none of it had reached the expedition directly.

But now it came indirectly. Some of it dripped with sulky reluctance from overhead; more of it came down the floor of the branch tunnel. The curved matting of wood became slippery under their feet so that their knees were soon bruised and bloody. The oruh slipped, too, sometimes, bellowing as they went down. Zero was afraid that a bad fall might send the oruh crashing through. In places he could feel the matting give way under his feet a little. It creaked around them.

But it maintained itself unbroken; stretching ahead into misty brown nullity. The rains steaming everything, making the Earthers slippery with sweat.

Zickorian and Calum climbed with great caution and—it seemed to the Earthers—left most of the work of managing the oruh to the others. The Pezz, with its malleable limbs, had no difficulties. It had volunteered to carry some of the baggage on its back to ease the weight on the oruh. Zero decided he definitely liked the Pezz better than the High Clansmen, despite its being far more physically alien.

"I really have got to get out of this thing," Angie said. "I can't breathe in here, it's so humid, and . . . maybe it's my imagination, but it seems as if this tunnel is one of those Chinese finger traps. Like, the more you go into it, the more it tightens up around you, and—" She shook herself. "God, listen to me."

"I feel the same way," Zero said. "Makes me feel better to hear somebody say it out lou—shit!" He'd slipped, hit his knee on the slippery wooden matting. "I think it's getting steeper. Christ, what's with this animal?"

The oruh had begun straining at its halter, stretching its neck out, snapping at the air.

"Rooooooooh!" it bellowed.

And then it broke free of him and scrabbled frantically up the slippery grade, disappearing into the mist.

Zero cursed and scrambled after it. The other oruh was straining at its halter.

Zero plunged into the mist. Up ahead was a shaft of light, projected from below. *And there was a pit.*

Zero stopped short at the rim of the pit, swaying, losing his balance, flailing for something to hold onto. Going to fall in . . .

He bent his knees, grabbed a ropy piece of the living floor, and leaned back.

He took a deep breath, knelt, and looked over the edge into the shining hole the oruh had fallen into.

Squinting against the light, instinctively holding hs breath, he made out the oruh about thirty feet down, spraddle-legged, head down, ass pointing up at him, looking silly. It was caught in the sticky sides of a funnel of flowers. And these flowers were fleshy pink, striped with blue, shaped like cactus flowers—or suckers. Each was connected to the others by a mesh of dull gray vine, visible only in a few rifts in the floral perspective; each blossom had a glistening dollop of stickiness at its center. Other animals struggled or lay shrunken and inert against the walls of the flower-funnel. Their shapes were blurred by the fringe of petals and the mist. One of those unmoving looked human.

In the distance the funnel narrowed to a diffused green-golden glow, a light from the lower levels of the forest. The oruh moaned and coughed and moved with a vague swimming motion, but it didn't seem to be trying to escape.

Its movements looked drugged. Zero had to take a breath and immediately felt dizzy. He sagged forward, feeling heavy, as if the funnel of flowers were somehow toying with gravity, drawing him in.

He wrenched himself back, and the motion sent him rolling down the slope to Yoshio, who was coming to look for him.

Yoshio helped him up. "What was that line from *King Kong*?" Zero asked. Asked himself, really. "Oh yeah. 'It was Beauty that killed the Beast.' "

There was just enough room to get around the flower funnel. The remaining oruh struggled the whole way, drugged and enticed by the cloying flowers. They only just barely kept it from leaping after its fellow.

It was growing too dark to go on, when the ascending tunnel ended. They emerged, gasping with relief into clearer, cooler air, a place of blurred, emerald-tinged light. The oruh emerged from the tunnel reluctantly, looking over its shoulder with grotesque longing . . .

The level they'd reached was a vast echoing space upheld by the pillars of ancient growths rising, knobbed and veined, through the tiers of interwoven foliage and branches. The matted floor stretched on and on, unbroken except for the gnarled boles and the abstracts. The abstracts—that's how Zero thought of them—were the iceberg-tips of growths starting on the forest floor many levels below; they were made of irregular segments of blue and silvery white and green. The segments were unified into shapes that might have been solidified ideas, twisting and veering experiments in organism but right-angled from the style of the organic to penetrate—just enough to be haunting—the realm of artificial design.

"Who created those things?" Yoshio asked breathlessly, staring up at them. They were enormous, with the presence of the great rocks studding the coast at Big Sur. "I mean, they look grown, but they look *made*, too."

"Maybe we did," Zero said, remembering the plant sculptures at the last camp.

"No," Yoshio said, gazing breathlessly at the abstracts. "They are very old. Very, very old."

"Those forms are not artificial," the Pezz said. "They are organism. It is something I can sense. But they are not without intelligence and have rearranged themselves in accordance with something like what you call vanity, or 'self-expression.' "

They were on—Zero supposed—the fifth or sixth canopy of the many-leveled forest. The matting rustled with life and steamed with evaporating rain. Tenuous clouds were stretched like spun glass between the boles, just under the ceiling of the next canopy.

They made camp on a relatively flat place, not far from the tunnel.

Building a fire on the matting was unthinkable. There was no telling how it might react. So it was a chilly, clammy, uncomfortable night. A night of rumbling bellies; half their provisions had gone into the hungry flower-funnel with the oruh. The mating was painfully irregular under their bedrolls.

In the morning the other oruh was gone. So was the Pezz.

But minutes after they discovered these absences, the Pezz came trotting back from the mouth of the tunnel. "I awoke from dormancy with a sense that something was missing. The animal's [approximate translation:] territorial expression had been removed. It was gone. I ran after it, but I must apologize and [untranslatable]. I should have aroused you to help me. I was not strong enough to restrain it. It has gone into the throat of flowers."

"Shit!" Zero said.

"Bacterially infested excretions!" the Pezz agreed politely.

"Well, at least we won't have to figure out how to get the damned animal down from up here," Cisco said. "Maybe it's, like, an act of providence. Like, it's our karma straightening itself out with—"

"Shut up, Cisco," Angie growled.

They'd removed the rest of their provisions from the oruh the night before, so they carried these on their backs. Zero and Angie had to insist that the Clansmen carry their share.

"It it not a work of our rank," Zickorian said.

"Our rank doesn't do that kind of work," Calum chimed in.

But they sensed Angie's seething irritation with them and remembered the solecism of the mistaken mating ritual. So they accepted equal loads and trudged across the matting after the Pezz and the Earthers to the north.

The Pezz seemed to know, through some vibration-sensitive organ in its legs, just how thick the mat was at any given place. It led them safely through the forest-walled gallery and into a zone of broken rainbow light. The sheets of polychromatic light were refracted through broad, crystalline leaves on great, man-thick vines that spiraled up around them and over them, stretching through the canopy.

"Here is the source of our light," the Pezz said. "There are lens-leaves on the roof of the forest. They magnify light, focus it, send it to lens-leaves at sublevels, which send it to others, which refract it to us."

The members of the expedition changed colors as they passed through the splinters of the prismed light; they were bathed green, scarlet, blue, and gold, by turns. They traveled between screens of growth abstracts, thin-walled corridors of the stuff arranged in wave patterns and zig-zags. like loopy room dividers. Close up, the wall's dense growth made Zero think of a brick of marijuana. But in other places the growths perspired big drops of ginger-fragrant pitch which hung like pendant jewels; and inside the pitch-jewels the living gallery's prismed shine was restored to a glow of pristine white. Zero found that if he stared at the drops of pitch they began to tremble and then slide into rows, the leaves between them patterning like the frowzy conceits of a Victorian facade.

The High Clansmen seemed to tighten into themselves, shivering, turning their enigmatic bands of gold to the right and left. "The animus thickens," Zickorian muttered. "This place is speaking to us in a language I don't understand. It is crowded with spirits like a gathering of tribes."

Hearing that, Cisco looked around at the living emptiness nervously, licking his lips.

The animals began to come.

They came with the sensation in the air; the feel of something unseeable lowering itself about them. All fatigue passed out of the expedition; the ache of carrying their supplies became a distant, benevolent glow in the limbs.

And the animals began to trot and slither and flap up to them. Small furry things; bulky things with wet palps for eyes, and bouncing things with lizard hides; trap-monkeys and flying lampreys; panthers made of sticky oyster-stuff; a small armored whatsit that rolled itself up, unrolled to look at them with a tongue that also saw, then rolled itself a little closer; petite creatures like Dali-designed jewelry with legs, emerald broaches that scampered, tie-clasps of diamond and blue topaz that scuttled near, trading colors with one another in the promiscuous light.

The animals approached silently, coming in a crowd, oblivious of their normal rivalries and instinctive fears, and the expedition froze with uncertainty. Should they run? But the animals were coming from both sides. From above and below.

The spontaneous menagerie came within ten meters of the expedition—and stopped. The animals seemed to be waiting for something. Zero looked at Zickorian. "What you think we ought to do?"

"Go on as if we are unafraid," Zickorian said. "Move with authority."

He and Calum began walking to the North, Zero and the Pezz following, Yoshio and Cisco and Angie coming close behind them. The animals began to move—parallel with them. As if escorting them. Their silence was terrifying.

"Maybe," Angie whispered, "they think we're Noah."

"They're going to be pissed when they find out we haven't got the boat," Cisco muttered.

A cloud of the small valving jellyfish of the air approached with a sort of purposeful Brownian Motion, and Zero worried that the expedition was about to be swarmed over, and drained. But the flying cusps stopped over the parade of animals, and began to parallel the expedition too. Looking at the cloud of cusps, Zero tried to see some pattern in their motion. Was that a whirlpool pattern? Yes, they were moving distinctly in a . . .

They were moving that way *now*. He frowned, and visualized a roughly oval pattern, like race cars chasing one another around a track. The flying cusps moved into that shape. He visualized a diamond shape. The cloud became diamond shaped.

Dizzy, Zero looked away, feeling a return of the horror of disorientation he'd felt his first day on Fool's Hope. Maybe this was all hallucination. Things were arranging themselves according to his imagining. Like when you took psychedelic mushrooms and looked at a blank wall, you saw patterns there that shifted according to your thinking.

What was his inside, here, and what was his outside? What if he lost touch with his borders and melted into things . . . Maybe the Pezz was right, maybe territory was important, especially in this forest.

The Pezz. Talk to it. It might help you orient yourself. (But don't look at it.)

"Pezz . . . uh . . . I'm beginning to feel like I did that night when we ate the fruit . . . "

"I, too," The Pezz said. "It is the IAMtons. They explain the animals' attentions, and the geometrical formations of the flying things."

"You saw that too? Good . . . You mentioned IAMtons before . . . "

Yoshio and Angie trooped up close to listen. Cisco came too, because he was scared to hang back alone.

Near the forest (the Pezz told them) is what appears to be a great wasteland. It resembles a salt desert, a place of crust-edged craters and crystal-formed pinnacles that rise and reform with the fluctuation of some fickle subatomic mood. These are the IAMton wastes, great deposits of a certain chemical impregnated with the subatomic particle, *the IAMton*. The IAMton is most commonly found in the organs of perception and cognition of any sentient organism. IAMtons are the essence of awareness.

The characteristic electromagnetic field generated by the cognitive organ of any sentient organism acts as a kind of net to trap and store some of these IAMtons. The more developed the brain, the stronger the field and the more IAMtons are caught. The particles work in collaboration with the inherent electrochemical actions of the brain to produce a psychically holographic entity, the 'Self.' Real awareness is impossible without IAMtons. They are the sentient beings' link to the universe's reservoir of collective awareness.

"The forest itself is impregnated with them—some places more than others—" the Pezz said. "—but not so much as the IAMton wastes. The electromagnetic churn in the wastes is so pronounced that nothing is stable long enough to grow there . . . We theorize—my people have made a study of IAMtons for many generations—that in sufficient concentrations external IAMtons interpret the electromagnetic noise of our brains telekinetically. Whatever is impregnated with IAMtons —the forest, the animals here—is psychoreactive . . . "

"You sure the animals won't attack us?" Cisco asked, looking at the polymorphous procession accompanying them. Muttering to himself: "If they *are* animals."

"No, I am not certain," the Pezz said. "But I think it unlikely. They are responding to the complexity of our fields . . . It seem to put them in some sort of trance of mindless attraction."

"Moths to lightbulbs," Angie said. "Hope they don't start bouncing off us."

"What's all that stuff?" Cisco wondered aloud, pointing ahead of them. The fence growths curved back for a wide-open area where the matting was thickly covered with curvaceous tendrils of pale blue-green. The tendrils swayed and rippled as if in a dozen conflicting breezes. Symmetrical patterns asserted themselves in the arrangement of plants and then broke up into other patterns.

One of the patterns in the field of plants asserted itself repeatedly. It was a mandala parity of lines, right down the middle of the field, like shimmer-vibrations spreading out on a struck cymbal. *Down the middle* of these lines rode Jack the Baptist, coming toward them with majestic ease, waving cheerfully at them, smiling as the tendrils stretched out past their normal length to affectionately clean away the grime from his face, to groom his hair and clean his teeth. He rode the wave up to them, carried on nothing but the tendrils themselves; they passed him one to the next like a man handed over the tops of spectators at a rock concert. The field passed him to the expedition. He alighted in the open ground as if he were stepping off an escalator. "How *is* everyone?" he asked, smiling beatifically. "Got anything to eat?"

Father's devotees were waiting for him when he returned to the Earther settlement. As arranged, his followers gathered outside the main gate with fronds from feather trees in their arms, waiting to greet him as he rode up on the oruh. He was dressed in white robes that seemed to share the glow of the dawn.

The crowd laid the fronds down before him as he rode slowly up to the gate, his face a study in wise humility.

Doggo and Sanchez and Jamie stood on the walkway atop the wall, looking down at Father as he rode into the courtyard. His head wagged slightly from the motion of an overburdened oruh as it clopped up to the wooden stage remaining from the Interspecies Festival.

Jamie and friends watched Father; someone else watched them all from the roof of the dorm building, crouched in the shadow of a half-fallen wooden shack that the Earthers had erected as a Meta Observatory— long abandoned for lack of observations. Swanee crouched there with his wings folded He focused his hearing on the Earthers standing on the wall, and extended his senses to overhear them.

"Look at them," Jamie muttered. "Like a lot of children waiting in line to see a department-store Santa."

"I don't hear the noise from his bug," Sanchez commented. "But maybe I can feel it, just a little."

"He killed someone," Doggo said softly, aside to Jamie. "There were witnesses. He's big, but if I call up the rest of the constabulary, we could take him."

"That crowd is with him," Jamie said. "Fiskle's scumbags are with him, too, outside somewhere. Not too far away."

Sanchez nodded. "Taking him could provoke more killings. But in the long run it might be smarter."

"Wait and see," Jamie said.

She leaned against Doggo and watched as Father climbed off the beast and went to stand on the stage. Someone led the beast away for him. Everything had been rehearsed. Father looked out at them. How many? Fifty? He sat down on the edge of the stage with one leg drawn up, his arm on the knee of his cocked leg, smiling faintly but radiantly.

"Sermon on the Mount," Sanchez muttered bitterly. His eyes were hooded, and he touched the wooden cross on its oruh-leather thong at his throat. Almost inaudibly he added, "Lower than blasphemy."

Swanee didn't need to focus his hearing for Father. Father's mutated voice carried up there.

"We call it a spaceship," Father's voice boomed out, forceful but measured. "Ezekiel called it a wheel of fire. The Emperor Harmony, whose servant I am, calls it . . . a miracle."

("Holy shit," Doggo muttered.)

("Exactly," Jamie said.)

"How can you simply accept what has happened to you?" Father asked. "How can you take the attitude that it was just a sort of interplanetary accident, a kidnapping by aliens? Faster-than-light drives are *just not possible*. Einsteinian physics makes it impossible. So how did we get here? We came here on the wings of grace, brought by a power that transcends the laws of physics —the only power that transcends those laws."

"Bullshit!" Doggo roared, unable to contain himself.

A few people glanced up at him. Loftily, Father ignored him.

"The only explanation is the intervention of God!" Father declared, managing to sound both humble and inspired at once. "God Himself has brought us here. And whatever happens here is ordained by God. I recall to you Job 38:4, 'Where wast thou when I laid the foundations of the earth? . . . Who hath laid the measures thereof, if thou knowest? or who hath stretched the line upon us? Whereupon are the foundations thereof fastened? or who laid the cornerstone thereof, when the morning stars sang together, and all the sons of God shouted for joy?' "

"God forgive him," Sanchez hissed between clenched teeth.

"You and I cannot pretend to know why God brought us here!" Father declaimed. "Or why He subjects us to our ordeal here. What is our ordeal to Job's? But there is one who hears God and speaks for Him. The one you call Fiskle, whom we call the Emperor Harmony."

"Now Fiskle speaks for God?" Jamie murmured. "When God hears this shit, *She's* going to be pissed off."

Swanee saw the one called Bowler, then, emerging from the crowd, pushing to the front.

"Did you say something before about the 'Emperor' Harmony?" Bowler asked loud enough for everyone to hear.

"He is a spiritual Emperor," Father replied evenly, "sent to guide us—"

"Spiritual Emperor?" Bowler interrupted. "You mean like Caligula?" There was murmuring in the crowd, some supportive of Bowler, much of it hostile to him.

"Cagligula was human," Father said, unruffled. "The Emperor Harmony is superhuman. He has undergone the Ascent, the spiritual growing that you call Twist, and has come out of it a higher being."

"How about that thing on your chest?" Bowler demanded. "Is that a higher—"

Bowler was shouted down by Father's supporters. Father sat up straight, crossed his legs yogilike, and spread his hands in benediction. He radiated paternal tolerance. "I have come here to ask one thing of you:

trust. A single morning's trust, and no more. Come with me to meet the Emperor."

"He'll put you in the Current!" Doggo bellowed. "He's got some kind of control over it"

"Then why doesn't he just direct it here?" Sanchez wondered aloud.

"The Current has never come into the settlements," Doggo said, aside to Sanchez and Jamie. "But Fiskle seems to be able to conjure it up, from what I've been able to find out, in certain spots."

"It is no accident that God brought us to a world where we are in conflict with aliens!" Father boomed out suddenly, standing. "The Emperor has spoken with the angels we call the Meta. They have informed him of what should have been obvious: God has brought us here to hone us, to improve us in combat with all that is diabolical! Do you really believe that the aliens are 'beings from other planets'?" He chuckled at their naïveté. "Truly I say unto you: They are beings from our own world—that part of our world we call Hell; *They are demons!*"

Thrum. Thrum. Thrum. Thrum thrum. Thrum thrum . . .

"Then let's kill the bastards!" someone shouted, and a roar went up from the crowd.

"That's all!" Doggo shouted, coming down the stairs, signaling for the pikemen. "He's using his Twist —that thing on his chest! Can't you idiots hear it?" He reached the courtyard, and two burly, tanned guards with pikes ran up to accompany him to the stage.

Thrum thrum thrum thrum.

Swanee saw the faces of the crowd open up. Secret doors in them were unlocked by Father's thrum and by their own need for release: release of pent-up fear, the restlessly corralled terror of life on an alien world. Father was offering them escape from that fear; Doggo was threatening that escape. It was as if he were slashing their rubber life rafts in the middle of the North Sea. The crowd roared and surged toward him.

Boom. Smoke and hellfire, as a blunderbuss roared from the stairs just above them. Sanchez had fired it in the air; he dropped it and unslung a second from his back. "Keep back from him! He's our law here!"

The crowd hesitated. There was a momentary stand-off. Doggo glared at a ring of hostile faces held in check by fear of the blunderbuss and the pikemen. Father pointed at Doggo and said, "There are aliens among us!" Thrum thrum thrum thrum. "There are demons among us!"

Doggo turned, snatched a pike from one of his men, and all in one smooth motion cocked his arm and flung the spear straight, with every iota of his strength behind the cast. Swanee braced himself as the pike sank deeply into Father's chest and jutted from his back, darkening his robe with his inky blood, piercing the thing that lived there.

Father fell back, writhing. Swanee, linked to Father as all Earther Twists were linked, bent double with empathic pain.

The crowd watched, stunned, as Doggo stepped close to Father and, with both hands, ripped the robe away from the shivering metal shaft. He exposed the insect thing, transfixed by the spear, its mandibles foaming, its eyes whirling with hatred.

Father threw back his head and gave out a shriek that came not from the human part of him but from the hideous chitinous thing on his chest. His eyes glazed. The dying thing at his middle spat venom at the crowd, black stuff that sizzled where it fell on exposed flesh, raising screams from the Earthers. Then the light went out of its eyes.

The thrum was gone. Swanee looked at the crowd, expecting them to turn on Doggo, to declare Father a martyr. But all eyes were fixed on the diseased thing that had lived in Father's chest.

Moving away to another roof edge where he would not be seen, Swanee took to the air. Shameful though it was, he was relieved that Father was dead. But he knew what it meant. Harmony was frustrated. Which meant that he would be profoundly angry. Was angry already. Swanee could feel Harmony's anger in the air itself, even from far away, could feel it like a sudden radical change in barometric pressure.

Now the killing would begin in earnest.

NINE

When Jack the Baptist led them onto the roof of the forest, Zero thought for a moment that he had brought them to paradise.

They emerged from another long, stifling tunnel through steamy twilight into sunny, clean, wide-open spaces. The feathery blossoms and wind-shivered tops of the taller trees, emerging here and there from the otherwise-flat canopy, only embroidered the soaring vista and seemed caught up in a subtle genuflection to the blue-green sky.

Yoshio breathed, "It's like a roof garden. The Hanging Gardens of Babylon."

The roof itself was made up of treetops, and leafy vines. The tufted branches and coiled around broad sections of transparent fronds like crooked skylights—the lenses that sent sunlight down to the lower levels. There were a few animals here. They'd left their escorting menagerie of wildlife behind on a lower level, when Jack had led them into the up-slanting tunnel to the roof. Jack had spoken a few gentle words to the animals and dispersed them. But here, at intervals that seemed almost garden-planned, little translucent creatures flew and fluttered around outcroppings of topaz blossoms, like spray at a fountain. Yoshio took a step from the tunnel toward the nearest of these.

And fell through the roof. Jack had already started after him; he lunged and caught him just under the armpits. Yoshio had fallen through up to his arms. He clawed for a hand-hold, hissing Japanese. Jack was lying flat, facedown across the roof, stretched out to him from the hardened area around the tunnel mouth.

"Hold still, Yoshio!" Jack said. "I don't want to drop you."

Zero wriggled out to help Jack Cisco and the Pezz held him by the ankles.

In a few minutes they'd pulled Yoshio back up. He was scratched and shaken but unhurt. "How are we going to cross this place?" he asked Jack.

"It must be persuaded to bear our weight," Jack said. He knelt and reached into the roof, his arm vanishing in the foliage. He felt around invisibly below. He frowned. He drew a trap-monkey from under the foliage, pulled his hand from its stomach, and irritably tossed the squawking creature over his shoulder. It scurried off as he wiped his hand and resumed fishing about beneath them.

"Ah," he said at length. He pulled something they couldn't see—and just in front of the tunnel the roof of the forest drew together with an audible creaking and rustling, knitting itself tightly, becoming a hard road of interwoven wood stretching ahead of them to the north.

"You going to explain how you do that?" Zero asked as they set off.

"It's a matter of intuition," Jack said. "You'll find it on your own."

He would say no more of this. He'd been equally close-mouthed about the pyramid he'd followed into the forest. "It was a sort of beacon," was all he'd say. "I went to speak to it, and when I did, I had a long and very strange dream."

The expedition tramped on through the morning and into the afternoon. Although the spontaneous road on the forest roof was solid, it was lumpy and bruised their feet. By late afternoon Jack called a halt.

Zickorian said, "What gives this Earther the authority to tell us when to stop and go?"

Sitting beside Cisco and Yoshio in the shade of a corkscrew-shaped upthrust of tubular plant-stuff, Zero said, "If he hadn't done it, I would have. I've got to take a load off for a while."

"A load of what? Off of what?"

"Never mind. Man, I'm thirsty. It's cooler up here, but that direct sunlight dries me out."

They'd sat across from an enormous purple bloom, nearly two feet across, made of four great rumpled, out-spread petals, fringed with a translucent beard of fine silky strands that sketched the breeze. It was beautiful, so that Yoshio groaned a little when Jack stepped across to it and made it disintegrate.

Jack had pinched a particular section of the stem between his thumb and forefinger and then stroked that section a little—and the plant fell apart, the whole thing, as if Jack had pulled out its molecular underpinnings. It had collapsed into a heap of fragrant, wet ash that quickly melted down to a puddle of perfumed water with a purple slick swirling across it. "You wanted water," Jack said, bending to drink.

Zero crossed to the puddle and knelt—then straightened up. "Smells like perfume. This stuff isn't going to make me hallucinate, it it?"

"Not at all."

"Good." He thrust his face into it and drank, and an alien fragrance suffused his brain with soft, purple refreshment.

"At least, not much," Jack amended.

Angie saw the glow first, just after sunset.

The colors of sunset had washed over them and receded, like the glow of their aching limbs, and evening had come with a long, leisurely twilight. Then they heard the sound; it was foghorn deep, a concord of voices, like an all-baritone choir hitting its lowest note as one. The sound rumbled toward them and faded. And came again, after a while—and faded. Angie said, "It's coming from the north. And there's a light there."

She pointed, and Zero made it out, a white shimmer at the northern horizon. What was it? Some marker set over the Progress Station by the Meta?

It was odd that they had ceased to speculate about the Progress Station, Zero thought, now that they were so close to it. It was as if they'd almost forgotten about the Progress Station itself.

'You're seeing the glow of the IAMton fields," Jack said. "It may seem strange, but when you're on the field itself, there's very little glow. It seems to be something you can only perceive from a distance."

"And that sound?" Cisco asked, shivering, as the baritone choir began again.

"The hills, singing," Jack said. "A related phenomenon. They are discharging their own IAMton excess."

Not only did Zero hear the sound, when the rumble swelled, he seemed to feel it, or something that accompanied it, rippling through him. And with it came the tingling, the electrical enormity he'd experienced the night Fiskle and Kelso had been caught by the Current.

Cisco said it aloud, his voice breaking, "It's the Current, man. I can feel it."

"No," Jack said. "It's something much more diluted. It's not the Current any more than a little St. Elmo's Fire is a whole lightning storm. But it may have some effect."

"I do not wish to be [approximate translation:] a Twist," Zickorian said. "Have you led us into this deliberately?" He was squatting beside Calum opposite the Earthers and the Pezz. If he'd had an Earther face, Zero would have thought he was glowering. His optical strip shone faintly against the dark backdrop of gathering night.

"I have not led you into danger," Jack said, "except what you knew would be here. I have led you into a circus of delights. But you have yourselves knowingly agreed to do without a safety net."

"The translator appears to be confused," Zickorian said.

"You are in no danger of the Current here," Jack said. His face was wrapped in the deepening shadow.

"I'm in danger of falling asleep sitting up," Angie said, looking around. "I just wish this stuff were more comfortable to lie on."

"I'll return momentarily," Jack said. He stood and moved off into the darkness, and somehow the forest knew to hold him up, although he'd strayed off the road. When he returned a few minutes later, he was staggering under an armful of fronds gathered from a droopy stand of treetops they'd seen just before camping. "These will make excellent bedding."

He dumped the thick blue fronds in the midst of the road where the light was strongest and said, "Now, what about some dinner?"

Zero awoke at the apex of the night. He had an uncanny feeling that the stars had nudged him awake. They were crowding the sky; they were all around him, searing and yet pristine.

Feeling noontime-black-coffee awake, he sat up— and found himself staring into Angie's eyes. "Well?" she said. "What did you want?"

"What?"

She made a small noise of impatience. "I'm sleepy." She didn't look at all sleepy. "Don't waste my time with games. You said you needed help or something. So I came over. You called me."

"Not unless I was talking in my sleep. . . . I think you dreamed it."

She stared at him. She opened her mouth to deny it —and then closed it. After a moment she said, "Maybe so. I feel strange."

"Me, too, now that you . . . now that . . . " He couldn't get it out. The sensation that had come over him was occupying his every muscle and cell completely, petrifying him with input. After a moment it ebbed a little, and he was able to move. He exhaled raspily and looked toward the white shimmer at the horizon. It had come from there: the north.

Angie was sitting beside him now, clutching his arm, digging her fingers into it, staring north.

"You felt it, too?" he asked.

She nodded. Her sharp intake of breath was the only sound that escaped either of them when the sensation rolled over them again—a feeling of drowning in warmth and sheer sensation, a feeling of profound inner weight, a resonance.

With Angie. He turned to look at her. "I felt you."

She was shaking. "Help me."

A trembling in the air threatened apocalypse. "I'm scared, too." He slid his arm around her, utterly without volition, carried on the wave that was passing through them again; and like two pieces of soft flotsam on a tide, they were washed together. Something hard in him became soft; something soft on him became rigid. They clawed and kicked their clothes away and stretched out on the bed of fronds and groaned when their skin made contact. Angie sobbed and ground herself against him, so that he felt a wet suction against his shaft, a purely organic imploring.

They meshed, and the circuit was completed. The energy flowed through them, and into the world, and back through them again. Zero knew then—the knowledge flowed through him like an inner river—that the psychoreactive tide of the IAMtons had brought them together. The radio emanation of their sexualities had signaled each to each in sleep, and their inhibitions and mistrusts had been overwhelmed in an arousal that transcended the biological. They danced horizontally to the soundless tune, choreographed by a limitlessly arrogant force that was utterly indifferent to their mawkish little individual preferences.

Zero came. But it didn't have the usual shrinking, depressed aftermath. His orgasm dulled his blade a little but didn't slow his chopping. He dug deeper into the sensation-core of her, and she clamped her legs around the small of his back and urged him on with a seamless flood of whispered obscenities and romantic endearments—*"Fuck me!"* and *"I love you, love me, love me!"* —overlapping and indistinguishable, for many hours. It seemed as if the stars were all around them, and beneath them, too.

The same night, a winged man all of black was poised on the edge of a roof, beside a giggling human skull.

Swanee perched just on the edge of the Pioneers' dorm building, steadying himself with his hands between his taloned feet, his wings folded back so as not to catch the breeze. He extended his senses and listened.

He could hear the man inside the room below him breathing in sleep.

"Yes," Swanee whispered. "Now."

Kelso, who was crouched beside Swanee, said "Goo-ooo-oood. I told the Phylum Twos." Kelso's telepathic rapport with the brutes was sharper than Swanee's.

"Best keep your voice down."

"Don't tell me what to do, sky-slitherer. I am the Emperor's favorite."

Swanee shrugged and watched the wall across the narrow way from them. He heard an Earther guard on the front wall; for the moment this building, near the back wall, was unguarded.

But the back wall was not unoccupied. A hulking silhouette heaved itself up over the wall from the other side. The enormous Twist found his footing on the wall, then turned to help a second over. Swanee was a little disappointed. He'd been hoping the rickety ladder would break under the weight of the Phylum Twos. But the Twos made it over the wall and onto the roof adjacent to it. They crossed the roof to the next building, the dorm, and came to hunker down, stinking, beside Swanee. One of them uncoiled a rope from his waist and lowered it over the edge. The nearer end was looped around him. He braced himself against the little wall edging the roof leaning back, holding the rope as the other descended it.

In a moment there was the sound of rending wood as the climber tore the shutters from the window and forced his way inside. There was a muffled cry of outrage from within.

Swanee saw a shape moving against the stars at the front wall: the guard, coming back their way. Maybe he'd heard the noise, was coming to investigate.

"I smell rotten, rotten enemy stinks comin'," Kelso said.

"Yes. I will take care of it," Swanee said as he leaped off the rooftop. His wings caught the air, and he tilted, climbed, then dove at the guard. He had a glimpse of a young, very startled face, a blunderbuss angling toward him. He grabbed the weapon; it came away from the surprised guard with hardly a tug of resistance. Swanee flung it over the wall and swung about, flapping at the guard to keep him confused.

The guard saw a man-sized bat-shape against the sky, perhaps glimpsed starlight on talons. As Swanee had hoped, he turned and ran. Swanee was relieved he wouldn't be forced to kill the boy. The guard was shouting, but hoarsely; terror kept the sound small in him.

Swanee turned and flapped back toward the dorm. He saw one of the Phylum Twos help the other up onto the roof; the second, the climber, was carrying a man slumped limp over his shoulder.

In three minutes, just as the other guards were arriving with torches and guns, the Emperor's faithful had carried their charge over the wall and out into the wilderness. And Swanee, with Kelso tucked like a complaining football under his arm, was flying above them toward the distant shine of the IAMton beams glimmering from the holes in the Rug.

Swanee several times had to fight the temptation to drop Kelso from way, way up.

"Yes," Angie was saying, "I think we'd have done it anyway, eventually."

"Then what does it matter?" Zero asked. It felt good to hear her admit it: the inevitability of their coming together. He'd known it already, of course; he'd seen it in the river of knowledge that had flowed between them in the night.

She turned and looked at the spavined dawn. From up here the light was half occluded by the forest's bulk.

"I just—I wanted it to happen because *we* wanted it to. More gradually . . . by degrees."

"Romantically?"

"Go ahead and sneer."

"I'm not sneering. I feel the same way. I'd have liked that. But I *do* feel romantic about you."

"I just feel cheated, that's all. I don't even know how to say what it was I wanted. But I know it was ripped off from me." She shrugged and nestled against him. He put his arm around her.

The others were just beginning to move about the

camp. The Earthers were careful not to look at Zero and Angie. It was respect, and a certain shyness, for their new intimacy.

Except for Jack, who grinned at them embarrassingly.

After a short, almost silent breakfast, the expedition set out. Everyone seemed distracted, brooding. The waves of sensation from the IAMton field had passed with the dawn, but there was a pressure in the air, an oppressiveness compounded of depression and a meteorological pregnancy. Zero and Angie walked side by side, not touching but somehow moving in partnership, Yoshio was just up ahead. Zero said, "Yoshio, did you feel that thing last night? I mean, did anything wake you up? Uh—I don't mean—"

"I know what you mean," Yoshio said, dropping back beside him. "I slept through it, but I felt it. It gave me nightmares, more vivid than I've ever had. I dreamed of the settlement. I saw a man with wings drop a skull on the settlement, and it exploded like a bomb, and then Fiskle came in." He scowled. "I don't think about it. I felt strange all night. Cisco did, too. I did wake up once, actually: The Clansmen were"—he lowered his voice—"terrified. Hiding in their bedrolls. The Pezz got up and ran in circles for a while, then started throwing up pottery."

Angie laughed. "Seriously?"

"Oh, yes. Gorgeous stuff. The Pezz buried it this morning. Don't ask me what that was about."

"What about Jack?"

"I don't know. I didn't see him."

The expedition had been a half-hour on the road when Yoshio pointed at the onrushing clouds. They felt the damp wind skylarking about them, tugging at the fringes of their clothing, whipping their hair.

The Pezz danced about excitedly. "Another living rain! We should take cover; [approximate translation:] Livid phenomena are afoot! And [untranslatable] commingle!"

Zickorian nodded. "It's coming quickly. In minutes."

Everyone looked expectantly at Jack. "Oh, very well," he said, shrugging. "Though personally I think you should enjoy it."

"I don't enjoy being flattened," Angie said.

Jack stepped off the road, knelt, and reached down to the vines. He pulled two out of the uneven surface and tied them together, then commenced to tug at them, first one way, then another, wtih an air of distraction.

In minutes a sort of igloo of forest life had bulked, rustling, up from the roof, and they'd crawled into its shadowy mouth—Cisco with some reluctance, muttering about being eaten by plant spirits—and huddled together away from the gathering force of the wind. Zero found himself pressed up against the Pezz; its skin felt like balloon plastic and was cool to the touch.

It surprised him by saying, "I forgot to tell you—congratulations on your marriage."

"Oh. Well, it's—" The sudden downpour interrupted him, smacking down on their inadequate roof with a thunderous clap. The igloo shivered and became a little more oblate, but held.

"Did you see him, too?" Angie asked, nudging Zero, shouting over the roar of the amino rain. Its salty smell and glutinous presence had transformed the world; already it was oozing through onto their necks in big sticky drops.

"See who?"

"The golden-eyed thing! That—that marsupial thing we saw in the clearing that day! I saw it just now. Just before the rain! It stuck its head up from below the roof!"

"You mean that thing Jack said was spying on us?"

"I can't hear you! Never mind, the rain's too damned loud, I'm going hoarse!"

Zero nodded and looked out the entrance of their igloo.

Things were happening out there. Towers raised themselves up. Inseminated by the bulky rains, shapes reared and shrugged into intricate convolutions.

When the rain stopped, the world outside was changed, and Jack said, "It would appear that Fiskle has erected an obstacle. And it's one I don't think I can do anything about."

I looked everywhere," Sanchez said, coming into the Council chamber. "He's just not in the settlement. His room is a shambles." He shrugged resignedly. "They got him."

Trish choked off a sob. "I always liked that guy. He was so sweet to me when I first came. He kept everybody off me and—God, he was just like this neighborhood cop where I grew up."

Jamie squeezed her hand and said, "We'll find him."

"You won't have to," Bowler said, appearing at the door. "He's outside."

Bowler led the Council outside to the front gate. They stood in the morning sunshine—it was a beautiful day—and stared at the gate.

Doggo's head, and most of his skin, stripped from his body, was nailed to the front gate. His hide was flayed,

with his intact head still attached. His head drooped
down over the skin, (the inner side of his skin, scraped
clean), which was nailed up like an animal hide in a log
cabin. Or like a parchment containing a papal bull.
Because on the skin, Harmony had written—with the
black poison that dripped from his fingernails—a sort of
declaration of intent, in baroquely calligraphed script:

BE IT KNOWN

IN PARADOX IS DIVINITY. THE PREVAILING ORDER OF
THIS WORLD IS A RULE OF CHAOS: A PARADOX. I,
THE UNDERSIGNED, EMBODY THAT PARADOX, THERE-
FORE AM I DIVINE: THE AVATAR. AND THEREFORE
BY DIVINE RIGHT AM I RULER OF THIS WORLD
WHERE CHAOS IS THE META'S ORDER. IF CHAOS IS
THIS WORLD'S ORDER, THEN THE RULER OF THE
WORLD IS THE EXECUTOR OF CHAOS. THEN CHAOS
IS MY LAW. AND MY LAW IS GOOD, AS ALL THAT
PROCEEDS FROM DIVINITY IS GOOD. AND THE CHAOS
OF THE LAND IS MY RAIMENT. FOR CHAOS SPARKLES,
AND SO CHAOS IS MY GLORY. MY WORLD WILL BE-
COME A SPLENDID CHAOS THAT GLORIFIES MY RULE.
AND BE IT KNOWN

THAT THE LANDS TO THE NORTH AND ALL
TREASURES AND GOODS TO BE FOUND IN THEM ARE
THE PROPERTY OF THE EMPEROR, WHOM CLEARLY
THE META INTENDED AS THEIR SPECIAL ENVOY; BE
IT KNOWN THAT ALL TRESPASSERS IN THE NORTH
WILL BE EXECUTED; THE DESIGNATION TRESPASSER
WILL SIGNIFY ANYONE I HAVE NOT OFFICIALLY
RECOGNIZED AS MY SUBJECT. ALL EXECUTIONS WILL
BE SWIFTLY UNDERTAKEN BUT SLOW TO CONCLUDE.

THUS IS ESTABLISHED THE FIRST LAW OF THE
LAND, BY ORDER OF HIS SUPERHUMAN MAJESTY,
EMPEROR HARMONY, THIS SECOND DAY OF THE
YEAR ONE, ANNO HARMONY.

He is going to come and kill us," someone said.

Jamie turned to a guard. "Take that thing down.
We'll cremate it. We'll hold a service for Doggo."

The guard stared at Doggo's head. One of Doggo's
eyes looked up at the sky; the other looked at the
ground. Worms crawled across the blackened, shriveled
tongue in his open mouth, a mouth rimmed with dried
blood. The hands had been cut away. The guard had to
be asked twice, but at last he raised his pike and began
to pry.

A tired old man named Carmody—he was only fifty
but in the months here had come to look seventy—said,
"They're going to come and kill us unless we surrender.
They can take people anytime they want. They have
magic or something. They can fly. They are too strong."

Jamie turned to the Council. "No," she said. "This
is grandstanding. And lunacy. We outnumber them. We
have the fortress. No."

Sanchez nodded. "Jamie's right. If we give in, he'll
Twist us or kill us. We'd live in a Hieronymus Bosch
place, shoving knives up our asses. No. We have to
fight."

TEN

The rain stopped, and after a while the puddles stopped crawling.

Zero and the others could feel the IAMton charge in the air as they stepped out of the wooden igloo. They could see it—no, they could *almost* see it, when they looked at the odd structures that had sprung up at the behest of the deluge. A sort of iridescent glamour clung to the new growths, a shine that was invisible except when the head was tilted just so and the eyes were squinted. . . .

The growths reminded Zero of the fifteen-foot termite castles he'd seen in documentaries about the tropics, although these were of something like plant matter and were more intricately studded and vented. There were eight of them in a semicircle around the igloo, neatly spaced twenty feet apart.

The great gray clouds were still breaking up overhead, moving with unnatural speed to race away like a panicked herd of elephants. The sunlight struck through in wildly dancing shafts, chased by shadows that crawled frantically over the semicircle of organic monuments and seemed to make them move and shift.

One of them *had* moved. Hadn't it?

Feeling giddy as he inhaled the mists rising in the aftermath of the downpour, Zero looked at Jack the Baptist. He felt a certain warmth as he saw Jack's mood of uncertainty. Jack had supposed these sudden growths in their path to be a sending from Fiskle, but he wasn't sure.

It was good to see him unsure. Easier to think of him as a friend when he was fallible. Zero looked at Jack more closely, trying to perceive him as an individual, as one does with real friends. Trying to see past the assumptions and misguesses, past the veneer others themselves generate defensively, trying to see the real Jack.

He saw that Jack was not there. It was as if, for a moment, he had become invisible, or opaque, or both. He was the silhouette of a man cut into the air, an outline with no interior detail.

Zero blinked and shuddered, and the effect passed. Jack looked normal. A puzzled, filthy, half-mad, long-haired, scruffy hermit, come out of his hermitage for a while like a precocious rat snuffling the daylight.

Jack saw Zero staring at him and smiled faintly. "Let's leave here quickly," he said. "These things are a function of the Overmind in an uncontrolled mode, and I mistrust them."

But Cisco was standing at the base of the nearest growth, staring at something emerging from its grainy, dirty-blue surface. "Look at this!" he shouted.

"Best that you not," Jack said.

But Zero and Angie had already gone to watch the thing bulging from the growth. It was an enormous gem.

So they thought at first. A great cats-eye gem, as big as a beachball, emerging like a blister in fast-action, pushing through . . . a blue-green gem, polished but smokily obscure within.

They all felt it. The tug. The overwhelming desire to reach out and touch the thing.

They were dimly aware that the Pezz and the High Clansmen were standing at other growths, looking at similar glassy swellings. And that Jack was speaking stridently against further contact with them.

And then Cisco touched the gem, and it burst. It split open down the middle and oozed out a blue-green gel that, on meeting the air, sizzled and then evaporated. In moments it had steamed away, revealing an object that had been hidden in the smoky interior of the gem-thing.

Something blurry . . . till Cisco touched it, and then it instantly reshaped, became almost recognizable. It was artificial but effortlessly so, as if it had grown itself, using a manufacturer's blueprint for its DNA. It was chrome and oblong, with artfully placed metal about it and glass panes that showed mysterious inner works defying articulation. Cisco caressed it and sucked in his breath appreciatively. He drew it out and cradled it and hefted it and felt it murmur against him.

"It's a—a . . . it's a—" he muttered.

Zero and Angie looked at him enviously. But they knew it was *his*.

As if in response to their inchoate yearning, another great gem blistered from the grainy blue stuff, and then another. Zero and Angie each chose one and touched it. Zero's burst and revealed a sort of camshaft-shape that played the tunes that drifted through the back of his mind all day. He could hear the songs whisper softly from between the interlocking, turning parts of the thing, as if it were cranking them out, an alien organ grinder playing bits and pieces of old songs and jingles that haunted every Earther brain, harmonizing all of them together with a marvelous connective drone. When he held the torquing white metal thing against him, its touch produced a quasi-sexual stimulation, a delicious electric shock, its movements triggering responses in the secret chambers of his epidermis.

He saw that another of the growths was hollowing itself out invitingly, and there was niche where the squirming camshaft songmaker would fit. He was quite unable to keep himself from carrying it to the niche and installing it. He returned to the first structure and found another gem blistering, swelling out, a precious bubo that split at his touch and produced something that shifted, under his attention, to become sharp-edged, compressed to glossiness in some places, fluffed to furriness in others, the essence of Tantalus in a material thing. It was a designer compact disc player; no, it was a gorgeous Mardi Gras headdress; no, it was a device with which, surely, they could communicate with Earth; no, it was a weapon, if worn just so on the arm, the essence of martial confidence and macho chic; no, it was a marital aid, an aphrodisiac if you merely gazed at it; no, it was . . .

Each object was heart-rendingly beautiful. *Don't take your eyes off it—it might vanish.*

The objects (some part of Zero's mind noted, behind the feverish wanting that occupied most of his consciousness then) were reminiscent of enticements seen in glass cases and expensive, artfully arranged window displays on Earth—but they weren't those objects. They were abstractions of the glamour of those objects, extracted from the unconscious. They were the secret paradigms of material perfection, clockworked into the engine of desire itself. Zero knew this; the knowledge like a draught from the inner river that flowed through him from the IAMton ambience. He knew this in the objective filmmaker part of him. But it did him no good to know. He was as feverish as an amateur Vegas gambler on a winning streak, scooping up his shiny loot—object after object, another and another, till he was breathless from exertion (more and *more!*), each radically different from the last but of the same continuity—and carrying it to the niches in the growths to one side.

Till he had a wall of them, whirring, cranking, humming, glowing, singing things, interlinked into a gestalt of sheer but unidentified appeal that made him buzz with possessive delight.

He was distantly aware that Angie was doing more or the same thing, at another of the growths; that Zickorian and Calum were taking tribal fetishes of some sort from their own gem-eggs, were twining them on themselves and hearing them sing out the cries of beasts from their home world, messages from the plane of animistic spiritism.

And Yoshio was at work on objects that seemed melded together of various cybernetic modalities, objects that were programmable, responsive, material things that spoke to you with digested concepts the way a guitar responds with attuned sounds. Yoshio chattered to himself in exhilaration. He, too, was caught.

It was as if they each had a hollow place inside, and now, holding the object, they felt it filling the emptiness, the hollow-place, snugly and exactly.

Jack stood back, saying something that wasn't quite

intelligible; the Pezz danced a warning and uttered cryptic squeaks that confounded the translator.

Zero was aware of all this through a sort of IAMton-fed psychic peripheral vision, but he was mostly indifferent to it. The thing he had been constructing in his niche came together as he'd known it would, forming a cinematic continuity, so that images flashed in membranes that stretched like soap bubbles between the exquisite materializations. He saw the movie from its beginning: his arrival on Fool's Hope; his struggle to accept his lot; the confrontation with the alien at the Neutral; his vision of an exile to drudgery in the settlement; his decision to seek the technological Ark of the Covenant, the Progress Station; his journey through sweet dreams and nightmares; Dennis's death and the teeming foreignness of the plains and forest; his sense of being both the manipulated and the manipulator; and their arrival here. All were neatly edited into a seamless cinematic flow, a thing with Kubrick's lucidity and scope, Roeg's luscious intricacy, Zefferelli's lyrical faith, and Wertmuller's moral force but this was *Zero's* film! His own! His own creation; His *raison d'être*, completed, here and now; The consummation of his life; The bits and pieces he'd taken from the gems were like jigsaw-puzzle parts connected into this perfect cinematic composition, so that he was sure that he had come here, to this world, for this moment, and—

"It's false," Jack said, gripping his shoulder so it hurt him. "It's a fake movie. It's not something you created. "It's an idealized hallucination."

Irritably, Zero shook himself free. "You're disturbing the images."

"If you let this thing capture you, it won't let you go."

"Why shouldn't it capture me? I filmed it, I created it to hold me."

"No, listen to me. You didn't do this. It wants you to believe that you did so you'll fall into it."

Zero snorted. Jack was raining on his parade; he was an obstruction to ecstasy. Zero turned his back to him and went back to his rapt, masturbatory self-congratulation.

He was distantly aware—and irritated by the knowledge now—that Jack was talking to Angie. "Angie, listen to me—*listen!* You're seeing objects that seem to embody your desire for a home and your ambition for a sort of matriarchal influence on your community. You want to be a woman with a family and a leadership role, too. So the objects seem to embody that. When people buy things on Earth, they're buying psyche-symbols framed to represent reassurance and resolution of uncertainties. The Overmind—at Fiskle's prompting—is doing the same thing to you now. You are being manipulated. Don't you resent it?"

Why doesn't he leave her alone? Zero thought. *Why doesn't he—*

"Zero?" It was Angie at his side now, tears streaking her face. He had never before noticed that her face was grimy, that her eyes were kind of funny-looking, that one of her front teeth was inexplicably more yellow than the other. Her breath was not as fresh as it might have been. Why didn't she go away?

She stepped between him and the construct, the perfect film. He raised his hand to strike her. She reached out and touched his lips with the tips of her fingers, sending something into him there, a pulse of knowledge she'd stored up from the night before.

Zero hesitated.

"Zero," she said, "he's right. We're being pushed around."

Yoshio was there, too. "She is right. When I heard her say it, I knew."

Zero shivered and felt dizzy, as if he'd awakened standing on the edge of a precipice. He stepped back and made himself look away from the growths. Sirens called to him from the far side of mythology. But Angie had tied him to the mast now, and he sailed past them.

"Come on," he said hoarsely, turning toward the High Clansmen, moving slowly, slowly, feeling he was moving through syrup. "Let's get Zickorian and Calum. We're going to have to take them by force. And then let's get out of here."

"We have asked too much. We have taken a great deal from the spirits," Zickorian said, "but we have given back nothing. They came to ask us a price, and you defied them. You carried me by force away from them. Now they will punish us. There is a beast we call [uncertain translation] the Unmasculator, who has a serrated mouth where his face should be; his teeth are his eyes; his teeth are his nose, too; his tongue is his heart; and his heart wishes to take your reproductive facility and grind it into paste, which he will spread on his Nightmare Eggs. This Unmasculator is the one who will come to punish us, Zero. Or his [uncertain translation] incarnation on this world.

"We have the tale of Erythmanna, who desired the soft pelts of the infant cave-diggers, the [untranslatable] lambs, and who roamed the countryside stealing the lambs from their cave-digger mothers and murdering them for their soft flesh and pelts. He could not pay his great debt to the growing places, and they sent, first, a warning, in the person of [untranslatable] feathers, which grew about his loins; and this feathered beast had no male sex about it. And when he did not heed this warning, and refused to make the Seventeen Submissions, and did not cease his lamb raiding, his four children were turned into belly-slugs with the heads of children, and they crawled into holes and cried out to him from within the dirt-places in horror; but still he did nothing. And a cloud came from the sky onto his wife and wrinkled her into a dried (untranslatable), taking her juices with it so that it was a great red cloud when it floated away, and all the female juices were gone from her; and still he did not see. And then the (untranslatable) beast itself came, and took his sex in its jaws, and chewed it slowly, carrying him about with it, so that he lived with his crotch in its wet jaws for one hundred fifty years precisely, whereupon—"

"That's quite enough, Zickorian," Angie said.

Calum reproached her. "But he has attempted to tell you the classic story of Erythmanna, who stole the (untranlatable) lambs and was visited with—"

"You too, Calum, or I'm going to start with Snow White and the Seven Dwarfs and go right through the story of Rudolf the Red-Nosed Reindeer and the Grinch who Stole Christmas," Angie snapped. "And when I get to the autobiography of Shirley MacLaine, you're going to be *really* sorry."

"Besides, Zickorian," Jack said, "all this prophecy is false prophecy."

"What if it's not?" Cisco said. "What if he knows the damned spirits better than we do? I mean—" He broke off, his lips trembling, his face pinched with fear he couldn't articulate. Zero watched him, wondering how much longer he'd last.

The High Clansmen fell silent and went on trudging. They were near the edge of the forest, Zero reckoned. He kept himself busy looking around at the details of things to distract himself from the sense of loss he felt at having left . . . the objects.

They were all depressed, their movements sodden. They were hungry, and irritable from being hungry. Their packs seemed nothing but irksome crosses to bear, and the pikes were painful weights in their hands. They had seen too much.

So they were relieved to be shed of this paradise when they reached the chute at the end of the forest, where Jack said, "Escalator to the first floor, ladies' shoes and imported cosmetics, no wheelchairs or baby strollers." And they descended the chute, left the forest behind, and stepped into the uncertainty of the Hillserlive Hills.

Swanee tasted pity in his mouth like bile as he watched the Groyn child playing by the creek-worm.

The Groyn kidling looked rather like a teddy bear. It was three feet tall and plump and brown and pleasantly furry and mild-muzzled. Almost disgustingly adorable. Nearby, at the far edge of the clearing from the kidling, was its shaggy brown mother, using a crude iron tool to root through the soil for the bulbous hibernating things—little round yellow creatures like puffer fish in the dirt—that she stowed in a leather bag slung over her broad back. Mother was less preciously cute: she was big as an Indian elephant. She had no legs, for in the second growth phase Groyn legs fused into a single supportive base that moved on thousands of tough cilia, surprisingly quickly. The adult Groyn, in fact, looked as if it were cut off at the hips. It moved over the ground like a snail, though faster, much faster.

It wouldn't be fast enough, Swanee knew.

It was another perfect day. If not for the burning weight of his duty, Swanee would have enjoyed it. The wind soughing through the coral trees, the cool *sssssssssss* of the creek-worm, the light playing in its dull, quartz-colored depths. Swanee shifted on his perch in the thicket of coral trees at the edge of the clearing; he was not far above the kidling but was out of its line of sight. Swanee looked at the creek-worm with a friendly appreciation, thinking what a benign marvel it was, what a challenge it would be to paint accurately. Unlike the Groyn, it was a native of Fool's Hope, a single being twenty or thirty miles long and five yards across (a little narrower here at this curve, a little wider there at that straightaway), curving through its own trench in the land, a mass of protoplasm that simply dissolved minerals from the dirt and dead proteins from mulch. A gelatinous, transparent thing made of the stuff you found inside earthworms back in Tennessee but without a skin and with no visible spine. (What did it use for nervous tissue or organs? No one knew.) Curving through the land, it looked exactly like a creek from a distance, with ripples on its surface. Only, when you got closer, the ripples were slow-motion wallows and freeze-frame waves, and the thing was moving only as fast as snake on Valium.

The Groyn kidling tottered on the edge of the creek-worm—and fell in, disappeared beneath its surface as if under hungry quicksand. The Groyn mother ran up to the edge, snarfling mightily. And then the surface of the gelatinous river erupted, and the kidling was lifted clear on an arm of protoplasm and set on the banks directly in front of its mother. The kidling was sticky and confused, but unhurt. The Groyn mother snarfed gratefully at the creek-worm in her own language and caressed its slow ripples once with her ropelike upper limbs (the creek-worm shimmied politely in response), and after soothing the child, she turned away, letting the kidling wander once more, knowing it was being baby-sat.

If only it really were safe, Swanee thought.

He looked up and saw the Meta's watching sphere, striped with shadow and sunlight, as it floated between the boughs of coral trees. It stopped over the clearing, fifty feet up, to hover expectantly.

There: an Earther, big and pink and mightily sexed, a Phylum Two, was huffing through the undergrowth. It paused and looked up at Swanee. He shifted on his perch to see the mother Groyn better. Yes, she was far enough away. He turned and, sadly, nodded to the Phylum Two.

The Two sprinted from cover, ran across the little clearing, grabbed the infant, and carried it away, flailing and whimpering, into the woods. Mother gave chase, but the Two ran into a thicket of coral trees that were too close together to allow her entry. She wasted time trying to push the outer fringe of coral trees down—and succeeded after a moment but only encountered more of the same. Realizing her error, she tried to circle 'round the thicket.

Swanee dove from his perch, angled down, and whipped close past the mother's head, shrieking at her. She swiped at him, so that he felt hot wind against his ribs. She pursued him, and he led her away from the thicket.

The kidling was lost.

Swanee eluded the Groyn, after enough time had passed, and returned to the Twist camp in the woods on the far side of the thicket, hoping to see to it that the kidling had a merciful end. But he was too late. His duty was a sulfurous smell high in his nose as he watched what was done.

The Groyn mounted a search party, eight enormous warriors, both male and female, caparisoned in leather harnesses that contained their throwing weapons. They traced the child quickly by smell, but they were far, far too late. They found the remains of the kidling spitted and roasted, its charred carcass already cool.

The Emperor sat back in his throne of flesh, and Swanee squatted before him, head inclined.

"A Groyn war party makes plans to march on the human settlement," Swanee said. "I saw them sketching a map of the settlement in the dirt. Like you figured it, they don't know about human Twists. They saw the Phylum Two and thought: *Earther*."

The Emperor Harmony's posture of easy recline informed everyone there—in lieu of a novel facial expression—that he was pleased. The living cave contracted the folds of its walls just a little to show its empathic pleasure in its master's happiness. Bella smiled and stroked the long penis of a Phylum Two like a spinster stroking a cat. The Two gave out an inarticulate sound of frustration as his erection sprouted. Bella made big eyes at the erection and pretended surprise.

Swanee watched in a torment of jealousy, although he knew she was only taunting the thing.

"Don't tease him, Bella," the Emperor said. "I've

told you before. It makes them bella-cose." Everyone dutifully chuckled at his little joke. He waved peremptorily at her. "Take him outside and make him mount one of his brothers. It's too crowded in here anyway."

"Certainly, my lord," she said. "Come on, Hunky."

Swanee flattened into the too-friendly folds of the living wall as she squeezed past. She smiled mockingly at him.

"Swanee, come here," the Emperor said in honeyed tones. He knelt before the Emperor. "You've done well."

"For once, for once, the sky-slitherer didn't shit it up!" Kelso snickered, scampering up and down the Emperor's leg.

"Really, Kelso, he has almost always done very well for me," the Emperor said. "Now I have something else for you to supervise, Swanee. You have seen, I trust, the pavilion of the Whorebugs in the Neutral. You are to—"

"Uh, begging your pardon, my lord"—Swanee had heard this phrase used in a movie about Elizabethans—"but I would be a bit obvious in the Neutral. Doggo's successor, Sanchez, is in charge there, and he knows about my part in Doggo's kidnap."

A great weight slid off Swanee when the Emperor said, "Hm . . . very well. I'll send Bella to do it. She's a clever thing. It's true: she can be disguised more easily than you. If we do it right, the Whorebugs will ally with the Groyn against the human settlement." He clapped his hands together. "What splendid colors I am bringing to the canvas!"

Jamie and Trish and Sanchez stood together on the settlement's front wall, looking over the small army of Groyn massing in the field outside. "How's the gate going?" Jamie asked Sanchez.

"It's shored up as much as we have time for."

"We wouldn't have any time at all," she mused, "if they hadn't decided to wait for something or other."

"They're aliens," Trish said. "They might have any kind of motive at all. A ritual or some certain time of day they prefer for attacking or . . . anything." She raised a hand to shade her eyes against the sunlight as she looked out over the field. The Groyn milled restlessly about, more like cattle than soldiers. But they were strapped with weapons, and armor of wood and iron. From here, blurred by the low clouds of dust rising about them, they were a little reminiscent of Hannibal's martially decked-out war elephants, sans riders.

"Maybe," said Trish, "we should try another emissary. He might've made a mistake."

Sanchez shook his head. "No. As lawkeeper I have to veto that. He didn't do anything wrong. They're just too pissed off to negotiate. One of their kids roasted alive— can't blame them. Even for that." He gestured vaguely in the direction of the red splash, halfway across the dusty field to the Groyn, that was all that was left of the last emissary. He'd come running back when he'd seen them charge him, and he hadn't run fast enough. "I I don't want to waste anyone else that way."

"We could send another emissary to explain that it wasn't us. A woman this time," Jamie said.

"What?" Sanchez looked at her, startled.

"Their leaders are women. They're matriarchal. Perhaps they'll sense another female, agree to talk to an equal. As opposed to talking to an inferior. Sending a male might have been an insult."

"An equal. I see. Jamie, we can't risk any of our women. We have too few."

Jamie turned on him, nostrils flaring. "You want to protect the female commodity for breeding, is that it?"

"I—frankly, yes. And we can't risk you, you're too valuable a leader."

She shrugged her anger away. This wasn't the time. Then she smirked. "You're discounting me as a breeder? I have news for you. I'm pregnant."

Sanchez's mouth dropped open.

Trish and Jamie laughed. With destruction shuffling restlessly outside the gate, it was sad, bitter laughter.

"Doggo helped us out on that," Trish said. "He was a nice guy about it, too. Very understanding."

Jamie winced. "Do we need to go into all that? It was brutish enough once, without having to relive it. Ugh. But I got pregnant and I always wanted to raise a family. And Trish had a hysterectomy on Earth. But I wish Doggo were alive to see the baby. He could've been godfather or something. And baby-sitter."

"He would've been something more than that to the child," Sanchez said, quietly simmering with disapproval.

Jamie shrugged diplomatically. She glanced back toward the back gate. All this talk was just to cover the anxiety of waiting for their other plan to come to fruition. They'd sent a runner to their allies among the other races, asking for help. If he'd got past the Groyn . . .

"This is all Fiskle, you know," Sanchez said.

Jamie tilted her head to one side and pursed her lips. "Probably."

"Not probably. Definitely. What happened to the Groyn child . . . we shouldn't be just sitting back letting him hammer at us. First he set up Father's little lecture series; then he murdered Doggo. Now this."

"What do you want her to do?" Trish snapped.

"Really," Jamie said, nodding. "I can never find the

bastards. We sent a party to try to arrest those big guys he uses, the ones who carried Doggo off. Took them three days to find one, and when they did, he killed two of our people and their oruh. He broke the oruh's back with his arms. We don't know how many of those things Fiskle has. Anyway, Fiskle has some sort of . . . some telepathic thing. He knows when we're coming. The one we caught was a fluke, and I wish he *hadn't* caught him. So what do you suggest?"

"We'll have to trick the son of a bitch. How, I don't know yet. But . . . Here comes our messenger boy." He'd spotted Warren trotting up the courtyard. The undamaged side of his face, contorted with the pain of exertion, almost matched the other side. He trotted up the steps to the walkway just beneath the defensive wall.

Puffing, he leaned on the wall and said, "Twists . . . broke into the Neutral, killed five Whorebugs, set 'em on fire. . . . The Whorebugs are joining the Groyn. That's what the Groyn are waiting for—the Whorebug war party."

Trish said softly, "It'll be soon. Things must be coming to a head. Look." She pointed upward. The Meta's watching spheres were there, a hundred feet overhead, a cluster of little silver spheres turning this way and that, like a group of toy balloons.

Jamie glared up at them. "Five of them. Plenty of camera angles," she muttered. "Bastards."

Standing on the strip of barren rock between the forest and the Hillserlive Hills, Zero watched the literal rolling of the rolling hills with queasy fascination. A great ripple went through the ground, and then another from the opposite direction; the two nearest hills seemed to roll toward one another. "This, Cisco," Zero said, "is what the word *awesome* really means."

The ground shook; small cracks in the strip of rock widened and extended just enough to be noticeable.

The hills were covered with a flat, dusty-blue growth identical to the Rug near the settlement. Zero looked at it nervously. He moved up close to Jack, who stood beside Cisco and the Pezz, watching the grumbling roll of the hills. "Jack, we going to see wheelers here? Under those hill-things, maybe?"

"No. None. What is under the Rug here are the hills themselves. Living things, relatives of the creek-worm."

The hills moved under the covering like a bull's muscles rolling under its hide. But they were big, so damned big. Zero felt dwarfed and lonely, looking at them. The vastness of them, like the great, storm-driven oceanic swells he'd seen off Oahu, gave him an agoraphobic sense of vulnerability.

As the nearer hills approached one another, dozens of slits opened in them like lipless mouths, giving out the baritone-choir sound that the expedition had heard earlier. The hills seemed about to collide—but instead they ground loudly against one another, as if they were grindstones working away under their Rug-like covering. And from the point of contact, yard-long spines of what appeared to be polished steel emerged, squeezed out as if manufactured by the junctioning of the hills. The hills stopped moving, and the spines toppled and clanged down into an untidy heap, flashing in the sun. The slits on the hills closed; the hills fell silent.

Jack pointed across the Hillserlive region toward the horizon. They could see, beyond a few miles of the hills, a shining band of white. "The IAMton wastes," he said. "We'll have to cross the hills, and then the wastes. Then we reach the Progress Station."

"And if we acquire the goods in the Progress Station," Zickorian said, "a very doubtful proposition—but if we do, we are expected to split their value with you, Jack?"

"He's earned the right to it," Angie said. "He's helped us."

"I agree!" the Pezz chimed in, rearing on his hind legs for emphasis. "I quite agree. He has demonstrated his value!"

"He was not part of the original agreement," Zickorian said. "His motives are suspect."

"I'm here because I'm concerned," Jack said, "because I love intelligent life and don't like to see it wasted. I have no desire for a share. Now, let us go. I am very hungry. There is food to be had at the swamp on the other side of the wastes. Let's hurry to it."

Zero looked at him. "Your style has changed. You talk more rationally, cooler. You were playing some kind of role before, right? How come?"

Jack smiled. "We really don't have time to chat. Are you all willing to make the crossing?" He looked around at them.

"It can't be safe to cross those hills, man," Cisco said, chewing a knuckle. "Maybe Zickorian's right. I mean, *anything* could sprout up out of those humps. Maybe that Unmasculator thing he was talking about. Some kinda spirits of the ground."

"It's perfectly safe, if you don't wake the hills," Jack said casually. He set off across the Rug.

Angie and Zero looked at one another. *If you don't wake the . . . ?* "Looks like we gotta," she said. "That way's north, all right."

"Yes, yes, this is the way, north, north!" the Pezz said excitedly. "The ones who live beneath the ground here—their territorial emanations are turned downward, toward the inner planet. They commune. Their exudations are foreign to me, but I sense deep planetary rapture and (untranslatable). Let us go quickly before their territorial fields are expressed upward!"

"It seems inevitable," Yoshio said resignedly. He hurried after Jack.

"It's all hopeless anyway," Zickorian said. "We die soon, it doesn't matter where."

Calum, crestfallen, muttered, "Die soon. Doesn't matter. And (subarticulate)." They followed Yoshio.

Shouldering their packs and pikes, Zero and Angie and Cisco hurried after the clansmen. Hurrying but treading lightly . . .

They crossed between the two nearest hills, entered a valley between a row of others, feeling the body heat from the great, anonymous humps beneath them. There was no shade out here, and the sun blazed down on them, sapping their strength, making them bow their heads. Jack led them to the middle of the valley and up to the shining heap of spines. They were long, barbed quills, Zero saw. Jack bent and picked one up.

"Uh, maybe we shouldn't disturb them," Zero said. "Maybe the hills wouldn't like it."

"It's quite all right," Jack said. "I advise you to get one each. They'll be useful."

"Just what we need," Cisco grumbled. "More to carry."

"They're very light."

Skeptical of this, Zero bent and picked one up. It was light indeed, like something made out of balsa, and surprisingly cool to the touch, but very hard.

They'd each picked one up when Angie said, "Uh-oh."

She was looking up at two Meta spheres that arrived overhead, forty feet up. Dolefully she said, "Must be we're in for a hassle."

"Very astute," Jack said. "Here it comes." He was watching something approach from the far side of a hill, circling its base to angle sharply toward the expedition.

Zero saw six clusters of internal organs, it looked like, winding through the air toward them. And then Zero saw the rest of the creatures, the transparent plastic bodies the sun had washed out at first, casting rainbows on the ground as they came, skating over the ground as effortlessly as expert skiers down a slope, coming right at them with a terrible, drawn-out squeaking sound that set Zero's teeth on edge.

And now he saw things whirring in their hands, bolas of some kind, spinning so fast they were just a blur unless you watched closely. *Spiked* bolas.

"Start backing up the hill!" Jack shouted. "Get up the slope!"

Backing away, pulling Angie with him, Zero remembered. He'd heard these creatures described. Vinyls, they were called.

"We should surrender to show our good will!" Yoshio said. "Then we can convince them we're not hostile."

"This race cannot be negotiated with once it decides you are the enemy!" the Pezz said, rearing up. "They regard all other creatures as subbeings!"

"They have been set against us by Fiskle!" Jack shouted. "Talk is no use! Climb the hill! Up!"

And then the Vinyls were upon them, streaking around them in a snappy ellipse, roughly human-shaped things, their features just dimples in their transparent heads. One of them zipped in close to Zero and whipped a bola at his face; Zero blocked with his pike and staggered back.

Another was upon him, but Angie was there, her pike braced against the hillside, catching the Vinyl in its gut. It squealed, and a comet of light flashed from its wound to spiral away into the sky. It collapsed, spurting an interior goo that smelled of industrial waste, but as she jerked the pike free of it, another came. Zero jabbed at it, but Angie had hit the first one just right. Zero's jab only just deflected the second Vinyl for a moment. It zipped back around as if on a rail, its frictionless feet never leaving the ground, and came at them again. Yoshio stepped in and karate-kicked it off balance so that it went glimmering down the hill, but the others were closing in, slashing at him with the bolas.

Zero saw Yoshio fall—then he had to swing the pike at another; it ducked and skated around behind him. He caught the edge of a bola on the back of his neck, and fell, tasting the hot iron of terror in his mouth, picturing them closing in on him, their squeaking bodies and horribly faceless faces blockng away the world. "Angie!" he shouted over the furiously squeaking passage of the Vinyls, as he skidded facedown. "Angie, get up the hill with Jack!"

He looked up in time to see the Pezz, with one rubber-band *ssswwwap* of its front legs, hit a Vinyl so hard that it flipped over backward, head over heels, and landed in a tangle of broken plastic and steaming liquid.

The ground was moving beneath him.

He heard Cisco shout, "They're coming awake— the hill spirits are waking up!" Panic pealed in his voice.

And then another Vinyl was looming over Zero, and the bola blurred down at him. Someone—Angie!—was blocking the bola with a pike, deflecting it only partly—

A hot flash of pain in the right side of his head.

It was only a minute later when he came to. Someone was dragging him up the slope by his wrists. Through a haze of pain he saw Cisco running wildly, trying to escape the hill, running down slope, and falling off the edge . . . the edge?

The hill had broken away from the others, was booming to itself in pain as Jack stabbed one of the pikes into it, bleeding pink glue-stuff from the wound as he drove it away from the Vinyls . . . leaving, at its edge, a ten-foot cliff that the Vinyls couldn't climb.

And the hill had torn the Rug, was carrying a piece away with it, away from Cisco and the Vinyls. Cisco looked up, screaming, as they closed around him. Squeaking. *Squeaking.*

Zero closed his eyes.

Zero was lying atop the hill, which was moving away to the north, shoving rudely between its fellows. An earthquake out for a walk.

"The Vinyls tried to control one of the other hills the way I did this one," Jack was telling Yoshio. "It trampled them. It has to be done just so. And I wasn't even sure *I* could do it. It was a great risk. Are you quite all right?"

Yoshio's voice: "Yes. The bleeding has stopped, I think."

Zero sat up and sucked in his breath sharply. Angie, sitting beside him, said, "You better lie down. You might have a concussion."

"It hurts, but I don't think there's any damage."

"Better lie down anyway," Yoshio said.

"Please recline, recline!" the Pezz said.

Zero lay back. He saw Zickorian off to one side with Calum, the two of them muttering out of translation-box range.

He saw the shining wastes to the north growing closer.

He saw the emerald ceiling of the sky losing its polish. Dusk.

He saw Angie smiling down at him, the dust on her face striped with tears. "I knew that guy a long time," Zero said. "Cisco was kind of a jerk, but—"

"I know," she said. "Rest. Just accept whatever happens here. Just accept it. Because otherwise . . . "

"Yeah. Otherwise."

He closed his eyes and let the growing susurration of IAMton energies whisper to him from the north.

ELEVEN

The Groyn only had to charge the gate twice. The second time, it splintered with a despairing groan. The men behind it screamed and were crushed under broken planks as the Groyn plowed through, rearing up on their back sections to slam down on the Earthers caught beneath, jellying them. Meanwhile the Whorebugs climbed the outer walls, scrabbling up them without handholds, ascending furiously on sticky clawpads. Some were struck from the top edge of the wall with pikes and blunderbusses; but others whipped lassos of Whorebug exudation over the battlement and noosed the Earthers and used them to pull themselves up and then finished the choking, clamping them with all their limbs at once in the lethal embrace of a preying insect. Glamorous in the light of sunset, jewelry-perfect and nightmare-disgorged, the Whorebugs showed a strength that seemed impossible for their slender limbs, dismembering their victims with methodical intentness.

The Groyn, though bigger and stronger, crushing men against the walls like ripe fruit, were nevertheless almost Earthly, were like angry, sentient bears or mammoths; they were furious and showed it, as animals from Earth did. But the Whorebugs were monsters of inscrutability, with bodies designed by some speed-freak paranoid; they were expressionless and mechanically efficient in everything, making not a sound as they killed, like bored workers in the slaughterhouse dispatching steer after steer.

Men were later found dangling from the walls, wrapped in the most bright and gorgeous Whorebug silk, intricately patterned and tightly bound, smothered inside it, buried alive in textile excellence. Sarcophagi for the fashion-conscious, Harmony would call them.

Now there was flame, as fallen torches ignited debris, and leviathans came bellowing, looming up in the smoke. Leviathan silhouettes resolved into Groyn flailing with their tentacular limbs to tear heads from shoulders and to smash leg bones into flinders, shrieking to their gods as they were impaled on three pikes at once. A child was glimpsed screaming and clawing the air as she was carried away over a wall by a Whorebug . . . Flame wagging out of windows like an angry neighbor . . . On the ground, red blood puddled with black blood, and both mixed with yellow effluvium.

Overhead, the Meta's watching spheres placidly took everything in.

Jamie and Sanchez and Warren and Trish remained on the wall fighting, shouting encouragement, struggling with panic. They crossed to the roof of the dorms, calling for the other Earthers to fall back.

At last the Earthers retreated to the main dorm, their numbers halved, knowing the barricade at the door of the dorms would not hold for long; choking on the smoke and the taste of impending probability.

That was when the Emperor Harmony made his

entrance: Swanee carried the shape-changer to the roof of the dorm, where Jamie and the Council were arguing about surrender and the consequence of it. And then Swanee was there, lowering the pink bar of flesh that was already writhing into another shape. Harmony's face showed on it, grinning, and then the rest of him slowly filled in.

The pikemen came at Swanee and Harmony—but paused at Jamie's order after Swanee shouted, "This is not the Emperor Harmony, but his representative!"

The "representative," in psychic rapport with the Emperor, took on the Emperor's shape and spoke what the Emperor spoke, safe in a far place. "They are too furious to stop now, even if you do surrender," Harmony said. "We picked them for that quality: that banzai rage against the enemy. But I know something about the Groyn that I can use—together with the strength of my Phylum Two Pragmatics, who wait outside the settlement—to make them give up the fight and accept a truce. If the Groyn back off, the Whorebugs will, too. All I require for this service is your simple loyalty. Your recognition of me as your Emperor.

"At this point I could take the place anyway, of course. But I want the ritual of coronation, I want your cooperation: it will be best in the long run. Choose. Death or a redefinition of honor."

"Fuck off," Jamie said.

"Go to hell," Sanchez said.

But Jamie and Sanchez were almost alone in their defiance.

The others stepped forward and voted to accept the new ruler. It was a matter of survival. Among them was Bowler, who perhaps saw an opportunity for revolution in the installation of a proper dictator.

"Here then, are the first commands of your new

Emperor!" The Shapehanger boomed. "First—you are all to remain here, while my people dispose of the aliens. Once that is done, we will begin reconstruction—"

At the back of the crowd, Jamie squeezed Trish's hand. She looked at Sanchez. He bent near them, whispered, "We have a few minutes . . . " He tilted his head toward the stairway that led onto the roof from the second floor terrace. Jamie nodded. She and Trish followed Sanchez to the stairway and hurried down it, quietly as possible. When they reached the terrace, Sanchez said, "I don't think Harmony knows about the back tunnels under the walls. You were smart to keep that under wraps, Jamie. You and Trish'll hide there, I'll head for the Neutral, try and drum up some alien support—"

"Look, if we run," Trish said, "it'll look like we're his Enemies for sure. He'll hunt us down. Maybe we can play along, then organize an underground . . . "

Jamie shook her head. "We *are* his Enemies, right now, and he knows it—" She broke off, startled by the crunching sound from below. The Groyn were breaking through the barricade. Jamie looked at Trish. "If we stay here, he'll kill us. That's what he's like. He'll weed out anyone he thinks would cause him trouble. We have to hide in the building—when the coast is clear we'll run."

Another crunch from downstairs. And then a scream.

The Pragmatics—Phylum Twos—charged from three directions into the herd of Groyn at the front door of the dorms. Fifteen of them, at Harmony's command, using crude iron axes, leaped astride the Groyn and hacked their tentacles away, sunk pitted iron blades into their broad skulls, axed Whorebugs into twitching segments. The aliens fell back before this onslaught as yet another Twist kited in over the wall: this was Sizzle, a new member of Harmony's troop. His head was human, and his hands and feet, but between them he was a membraneous thing that glided through the air like a flying squirrel. The thin pink-and-blue membranes were stretched between his flattened pitted torso and limbs; his expression was imbecilic. He was shaped, overall, like a slightly concave disk—the convex side upward—and clapped down over his prey from above. Now, protected by the phalanx of Phylum Twos, Sizzle dropped down over a Groyn and enclosed its head and upper parts in his cuplike membrane, closing over them like an octopus over a fish—and exuding powerful acids from his underside. The Groyn shrieked as the acids melted into it, breaking it down into living mush, crumbling bone and melting muscle, pressure-cooking it in seconds so that a bubbling organic soup cooked from the Groyn's flesh bubbled out from around Sizzle's edges and spattered the ground. The Groyn collapsed to a shapeless white lump of anonymous *stuff*. And then Sizzle sprang into the air like a mongoose and came down on two Whorebugs, closed around them, tittering like a lunatic squirrel as they melted beneath him, held helpless by the paralytics in the acids.

Three Phlyum Twos surrounded a great, shaggy female Groyn who'd stayed in the background bellowing commands, who had not entered the settlement till the Earthers retreated to the dorm. The Pragmatics dragged her away from her consorts. On seeing this the other Groyn froze where they were and waited.

Swanee, carrying a translation box, appeared in an upper window and said, "People of the Groyn! We have your Chief Mother, and we advise you to accept a cessation of hostilities. You have many times over avenged the death of one of your own. Let it rest here, and your Chief Mother will go free, unhurt. We require your Soul Boulder agreement on this."

The Groyn gave out a moan of defeat, hearing the invocation of the eternally binding Soul Boulder. But they consented, and the Chief Mother was set free. They filed out of the settlement; the Whorebugs accepted the peace as equably as they had accepted the war.

And the Emperor Harmony arrived and toured the settlement so as to choose a proper site for his throne room.

"We should have gone with Sanchez," Trish said. "There's food at the Neutral."

Jamie sighed. "Yeah. We got 20-20 hindsight. But we can't make it now with Fiskle's guards on the walls, watching everything outside . . . I'll be back in ten minutes." Jamie kissed Trish, deeply and languidly. They hugged, and then Jamie turned and crawled out through the tunnel, into the torchlight.

She had come out near the scum-pod worksheds at the back of the settlement, and there was no one around. She froze, hearing the roar of some great beast of the night, a beast with a hundred throats—No. It was a crowd, chanting something: the "Emperor" was holding a rally; the noise was coming to her from the distance, distorted by the crooked streets. *Or maybe,* she thought as she ran up the road, going for the food stored in her dorm room, *Maybe it wasn't distortion. Maybe it was the truth behind it. The roar of an animal.*

She saw one of the animals, then. She turned the corner and there it was, looming over her, pink and contentedly bestial. It was ten feet away but she could smell it: the rotting essence of male. Its muscles rippled as it moved toward her; its ropy penis stirred.

She tried to circle it, to walk past, hoping the Phylum Two would ignore her. Maybe it didn't know who she was . . .

But it knew. She tried to run when its fingers went around her neck—easily encircling her neck with its one hand—and it jerked her from her feet, snarled at her. It lifted her by the neck so that she hung struggling and kicking over the ground. It carried her like a spitting, ill-tempered cat, almost choking her. Dangling her feet over the ground, it struck off down the street. She was to be a gift, given to the Emperor of all the world.

They stood on the edge of the IAMton wastes, their backs to its teeming expanse of emptiness, and watched the hill roll away like a disenfranchised wave rumbling back to rejoin the sea.

"Now the spirits abandon us," Zickorian said.

"He's leaving because he's fed up with us," Jack replied. "Wouldn't bear us an inch farther. Well." He turned and looked at the IAMton wastes.

Angie said, "Looks like Death Valley. Sort of."

"*Death* Valley would be a misnomer here," Jack said. "Let's camp, so that Yoshio and Zero can rest. They're not badly hurt, but let's not take chances when we haven't got a doctor. And"—he brightened and rubbed his hands together—"I suggest we eat the last of our provisions all up completely, like pigs. There's food a few hours' march from here, across the wastes."

"Look like the salt flats to me," Yoshio said as they laid out their packs. Yoshio grimaced from the pain of his wounds, bandaged in crude-cloth. "Except for those clinker-type things. Those crooked little towers and that violet stuff." He meant the small violet lightnings that crackled intermittently over the ground. Just overgrown sparks. "Will we get a shock from those discharges?"

"No," Jack said, opening the provisions pack and frowning as he inspected the interior. "We'll be appropriately grounded. It's not actually electricity, as you mean it. What have we here? A little dried crustacean left. Some dried fruit of a disappointingly nonhallucinogenic variety."

Zero sat down on his bedroll with a sigh. His own bruises ached, fussed at him when he moved. His ears still rang, and his head throbbed from the blow to his skull.

They ate what remained of their stores ("Nothing matters now," Zickorian said. "Therefore, why not?") and prepared for a night's rest.

Zero expected more of the psychic intrusion from the IAMton field that he'd felt on other nights. "It won't come as powerfully as that here," Jack said. "You are on the edge of the field now. It's like being in the eye of the hurricane. But there may be *some* effects. It knows we're here."

The expedition settled in, and full darkness closed in on them. Its way prepared, the hourglass moon rose in the sky. The violet glow of the IAMton field was faint, ghostly, haunting. The stars crowded around to outshine it, the Frost rose like a white-hot interstellar battle flag, and the expedition, each in his or her own way, retreated from the fearsome surveillance of these energies, from the sense of being spied on by the perpetually burning gods.

Zero and Angie lay on their sides together, fitting like spoons, Zero with his arm around her. But within their own heads they detached from one another for a while and went away into the private places of the mind.

One astronomical pulse away from dawn.

A strange taste in Zero's mouth awoke him. It was a sharp metallic taste. A smell accompanied it, of electrical burning. And a sensation on the skin, as if he had a sunburn under his clothing.

He sat up, looked around, and saw that, restless in sleep, Angie had rolled away from him in the night. She was ten feet away, making abortive inchworm motions in her sleep. He saw another movement from the corner of his eye, turned his head to look—and froze. A chandelier was hanging in midair. No, it was more like a man-of-war jellyfish, as big as a condor, translucent violet and fluorescent, training long, scintillating streamers from its underside. It tinkled softly to itself, chiming like wind chimes as it drifted above the sleeping camp and came to rest over Yoshio. A second one drifted in from the IAMton wastes . . . and Zero saw a third emerging from the violet shimmer of the ground itself, like a bubble appearing on the surface of a pond, growing out of it. The chiming thing—clearly something alive and aware—mounted buoyantly into the sky, where it was almost lost against the stars. But he could make out its outline, smearing the stars with violet; it drifted twenty feet up, coming closer, angling now, floating toward—

"Angie!" But it was too late. The limp violet streamers of the thing had already insinuated around her head, crackling out blue fulminations, and he knew without needing proof that it was changing her. He was up, shouting, waving at the thing, and it backed off.

He turned to Angie and found her sitting up, reaching for the empty provisions sack lying beside her. Hands trembling with urgency, she tore it along a seam and drew it over her head like a hood so it locked her face into shadow.

In the faint light from the eastern horizon he saw Yoshio sit up and look around at the expedition as if he'd awakened to find himself among strangers.

The third jellyfish floated toward Zero. He made a dash at it, throwing one of the light metal spikes produced by the living hills. Halfway to the thing, the metal spike started turning end over end, and fell through it from above—and the diaphonous creature vanished in a fireworks of glitter.

"Don't do that," Jack said, coming up behind him.

"They did something to Angie!" Zero knelt beside her, reached toward her. "Angie . . . hey, you okay?"

She drew back from his hand and spoke in a deadened voice, a monotone: "Don't touch me." And then something more in nonsense syllables.

Zero stared at her in shock.

Jack laid a hand on his shoulder. "Leave her alone for now."

"But she's—shit! What happened? I mean she—"

"Leave her alone. It's what's safest for her, for the moment."

Reluctantly, his mouth dry, Zero stood and took a step back from her, staring. She just sat there, face concealed, hands clasped in her lap, a little hunched over.

Zero heard a clacking sound, looked up, and saw that it was Yoshio piling large flat rocks from the edge of the wastes onto one another. He moved stiffly, but the Vinyls hadn't hurt him badly.

The formation he'd constructed, a low, precarious

wall of rocks, described a crude spiral about eight feet across. Yoshio knelt beside it, laid his hands on it, and said, "I am descending to the Higher; I am de-escalating to the Upper. I am debasing to the Tower. I begin again in each minute that arrives." And then more in Japanese—and in another language Zero had never heard before.

"Oh, dear," Jack said, staring at Yoshio, "I fear he is going to be violent."

The Pezz bounced up to pose springily beside Jack and said, "Yes, completely and with verification: yes. I have heard that chant in translation before, just prior to the skirmishes of [untranslatable term for the speaker's own people] and the Mack Nary."

"I agree, a Mack Nary declaration-of-evil construct. The descending spiral."

Zero turned fiercely toward them. "Are you going to explain, or—?"

"It's not the same thing that has Angie," Jack said. "I believe she's a Solips now. Yoshio, judging from the way he's now rubbing sand in his face and generally debasing himself, is working his way up to a ritualistic Mack Nary killing frenzy. There was a Mack Nary on the planet for a while, a Murderer as Earthers call them. It was killed by the Whorebugs. Its consciousness was, I suppose, drawn into the IAMton fields and now has been transferred into our Yoshio." His voice was distracted. But he went on. "The Mack Nary are the monks of a race of beings who are by nature utterly benevolent, almost unnaturally sweet of disposition. In contrast to most beings, which are instinctively aggressive around competing races. This nearly caused the decimation of their race, and they came to believe it was a serious imbalance in their relationship to the universe. They believe that the great object is to merge with the base clay of the universe, the most primitive forms of life. They believe that these forms are closer to God than the complex organisms because most of the universe is made up of raw material, of primitive stuff. They attempt to redress this imbalance and to achieve oneness with the lower forms by forcing baseness on themselves—especially by doing pointless evil. They overcompensate, you see. They see that the lower animals are predatory and that unevolved races are sadistic and cruel—they aspire toward this, and constantly struggle against their own natural predilection for saintliness."

Zickorian and Calum had joined them. "The spirits have taken two more, I see," Zickorian said.

"Two more are gone, we see!" Calum intoned.

"Shut up," Zero snapped, bending to try to see Angie's face. "She hasn't gone anywhere." He looked up at Jack. "You say she's possessed?"

"In a sense. I suspect her to have become—psychically—an alien we call the Solips. When they're around others, they don hoods and behave with the maximum characterlessness. Try to become ciphers. They are strong individualists and live in fear of being 'eaten' by society, of being pressured into conformity. So they live in solitude, except in childbearing. They simply don't want their personalities subsumed in others, so they communicate in this safe, distancing mode, which refuses all commitment."

"Great. Fine. Now, *how do we get her out of it?*"

"Don't shout, Zero, you'll provoke the Mack—uh-oh."

Suddenly Jack lunged for Zero, tackling him about the middle, knocking him flat. A pike flashed through the air where Zero had stood a moment before. Jack had saved his life.

Zero and Jack were up in time to see Yoshio—with the Mack Nary controlling him—reach for another pike, his face contorted in self-hatred, eyes filling with tears. "I *am* sorry about this," the Mack Nary said. "It is *so* distasteful. But I really must impale the lot of you and let you die slowly on the spear. Twist it in your guts, that sort of thing. I *do* hope you understand." The voice —it was not Yoshio's voice—was unctuous with sincere apology.

The Pezz danced toward Yoshio and danced back, snagging his attention. Yoshio jabbed awkwardly at the Pezz with the spear, missing by a good margin and muttering, "Drat. I feel so odd. Hard to control this body." Something in Japanese, and then the alien language. And then in English, as he made another fruitless stab at the Pezz, "I really wish this wasn't necessary, but I'm sure you understand—must get back to basics, you know."

Jack stepped into the wastes and circled stealthily around behind Yoshio.

Zero couldn't hold himself back any longer. He squatted beside Angie and put his hands on her shoulders, shook her. "Angie, fight the damn thing!"

"This physical contact is embarrassing, disgusting, imperialistic, and tasteless," she said in a monotone. "Please withdraw." Not waiting for him to obey, she drew away from him and turned her back.

Zero heard a shout, turned, and saw Jack straddling Yoshio, who was making feeble struggling motions facedown in the dirt. Jack drew a piece of line from inside his tangle of clothing and tied Yoshio's wrists together with it. The Pezz took a turn sitting on Yoshio as Jack returned to Zero.

"More of the spirits have arrived," Zickorian said, pointing. Zero looked and saw three more of the fluorescent aerial jellyfish drifting toward them. One of them was on a trajectory that would take it to Angie.

"Just what she needs," Zero muttered.

Zero snatched up another of the metal spikes and took aim at the delicate being daintily approaching Angie.

"This wrestling is getting very tiresome," Jack said. "But . . . " He clamped his arm around Zero from behind. "Mustn't interfere, Zero," he said.

Zero struggled and found that Jack was impossibly strong. He felt like an infant gripped by an adult in Jack's arms.

The jellyfish approached Angie from behind. She sensed it, turned, tried to back away—and tripped. She fell heavily, and the thing was upon her. She froze into paralysis as the tendrils shot sparks into her skull. "Zickorian!" Zero cried, anguished. "Stop the fucking thing!"

"I don't believe it is having sex with her," Zickorian said. "And it would be wrong to interfere with the spirits."

"*Now!*" Jack said, suddenly releasing him. "Chase it away now—but don't hurt it!"

Zero ran toward the thing, yelling, waving the spike. It drew hastily back and returned to the IAMton wastes.

Angie sobbed and clutched her head. Zero knelt and put his arms around her. Relief cascaded through him as she returned his hug.

"God, my head hurts," she said.

"The second visitation drove out the first," Jack said. "And we drove the second off before it could possess her. They are not spirits; they are plasma vessels generated by the IAMton field, carrying records of psychic imprints that—" He broke off, staring at the

Pezz. Another of the things was drifting toward the Pezz and Yoshio. "Friend Pezz! Back off, my friend— let it get at Yoshio for a moment! Let his second visitor drive out his first. And then we shall see."

An hour later they were standing on the edge of the IAMton desert, squinting against the reflection of early morning sunlight off the white expanse. "Still looks like the salt flats," Yoshio said dully. He winced. Saying even that much had hurt his head.

"It feels exactly like a real, real bad hangover," Angie whispered to him. "Doesn't it?"

"Yes," he said as softly as he could and still be heard.

"We shouldn't make them march when they're feeling like this," Zero said.

"We are out of food," Jack said.

"Food is a big priority with you apparently," Zero said brusquely.

"Yes. It has to be."

"We could go without for a day."

"I urge that we don't wait here any longer," Jack said.

"The hell with it," Angie said, wincing. "Let's go. He's been right about everything else. We're just scared to go into this thing. Making excuses. The hell with it. Come on."

She started off across the wastes, and reluctantly, carrying their packs and the metal spikes, the others followed.

The boy screamed and writhed, and foam flecked his lips.

"You're fortunate I'm here to deal with this matter," the Emperor said. "The wounded are fortunate, too.

They need someone who's not squeamish to rescue them from their suffering. Do this one now, Bella."

Making a kissy-face and batting her eyes at the teen-age boy, Bella knelt and lovingly cut his throat with a ragged-edged machete cadged from a dead Groyn. The boy's screaming became a gurgle, then silence.

Sadly, Swanee realized that this was the boy guard from the night they'd taken Doggo. The boy he'd frightened off, trying to save his life. Well, his lower half was crushed; he'd have died anyway. And now the screaming was stopped. But did Bella have to enjoy herself so much?

Bella, Swanee, two Phylum Twos, Jamie, Kelso, and two air-sharks accompanied the Emperor Harmony on his continuing inspection of his new residence. The air-sharks circled the group restlessly in opposite directions, one a little higher than the other; they were waiting for another chance to feed, eyeing the cadaver of the boy, champing their beveled jaws.

Jamie stood grimly rigid in the enormous hands of a Phylum Two, who imprisoned her effortlessly, clamping her arms to her sides. Now and then he nudged his semitumescent penis against her rump, and she ground her teeth in bottled-up fury. Swanee could see it in her eyes: she was imagining just how she would kill this creature once she had the opportunity.

The room had once been a large workroom in the back of one of the open-air shops and was now a repository of broken crockery, shattered pots, overturned furniture, and a heap of gravel where one wall had collapsed.

"There's another over there, there is!" Kelso cawed out, hopping from foot to foot on Harmony's shoulder. His stunted wings flapped his excitement; drool leaped from his skull's mouth; and his lidless eyes dilated and pinpointed and dilated and pinpointed.

Swanee had to suppress an imprecation. He had hoped that the Emperor wouldn't see the scarred fellow, just a boy himself. Warren. He was lying on his back, half covered with debris, mostly hidden by a wooden table lying on its side.

Harmony turned to look. The camera lenses occupying his eye sockets whirred, focusing; the mechanical iris inside them opening as he looked into the dark corner of the room.

Bella threw the table aside. Jamie sucked in her breath audibly. "Warren!"

Warren grinned lopsidedly at her. It was a weak grin. His side was stoved in; blood glued gravel to the floor.

Then Jamie glanced guiltily at the Emperor, who had turned his changeless features toward her. "He's a friend of yours."

"I know everyone here," she said, shrugging. "I even used to know you when you were human."

"Is that supposed to be an insult? If it is, you're an ignorant girl. A silly airhead, like all females." He snorted with pleasure. "I see you don't like that remark. That's nice. Listen: I'm going to let the air-sharks play with your friend here. Unless perhaps you'd like to tell me where Sanchez and your little lesbian whorefriend are hiding?"

She was fighting tears. "I really, honestly *don't know.*"

"I could Twist you, and then I could read your mind. But I don't think I want to see what you'd become, and anyway the process takes too long. Well. The sharks."

"Look, leave Warren alone. He could be useful to you," she said desperately, a catch in her voice. "He might live. He's a good fighter."

"That's what worries me. But he'd die anyway. The wounded are all impossible to care for on Fool's Hope. Stupid to try to save them unless their wounds are minor. No, he'll die. But if I give him to the sharks, it'll be . . . well, they like to play with their food."

"Look, I'll help you any way I can. You're in power, so putting this moron on me is unnecessary. But I don't know where Sanchez and Trish are."

He snorted. "As if the whore would so much as go for a tinkle without telling you where she was doing it and how much came out."

"Hey, Jamie." Warren's voice was a rasp. "Forget it. I'm goin' anyway. I like the idea . . . the sharks. Always knew sharks'd get me. A surfer way to go. One of the risks of living freestyle."

"You think you'd like the idea, but you won't," Harmony said nonchalantly.

"You won't like it you won't like it you won't!" Kelso sniggered.

Harmony gestured, and the two air-sharks dove. One of them clamped Warren's head in its jaws—not hard enough to kill him—and pulled him from the debris. He choked off a scream. It carried him about the room, dangling him awkwardly from its jaws, as the other worried at his thighs.

Swanee shouted, "Shit!" He stepped in and slashed out Warren's throat with his talons as the shark swept by.

He turned instantly to Harmony, fell to his knees, and bowed his head. "Forgive me. I couldn't bear it: I am weak. But I am loyal. Kill me now. My essence is yours."

Harmony said nothing for a moment. The only sound was the crunching, sucking noises as the two air-sharks fought over Warren's remains. Jamie was alternately sobbing and cursing.

Swanee couldn't bring himself to look up at the Emperor.

Finally, Harmony said, "You could have been my favorite. But I have always perceived this—this simpering indecision in you."

"He has misgivings," Bella said. As always, her voice was a velvety tease. "But he does what is required. He can fly: he is useful, my Emperor. One who serves even in the face of his doubts is finally more devoted than one who serves unthinking. The unthinking servant might one day think and turn. This one has shown that he is yours no matter what occurs to him."

Swanee was staring at her in surprise. She looked at him languidly, with cool objectivity. There was no hint of affection or regard in her gaze. But she had spoken up for him. Which meant that she was willing to take a risk for him.

"Still, he has defied me just now," Harmony said. "He knew I meant for the little asshole to suffer. Oh, very well. But go from my sight, Swanee. Quickly. Make yourself useful restoring my throne room. Go!"

Bowing his head to conceal his relief at being allowed to leave, Swanee backed away, out the door, and then leaped into the air. He climbed the sky and, feeling strangely giddy, circled the settlement, looking down at the restoration activity, wondering about Bella. Wondering how he could care about so cruel a creature, and how so cruel a creature could care about him.

Below, workmen under the watchful eye of various Twists were loading wreckage onto oruh carts and shoring up the gates against hypothetical attacks. Others had begun work converting the warehouse into Harmony's throne room. *"Save the skulls,"* Harmony had told them. *"Keep the skulls of all the dead. The old era has expired; the skulls will symbolize the death of the past. The new age is here: the new age of Harmony."*

Oh yes, Swanee thought. *The new age.*

The sunlight glanced off the clinker tower of crystal up ahead and speared into Zero's eyes. He squinted against the reflection and the glare of the pitted white plain. Abruptly, the forty-foot tower collapsed into itself, crackling and thudding. Section by rough-faceted section shunted jerkily into the desert surface as if it were being pulled into a tube from underground. And as if in response, another rose off to the left, rising shakily from the plain with a *chuck-chuck-chuck* sound, an irregular construct like a precarious pile of badly worn children's blocks just waiting for someone to push it over. In the distance, against the horizon, yet another tower built itself out of nothing, while a third tower deconstructed.

"That a reaction to us?" Zero asked Jack. The Earthers were together; Angie, Jack and Yoshio were walking abreast. The Pezz trotted up ahead, very nervously indeed, muttering to itself. Zickorian and Calum followed disconsolately behind.

"The towers? A reaction to us?" Jack seemed distant and less animated than usual. "No. It happens all the time out here. Some electrochemical activity I don't pretend to understand."

"It's funny, the things you *do* understand, Jack," Zero said, watching him, "and the thing you profess not to. You seem to know what you need to know when the time comes for it."

"Very good," Jack said wearily. "I have traveled many times farther on Fool's Hope than anyone else who was kidnapped to this world. I entered its wilderness alone in order to make its acquaintance. Its Gaea, its Overmind, its ecological network—it is there to talk to you if you learn its language. It tells me what I need to know."

Zero kept watching him. It seemed to him that Jack was a bit more frayed around the edges than usual. Not his clothing or the dirt on him, not the depredations of travel; no, instead, Zero thought, it was the total picture, the gestalt of him. There was something . . . something . . . thing . . .

"God, I'm hungry," Angie said suddenly, bitterly, "and thirsty. No more water. I hope to God you're right about that swamp. It seems so dry here."

"We encountered that phenomenon before. From dry to wet, just like that," Yoshio said.

"And my head is killing me," she went on, scowling. "I'd kill for an aspirin. Okay. I wouldn't kill for one. But I'd *maim* for one. Or maybe a couple of Tylenol. No, make it Advil. Three Advil washed down with a glass of fresh-squeezed orange juice. Chilled."

Orange juice, Zero thought. *Grapefruit juice, apple juice, strawberry-banana milkshakes: never again. Change the subject, quick.* He said, "The thing that happened to you this morning—the alien, um, borrowing your body, sort of." He didn't want to say *possessed.* "You really don't remember any of it?"

Angie shrugged glumly. "Not anything that happened. Just a feeling. Like an aftertaste. Fear. Like, a fear I was going to be eaten. Wanting to escape, find isolation. Just a general sort of feeling."

"Same here," Yoshio said. "All I can remember about the alien is a mood. A sense of regret and being angry at the regret."

Zero understood. He felt a sharp, empathic sense of what they were describing. *Too* sharp. The IAMton field was enhancing his intuition, leaking bits of telepathic signals to him. And it was growing more intense.

For a while the only sound was their footsteps crunching across the acrid crust of the IAMton wastes. The dust they raised stung their eyes and made their mouths dry and puffy; it burned in Zero's split lip and worked its way under the bandages to Yoshio's wounds.

All at once the Pezz froze in its tracks. Then it began to back toward them and turned, very slowly, as if struggling with a mysterious inertia. Zero had been around it long enough to know this was an indication of real fear.

"I cannot continue," it said.

"It isn't much farther," Jack said. "I can smell the water, the grass. We could carry you if—"

"No, no, I am not weary. I am . . . there are too many others here. Invisible ones. The territorial impingement is great. I violate them; they violate me. We are [untranslatable]."

"I sense them, too," Zickorian said, moving up from behind. "The beast-ancestors of this place give us our final warnings."

Zero felt a prickle of sourceless anxiety himself, had been feeling it for a while. The sunlight seemed intrusively bright. He closed his eyes for a moment to rest them.

And then it washed over him: a vision, styled cinematically. Pan over a cavern of verdigris, artificially lit from within artfully arranged wall-niches. The big cavern's gold and green-streaked walls are honeycombed with elegantly carved-out holes, cave-mouths tastefully bearded with something like sparkling macramé made of cotton candy. Truck in on one filigree-trimmed cave in particular. Someone looks out of one of the holes. It exudes a tangerine mist that clings to it, obscuring its inner form. But he knows what this person is like under the clothing-smoke: like a leathery vacuum cleaner hose articulated with animate hairs and pincers. *Zzzz,* but it is good to see her! A warmth rolls through him at the sight of his sweet mother.

"Zero!" Jack's voice, from somewhere. "Clasp it! Close your hands over it!"

Zero felt something cold in his hands. The cold was like the cold pang of separation from a loved one: he'd lost his mother.

Reeling from the loss, he opened his eyes and saw himself surrounded by strangers. Aliens. *"Zzzz?"*

"Oh, God," Angie said. "Zero!"

He looked at her, and a filter was withdrawn from his mental camera. Her features shifted from alien to familiar. "Angie . . . " He felt spaced out and his head ached, but the vision and the strangeness had gone. He opened his arms to embrace her. She melted against him. He closed his eyes to savor her—and then snapped them open. He'd seen pictures against the darkness behind his eyelids. A city of interlocked glass toroids; a red sky thronged with flying creatures moving in strict ritualistic formations.

"Don't close your eyes except to blink," he told the others over Angie's shoulder. "You'll see things."

"You see how it is?" the Pezz said, turning to Jack. "They are everywhere, here."

"It's not them, actually," Jack said. "It's a sort of record of them, impregnated into the ambient IAMton field. But I see your problem. You feel you are transgressing?"

"Yes," the Pezz said. "I am unclean and in danger of becoming absurd."

"Talk about closing the barn door after the horse is gone," Angie muttered.

Zero turned to the Pezz. "Don't you have some kind of—some sort of official diplomatic apology you can make for, uh, transgressing? Maybe something traditional among your people?"

"Yes, the Traveler's Obsequy. It would not be enough."

"It might be," Jack said, "combined with this." He bent and unwrapped the metal hill-spikes he'd been carrying wrapped in cloth. "These can be dangerous. I didn't want to break them out till they were really needed." He gave one to each of the travelers. "Now, be careful how you hold them. They will act as lightning rods of a sort for the psychoreactive energies. They are to be used with a firm grip, held just so." He held his own shining metal spike out to the side like a canoe paddle, its lower end touching the dirt. "It must drag in the dust. It will be uncomfortable, hunched over like this, but we haven't got far to go, and you can take frequent rests."

"Why do you say 'Keep a good grip on them'?" Yoshio asked, sounding worried.

"Because when they pick up an IAMton surge, they might react by turning in your hands and attracting to your center of psychic polarity. That is, if you don't hold them firmly, they'll whip about and sink themselves into your skull. They're attracted to your brain like a pin to a magnet, you see."

Zero's knuckles immediately whitened on the spike.

"I refuse," Zickorian said, casting his spike down. It clanged onto the salt crust and trembled as violet sparks shivered up and down its length. "It is wrong to defy the spirits. If they desire to enter us, it is for good reason. We should commune with them."

For a moment Zero found himself wondering if Zickorian were right. He shook his head. He didn't want to go back to that verdigris cavern.

"Do as you prefer, Zickorian," Jack said. "And I wish you farewell."

Zickorian turned a rather human expression of accusation at Calum, who reluctantly dropped his own hill-spike beside Zickorian's.

The expedition set off once more to the north, toward the Hungry Punkin' swamp and the Progress Station. The Earthers and the Pezz were moving clumsily, having to drag the "lightning rods." Zickorian stepped out well ahead of the others; as if setting himself apart from them and challenging "the spirits" to take him. Calum hung back. Zero noticed that he walked between Angie and Yoshio, close between their hill-spikes, as if hoping their close proximity would protect him. Apparently it did.

For he was untouched when, minutes later, Zickorian gave a shout and went rigid, his arms stretched overhead, reaching for the jade sky. And then he bent double, clawing at himself. Zero and Jack ran up to help him, but it was too late. Zickorian had drawn a knife from his boot and was using it to slash himself. The alien within the alien, the alien mind that had taken over Zickorian, had seen hideous things sunken into his underside—what the Earthers called legs—disgusting growths trying, perhaps, to eat him alive.

Zero gathered something of the sort from the few fragments of Zickorian's babbling that the translator-box could manage. And then it translated Zickorian's death-scream as "[Untranslatable]."

Before Jack and Zero could wrest the knife away, Zickorian's random slashing found a vital organ.

Silently, Calum buried Zickorian and inscribed the appropriate runes in the dust over the shallow grave.

The Earthers stood gloomily by while this was done. There had been much friction with Zickorian. But he had traveled with them a long way, had undergone the same privations and confusion. They had come to identify with him, to think of him, like every member of the expedition, as an extension of themselves. He had been part of their island of familiarity in a sea of the alien. Piece by piece their island had been swamped by the sea: Dennis, Cisco, now Zickorian. Losing Zickorian made them feel small and lost and sorry they hadn't tried harder to understand him.

Zero's own sense of loss was complicated by the after-taste of the alien consciousness he'd shared for a few moments: the alien's sense of loss for its mother.

The horror of that intrusion, the longing for the embrace of that *thing*, nagged at the back of his mind.

Don't think about that, Zero told himself. *Bury it.*

But he wondered how much longer he could keep burying his shocks and stay sane.

Zero slipped an arm around Angie's waist, and for a few minutes they leaned on one another.

Then Jack said, "We'd best go." Calum nodded

and hunkered beside Jack, sharing his hill-spike. Walking like Groucho, they continued on their way.

When the back pain could no longer be borne and the irritation of the dust in their eyes threatened to blind them, Jack announced, "There, up ahead, see it? The stand of ghost trees?"

With watering eyes they peered through the haze of dust and saw a thatch of wavery plumes at the horizon. Like filmic superimpositions of trees, Zero thought, but without color. Misty gray.

"That is the edge of the swamp," Jack said. "The turf of the Hungry Punkin'. And the place where the Progress Station is supposed to be."

TWELVE

"I knew we'd find her," the Emperor said, turning his camera-lens eyes toward Trish. "Something as sweet and delicate and *valuable* as this silly creature couldn't be hidden in the settlement long. I'm deeply annoyed to learn that there were escape tunnels dug under the settlement for her to hide in. I really had no idea they were there. I'm going to have a bit of advice sewn into a sampler: *Never have too much faith in your own intelligence service.*"

Swanee was lying on a wooden scaffold on his back, gluing snail shells to the ceiling. They weren't really snail shells—the creature who'd lived in them was more like a spider—but they looked a lot like them, with their spiral formation and their delicate patterning, and they were perfect for a ceiling mosaic. He was using them to delineate patterns of power radiating from the central figure of the ceiling, the Emperor's face, which was forty feet across from ear to ear.

The throne room—which, because it was so fussily tended by the dwarf-pig, Harmony called the Porcine

Chapel—was to be decorated wall to wall, ceiling to floor, with murals and mosaics depicting the Ascent of the Emperor, in Harmony's own fanciful version of the story.

Swanee shifted a little on the scaffold and grunted with pain. This was very hard on his wings. They were flexible wings, almost rubbery, but they were not unbreakable. Also the smoke from the torches had collected near the ceiling, making him cough. He had run out of shells up there. A good excuse to quit the scaffold for a while and work on the walls.

Swanee wriggled free of the scaffold and slid down a rope to the floor, giving his wings a few tentative twitches to restore circulation.

"Watch out with thothe wingth!" the dwarf-pig lisped indignantly. "You almotht knocked over the royal chamberpot!"

"Thorry—I mean, sorry," Swanee said, looking over his shoulder. The dwarf-pig was carrying the chamberpot proudly out the front gate, where two Pragmatics stood guard.

Swanee looked around. It would be a very busy room, in the design sense, when he was finished. But it was not for him to dictate the Emperor's taste.

It was high ceilinged, the biggest room in the settlement. It was empty except for the ceiling decorations, the scaffold, the throne at one end, and a red rug of of Groyn hide running from the throne to the door opposite. There was a door behind the throne leading to new jail cells and to the Emperor's quarters.

The Emperor was humming as he supervised the hanging of various ceiling decorations and of various people, and these two decorating tasks were indistinguishable. He hung two of the textile sarcophagi of the

Whorebugs above and to either side of his throne; the windings were cut away in one spot so that the genitals of the men who'd died in them were exposed, dangling like shriveled blue tassels. Others, two men and two women who had resisted his takeover—in fact only one of them had; the others were executed for not completely contradicting the dissenter at once—had been hung by the neck, and then, after Swanee had dutifully painted pretty Art-Decoesque designs on them, were dipped in a lacquer made from oruh hooves to preserve them. Mummified, eyes bulging and tongues protruding under their yellow coating, they were hauled by pulley into place, dangling from the ceiling by their nooses like morbid chandeliers.

"When we get the electric lighting worked out," the Emperor said thoughtfully, "I really must have some bulbs put in their mouths, or perhaps in their rumps."

Trish was tied hand and foot, lying at the foot of the Emperor's throne. Her groin was bloodied; the Emperor had let the Phylum Twos use her. He'd watched, absently caressing himself the while.

"Look at yourself, you animal!" Trish had screamed at Harmony as the Phylum Twos dragged her onto the mattress. "Look in a mirror! You call that exalted? Divine? You're being *punished*, you dumb backward intellectual *slob!*"

Harmony had laughed at her. "Punished? If this is punishment, give me more—because I'm very happy! How could punishment make a man so happy? And do you think I don't look in the mirror, dear child? I do so, lovingly, every day! Do you imagine that this is some Dorian Gray retribution for me, my transformation? Should I want to look human? But humans are base things. Lower animals. That's like a human wanting to resemble a chimp! What divine being ever looked really human? No one interesting. Have you seen paintings of Krishna, of Kali, of Shiva? I never liked my former face. This"—he indicated his own face—"now this is an idea made flesh. It is purity, my dear. To me it's very beautiful."

But she hadn't heard him; she'd been penetrated by the Phylum Two just then and was occupied with screaming.

The Emperor's shape-changer had assumed the shape of a throne. A throne of living human flesh, of soft pink skin, veins and sinews and muscles articulating an imitation of an Earthly throne's marbling and baroque inlays. It was outlined in blinking, rolling human eyes, and its cushions were pulsing and warm. The Emperor strode to it and sat down with a sigh of pleasure. Kelso was asleep, eyes staring, glazed over, on the back of the throne. He woke with a snort when the Emperor sat down, flapped his truncated wings; his long tongue unwound as he yawned hugely.

Swanee watched the throne with sidelong glances, looking up now and then from his palette and his brushwork.

The Emperor looked down at Trish, and a reflection of a wall torch glimmered in perfect miniature in his camera lens. He spoke aside to the dwarf-pig. "Have the guards bring in the little bird's new cage."

"My ethenth is yourth, Your—"

"Yes, yes, just do it."

The dwarf-pig scrambled to do the Emperor's bidding. Swanee could *feel* the Emperor's gaze shift to him, to his work at the wall mural. It was like hearing a wasp buzz at the back of your head; you were afraid to move, afraid to provoke it into stinging you.

Swanee was using a crude brush and a palette of crude but vivid paints to fill in the details of a mural depicting the transformation of the Emperor. The figure of the Emperor was the center of a pastoral design, and the trees, the undergrowth, the gathering of animals and awed worshippers all seemed to emanate from him in the stroke-emphasis of Swanee's stylization.

"Very pretty," Harmony commented. "But it's rather . . . there's a sort of angry undertone, don't you think? Rather like Van Gogh in his last phase. Emotional strokes, so vivid as to be hostile. Could this express some inner turmoil on your part, Swanee, hm?"

"No, my Emperor," Swanee said as evenly as he could, blanking his mind to discourage letting go a telepathic contradiction. "To be honest, what it expresses is the crudeness of my tools and paint. It just comes out that way with these brushes and this unsubtle goo I'm stuck with." He tried not to hope that the lie would work. The Emperor might pick up on that hope.

"I'm dubious. It's vibrancy is—ah, here's your new home, Patricia."

"Fuck you, scumbag," Trish said, articulating clearly.

"The sun-monkeys made this cage for us," Harmony said conversationally as his entourage entered the throne room. The wrought iron cage was carried in by the newt and snakelegs and the beetlewingface and El Chingadero—who had a new victim, a teenage boy. "They're quite good at ironwork, the 'monkeys," Harmony went on. " . . . Ironic all this dealing we're doing with aliens. Considering what we've got planned for them. I think it wise we find out which ones are most useful to us. That way, before the extermination, we can select a few for slaves . . ."

The cage, with its floral pattern of black metal, was about four and a half feet high, three in diameter. It was shaped like an outscale parakeet's cage except that inside there were hundreds of tiny barbs.

They opened the cage door and pushed Trish in. She bit off a scream. They locked the door and reached through the bars to cut her bonds. Running a chain through the iron ring at the top of the cage, they hoisted her twenty feet into the air, just in front and to one side of the throne.

Trish writhed, and her blood, released by the hundreds of barbs on every interior surface of the cage, began to leak almost immediately through the holes in its floor. Trish hunched herself, trying to avoid the barbs, but could find no place where her weight didn't bear her down on them.

"Actually, I borrowed this notion from Elizabeth of Bathory," Harmony said. "We really should have gagged the pretty little lezzie—the noise is . . . oh, good." This last as the guards—two scared-looking humans—brought Jamie in and tied her to a ring in the floor, directly beneath the cage.

"You needed a shower, you dirty little dyke," the Emperor said.

Kelso howled with laughter at this. "Yes, stinky dyke needs fuckin' *show*-wer!"

In trickles and drops, Trish's blood rained down on Jamie. Jamie sobbed and tried to strangle herself on her ropes. The guards prevented her. She convulsed and bent double, clutching her belly. On her thighs, her own blood mixed with Trish's.

She's having a miscarriage, Swanee thought dully. The paintbrush seemed heavy in his hands. He felt numb except for a distant, roiling nausea.

"I'm hungry I'm *hung*-reeeee," Kelso said "I want to eat little furry things like Swanee, Emperor lovey-sir! You said he could take me to get some, you said he could!" Kelso capered on Harmony's shoulder, nuzzling and begging.

"Oh, very well. Swanee, take him out and feed him, but don't dawdle. Bring him back soon and return to work."

"My essence is yours," Swanee said. Despite his disgust at the thought of physical contact with Kelso, he came alive inside knowing he was to be released from this scene. The girl writhing in the cage, the blood raining on her lover. *Get away,* he told himself, *before the Emperor reads you.*

Fortunately, the Emperor was fully involved in enjoying his new toys.

With Kelso tucked under his arm, Swanee hurried into the sunlight. Even out there he could still hear the screaming.

Get away. Get gone. Go!

He leaped into the air and mounted into the sky with laborious heaves of his wings. As he did so he was aware that he'd made a decision. The leap into the air and the decision had come simultaneously.

He climbed and climbed till the soft green sky cooled him with an amber-tinged cloud and the winds drowned the scream of the young woman in the barbed cage. (All those little holes—how long would it take her to bleed to death?)

"Where yuh *go*-in'?!" Kelso yammered. "Whatcha

doin'? The woods is the other way, that's where thuh little ani-mules is!"

Swanee ignored him. He soared, gliding toward the Neutral. Presently, through a gold-limned break in the clouds, he saw it below, looking as if Stonehenge had multiplied. He dove through the break and spiraled down toward the Neutral, wondering where to begin. "You're gonna get in trouble," Kelso complained. "I'm gonna call the Emperor!"

"Oh no, I don't think so," Swanee said. "I've been waiting for this moment for a while, Kelso."

He was still a quarter-mile up when he lifted the living skull over his head and flung it downward. Babbling obscenities, making futile flaps with its Thalidomide wings, the skull turned end over end as it fell —and in a few moments it was a white-flecked red splash on the empty blue road, a few hundred yards from the edge of the Neutral.

Swanee had felt the ripple of empathic pain go through him—and it bothered him not a whit. He laughed and spiraled lower yet and saw that the road wasn't quite empty. Bella was there, staring at the splash on the road. Swanee grinned, pleased to see an expression on her face that had nothing to do with her Queen of the Night role.

Emboldened by her amazement, he fluttered down across from her, the spin-painting that had been Kelso between them.

She closed her mouth and regained her aplomb. "Your prettiest artwork," she said, nodding toward the splash. "Very modern. I like it. I could never stand the little snitch."

"I feel like I've just pulled a tick off my back," Swanee said.

"I have to turn you in, you know. And the Emperor will kill you."

"No. I'm leaving. And I'm going to see him brought low. He did something today . . . I just couldn't stand it anymore."

"You don't really think you can just fly off, do you? He'll reel you back in, Swanee." She came around the circle of blood, making motions with her hands as if pulling on an invisible line that brought her closer to him till she was standing body-warmth close , the tips of her breasts just touching his leathery black chest. She tapped Swanee's forehead. "He'll reel you in up here."

"He'll try. He succeeded before. But I'll fight him. This time I'll win. Something busted open in me back there." He looked into her eyes, searching for warmth, compassion. He saw only a vibrating void. He shook his head. "You wouldn't understand." For a moment he thought he saw it. Just a flicker.

It occurred to him that she might be planning to kill him. To curry favor with Harmony.

He took a step back and tried to see past the styling of her Twist. Even here in the sunlight she was Queen of the Night. In the darkness she carried light with her, an unhealthy swamp-gas glow. In the daylight she carried a corona of darkness, her own capsule of night, a backdrop that went with her wherever she went.

He remembered going to the state fair as a boy. There had been a Haunted House—just a big trailer, really, with a facade that unfolded, that showed cartoony ghosts and ghouls wreathed in mist and climbing from mossy graves beneath crooked gravestones. And he'd paid his fifty cents and entered this thing from the bright daylight, and inside it was pitch dark, narrow, zig-zagging corridors lit every so often by a little alcove

with a black light and a Day-glo monster mask in it;
maybe, here and there, wispy stuff hanging from the ceiling tickled the back of his neck; cold air blew from a
hole somewhere in the floor. But for a nine-year-old,
they'd successfully created the right atmosphere. The
tacky atmosphere of the American Halloween, of Disney
movies about witches, of Abbott and Costello movies
about ghosts.

And this superbly tacky rendition of supernatural
darkness was something Bella carried with her like a
negative aura.

Combined with Bella's maddening voluptuousness
and her skin-tight black and scarlet costume that was a
kind of lingerie to wear in public . . . it gave Swanee a
hard-on.

He turned away from her and glanced down at himself. The hard-on bulged beneath the skin of his belly.
So it *was* in there. A mental image came to him, a motion
of his hips that would unleash the organ, snap it into
the open.

"Take a walk with me, and we'll talk about it," she
said, coming up behind him, taking his arm.

Mouth dry, he looked at her. "Talk about, uh, it?"

She smiled wickedly. "About Harmony, silly."

"Oh."

They strolled down the road between the bogs, distantly aware of jumpskeeters splashing, the life of wet
places carried to them on the smell of the alien breeze.
It was hot and humid, and walking along the road beside
the swamp was a *little* like walking through the Deep
South countryside, like an afternoon of that summer
he'd spent in Georgia. Almost.

"He'll know Kelso is dead by now," Swanee said.

"He'll have sensed it. I should go. He'll send some-one after me." He looked at her. "Perhaps he already did."

"Nope. Not me. I was coming back from the Neutral to report to him about Sanchez. He was right: Sanchez is hiding in the Neutral. The Pezz are hiding him."

"Is he?" He watched her sidelong. "Still, you said you have to turn me in—and he'd know if you let me go."

"I changed my mind. He can't read me like he can the others. I let him hear what he wants to hear. I'm . . . telepathically selective." She stopped and turned him to her. Her hands burned across his pectorals, down his ribs, coming to rest on his hips, where there was just a suggestion of a *pull* in them. "I know how you feel about me," she said. "I am not . . . invulnerable to emo-tion." Her voice had gone husky.

Could he believe her? He wanted to back away. He couldn't.

"Swanee . . . " Her eyes were windows into under-ground rivers; her voice was thick now with invitation. Her cleavage sang to him. "What you did to Kelso—I mean, defying Harmony—that turns me on. Got me all . . . *you* know."

He pulled her close and felt her, firm but yielding, a communicative heat against him. (He managed not to think about the fact that she used to be a man, a pro *football player.*) And they kissed, which was a storm on a midnight sea, and then she raked her lips from his, across his cheek to his ear, and, with her hips grinding sotfly against his hard-on, one hand caressing his wings (an erogenous zone, he discovered), she whispered, "It's so hot here on the road—take me up into the sky. Fly with me. Make love to me up there in the clouds, where it's cool and private."

He blinked in surprise. "I don't think I could. I'm— uh, not strong enough. . . . I mean, it's not that you're overweight, but—"

"My weight is my whim. I can cancel my mass, dear, with a field I don't really understand. It works for a time, darling, my darkling darling. Take me up, take me up."

"I'll try."

He gathered her in his arms, carrying her like a groom toting a new bride across the threshold, and found that she *was* strangely light. So he ran and leaped, and his wings climbed the air-pressure ladder till they were mounting the sky and she was laughing and kick- her feet with happiness. He grinned at her and took her up, took her up.

And then they were in the clouds, in damp silence and muted, pearly light, and it was cooler there. She touched something at her crotch, and her clothing melted away, and he did that thing with his hips, glanced down and saw with relief that his organ was not particu- larly Twist, it was simply very big, very black, and very hard. She ground her sticky-wet parts against him, and he thought, *She smells like a spring in the Okefenokee swamp, the smell of swamp rot mixed with blooms.*

His wings kept them climbing, but slowly now, a few inches at a time. He explored her breasts and found them impossibly firm and resilient and magnetically charged, his hands positively charged, so that *click*— they locked together. The light diffused around them, leaving them in a sweet gray limbo with nothing to distract them from one another. God, the smell of her hair, its gloss, the cloud moisture beading like diamond chips on the exquisite line of her throat, the swell of her hips inviting him in. . . . He tried to enter her, and she said, "No."

"*No?*"

"Not till we're farther up—and then *stop flying.* Fold your wings. Dive. Do it to me then. When we're diving."

"But we'll—"

"I trust you to pull us up before we hit. Please. Please. I'd come then. I'd come hard for you."

Too feverish to think twice, he climbed, kept climbing till they'd broken from the cloud. And for a moment they hung in the air at the roof of the cloud with the emerald sky arching above and the soft, light-infused infinite fluff of the cloud's roof stretching out to either side like their Elysian marriage bed, and she said, "Now!"

He drove himself into her. He moaned and couldn't have flown then if he'd wanted to. He was too wired with sensation, savoring it, then pumping for more of it, digging deeper. A miner in a delirium of lust when he's found a millionaire-making vein of gold; dig into the gold, follow it back into the darkness of the world's secret interior places . . .

Swanee was not aware that they were falling till they'd broken from the bottom of the cloud and were plunging through a plane of sunlight and she was howling with happiness, urging him on, bucking wildly against him, her eyes lit up with suicidal glee, with kamikaze devotion to some sexual absolute. The wind ripped the breath from his lungs, the sky screamed past him, sucking the moisture from his eyes as they fucked in freefall turning over and over, clouds and sun above, strobing, alternating with the glimmering topography of the bogs down below as they spun, adrenaline shouting through him and mixing with hot Twist semen as she screamed, "I'm *coming!*"

The ground rushed up at them. From the corner of his eye he saw a spike of glass in her hand and caught her wrist in his taloned fingers.

He shrieked like a man whose wife has metamorphosed into a black widow. He wrenched free of her, wings flapping desperately for purchase on the air, backing away from her. He saw the long thin glass needle in her hand, like a hatpin but exactly as long as his penis, glimmering in the light as she slashed at him again with it. She missed but screamed with delight, still bucking in orgasm.

Swanee was still falling, but he twisted away from her slash and angled down, then arched his back to ascend, to glide, fighting his momentum, terrified by the rush of the bogs toward him. He fought and found a grip on the air. The approach of the ground slowed, stopping as he raked upward. He thought, *My God, I've let her fall.*

But she was floating in the air, her arms and legs moving like a frustrated spider dangling on a webstrand. She drifted downward very slowly; she would make the ground safely, he saw. Despite his bitterness, he was pleased.

He heard her think a parting message to him as he flew away from her: *"I meant everything and would never have wanted anyone else. But I had to try to kill you anyway. I really tried. And I'm almost glad you got away, darling. . . . Keep fighting. . . . I love you. . . . I'll kill you if I get the chance. . . . I love you."*

Swanee closed his mind to her and flew faster to put more distance between them. He angled for the Neutral and his cock—dripping, feeling cold now in the open air—drew itself into its sheath, like a frightened turtle into a shell.

Feeling drained, he fluttered down to the Neutral, dropping into the midst of the Pezz's pavilion.

"Where's Sanchez?" he asked them wearily. "I want to save his life."

Zero felt relief here on every level. Relief from heat, from hunger and thirst and the burning in his eyes, relief from exertion and especially from the pressure of alien minds. The prickling anxiety had drained away the moment they'd stepped out of the IAMton wastes.

And it was soothing here among the ghost trees. The ghost trees were living organisms, Jack had assured him, but they were so diffuse—as limpid as steam, etiolated and fine—that they looked like mist, mist carved into the shape of elms seen in the foggy distance on an autumn day. The dramatic upward lift of the trunk, the expressive articulation of branches and leaves, all blurred into fog. But they were in their reproductive phase now: every few minutes they spawned seedlings with meteoric bursts of colored rain, colors of rainbow purity showering miraculously from colorlessness, silting brightness to the ground.

Cooled by a fine spray from the ghost trees, Angie and Zero and Yoshio and Calum sat together against a hummock that rimmed a swamp-pool. They had washed in a clear, cold pool of spring water. They'd eaten crustaceans and something Jack called swamp bulbs; the bulbs looked like onions, growing underwater along the edges of the pools. They tasted like papayas dabbed with catsup.

Stomach full, the Earthers and Calum sat waiting

for Jack and the Pezz to return from reconnaissance. They sat contentedly, watching the ghost trees become more solid with the thickening of dusk.

"I suppose we ought to be worried about the jumpskeeters," Yoshio said. They could hear those and other creatures buzzing and whirring and splashing behind them.

"The hell with the jumpskeeters," Angie said listlessly.

"The Hungry Punkin' is the real problem child around here," Zero said.

"The hell with the Hungry Punkin'," Angie murmured, her eyes drooping.

"Perhaps we should seek out the creature," Calum said, "and kill it. Take the offensive. Lay a trap for it."

Zero looked at him. "Huh! That sounded like initiative. Like an idea all your own. Not something I would expect from you, the way you parroted Zickorian."

"Truly," Calum said, "you don't know our customs. I repeated what he said because I am underage, and he is my [approximate translation:] Boy Scout troopmaster. And that is our way. Without him, I am a free agent, permitted to express myself independently."

The Earthers gaped at him. "Christ," Angie muttered, "I wonder what else we misunderstood about the High Clans. About *everyone*."

Calum craned his neck, looking around. "Jack and Yoshio have been gone a long time," he said.

Zero nodded. He'd been worrying about it. "They could be lost. Maybe we should look for them."

"Then we'd *all* be lost," Yoshio said. "Anyway, you really think Jack is ever lost?"

"No," Zero admitted. "I guess what really worries me is that we can't be the only people doing recon for

the Progress Station. The Vinyls must be around somewhere. Maybe . . . I dunno. Others. Or the Punkin'."

"You mean they could've been ambushed."

"We weren't," Jack said, stepping into the little
white-sand area that had sprouted the ghost trees. "But
we were followed."

THIRTEEN

"We saw the [untranslatable]," the Pezz said. "From a safe distance."

"He means the Hungry Punkin'," Jack said. "The Punkin' spotted us from a ways off. It followed us, clearly intending to kill us. But I *think* we lost it."

"We have found the Progress Station!" the Pezz said, prancing excitedly.

"It's a sort of bunker," Jack said, "made of the same stuff the settlement is made of, on a little island in a lake. I've never seen a Progress Station—it wasn't here before. But I'm pretty sure that's it. But in the lake . . . " He hesitated.

"The bodies of the dead," the Pezz said. "They are floating in the lake. Among them is the creature who spied on us in the woods. It is dead. Also some Vinyls, and some creatures I've never seen. They're badly deteriorated."

"The creature who spied on us?" Angie said. "That thing with the big golden eyes?"

Jack nodded. "One of Fiskle's pets. Its head is half torn off, and those big eyes are quite gone."

"What was the Punkin' doing when you saw it?" Yoshio asked.

"It was sloshing through the lake—the water's very shallow—and we saw it kill a marsh weasel, and a flying dog, and a rope worm. It simply likes to kill things. I wonder what it used to look like.

"Used to?" Zero asked.

"I don't believe the story about their representing psychotic alien races. I think they're Twists from the races we know here. I think it's what happens to most Twists eventually if they haven't got the right sort of psychological underpinnings. Well, what do we do?"

"Perhaps we should go now," Yoshio said. "Maybe the darkness would work to our advantage. We could pass the creature with stealth."

"I suggest we rest the night," Calum said, "but leave shortly before dawn, before first light. Then perhaps the creature will be dormant. If not, we will see if darkness works to our advantage—and if it doesn't, it will shortly be day."

Jack and the Pezz looked at Calum in surprise. Zero and Angie laughed.

The Pezz had taken the first watch. The watch's job was not only to watch for the Hungry Punkin', and other hostiles but also to slap away jumpskeeters and spongesuckers with a stick. The Pezz was very good at this, and when Zero awoke to take his watch a few hours before dawn, he found a ring of smashed jumpskeeters around the camp.

As the Pezz went rigid with dormancy, Zero moved around the camp, stretching, taking deep breaths, trying to clear the cobwebs away. He'd been deeply asleep, and coming back from it was an ugly affair.

Starlight limned the ghost trees and made the white sand seem fluorescent. Beyond the rim of the swamp pool, clumps of bulbous bushes alternated with stunted coral trees that hooted and clicked and rattled softly to themselves. The jumpskeeters had done for the night, but other creatures slapped the water of the pool and clattered in the crystalline hoop-grass.

Zero turned to look at Angie; her sleeping face was angelic in the starlight.

Zero's head snapped up; he froze, listening.

Something large was shouldering through a thatch of blue spindle-shaped growths about forty feet away, just on the other side of the swamp pool. Zero heard a crackle of electricity and saw a strobe of sparks jump through cracks in the brush.

"*I think we lost it,*" Jack had said.

"I think it found us again," Zero muttered.

And then it bounded from cover and splashed into the pool, waking a group of jumpskeeters; it stood there trembling with fury, glaring with every inch of itself.

"Shit!" Zero yelled, bending to fumble for a pike without taking his eyes off the thing. "Yo! We got a visitor!"

The Hungry Punkin' was fifteen feet tall, with long, lean, corded arms and taloned hands dangling near its double-jointed knees. Its hands looked almost detached; its loose claws were like the mechanical grabber in the arcade game where you operate a crane to pick up the prize. It had a big orange head like a pumpkin—no features, not even eyes on it—and a two-foot-wide mouth that opened in its belly where its navel should have been.

The Punkin', Zero had heard, would stuff anything that had body heat into its belly-mouth. As if to confirm this for him, it grabbed one of the crow-size jumpskeeters and crammed it buzzing, whole, into its maw. The Punkin' had four organic cables dangling from its neck, spitting out sparks like Fourth of July sparklers—but bigger sparks, deadly ones.

As the Meta's watching spheres gathered overhead, the others, awakened by Zero, snatched up their crude weapons and stood on either side of him. The Punkin' came sloshing toward them, sparking and roaring. Unprepared and disoriented, they babbled suggestions at one another, everyone talking at once, while the Punkin' climbed over the rim.

"Surround it!" Zero yelled as it came on.

They formed a rough circle around the Punkin', trying to confuse it, keep it off balance, jabbing at it with their pikes.

Its arm lashed out and grabbed Yoshio's pike; he wouldn't let go. The Punkin' lifted him into the air, so that he dangled from the pike, then whipped him hard across the face with a sparking cable. Yoshio screamed and fell away, rolling—then lay still.

Another swipe with its free talon, and Punkin' sent Calum flying through the air, falling heavily on his back, coughing and shaking. Then it snapped Yoshio's metal pike in two and threw the halves contemptuously aside as Jack lunged at it with a pike from one side, Zero and Angie from another. The Pezz tried to use a pike but could handle the weapon only clumsily. Zero's jab glanced from the Murderer's head, leaving a waxy streak across it; it weaved like a boxer, and Angie missed it entirely. Jack stepped in close and tried to jam the pike down its throat. It closed its jaws on the spear and wrenched it away, at the same time slashing at Jack with its claws—

—and ripping his face away.

The claws had caught Jack's face at the side of the jaw and neatly sloughed it off his head. And what was underneath made the Murderer stagger back, disoriented. It was a light.

Jack stood there shaking as the skin began to peel away from the rest of his head, as his neck began to crumble into paste that fell in clots at his feet. There was no blood.

What remained was a smooth, glowing bulb shape, a shining head-size light bulb floating over the shoulders, without a neck at all. Upheld by an electric field of some kind, Zero supposed. The rest of Jack's veneer peeled away in seconds, as if he were coming unraveled. The torso was human-shaped but made of the same shining white stuff. The glowing legs and arms floated near it but weren't directly attached.

For a moment everyone stared at what had been Jack the Baptist—and in that moment Zero and Angie and the Pezz and the Punkin' were all members of the same group, sharing their amazement. Zero felt like turning to the Murderer and saying, "Can you beat that? Man, you never know, do you? I mean, Christ, did *you* know that he was—?"

But what he said was, "Fuck!" as the Punkin' recovered itself and lashed out at him with a cable. It wound around his pike, and Zero was knocked off his feet with the electrical jolt that came through it. He found himself lying on his back, his hands aching, wondering where the pike was. He sat up and saw that once again Jack had startled the Punkin'.

The glossy surface of the shiny creature who'd been

Jack the Baptist was emitting a tan foam that was quickly reshaping itself, hardening, changing color, becoming . . .

Another Hungry Punkin'. A smaller one (a female? Zero wondered), that was backing away from the creature. The real Punkin' took a tentative step toward it. The Jack-Punkin' picked up one of the hill-spikes they'd taken from the Hillserlive. The real Punkin' followed, fascinated.

Angie knelt beside Zero and caressed his head, took his hands in hers. "Are you okay? Maybe you better lie down."

"No, I'm okay. Little spaced out but okay." He watched the real Punkin' follow the simulacrum. "Not too bright, is it."

"Uh uh."

Jack and the Punkin' reached the edge of the wastes and stepped into them. He—or it—proffered the hill-spike to the Punkin', as if offering a gift. Hesitantly, cables waving in confusion, it took the spike in its claws. The spike began to waver in its uncertain grip—and then, as if propelled by poltergeists, it spun and aligned itself with the Murderer's pumpkin-head and flew the intervening few inches to spit its brain, skewering it through. The Punkin' fell, twitching, and its sparking ceased, except along the hill-spike. A violet crackling traveled the spike as the Murderer's essence drained into the IAMton field of the white desert crust.

Zero heard a groan and looked over at Calum. Calum turned over, gasping, muttering. He was alive. Yoshio was breathing, too, but was still unconscious.

"Zero," Angie said, "he's coming back. The . . . the Jack-thing."

He hugged her as they watched the Jack-Punkin' begin to change. Bits and pieces of its false exterior curled off from it, as if molting, falling away as it came back to the camp. When it came within twenty feet of them, it paused as if uncertain of itself and was just the glowing light-bulb man again, shining against the darkness.

Zero wanted to do something to help Yoshio and Calum, but he was afraid to take his eyes off the alien they'd called Jack the Baptist. Now that the thing's secret was exposed, it might do anything.

A voice came from a slit of dimness that appeared in its chest. It was Jack's voice, but it sounded oddly reverbed now. "I would like to talk to you. I have much to explain."

"Are you . . . the Meta?" Angie asked.

"No. But—"

It hesitated for a moment. The hesitation hung in the air, vibrating. It was a long, long moment.

Swanee swam through darkness.

That was the way it felt, with his wings so leaden, his chest burning with the effort. The weight of the man hanging from him seemed to increase exponentially with each minute, as if he were a seagull in an oil slick; Kelso's epithet was a prophecy.

He was carrying Sanchez in a leather harness that the Gatermen had made; Sanchez dangled in his crude seat a couple of feet below him. A small guy, Sanchez, but he was almost too much for Swanee.

Now the sea of darkness had become a sea of pain. His joints creaked, his muscles screamed, his breath threatened to stop coming. He could hear his own heartbeat in his ears. And there was still a long way to go.

He almost laughed when Sanchez said, "Listen, Swanee, I really need a rest. This harness is cutting off my circulation. It's killing me."

Grateful for the excuse to set down his burden, Swanee grunted assent and spiraled down toward an enormous treetop nest. Flapping his wings to stay in place, he lowered Sanchez into the nest and then squatted onto the bed of interwoven twigs and grasses, wheezing and coughing, letting the ache flow out of his wing muscles.

"*Madre de Dios,*" Sanchez said, "I had no idea you were suffering like that. Stupid of me—it must be hard for you, carrying me. Let me help you off with that harness. Hold still, I don't want to hurt your wings. There."

Sanchez sat back carefully, taking the harness off; he folded it up, and used it for a pillow.

Swanee furled his wings and leaned back against a branch padded with nest. He could see better than Sanchez in the darkness. Sanchez could see him as a silhouette, maybe a few details from starlight, but he could see Sanchez quite clearly. The little man was squinting at the tangle of bones and hide and hair on the bottom of the nest. They could smell the beast's battery-acid sharpness, counterpoint to the dull reek of carrion.

"Whatever lives here," Sanchez said, "eats people. And it might be coming home to roost soon. Maybe we ought to climb down."

"We'll need the elevation to take off after we rest. Anyway," Swanee said hoarsely, "it won't come back. It's dead: I killed it. I was flying by here once, and it attacked me in the air. If I hadn't been the smarter one, it would have added my bones to those." He yawned. "We'll rest a few minutes and then we'll take off again."

"We've been flying for hours. I don't think we should go on until we both sleep," Sanchez said.

"The expedition has already reached the Progress Station. If we don't hurry, we could miss them. Or the Punkin' will kill them."

"If you kill yourself first, we won't get there at all," Sanchez said. "Don't squander your resources."

"Funny. That's what Harmony—"

"You mean Fiskle. He doesn't deserve any fucking titles."

"Yeah. Fiskle. That's what Fiskle said once. He was going to send me to fly to the Progress Station. But he decided that the Punkin' would probably kill me, and he'd be squandering his resources, killing his only aerial scout. The air-sharks are too stupid to be of much use as scouts or for anything besides killing. He's been trying to develop new Twists who can fly, to work up an expedition that could beat the others there. But all he came up with was Sizzle, who's too crazy to control very well."

"He should have sent his ground forces. Big mistake. The turtle wins the race because the hare is overconfident. So Fiskle controls the way people are Twisted?"

"Um-hm." Swanee was drifting off. "Sorta. Influences it with mind ripple. . . . Don't let me sleep long. We got to go. Get whatever is in the Station. Use it against Fiskle, if it's the right kind of . . . thing. . . . " He couldn't keep his eyes open any longer. Sanchez became a voice out of darkness.

"Maybe it was a mistake to bring me. Maybe you should've gone by yourself, brought it back."

"Told you. Can't. Can't come back. Fiskle would regain control of . . . me . . . you—" Swanee yawned hugely.

It felt good to let go, to slide into sleep. But then the dream swallowed him up, and in its belly he found Fiskle waiting for him.

"I simply felt that you would not have trusted me enough if you had known I wasn't of your race. People in the settlement would not have spoken so freely around me. My appearance seems to startle humans more than, say, the High Clansmen or even the Pezz. I wanted you to accept me as one of you. It was for the best."

The Jack-thing had foamed over again and regrown the form of Jack the Baptist, complete with clothing. Now he sat across from Zero and Angie, his back to a mossy hummock, his knees drawn up, arms locked around his knees, seeming very casual and very human. The completeness of its disguise was unnerving.

"I saw you eat like a human being," Angie said. "You swallowed everything you ate. Of course, I never saw you, um, eliminate wastes."

"I *did* eat. It went down a tube to the speech-slit where it was disintegrated and converted to energy. Nothing is wasted. I had to eat rather often—as you may have noticed—to maintain my disguise. It had to be constantly shored up."

"You holding anything else back from us?" Zero asked sharply. "Maybe about the Meta?"

"Not exactly. I understand what the Meta are doing, but I think when you get to the Progress Station, you'll see for yourself. If I try to tell you, it would be confusing."

"Try."

"Wait till the morning. If you don't understand after you use the thing in the Progress Station, I will try to explain. But I will be honest with you and tell you everything about myself. For example: I am not only alien to you, I am what you call a Twist."

Hearing this, Zero and Angie tensed and looked at one another. Zero looked around for a pike.

Jack shook his head. "You misunderstand. I am not dangerous to you. Not all Twists become . . . Twisted. I am simply more of what I was before. Mine is an intuitive race. I am, just as I told you, in deep communion with this world, with its Overmind. The Overmind is not a thinking being, like you and I; it cannot articulate words or even ideas. But still it is a mind, and still it communicates. I read in the Overmind that you, Zero, bear the fullest potential to conceivably take the Meta's game—if you choose to think of it as a game—into the next phase. I wanted to accelerate the coming of that phase. It will improve things. It will leave Fiskle broken. Or it will end our suffering with death."

"But—was there a human Jack once?" Angie asked.

"Yes. He stumbled into my Hollow of Meditation in the wilderness. He was dying. He laid his head in my lap, thinking me an angel, he said, and I had no heart to contradict him. As he died, his mind unraveled and I watched it decay, and I remembered all that was released in its decay. Hence I speak your language, know your ways. Hence I wrapped myself in some part of Jack's personality."

"Do you have a name?" Zero asked.

"A description, used as a name. It translates to something like 'A Zany, Self-Indulgent Overflight.' But the translation is too inexact. I think you should call me Jack."

Calum, who had been lying unconscious nearby, awoke just then, the light flicked on in the dark strip of his ocular organ. He made a miserable chirring sound in his throat as he sat up. "I am . . . not feeling [approximate translation:] at the top of my form. But I seem . . . intact."

"You are all right," Jack said. "But Yoshio is comatose. His outcome is unforeseeable."

"Where is the beast?" Calum asked.

"It is gone, dead," Jack said. "You call it a beast. You don't regard it as a spirit incarnate, as Zickorian would?"

"I suppose it had spirit in it. But Zickorian was very old-fashioned. Don't tell anyone, but I am a neo-materialist."

"The young always react in excess," Jack said. "Well, we had better go to the Progress Station. It will be dawn soon. There is nothing to keep us from claiming the prize now—unless someone beats us to it."

"We'd better explain about you to Calum," Zero said, looking squarely at Jack. "There should be no more deception."

"Of course. When we return. I urge that we hurry. The new phase and the object in the Progress Station are one and the same, Zero. And the new phase is overdue."

"Am I here?" Swanee asked.

"Yes," the Emperor said, "you are. Don't you feel like you're here? Touch yourself."

"I feel . . . strange but . . . it feels real. I was dreaming, though. This must be part of the dream."

— 310 —

"Does it feel like a dream?"

"I *couldn't* be here! I was in the nest!"

Harmony shrugged imperiously. "I brought you with a snap of my fingers. I can do anything."

"You'd like me to believe that. But I don't think I do."

They were strolling in a small courtyard behind the palace. The time, Swanee supposed, was somewhere deep in the night, a time too deep to see clearly.

A Phylum Two lumbered along behind them, carrying a torch. An air-shark circled them sleepily.

Harmony had had the paving ripped up here, and the dirt churned into the beginnings of a garden. Rows of exotic plants had been transplanted from the gulley. Haggard human artisans were working by torchlight to glue bones and teeth and hanks of hair and bits of shell to the garden walls, making baroque mosaics in accordance with the Emperor's sketches.

"Here are two people you might remember, Swanee," Harmony said. They'd come to a line of five humps, like graves without tombstones. From each sprouted a cluster of translucent tendrils, as fine as fishing line. Some of the tendrils groped through the air blindly, seeking here and there with the tiny filament tufts at their ends. One of the tendrils had found a home in the back of Jamie's neck. She was wearing rags, was squatting on the hump, patting dirt over something Swanee couldn't quite make out. Her face was empty of expression except for a certain intentness.

"These are the Phix," Harmony said proudly. "They'll be the centerpiece of my garden. They're really a prize. The bulk of their bodies are underground. They're related to the charming creatures that eliminated the little cockney fellow—ah, Dennis, I think his name was. The Phix send out these seeking spines, which, before you know it, latch onto you and sink their filaments into your brain from the little hole at the base of the skull and take control. Make an obedient little robot of you. To prevent any struggle before they take complete control, they inject their hosts with an enzyme that finds its way into the victim's pleasure center and stimulates it. Seems to work for most animals. People writhe in ecstasy when the Phix first makes contact. In fact, if you try to release the victim, the victim will fight you tooth and nail.

"Once the filaments are deeply into the brain, the pleasure stops and the work begins. They send the victims out to gather food, so the Phix can be nourished through them; the victim—or host, if you prefer—maintains the ground around the buried body of the Phix, chases away anything that threatens it. It's marvelous! A classic reward-conditioning system that evolves into a control system. A blueprint for the ideal monarchy, Swanee. I've made quite a study of it, as you can tell."

"You said that there were two people here. I see only one."

"Jamie is burying the pieces of the other one for later use as food. That one will nourish the Phix. I'm sure she'll be quite a delicacy."

Swanee glimpsed a swatch of blond hair in the dirt under Jamie's knee. Stomach lurching, he turned away.

"I wouldn't advise you to turn your back on these creatures. We really shouldn't be standing so close, in fact," Harmony said. They moved away. Swanee thought he'd like to snatch up a chisel that one of the craftsmen was using and drive it through Harmony's skull.

"I didn't quite get the details of that," Harmony said, "but I grasped that you were thinking of killing me. Don't try. You can't, since—well, it's quite hopeless. Trust me."

"Trust you? I assume you've brought me here to give me to your Phix. I notice there are several without hosts."

"You? No. There are others who'll grace my garden. Our friend Sanchez, for example. I am prepared to forgive all, Swanee, to welcome you home with open arms, if you'll tell me where he is. Precisely, I mean. We have only the vaguest idea as to where this nest is that he's sleeping in."

"Only the vaguest idea? Then how did you bring me here? You must know where it is if you brought me here from there."

"Actually, we don't. We, ah, had the coordinates and lost them after we brought you over." The Emperor's voice was colored by irritation. He was too pompous to be a good liar.

Swanee turned to look at him. "I thought I felt strange. Kind of heavy, uncoordinated. I'm asleep, back at the nest. This isn't my body at all, is it? This must be the shape-changer, shifted to resemble me, acting as a sort of container for me. Yes." Swanee could sense the shape-changer now. It was a presence squirming like a tormented amoeba, away off in the darkness somewhere. "Yes, there he is. I wonder if I and the Phix and the changer can coexist."

"Don't!"

But Swanee turned and threw himself onto the grave beside Jamie, trying to yank the tendrils out of her, to give himself to it. Then he felt a sting at the back of his neck, heard a hum of high-tension wires in high winds, tasted dirt. He knew another one of them had got him . . . felt his limbs go numb.

A cold, vindictive, hungry presence was all around him. The Phix.

And then he was standing over himself. Over the shape-changer, which was wriggling out of the Swanee shape and into a series of halfway shapes, expressing uncertainty and desperation—and then ecstasy.

Swanee looked down at himself and saw nothing. He heard Harmony whining at the top of his lungs in infantile fury.

And then a black wind picked him up and flung him into the stars . . . The stars spat him out onto the nest.

He sat bolt upright and stared at Sanchez, who was still snoring a few feet away.

Swanee looked down—and saw himself. He shuddered, and lay back, determined not to sleep again that night. The tree creaked and swayed a little in the breeze.

He needed something to keep sleep at bay. So he thought about Bella, and the pain of it kept him awake.

The faint green light of predawn slowly drew away the veils of shadow, as Zero, Jack, and the Pezz toiled across the hummocks of mud between the ponds. Angie had remained behind with Yoshio and Calum. The Progress Station was a short journey from their camp and, now that the Punkin' was dead, an uneventful one. But on another level, things happened around them; the miniature world of the local ecology was rearranging itself, shifting from its nocturnal web of relationships to its diurnal configuration. From a nearby mudbank something slipped heavily into the water and cruised with dark grace just under the surface, leaving elliptical ripples. Other things were waking; a thing of rhinestone scales said *Skrank! Skrank!* as it flapped from bush to bush; ten-fingered hands sucked themselves into their stems; something else unfurled from a tube hanging over the pond, like the tongue of a yawning dog. Insects rattled and hummed. A concealed animal slurped loudly.

The place smelled wet; of cheerful decay, and morbid life.

The dawn took a deep breath, and another degree of blindness seeped out of the sky. Up ahead a chain of ponds fed streams that pooled into a broad lake. It was shallow, and its surface, between the black outlines of corpses, quivered with reflected silver and green. On the little, almost barren island in the center of the lake, about fifty yards from the bank, was the white hump of something artificial.

"That's it," Jack said, when they'd reached the bank. "The Progress Station."

Between them and the mud island, bodies littered the lake as if the morning had overlooked them. They bobbed slightly in slow, vague vortices. A few might have been human. One appeared to be a Phylum Two. There was the deflated, torn shape of a Vinyl, and a much-decayed Pezz. Seeing this, the expedition's own Pezz muttered to itself. "We are all food-scraps for the microscopic."

"The lake is shallow," Jack said. "We can simply walk across."

"You're certain nothing else guards the station, Jack?" Zero asked.

"We have a saying on my world," Jack said. " 'Nothing is certain in life.' "

"We have the same saying," Zero said.

"So do we," The Pezz said. "It is one truth everyone agrees on."

Zero sighed. "Let's do it."

He stepped into the water, and sloshed toward the island. Jack picked the Pezz up in his arms and followed.

The water was warm; it soaked through Zero's pants, and lapped at his thighs. Mud sucked at his shoes. The smells of lake life and carrion curled around him.

The body of a chitonous alien with a head like an overlarge hermit crab spun slowly past, trailing a stink that nearly turned his stomach inside out. A creature of tawny fur and limp tentacles drifted by; a huge wound in its side was a home for a squirming puddle of alien shrimp. A human skull, still attached to a purple, bloated corpse, looked like a yellow fishing float in the water. The water around the corpse swirled with the sick iridescence of a petroleum slick as the body's fats exuded decay.

Gagging, Zero sloshed faster, harder, till at last he reached the island's shore. He fell to his knees in the yielding mud, drinking in the fresher air. The Progress Station was but a hundred feet away. Its entrance gaped wide, waiting for him.

There were no McMahons in the Progress Station. There was only the glossy black-plastic box, sitting in the center of the blue concrete floor. Zero walked around it and saw that on the far side a miniature translation unit was affixed to the center of that face of the box. On impulse, he knelt beside the translator, and said, "What do I do now?"

A falsely sweet, artificial voice spoke from the translator; the voice the McMahons had used. "Pick up the box and press it to your forehead."

Zero glanced up at Jack. "Now that," Zero said, "sounds risky."

"After all you've come through, it's too risky?" Jack asked him in a tone of disbelief.

"You have a point." But Zero only stared at the box. He chewed the inside of his lip. He looked up at Jack. The dawn light framed him in the doorway, and for a moment he looked like a Russian saint. "What's in it for you, Jack? I mean, why not take the thing for yourself? You expect me to believe you did all this for us just because you want to bring on the millennium or something?"

"You're stalling," Jack said. "But all right. I'm doing it for a selfish reason. Partly. The selfish reason being my own comfort. As long as Fiskle influences the Overmind, the IAMton fields, the intelligent life on this world—as long as there is false conflict, I'm in pain. It's a pain that's induced psychically. It's my empathic nature. I'll be healed in the next phase. Or, as I said, I'll be dead."

"You're suffering all the time?"

"Not always. But often. Yes. Are you finished stalling?"

Zero smiled crookedly. "Yeah." He lifted the box in his hands. It weighed about ten pounds. He pressed the nearest side to his forehead. He closed his eyes.

The box moved against him.

He jumped back, startled. It fell to the floor and didn't break. It had altered its shape, become a sort of double mask. The comedy-tragedy mask. He saw nothing inside it. It didn't look like a device. It looked like a mask and only a mask.

"Proceed to a center of IAMton activity," the sweet voice said. "Take me with you."

"Oh, man," Zero said, picking up the mask, "I got this bad feeling. . . ."

But walking beside Jack and the Pezz, and carrying the mask, Zero waded through the lake and followed a trail between bog-ponds back toward the IAMton wastes.

The light of day was still in its infancy, little more than dawn. it silvered the blue mists rising from the ponds, and when something many-legged and glossy black rippled the surface, it painted the widening circles of ripples with white-gold.

As they walked, Jack talked softly, coaching him. "The IAMton wastes are like a battery or, again, like a computer memory for the planetary Overmind. The Overmind stores things: energies and idea-structures. The Overmind automatically—but not maliciously—tries to coopt everyone into itself. As it did with Zickorian. As it does in a different way with the Twists.

"With Fiskle's Twists and the Murderers, the Overmind has released the dark aspects of their personalities, making them over according to their perverse obsessions, because that way they lose their free will. They think it's the opposite, of course, but once you're doing something compulsively, you've lost control of yourself. And then the Overmind has absorbed you, though you may continue to walk about the world as if you were free. What you have become is a living principle, a walking urge, a plaything of the Overmind, and nothing more. Except, perhaps, very dangerous, like a tornado. A tornado is simply a part of the weather system, but it moves about as if it's independent and is very dangerous indeed.

"The Overmind tries to keep us all in stasis and controlled and absorbable—but not out of any conscious purpose. Not because it chooses to. It does it because it's in its nature, just as it's in the nature of air to rush in and fill a vacuum.

"All intelligent beings face the same dilemma, Zero. How to communicate with the world, how to have a relationship with it without losing themselves to it—without losing their free will. Both things are important. To resonate with the universe; to maintain a personal perspective, an identity, a will. That is how you should approach this thing. You will have to do several things at once. You will have to commune with the Overmind through the IAMton-ambient field, and at the same time you will have to retain your free will, your individuality, without letting it exaggerate your obsessive side, without letting it trick you in that way or any other way. And the way you'll do that is with self-expression. With art. It's no accident that so many of those brought here are artists, Zero."

"Look," Zero broke in as they reached the verge of the violet-flickering white expanse of the IAMton wastes, "what does this thing *do*?" He tapped the box in his hands with a thumb. "I mean, how is this thing going to help the settlement?"

"It has a lot of potential, Zero. One thing it does, if I understood the Meta properly—"

"When did you talk to the Meta?" Zero demanded.

"The pyramid-thing that floated to me in the forest. It was a sort of signal beacon for them. They sensed I was . . . unusual. They enlisted my help."

"You *are* working for them!"

"Yes and no. Zero, if you want to understand, use the Progress gift. Use it. With it, you can communicate with the Meta. You'll understand how when you put it on. It'll come naturally."

Zero swallowed. His throat was charred with fear. He looked over his shoulder at the camp, a few hundred yards behind and to the left. He saw Angie and the Pezz watching.

With Angie watching, what else could he do?

He put on the mask. The comedy side was on the left half of his face; the tragedy on the right. He stepped out into bright shimmer of the IAMton wastes. Almost immediately he felt the psychedelic charge of the place. The electricity of it lighting up his bones, crackling between his teeth. His senses expanding . . .

The world. The world! It came to him on a tsunami of input, and he fell to his knees with the impact, a twig swept away in the Biblical flood. The vast matrix of it towered over him and threatened him with his own insignificance. He was nothing. He had to be something to survive this. What?

He looked for something strong and coherent in himself.

He glimpsed it: a star, a larger-than-life media figure of perfect features, ready wit, bristling awards, overarching charisma; a magnet for women, and an influence; a power, a power, a . . . a Twist.

"Not falling for it," Zero said aloud. "Got to be another way." But it had to be quickly. He could feel himself dissolving. He was a speck becoming a microdot becoming a microorganism blown away on the wind. *You're born, you blink, you're gone, pal. Gone. What's the point? It's a pinpoint. Now you see it, now you don't. Because it's nothing. You're nothing.*

Desperately, he reached out for something, past the Twist version of himself. There must be something else.

His expanded senses told him that *they* were there watching, somewhere overhead. The Meta.

Anger boiled up in him. He remembered Dennis. Cisco. Zickorian. Now Yoshio. Yoshio the wistful, the dutifully centered, the intellectually elegant. Dying.

Himself and Angie ripped from their own lives and pasted like collage figures onto Fool's Hope.

Tell it, man. Get off your knees and tell it.

He stood up. *Sing it.*

The first time Zero saw a movie was like the first time a sculptor saw clay, the first time a painter saw a color wheel. He recognized his medium as innately as a newborn turtle knows to crawl into the sea.

Now he recognized it again in another kind of theater, with another dimension added. But it was the same medium. He could feel it crackling at his fingertips. He raised those fingertips and reassigned the energies there, to the sands.

The Meta were watching. They were an audience. And he had something to tell them. Tell them about the anger, man. *Tell it.*

Obediently, the crust of the IAMton wastes rose up; their sands surged and rearranged and conformed to his vision. The IAMton desert was his canvas, and on it he created a moving painting, a three-dimensional film. It rose up from the colorless sands in colors given to it by his will; it rose up, holographically but touchable and on a gigantic scale, so it could be seen from a long way away, from above. In his mind's eye, he saw it from above. From the sky. As the Meta would see it.

Men on Earth. Huddled in the rain, under overhanging branches, stinking and crusted with sores, and shivering.

Men huddled in a hut, suffering from sickness.

Women protecting their children as other men entered and began raping and butchering. Protecting the children was no use.

Men enslaved by other men, building monuments. Pyramids rising; their stones cemented together with blood. With pain.

A city choked with the dead; the faces of the dead mottled with blisters, and bloated purple-black. The Black Plague, eating Western civilization alive.

Another civilization murdered by a plague of men from the East. The Aztecs, the Maya, their temples thrown down and their children slaughtered. The American Indian, massacred and massacring.

Four hundred thousand men murdering one another on a European battlefield in World War One, all in a few days—and not twenty feet of ground was gained by either side. Four hundred thousand men wasted.

Children herded into a gas chamber in Auschwitz, into a trench in Poland. Gas, machine guns.

A thousand faces dying of a thousand diseases. Their prolonged suffering.

A child playing in Hiroshima. The child looks up. . . .

Once Zero saw a videotape made in El Salvador. The face of a dying woman. Now he reproduced her face gigantically, a mile across, in the IAMton wastes, suffering with disbelief, the betrayal of it. While around her the events that had brought her to this were replayed. She was eight months pregnant, walking through a plantain field, when the soldiers came. American advisers had informed the soldiers that there were antigovernment guerrillas hiding in the woman's village. The woman had never met one of the guerrillas—not knowingly—and no one in the village had joined the uprising. But the soldiers had their information from the CIA, so it was not to be doubted. Everyone in the village, they were told, was a collaborator.

This was good news to the soldiers. This meant they could do anything they wanted to the people of the village and no one would arrest them for it. The first person they came upon was the woman, carrying her basket of plantains. They knocked her down with a gun butt, and then two of them held her while three others had her. Their CO told them to stop wasting time. Leave her as a message to the ones who escape, he said. So they stuck the bayonet in her swollen belly and opened it like a ripe fruit, exposing the baby, which shrieked when they skewered it and took a while dying itself, lying across her lap, still attached to her by the umbilicus.

The soldiers went on their way, closing in on the village. Half an hour later a group of Italian journalists arrived on the scene and found the woman and filmed her, going in for a close up of her disbelieving face, the camera's cool objectivity nonchalantly framing the unspeakable magnitude of her suffering.

Zero coalesced the segments of the image so that the image of the woman's living, real-time, dying face grew and filled his canvas. Close up.

"Look at that!" he told the Meta. He knew, intuited, that they could hear him through the Progress Station device. "Look! You put us here on this world, Meta! You pitted us against one another, indifferent to the suffering you caused except, I guess, for its scientific interest. Or whatever you're getting out of it. *But look again.*"

And then he made the image a part of a vast single-frame cinematographic composition, one constructed of ten million million grains of sand, sands in which every pigment existed, if you looked at them individually—and the image depicted the tapestry of suffering on Fool's Hope. Suffering both human and alien. In its individual parts, the image showed the suffering on Fool's Hope. But as a whole, it coalesced to recreate the face of the dying Salvadoran woman.

"You're alien to us. But you've studied us. You know what suffering is. You know."

He sustained the image as long as he could. It was too big to hold. The strain exacted its price.

Zero collapsed.

Just before he fell, as consciousness fluttered away like a startled bird, he saw the silver spheres, the Meta's watchers, forming patterns on the sky.

FOURTEEN

"Zero, you okay?"

"Mm. Yeah."

"Good," Angie said, "because there's something coming down. In both senses of that phrase. You better see this."

Zero opened his eyes. He saw Angie's face upside down. He was lying with his head on her lap. He sat up, expecting some sort of hangover pain—and felt only normal. Beside him was the tragedy-comedy mask.

They were at the camp. To one side were smoke trees. Above them was a spaceship.

"Anyway," he murmured, "I *assume* it's a spaceship."

It was about five hundred feet up, hovering over the IAMton wastes beyond the trees. It was enormous— two football fields of it—and hemispherical. It looked olive green one moment, rosy tinged the next. It was smooth, featureless all over.

Except for a little nubbin on the bottom, which

grew and became a pyramid. Relative to the ship it was a small pyramid, growing out of it and separating like a drop of water from ice, dropping from the underside to hover in the air, apex upward. It was mercuric and yet perfectly pyramidal, slowly rotating as it drew near, floating down toward the expedition.

The pyramid paused just in front and about thirty feet above them. It was ten feet high, seven to a side at the base. It rotated very slowly. At the apex of the pyramid, was an eye. It was more or less of the human sort, but its color was that of the spaceship: mercurial, uncertain. The eye seemed to float in front of the pyramid, in some way connected to it but not part of it physically. Like Jack's head with his shoulders, Zero thought.

From somewhere inside the pyramid came the sound of a translator box. It said, "Why didn't you say so before?"

Swanee had to concentrate on each sweep of his wings, one at a time. Mentally, he maintained a drumbeat to pace each stroke. Otherwise the pain made him falter.

The harness, with Sanchez dangling in it, creaked and swayed. By minute degrees, but steadily, the pain grew.

They were flying through the sunlight, not far over the cloud of dust that choked the plain.

"I'm glad we're skipping *that*," Sanchez said, looking down.

You may be walking through it on the way back, Swanee thought. But said nothing aloud.

Beneath him, Sanchez swore. Swanee glanced down and saw that a little blood had dripped onto Sanchez's cheek. It had dripped from the shallow groove the harness straps had cut into Swanee's shoulders, sawed by the constant motion of his wings.

Sanchez said, "For God's sake, Swanee, put me down! Let's treat that wound! We could pad it or something."

"No . . . time . . . ," Swanee croaked. "I can feel it. No time. Harmony wants to . . . start a war. With aliens. Every minute brings it closer."

"There's no guarantee the thing in the Progress Station will help."

"I sensed . . . something . . . from Fiskle. He's going to try to get it for himself. Before us. Thing in the Station is something important. Unusual."

"Look, man, you're killing yourself!"

To change the subject and to ease a certain emotional pressure, Swanee said, "Sanchez, what if you thought that you were evil . . . You . . . hated yourself for it . . . but . . . you fell in love with someone, and that made you feel like you . . . like you weren't so bad . . . but when you made love with her, she tried to . . . tried to kill you . . . How . . . would you feel?"

"Lord," Sanchez said. His voice was almost drowned by the wind. "I don't know."

Up ahead, the plain ended in hills that became a ridge. Beyond the ridge, just visible at the horizon, was the edge of a great forest.

"Yes, we knew you were suffering," the Meta said. "But suffering is the natural state of living creatures. We merely transplanted your suffering from one planet to another and gave it a different character. You have spoken to us in a higher language, in the poetry of vision, and we are compelled to respond. But we have no regrets."

"But why did you do it at all?" Zero asked. He was standing up now, gazing up at the thing, arms rigid at his side, fists balled. Angie and the others were huddled in a group nearby. "Why did you bring us here from Earth?"

"Why? Because we are like all evolved creatures, in search of spiritual exaltation. This we achieve through artistic creation.

"Every creature that lives is a part of the universe. Subatomically, all things merge into one in the great sea of energy, of which matter is only a particular series of wavelengths. And yet units of this greater body perceive. A creature perceives; therefore the universe, of which it is a part, perceives through it. God manifests Its perception in individual creatures in order to experience Its various parts from a subjective viewpoint. God, the Great Narcissist, is always looking out through our eyes or whatever perceptual organs we use; God is detached from our consciousness but sees through it like a cinematographer looking through a camera. This you should be well suited to understand, Zero.

"If a creature has perceived, then no matter how base the creature, God has perceived through it. God does not control the universe, as you would understand the concept of control, but It stages events in the universe in Its own way. Scientists of your own world have begun to see—in studying turbulence, in what they call Chaos Theory, and 'self-propagating reactions'—that structure spontaneously develops in any excitable matter/energy medium, as a response to the *intrinsic* nature of things. Things don't evolve purely by accident—although accident is part of the formula. They are programmed to evolve, atomically. In this way, and with other subtle influences, God stages dramas on the great stage of Its body, the universe, so as to investigate Itself. This is simply Its nature.

"To be in harmony with God, we aspire to Godlike artistry. We offer up this artistry to God. It is our form of prayer. It is the medium through which we speak to God and aspire to merge with God's divinity. We exist only to take part in God's art—and to create art of our own. All that remains aside from this is the process of reproduction and survival. Which is to say, tedium. The small rewards, the pleasures of mundane life, without art, are ultimately not enough to justify the difficulties of living. Not for a highly evolved being.

"Living only makes sense when it is framed by art, Zero, or composed into art. Interpreted by art. Art elevates perception above the perpetual struggle against entropy—because in the instant the viewer has perceived the art, God has perceived it, and recorded it in Itself, and added it to Its store of order-paradigms. Do you understand?"

"I think so," Zero said, amazed at the gall of it. "You're telling me that you kidnapped us because you're pious. To me, that's absurd. But I know what you mean about art redefining life. I've thought about that sort of thing looking at Picasso's *Guernica*, some stuff by Goya, Munch. They painted war, suffering, depression, but, uh, in the context of the composition the suffering becomes a thing of beauty."

"Yes. The beauty is achieved through a perfect balance between empathy and objectivity; between insight and unaffected appraisal. If we allowed ourselves to become empathic to your suffering—beyond what is needed to appreciate the fullness of our imagery—we would lose that balance and lose the insight."

"And all of us on Fool's Hope are part of your staged

drama? You're staging a drama using real-life players who don't know they're playing in a drama? Are you manipulating things in some way? Controlling the outcomes?"

"No. Except in our arrangement of the borderlines, the various limitations we impose, and in our choices of the various personality chemistries, cultural chemistries, and other elements to be included. And in the selective introduction of IAMton currents. We know that putting *A* together with *B* will elicit certain probable reactions; we can predict to some extent the direction of the drama. Not the details but the overall pattern. And when we are surprised, it is all to the good."

"You simply drop the players onto the stage and let them go at it?"

"Largely, yes. Setting elements are controlled. The environment, access to tools and shelter, Progress Station motivational factors. But randomness is the choicest element, introducing just the right degree of chaos: a splendid chaos, to quote one of your people, that elevates the drama to the cosmic because it adds in a collaboration with the universe's own principles of mathematical completeness."

"And the interspecies conflict, I suppose, gives you good, sharp, well-defined imagery."

"Your instincts are sound."

"And the watching balls—they record the art, then you guys edit it?"

"Yes. And transmit the results to our people. So that God can watch it through them."

"God watches anyway. Why make drama for God if God is already enjoying our dramas from, um, inside us?"

"It is like building a temple to celebrate God. It is a way of communicating with God. It is prayer without petition. Finally, we do it because it is the task we were created for, and to do otherwise would be to refute our creator."

"Yeah. Right. Do your people live, uh, somewhere on this planet? Or in the moon?"

"This is not our world. The moon of this world is our outpost. Our directorial vantage. This world is our canvas or, if you like, our set."

"So why talk to me now?"

"You have demonstrated a high order of artistic composition in your manipulation of IAMton energies to create images. It is an unusually high order for so low a creature, for IAMton mastery is difficult, it is a demanding medium. You were the best qualified to achieve this mastery, and we encouraged you, as it is time for the composition to come to its denouement."

"You say I'm a low creature. I am not low enough, Meta, to steal *you* from *your* world, even if I had a way to do it, nor low enough to throw you in the midst of hostile aliens."

"You are not high enough to do that."

Exasperated, Zero blurted, "Look, why does the 'drama' have to be so melodramatic, full of killing and— big splashy events? How about a nice little nonviolent drawing-room comedy, say? You know, something with some subtlety?"

"Our audience prefers a big canvas. Small, subtle events are not easily perceived on it. Furthermore, we are of the Historical Galvanization school of four-dimensional drama creation."

"Your audience prefers! Are you telling me it's a matter of *ratings*?"

"No. But rapport with the audience is an important element of the process of worshipping God through drama creation."

"Maybe orginally. I'm beginning to wonder if you haven't lost sight of your original motivations."

"Permit us to maintain our own aesthetic imperatives."

Inwardly, Zero fumed. But he sensed the futility of further argument. He and the Meta would have to agree to disagree on some points.

"Bring the composition to its fruition," the Meta said, "and your people will be allowed to triumph over this world and all competitors. World is world, Zero. You represent the empathic principle of your species' consciousness. That's why you're a filmmaker; the non-empathic, self-oriented principle is represented by the one called Fiskle, the Emperor Harmony. Resolve this conflict by bringing it to consummation. And then we'll talk."

The Meta began to move, angling down and to Zero's left. It lowered itself over Yoshio. The expedition stood, paralyzed by indecision, as the Meta seemed to bathe Yoshio in the essence of itself, for a few moments saturating him in its interior. Then, leaving Yoshio behind, it lifted away and in seconds was merging once more with the starship, which itself merged with the heavens.

Yoshio yawned and sat up, looking spritely and refreshed. "Is the Punkin' gone?"

"Why did they help Yoshio?" Angie wondered aloud.

Zero shrugged. "Can't say. Seems out of character, since they let so many others die. I guess the Meta were right there, and their 'empathic principle' got out of hand. They acted on impulse. Nice to know they have those kinds of impulses."

"Mostly they seem to be careful not to have them."

"Yeah." It was sunset, a bloodred sunset that seemed to give energy to the violet glimmers in the white expanse of IAMton desert. They were strolling along the edge of the desert, the swamp on their left an oasis; the wastes to their right. A few towers rose and fell out on the white crust in a desultory way.

"I wonder if just anybody could put on that mask-thing," she said, "and make something like what you made out there."

"Probably." But he didn't believe it. He was hoping she wouldn't try. It was dangerous. He'd almost blown it himself.

She stopped and looked at him. "You really did it, though. You contacted the Meta. I don't care what my mom thinks: I'm proud of you."

He smiled. "I haven't said anything about it, but I haven't forgotten: you saved my life, Angie, on those hills. You stepped in and stopped the Vinyls from killing me. Thanks. A lot of people—even people in love—would have panicked and run. You were brave, you were fast, and you were smart."

She seemed to bloom, hearing that. "I was, wasn't I?"

"You know what I want to see? I want to see you dance."

"What, you mean like a belly dancer in a skimpy costume? Sexist." But she was joking. Her insecurity was gone.

"I love you," he said, and kissed her. The IAMton field tingled around them, between them, made the kiss into an electric event. Things began to come together in his mind, organizing as order spontaneously arises from chaos, like self-propagating reactions. A surge of good feelings rose up in him. Triumph, love for Angie —and something more. A sense of being *home*.

Suddenly he was brimming with things to tell her. " 'World is world,' they said. Yoshio said something like that once. Angie, when I was out there, I felt the whole world moving around me. It made me feel small, threatened. But at the same time I got a hint from it, a sense of its identity. As if the Overmind told me its name."

"What *is* the Overmind?"

"The planetary matrix, Jack told me. The gestalt awareness of a biosphere. The Gaea of a world. Here it's more defined than on Earth because of the IAMton concentration. I saw it in my mind's eye. I saw ten million million little animals procreating and"—he struggled for words—"and growing and feeding on each other and just being part of the process. Plants and animals, struggling, competing, in conflict but at the same time part of this big system. And it was alien, but, Angie, I *recognized* it. From Earth. We *can* relate to this world. We *can* be part of it. Because two symphonies might be in different keys, with different, um, different styles, at different times but *they're both played by the same orchestra*."

She looked at him, and he looked back, and together they were a matrix, a gestalt, a Gaea, a world, and they fell to the ground together and began procreating, ecstatic in the release of recognition, making love on the breast of their home. The IAMton field reacted by creating spontaneous structures in the desert beside them, miniature temples growing out of the white crust, thrown up instantaneously by the completeness of their sexual union, rising and falling with the surge of their mutual pleasure.

Later, Zero and Angie sat by the ghost trees, feeling pleasantly drained and thinking vaguely about what to do next. The Pezz and Calum returned. Calum was carrying the IAMton device Zero had found in the Progress Station. It was shaped like a winged helmet now. Calum set it at Zero's feet, and it became, once more, a glossy black box. "I tried," Calum said, "but the thing nearly took my mind away. I cannot use it. The Pezz does not wish to try. We give it into your keeping, with the understanding that our people will share equally in any benefits that derive from this find."

"Okay. I hope your people trust me as much as you do."

"They will have no choice," the Pezz said. "It is clear that the thing is intended for you And you have spoken with the Meta—you are their chosen."

"Not sure I want to be," Zero said. But he picked up the box and pressed it to his forehead, and once more it was the tragedy-comedy mask, all of glossy black.

At dawn, as the expedition prepared to set off for the south, they spotted Swanee and Sanchez approaching over the desert. Amazed, they stared at the incongruous figures, thinking that Fiskle had sent Swanee to stop them, to steal the Station's gift.

Zero hefted a pike.

"That's no longer your weapon," Jack said.

Zero dropped the pike and picked up the glossy black tragedy-comedy mask.

But then Jack said, "That's Sanchez, I *think*. He's not one of Fiskle's cronies."

"But the batwing guy," Angie protested.

"I sense no hostility in the Twist," Jack said. "Pain, disappointment, self-disgust. But no hostility. No Fiskle influence. His name is Swanee." After a moment he added, "But there's a Murderer coming." He pointed to the sky above and behind Swanee. "There."

Zero saw it then. A second flying thing. It looked as if it were gliding more than flying. Every so often it pumped itself like an octopus, jetting up for a little more elevation. Then a long glide . . .

"Never saw it before," Angie said.

"It is a stranger to me, too," Calum said.

"Its name is Vanderman," Jack said, staring at the distant silhouette, frowning. "No—that was its old name, before the Twist. I pick up . . . Sizzle. The Emperor calls it Sizzle."

"The other one looks weak," the Pezz said.

Swanee's wing-strokes were uneven, shaky. "He's exhausted. Dangerously," Jack said.

They were close enough now that their faces could just be made out. The exaggerated expression of idiotic glee on Sizzle's face made Zero's stomach turn.

Suddenly Sizzle angled down toward Swanee, diving to intercept him. "He's going to kill him!" Jack said suddenly. "He'll burn him with acids!"

Swanee braked with his wings, backpedaling, and Sizzle overshot him.

Sizzle came about and pumped up his elevation, prepared for another dive. They were lower now, only a hundred feet over the desert. "He'll get him this time," Yoshio said. "Swanee's too weak, he's barely maintaining up there."

Zero ran, fitting the mask over his head as he went. He skidded out onto the IAMton wastes and told it what to do.

The sands of the IAMton desert boiled up and solidified into a structure that rose, rose, branched out, and enclosed Sizzle in midair. He was trapped, fluttering angrily, caught in a cage of solidified sand, visible through the bars Zero had constructed. Sizzle latched on to one of the bars, wrapping himself around it. The bars began to smoke as he commenced burning his way through.

Zero said, "Forget it." He visualized, and the sand structure responded. It closed around Sizzle, clenching, shutting like a mousetrap, crushing and dragging him down, burying him alive in the desert sands. A hump of sand shook for a few moments and then lay still.

Swanee came toward them like a plane with its engine out, losing altitude rapidly, his wings sagging, dipping. He angled for the nearest bog-pond. Sanchez had to yank his feet up to keep from losing them in the little coral trees. They hit the pond with a double splash.

The expedition waded out to get them, but Sanchez was already free of the harness when they got there, carrying Swanee in his arms. Swanee was limp. His wings trailed in the water.

"He's dead," Sanchez said, his voice thick with grief. "He wouldn't put me down. I tried to talk him into letting me walk, but he wouldn't. His heart just gave out. I guess it's what he wanted."

Bowler shook his head and growled. "No! No! He doesn't know everything. He isn't all-powerful. If he were, he would have busted us by now. We've had four meetings. Harmony won't tolerate dissent. He doesn't know about us."

There were six of them in the cell, crowded into a corner of the tanner's workshed. The hides of oruh and slug-lizards hung from pegs at Bowler's back. The place reeked, but you got used to it after a few minutes. They used it because the smell discouraged the guard from coming in.

Bowler lit a third candle to give them a little more light. The gloom was disheartening.

"It's not just the risk of it," Brindle said. He was young, thin, with a wispy red beard. Had been a sculptor on Earth. "It's the—the futility. Everyone is scared, really scared, of Harmony. He's got them all jumping when he snaps his fingers. They saw what happened to Doggo. Trish. They've seen Jamie. They've seen that big thing wandering around that looks like it's made of scrap iron. God, Harmony told it to kill someone who was looking at him funny, and it sucked the guy into itself like a human garbage disposal, grinding him up. And that Sizzle thing and those vamps and—"

"Don't forget the Pricks," Carmody said, meaning the Phylum Twos. "That's his real power."

Brindle added, "And anyway, the guy is telepathic."

"Not with just anybody," Bowler said. "Just with—"

"The point is, people think he's a supernatural power. Some are starting to worship him!" Brindle said.

"I'll bet he sucks that up," Bowler said.

"You bet your ass," Brindle said.

"I *have* bet my ass," Bowler said suddenly, seriously. "I've put my life on the line. I've decided it's better to die fighting this thing than to live with the whims of our own private Caligula. I thought you people had made the same decision."

Brindle looked at the bloodstained floor. His voice broke. "I don't know. I don't know. I think you're right, that this world is our chance for a social system that really works. I think you're right that it's no good living this way. But it's useless. And I'm scared."

Bowler took a deep breath. He decided he had to take the chance that one of them might get caught: he had to tell them. "I got the explosive," Bowler said.

Everyone stared at him. Bowler smiled. "Stole a nice quantity of it. It's just a matter of timing."

The return trip was faster. The Expedition crossed the wastes in minutes, carried in a great cupped hand created by Zero's control over the IAMton deposits. "The atom," Jack explained, "is only a superposition of possibilities, on the quantum mechanics level. And it is on that level that the IAMton works, when it is directed by Mind to reorganize the material world. It applies itself to the collapsing waveform at the root of atomic structure, and asserts the mind's probability of form over the infinite range of possibilities vibrating in the heart of wave-function."

"Whatever," Zero said.

Responding to Zero's new IAMton awareness, the forest carried them all as it had carried Jack, and they passed through it with equal ease. After the forest, they had to walk for awhile—till they reached another IAMton deposit, which Zero accumulated beneath them into a sort of abstract engine. The violet, powdery engine carried them in a chariot of maybes across the plain, till it lost its charge at the edge of the swamplands that lay between them and the Neutral . . .

Two weeks after Swanee brought Sanchez to the Expedition, Zero was one again staring at the gates of the settlement. He was almost unnerved. He lay on his stomach beside Angie, Yoshio, and Calum, atop the ridge that separated the settlement from the Rug, staring down at it. It was an overcast morning; in the dull light the settlement's new embellishments seemed to clutch the shadows to them.

Every visible surface of the fortress and the settlement walls had been covered with an intricate mosaic of bones, teeth, preserved fingers, and other body parts, together with red and black agates. The designs were lush with flourish and self-congratulatory excess. The skeletons of the Groyn killed in the battle had been hoisted to the outer walls, where they were arranged symmetrically, to lean outward like gargoyles. Minarets of wood, eccentrically notched and intaglioed, and fantastic structures with no clear purpose had been erected, making a mad tangle of the skyline. Phylum Two guards stood scratching themselves and leaning on their pikes at the gaudy parapets.

Another Phylum Two, in the early stages of its Twist—only slightly bigger than average human size—came lumbering out the front gate. The expeditioners watched it cross the several hundred yards of open ground between the fortress and the ridge, where they were hidden among the outcroppings. They watched him, unmoving, as he strode directly toward them. His eyes locked on Zero's as he caught sight of him. He came closer, and still none of the expedition moved.

The Phylum Two climbed over the rimrock and slid into the crater behind it, close beside Zero. Jack's voice came out of him. "It hasn't taken him long to put his stamp on it, on every level."

Gradually the Phylum Two exterior began to slough off, and in the gaps thus created a tan foam bubbled up. The alien recreated Jack the Baptist. He went on. "I heard no one bitching about him, but resentment was on a lot of faces. Others seem resigned to him. The ones in the court—the humans he's dressed up like courtiers

—seem to be enjoying themselves. He has a certain charisma. And he encourages their sadistic side. Some people like that. A human and a High Clansman were tortured and murdered while I was there."

Calum made an inarticulate sound of suppressed fury.

Jack went on. "There are more human skins—with the heads attached—nailed up here and there around the settlement, with more 'proclamations' from Harmony written on them. A spaceship dropped off another forty people from Earth a few weeks ago, and apparently some of them were rebellious. A couple of them were added to his garden. Given to the Phix, like Jamie." He told them about the Phix.

Angie's eyes filled. "I can't believe it . . . doing that to Jamie . . . making her . . . "

"We'll get her out," Zero said, squeezing Angie's arm.

"How many Twists are there?" Calum asked.

"I'm not sure. Perhaps only a hundred, or fewer. Fiskle converts humans into Twists at the rate of only one or two a week, I gather. Perhaps it's a great effort for him, or perhaps not everyone is a suitable candidate."

"Today's a Feast Day," Jack went on. He had finished his transformation. He paused to rest a moment. Durng the interval the Pezz arrived, with Sanchez; Sanchez climbed laboriously up from behind, and the Pezz climbed the slope easily, like a mountain goat. It came to stand beside Angie; she patted its back. It wriggled happily, then settled in beside her to listen as Jack went on. "He declares Feast Days every so often. Mostly only the Twists and the Emperor's sycophants are invited to the feast. In fact, the others are on half-rations.

The Earthers outnumber the Twists, but no one rebels because they're scared of the Phylum Twos— and the aliens."

"Why are they frightened of aliens?" the Pezz asked. "They have a truce."

"It's just barely holding. Harmony has made his intentions clear. The alien races are preparing for war with him. Some of the alien races have been raiding humans who step outside the settlement. It could blow up into war any day now. This is all Harmony's fault, but the Earthers are afraid of the aliens now. They see him as protection from them."

"What happens on a Feast Day?" Sanchez asked.

"They feast. They get stoned on wheeler-brain. The Twists have begun eating human flesh: anyone Harmony has designated criminal is publicly tortured or given to one of the creatures in his menagerie—wheelers, slug-lizards, Yellow Vampires, and a couple of alien Twists—Murderers he's caught. One of them is remarkable: the Widow Window, Harmony calls it. It teleports people *into* things."

"Skip the details about that one," Angie said.

"Did you find Bowler?" Zero asked.

Jack smiled. "I did. I have established psychic rapport with him. I believe I can locate him when I need him. He has a plan you should know about."

Zero turned to the Pezz. "Any luck?"

"If I understand you correctly, yes. Events transpired usefully. I have spoken to the Groyn and my own people. They are amenable. Perhaps others will come, too."

Zero nodded. It occurred to him that he had become the leader of their little group, seamlessly and without misgivings. And that their expedition had become something else: a cell of revolutionaries. In a way it was annoying—it was so clearly part of the Meta's drama. But there was no other way to play it. He shrugged and thought, *So be it*.

"What was Bowler's plan, Jack?" he asked.

Bowler was on the verge of telling the others in the cell everything when the Phylum Twos burst into the tanner's workshed and dragged the rebels out into the street. The morning clouds had burned away, it was a sunny noon, and everything was so starkly, bright lit up, it looked unreal. The crowd looked confused. A frightening number of faces in the crowd looked at the rebels with angry satisfaction, glad they were taken; others looked afraid, uncertain.

The crowd was made up of males except for a couple of women past childbearing age; that morning, the Emperor had sent his thugs to arrest all Earther women. They were taken to detention, where they were to be methodically impregnated—by anyone Harmony designated—in order to produce children as efficiently as possible. What is an Emperor without a population to rule over? One of the women had escaped and run to Bowler, and Bowler had called the meeting to decide how best to help her.

They were brought to the Emperor's garden. Jamie —her hair gone white, her face aged ten years—crawled in aimless circles on a Phix hummock. Two others Bowler didn't know were attached to the Phix behind her; dull-eyed puppets. Feverishly overgrown exotic plants curled and towered, the color of bruises and sores. In one palpating, oversize bloom, the shoulders and head of a man were just visible in the folds of blossoms. He was the same mottled purple as the petals, now; it was hard to see him. In the center of the garden a High Clansman, recognizable by his hands, was being turned on a spit over hot coals. His head was gone. On a table was a bowl of wheeler-brain mixed with a fermentation of swamp pods.

Smoke from the barbecue oozed greasily over the various Twists and courtiers in the garden; it assaulted Bowler's gut with the smell of cooked flesh. The courtiers were tarted up with Whorebug tunics of bright cloth that Harmony had awarded his favorites, and with gaudy makeup—paint, really—that made them look like inexpert drag queens. That turned Bowler's stomach, too.

Bella, and the two identical Adonis types, and El Chingadero, and the diaphanous vamps, and the junk-yard beetle-wing man, and the newt, and the dwarf-pig, and the pretty little girl all in white—a gleeful murderess, Bowler had heard—all of them and others, guarded by air-sharks and the overmuscled, naked guards, were gathered around the Emperor, who was sitting on his living throne in the open air.

Bowler and the other members of the cell were hustled up to the Emperor and forced to kneel.

Harmony took a deep breath and sighed, as if enjoying the air. "A backyard barbecue. There's nothing like it to bring a family together," he remarked, sounding perfectly serious. He looked at Bowler. "We knew you were there, but we didn't know quite where. It was your friend the tanner who turned you in. It appears he had an attack of paranoia. He was sure I was reading his mind. Thought he'd wheedle a pardon from me for ratting on you. That's him over there, feeding my blood-orchids. Fed to them, anyway. Want you to meet someone else. Window!"

From behind the Twists, escorted by two Pragmatics who kept it between them bound in thick crude-iron chains, stepped something that looked to Bowler like a giant tortoise, almost eight feet high, six wide. It stood on three legs at the bottom, like a tripod. Its hooded black eyes were motionless and ancient; its beak-mouth opened, and it chattered something in an alien language. Its flat stomach was composed of black plates folded one over another to make a spiral pattern. "He's a Twist of some alien tribe," Harmony said. "Just wait till you see what he can do, Bowler, it's wonderful. It's just lucky he can only do it with organic things, living things that have biofield—otherwise he'd teleport his chains, I suppose," He turned to the Phylum Twos holding the alien. "Let him at them."

The Phylum Twos paid out some slack on the chain, and the Widow Window stepped forward purposefully. It snatched a Hispanic girl, Carmen, in its stubby, scaly hands and thrust her against its middle—which dilated, opening to reveal a crackling black vastness. A window on noplace. Carmen screamed as it shoved her through. She vanished inside.

"Now, let's see where he teleported her to!" the Emperor said. He looked around eagerly. "I do hope it's handy. Ah!" He pointed up at a spot in the sky. The spot grew and became a falling woman, turning end over end. The crowd moved back for her—and she hit the ground just in front of the throne, splashing nicely. Harmony clapped his hands. "Oh, I *am* sorry that Kelso isn't here to enjoy this!" The evil little girl went to the shattered corpse and began to toy with it, singing a childish song without words.

Bowler shouted at the courtiers, "We have brought Hitler from Earth! Caligula, de Sade, General West-

moreland, Lieutenant Calley, the Ayatollah Khomeini!
It's as if we carried syphilis here with us! You don't have
to be part of this disease!"

Harmony laughed, and everyone obediently laughed
along with him. Sixty feet overhead, a trio of the Meta's
watching spheres bobbed in the sky. Bowler gave them
the finger.

Carmody was next: the Widow Window sent him
halfway into the garden wall. He shrieked and convulsed, melded with stone from the waist down; still, it
took him a noisy while to die.

"He'll make a nice decoration," Bella said. "We
could lacquer him."

"Let's do Bowler next," Harmony told the creature
through a translator. "And send him to the sky."

As a small boy, Bowler had seen a Bela Lugosi movie in
which a man was crushed as the walls closed in on him.
The man had been reduced to paste between the slabs
of rock. The young Bowler had tried to imagine what
that would feel like.

The transit through the Widow Window felt like
that. Only the crushing happened faster, in just under
two seconds. Abruptly, the unspeakable pain was gone,
and he was in an infinite vault of green, and he was
weightless. Drifting free, the wind singing in his ears.
And then he saw clouds, and the settlement far below,
its structures like lines on a blueprint from up there, and
he knew he was falling from the sky. He had no air in
his lungs to scream with. No audience to shriek defiance
to. Nowhere to go but inside himself and down.

And then he felt a jarring, a sharp jerk that clacked
his teeth together. The wind stopped whistling. He had
stopped falling. Something was holding him up. He

could feel it invisibly gripping him around the middle. He was moving again, but parallel to the ground, still far above it. Something was carrying him somewhere— probably somewhere that Harmony didn't intend.

His first thought was, *The Meta.*

He was heading out over the Rug . . . and he found himself descending now, into one of the "holes in the Rug" that sometimes gave off light.

As he descended the shaft, neatly down the middle, he saw faces looking up at him, illuminated by a faint glow from beneath. There was a man wearing a shiny black tragedy-comedy mask. With him was Angie. Yoshio. Sanchez. Also a Pezz, a Whorebug, a Groyn, an Arthropod with its jeweled shell, a High Clansman, and what appeared to be Jack the Baptist.

The invisible hands lowered him gently to a floor of white crust that shimmered with faint violet overtones. The man with the mask removed it.

"Zero! What the fuck! How'd I get here? What—"

"I brought you here."

"You? *How?*"

"IAMton enhancement of telekinetic potential. This thing was in the Progress Station. Helps me control the field. Apparently I've got the right visualization talent for it."

"What field? What's an IAMton?"

"Later," Jack said. "What about the explosives?"

"Uh . . . God, it's hard to think after all this. . . . Well, by now Harmony must have scared it out of Brindle or one of the others. He'll have told them where they are. I put a big hunk of blunderbuss powder, some other stuff the sun-monkeys told me about, set it up in the throne room so that if they try to detach it, it blows. I figured Harmony would be in the throne room today."

He sighed. "But it was 'such a nice day' that he took the court out to his 'garden.' So much for my plan to get most of them in one swoop." He looked around. "What the fuck *is* this place?"

"It is potential," Zero said. He put the mask back on. "I'll show you."

When the throne room blew up, Harmony just stood there, camera lenses dilating, closing, dilating, closing, hands opening and closing, mouth opening and closing. Silently. Staring at the wreck of the old warehouse building and the smoke churning up from the caved-in masonry. Seven Phylum Twos, sent to find the explosives and carry them to a safer place, had gone up with it.

At last Harmony strode to what had once been the dorms and was now his quarters. He climbed the stairs inside and flung open the shutters of a window on the second floor. He glared out at his followers and the human crowd. He pointed into the mass of humans. "Punish them!" he shrieked, his voice falsetto. "Just throw them through the Widow Window till I tell you otherwise! They all must have known!"

The crowd cried out and turned to run, stampeding. Phylum Twos and other Twists grabbed the laggards and began feeding them into the Widow Window. In seconds the air was lacerated with the screams of its victims as it rained bodies over the settlement. "Rains of frogs!" Harmony bellowed. "Rains of fish! Rains of giant hailstones and UFO crankshafts! Rains of blood! *Rains of blood!*"

The air-sharks went mad with the smell of blood and began swooping, biting, darting into the crowd, carrying pieces of people away, blood dripping from their jaws.

And then the cry from the guard reached Harmony,

barely audible over the pandemonium of the terrified crowd. It was a human guard on the walls, pointing at the countryside. "The Current! The Current is coming!"

"In the daytime?" Harmony muttered. "Never in the daytime! And never in the settlement! Not possible!"

But when he went to the roof he could see it wending eerily across the landscape, making everything it touched look Halloween, discharging violet sparks at its borders.

A hush fell. Or did it? Perhaps it was the silence in Fiskle's head. Silence as he watched the Current come. He seemed to hear a rising and falling of static sounds, of white noise, and nothing else.

In seconds the Current had borne down on the settlement, had washed over it. And Harmony felt the Other One. He felt Zero, was aware of him immediately, as the Current oozed around him like the ghost of some vast dragon.

Harmony was distantly aware that the Meta's watching spheres were gathering overhead in unusually great numbers.

Harmony could feel ideas approaching. They were carried on the Current, and they were crystallizing around him.

The Overstructure was appearing. Ornate structures were solidifying out of nothing and forming over the settlement like the Platonic ideal superimposing over the mundane world. They were crystalline and translucent, composed of segments that were bright with primary colors; they were architecturally vast, but formed arches at the base to accommodate people, so no one was trapped in them. No one yet.

They were concepts growing up level on level, each

level representing a paradigm, and growing out of each paradigm was a theory. They were like computer models of ideas, but three dimensional and solid. Some of them were clearly of Earth culture derivation, looking like variations of Greek temples, Venetian architecture, Japanese architecture, the Lincoln Memorial, sculptures by Rodin and Michelangelo and Brancusi, and Arp and Calder, all of these incorporated, intertwined, and neatly juxtaposed into one never-completed composition.

Other facets of the structure were alien; the Numinous Nets of the Groyn—mandalalike nets woven to catch Groyn who, in religious ecstasy, throw themselves off the roofs of their temples. The Groyn worship Gravity, the Mother of All Homes, which is the one invisible force that demonstrates its power without cease and not only holds things together but instantly punishes those who don't abide by its rules. In gravitational meditation the Groyn throw themselves off high places so that, on the way down, they can experience gravity fully, till they're caught in the net woven with symbols of apology to the Gravitational Mother.

And incorporated into the Overstructure were abstractions of microscopic cellular structure created by the Arthropods, who are believers in maximizing harmony with nature. It materialized bas-reliefs of the scaled-up interior of an Arthropod brain cell; and around this, giant models of DNA molecules twined and writhed up the length of the great tower.

The Whorebugs contributed their philosophical orientation of enlightened materialism, their belief that highly ordered property is the only hedge against mortality, a record of their activities that survived them; their segment of the Overstructure used Whorebug weaving patterns depicting their mansions and acquisitions on their home world.

Jack contributed a section representing the primacy of sheer organization in the evolving universe, the antientropic forces that organize things into organic structures, expressed in the great Overstructure by a series of sections that constantly mutated from one symmetrical geometric form to another, each a variation of the last.

The High Clans' shamanism made its imprint of animal-worship imagery on the Overstructure; the Pezz's fascination with boundaries, with interfaces and interchanges between borders, insinuated itself in marblesque veins and wood-grain patterns.

Yoshio's native Japanese cultural perspective arranged these alien and human concepts with respect to one another like the deft strokes and eloquent spaces in Japanese painting and gardening. Zero and Angie and Bowler and Sanchez infused the shape with humanistic ideas. Sanchez's contribution included a monument to Swanee: his image a hundred feet high, and despite his leather wings, he was styled more like an angel than a demon.

The Overstructure rose story on story into the sky, transfiguring the consciousness of all who looked at it—all but Fiskle, the Emperor Harmony, who resisted it with his own assertions.

Harmony plugged into the Current and began to create his own counterstructure, trying to overwhelm Zero and friends with a dark tower that rose up from his roof in counterpoint, spiraling, torquing, attempting to entwine and encompass, to smother the Overstructure. Harmony's dark growth wriggled with moving friezes, images of animals eating other animals; of people performing the basest acts of self-degradation and self-destruction; of women debased to slaves; the Emperor himself triumphing over Zero and a thousand other enemies; battle scenes dripping with blood and drooling entrails and spilled brains. Out of this Wagnerian display a Fiskle superman arose from a baptism in flames, rising like a Titan above the maggotlike swarming of his enemies, the aliens and the traitor humans: the triumph of the will. Social Darwinism and jingoistic fanaticism coalesced into a kitschy design that might have been the work of Frazetta or Boris Vallejo.

The two structures, Zero's and Fiskle's, interlinked and grew like competing vines, climbing one another, lofting into the sky. The underpinnings were stationary, but the upper segments showed scenarios restlessly acting themselves out. From the Neutral it looked like an Olympus that was creating itself moment by moment. A Jungian principle, materialized.

Zero's part of the structure didn't buckle under Harmony's fierce imagistic fecundity but continued to grow. The alien concepts mitigated the human concepts, and vice versa; they fused and synthesized, and as they did so the humans and aliens involved saw one another, began to really understand one another, for the first time. In their mind's eyes the alien symbols were translated into their own visual-symbolic terms. Their assumptions reeled, and their attitudes staggered for new footing.

Some more than others. Zero could sense them out there—the men and aliens who were particularly in congruence with his basic sensibility; those who were responsive to an effort at finding points of agreement and areas of commonality and compromise with aliens.

Using the comedy-tragedy device, he involved their psychic energies in his creation.

And found the additional energy he needed. He triumphed over Fiskle. Fiskle-Harmony was surrounded like a piece on a *Go* board by Zero's final gambit and locked in place. Checkmated. No more room to move. Caught.

Seeing the Overstructure rising a mile into the sky, the other races came from their various settlements to investigate. They were impressed by its incorporation of diverse themes; its responsiveness, in certain segments, to their own ideas, which they could see played out and recorded in the great fractal intricacy of the thing.

And they were pleased to see that their enemy, the one who'd called himself Harmony, was trapped in a crystalline cage, permanently entombed there, preserved alive, forever raving mad: a living cautionary sign, a warning about intolerance.

Onlookers could see into the cage atop what had been the dorm roof; Fiskle could not see out. Inside the cage he was surrounded by mirrors, alternating with panels showing the twisted imagery he contributed to the dark side of the Overstructure. The imagery was infinitely reflected in the mirrors, and Harmony quite lost his mind in it.

The aliens were further reassured seeing the other human Twists in their own cells. Those, anyway, who were beyond saving. Some few, like Bella, reverted to human in the IAMton adjustment sections of the Overstructure and were freed from Fiskle's influence.

The Meta's watching spheres recorded it all. Then, after a time, they drained away into the sky.

Zero, Yoshio, Jack, the Pezz, and a few others from the human settlement were gathered in Harmony's garden. Zero bent and cut Jamie loose from the Phix. She collapsed, twitching. "I've killed her!" Zero cried.

"No," Jack said. He'd shed his human camouflage and reverted to what Zero thought of as "the light-bulb man." "She'll be okay in a few days. Well—she will never be okay, not after what happened to her lover and her child. She will never be a leader again. But she will survive for a while."

As the settlement's amateur doctor laid Jamie onto a stretcher, the Pezz asked Zero, "Who will be the leader of the human colony now?"

"It'll be Zero," Yoshio said.

Zero shook his head. "I'm going to work on creating some kind of working relationship with the other races. Maybe be a minister of culture of some kind. But Sanchez is going to be the new Prez. He's suited for it. Anyway, he'll be Prez of the human settlement, but we're going to have to form some kind of interspecies nation so the conflict ends for good. Elect a council of Earther reps and reps from the other races." He said all this distantly, sadly, as he watched the doctor and his assistant carry Jamie out of the garden. "But first," he added, with more animation, "I think we ought to uproot this fucking garden. Turn it into a handball court or something.

"The drama has reached its denoument," the Meta said. "The planet is yours."

It was an hour after dusk, the day after the fall of Fiskle. Zero stood on the highest point of the Overstructure, having ascended with IAMton energy. He stood on the parapet with a wisp of cloud trailing past him, gazing up into the eye of the pyramid. He had come here in answer to the Meta's call.

"The planet belongs to all the races who live on it," Zero said.

"That is your decision," the Meta said. "So it will be."

"Actually," Zero said, "they can *have* it. Look, I'm not going to ask for residuals on this film of yours. No points, nothing. Just cab fare, okay? Can you take us home? Me and the Earthers, at least?"

"No."

"Why not?"

"What you have created is a self-perpetuating pattern. To disturb it would be vandalizing a work of art. Never. Besides, the planet you call Fool's Hope is your home."

"We dropped the 'Fools's' part," Zero said absently. He gazed out over the misty reaches of landscape, out into the green sky. "Yeah. It's my home. World is world."

"Still, we are balancing out the picture a little. We are bringing more females from your world. This will be the last shipment from your planet, or from any other, to this one."

"Bringing females. *Mars Needs Women*, huh?"

"The reference escapes me."

"Never mind." He patted the translucent railing of the parapet. "What's this thing made of?"

"We don't know. Haven't analyzed it. The Overmind built it in response to your wishes out of the local agglomeration of molecules. We know that it channels IAMton energies harmlessly—it will prevent any more malicious Currents. It will be a focal point of a harmonious interspecies society that you will be instrumental in organizing, involving all races now living on this world. In time, we project, your race and the others will develop a society that will find its own sociological and even ecological symbiosis. The structure will also provide you with a means to manipulate matter through IAMtons. We predict, therefore, a renaissance in your relationship with the environment."

"Oh. But you don't know what it's made of?" Zero asked dryly.

"No. It incorporates much IAMton energy; IAMtons are locked into its molecular structure. It was we who impregnated this world with the compacted IAMton deposits, but we don't pretend to fully understand the working of that particle. We are still struggling with the question. IAMtons don't like to be looked at too closely."

"You going to just abandon us here, then?"

"We may look in from time to time. We project that your associate, Bowler, will form a splinter society based on a much more communal, anticompetitive system than your own. It will be interesting to see whether the two Earther systems coexist peacefully."

"Great." Zero laughed. "Just great. We'd better start the diplomacy *now*." He looked up at the ship, hovering like a thundercloud beyond the pyramid. "I should hate you because so many people have died here because of you. But it's true: There's suffering everywhere. And Bowler's right about one thing: This place is a chance to escape the suffering people have locked themselves into on Earth. Where you going to go from here, Meta?"

"We are moving into a new school of our art. We are going to be impregnating already occupied worlds with IAMtons and then adding some energetic new races. It should be interesting as it involves only worlds that are already quite crowded. Farewell, Zero. We wish you artistic satisfaction."

The pyramid merged with the hemisphere, and both were drawn into the green bowl of the sky.

Zero looked out at the circle of the horizon. He could see infinity and he could see limits. "World is world," he said.

EPILOGUE

On Earth, in New York City, on a sultry September day, everyone was talking about the announcement that had come that morning on network television. Astronomers and other scientists, using satellite telescopes and a variety of other devices, had confirmed what lay observers had been able to see for some time.

There was a second moon in the sky. It was shaped like an hourglass.

The End

A Selected List of Current and Forthcoming Mandarin Science-Fiction

While every effort is made to keep prices low, it is sometimes necessary to increase prices at short notice. Mandarin Paperbacks reserves the right to show new retail prices on covers which may differ from those previously advertised in the text or elsewhere.

The prices shown below were correct at the time of going to press.

☐ 7493 0006 X **Exile's Gate**   C. J. Cherryh   £3.99
☐ 7493 0007 8 **The Chronicles of Morgaine**   C. J. Cherryh   £4.99
☐ 7493 0021 3 **Kinsman**   Ben Bova   £3.50

Available June
☐ 7493 0041 8 **Chanur's Homecoming**   C. J. Cherryh   £3.50
☐ 7493 0068 X **Pride of Chanur**   C. J. Cherryh   £2.99
☐ 7493 0037 X **Ravenmoon**   Peter Tremayne   £3.50
☐ 7493 0038 8 **Highway of Eternity**   Clifford D. Simak   £2.99

All these books are available at your bookshop or newsagent, or can be ordered direct from the publisher. Just tick the titles you want and fill in the form below.

Mandarin Paperbacks, Cash Sales Department, PO Box 11, Falmouth, Cornwall TR10 9EN.

Please send cheque or postal order, no currency, for purchase price quoted and allow the following for postage and packing:

UK   55p for the first book, 22p for the second book and 14p for each additional book ordered to a maximum charge of £1.75.

BFPO and Eire   55p for the first book, 22p for the second book and 14p for each of the next seven books, thereafter 8p per book.

Overseas Customers   £1.00 for the first book plus 25p per copy for each additional book.

NAME (Block Letters) ....

ADDRESS ....

....